MANI

This is a work of fiction. As such, any persons, places, things or ideas appearing in this book that resemble those of the real world, living or dead, ugly or beautiful, are either coincidental or used fictitiously.

MANI
Book One of the Mother Trilogy

First Edition

Text copyright 2024 Jacob Gamber
ISBN: 978-1-964257-01-3

Cover art and design by Ferdinand Ladera
Map by Jacob Gamber

Font: 12 pt Sylfaen
118,000 words
Printed in the USA

Idea Engine Press LLC
850 Euclid Ave Ste 819 #4020,
Cleveland OH 44114, US

The Mother Trilogy: Book One

- M A N I -

JACOB GAMBER

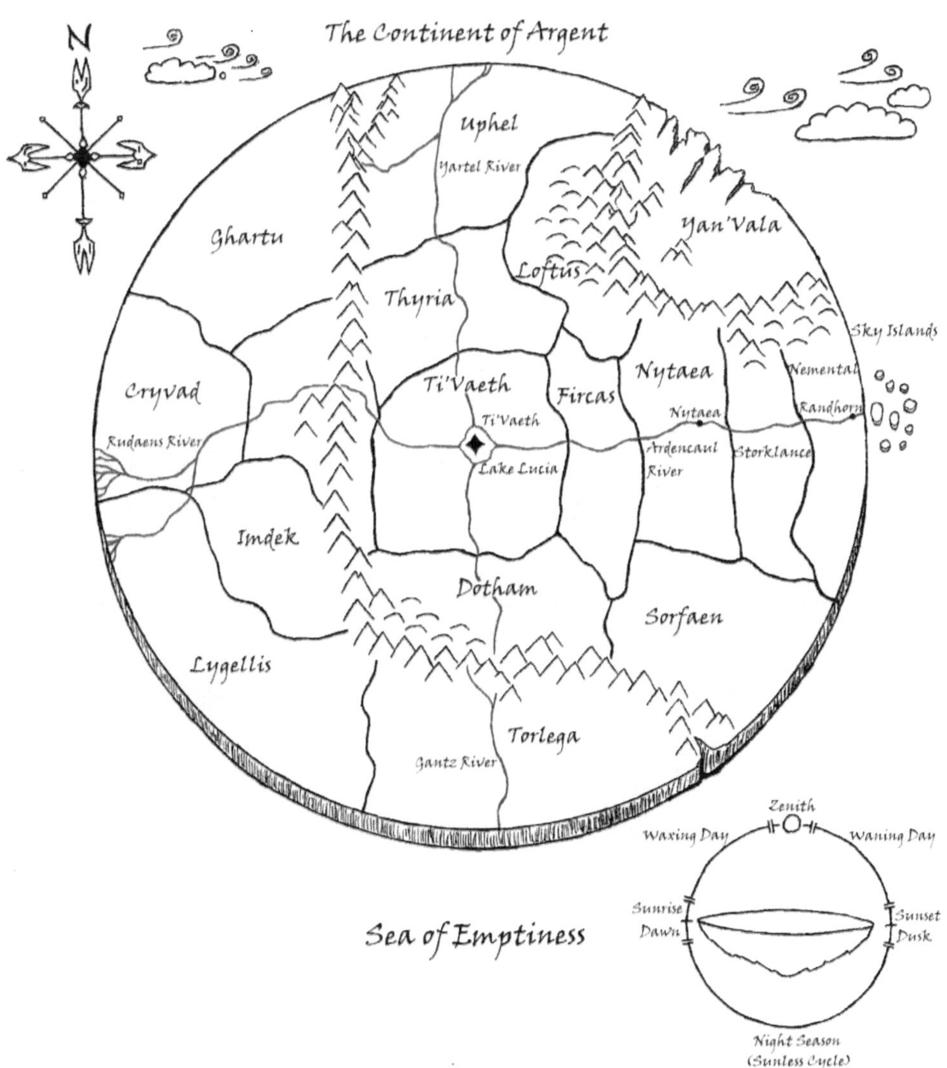

The Known World of
Mani
The Continent of Argent
N
Ghartu
Uphel
Yartel River
Yan'Vala
Thyria
Loftus
Sky Islands
Cryvad
Ti'Vaeth
Fircas
Nytaea
Nemental
Ti'Vaeth
Nytaea
Randhorn
Rudaens River
Lake Lucia
Ardencaul River
Storklance
Imdek
Dotham
Sorfaen
Lygellis
Torlega
Gantz River
Sea of Emptiness
Zenith
Waxing Day
Waning Day
Sunrise
Dawn
Sunset
Dusk
Night Season
(Sunless Cycle)

Dedicated to
My greatest inspiration
You are my favorite*

*Of my sisters. And yes, that's two syllables.

Contents

- Acknowledgments -

Praise God from whom all blessings flow! I am so grateful for the ability to write and the opportunity to share this story with others—and incredibly honored that you picked it up to read! But there are others for whom thanks is in order:

Firstly, I'd like to thank my wonderful wife Molly for all her encouragement, and my baby girl who cheers me up every day with her irresistible smile. My parents as well, for their longtime support, and many others who . . . well, maybe they used to look at me like I was crazy when I'd tell them I wanted to be a writer someday, but not, y'know, too crazy. So thanks. Especially my dad, to whom I credit my sense of humor and backhanded compliments.

My talented sister, Joanna, has inspired me to write and be creative from a young age and has been steadfastly supportive, so dōmo arigatō from the bottom of my heart. Also my brother Jeremiah, with whom I've swapped many creative ideas, and my cousins Owen, Rachel and Lydia—fellow readers and fantasy enthusiasts.

Ferdinand Ladera produced an absolute masterwork for the cover, bringing to life the Sea of Emptiness more wonderfully than I could have dreamed. Working with him was a pleasure.

And let's not forget the whole slew of folks on the internet for their help as critique partners in either the shorter or longer term. (No, seriously, I appreciate you guys and all your feedback.) Also a host of alpha/beta readers I managed to snooker into reading various early drafts—including the original way back in 2016. It's been a long project, so thanks for being a part.

Lastly, a quick note to the reader: should any confusion arise concerning terms, characters, pronunciations . . . there's an appendix at the back with full explanations, so don't hesitate to use it—just beware of minor spoilers.

— Jacob G.

- Prologue -

Beauty in Weakness

Dear Mother,

There is something I must tell you, and I am too afraid to say it.
Not to mention I know that you would stop me. So . . . I am
leaving you one final letter instead. I have decided to go. I
cannot say if I will be back, so I will make no promises. Know
that I love you more than all of Mani. But you know that this is
more important than you or I, or even this silver shell we call
home. And so, I must go. I must. I will see you again, whether
in this world, in the other, or in the afterlife.

Goodbye

(Planet Mani—Nytaea
Mani'Tor 20, 984—Night Season)

Lynchazel gathered her strength and leapt the city wall. She clutched her precious bundle with her left arm, extending upward with her right, as the force of her jump carried her through the air. Her ascent slowed just as she came within reach of the stone battlement at the top of the wall, some thirty feet in the air. Her right arm grasped the stone and she pulled herself onto the wall. Movement in this world was absurdly easy.

Here she stopped, looking both directions. The stone walkway on top of the wall was only about four feet wide, just wide enough for two of these lightworld men to walk abreast.

Fortunately, there were none in sight at the moment.

Lynchazel turned, scanning the horizon behind her. Still no sight of Sol. She was pretty sure this was the third day she'd been on this world, and yet no dawn. The dark sky changed color and the auroras came and went, almost like a normal day cycle, but who could say when full daylight would be back?

Twenty-eight days, he said. Fourteen days of sun, fourteen days of night. A strange world, this Mani . . . the thought of living here made her shiver, despite her certainty that it was a far better home for her daughter.

Lynchazel turned back toward the city. Nytaea, he had called it. The land of her child's ancestry. She scanned the alabaster buildings and watched the starlight play off of silver-plated rooftops. The white Nytaean Palace loomed high over the other buildings, at the center of the city. Weak though this world may be, she had to admit . . . it was quite beautiful.

She glanced down at the bundle in her arms, which she unwrapped gently—just enough to reveal the perfect face of her first and only daughter, named after herself.

"Lynchazel," she said softly. "We're here. Your new home."

- Exordium -

(From the Vault of Lyn of Nytaea, Mother Heiress Hersta 11, 2336)

I am getting really sick of your world.

Not very impressed so far, between the harsh conditions, the whole thing where I got imprisoned almost immediately, and the *terrible* food. I mean . . . just atrocious. You'd think these Hellebes scientists could give me something slightly more palatable than mystery lab chow while I twiddle my thumbs and wait for them to decide how next to experiment on me.

Oh, and my friends are all dead now. They didn't make it through the Gate, so I'm stuck here alone.

So yeah . . . not impressed. Can I go home now? Back to Mani?

I know, I know. I can't. You probably think I deserve this, or that it's necessary. I'm just a monster. Mother this, goddess that. I get it.

I also realize not all Hellebes are that bad. Look at Captain Zent —he was great. But he still left me here at the mercy of the Senate. I'm recording this in my Vault—being a Hellebes, whoever you are, you know all about Vaults—in order to leave a methodical account of the events that led me here. After all, I'm sure you haven't heard the full story.

I was an orphan, and I came from a city called Nytaea where orphans were considered illegal citizens. My mother brought me there as a baby. Nytaea, gleaming city of alabaster and silver, was made by an order of magi long ago. Magi are Legaleians who wield the 'Authority' of the elements, that is to say they can control nature. Magic, you might say.

The Legaleians, of course, are the people who live on Mani. The Exiled. On Mani, there is no moon, and only one day passes per month. Two weeks of day, two weeks of night. There are few men there, believe it or not, as far more girls are born each year than boys. Sounds weird, I know, but . . . it gets weirder. But I won't overload you—let's just start from the beginning.

PART ONE

- Disguise -

- Chapter 1 -

The Fate of the Innocent

Silver has always been a part of Mani. Quite literally—the bones of this world are molded from pure silver. Not only is this metal plentiful, but it possesses many strange properties.
— From *Secrets of Mani,* by Sor the Lark

(Planet Mani—Nytaea
Fynle 26, 997—Sunrise)

It was the second day of dawn. Sol hung full above the horizon, casting pale orange light over the white city of Nytaea. The light filtered through the streets and played on the silver rooftops as Mandrie led us back to the orphanage. We could see the smoke from a street away.

Our orphanage was in flames as Kaen and I rounded the last street corner and caught sight of it. That old, beloved house where we grew up, the place I called home ever since I was a little girl . . . burning.

She was right, I thought numbly as I stumbled to a halt, struggling to grasp the scene before my eyes. Two stories tall, the quaint building was made of wood instead of the more usual white stone. By now, however, multiple walls were beginning to cave in. Standing in the front courtyard were some dozen ruffians. Their leader stooped in front of two women held by his henchmen: Lentha, our aging caretaker, and Phoebe, an older girl of sixteen years from the orphanage. Phoebe was thrashing around in her captor's grip and spitting angry words at the thief leader, while Lentha just hung her head.

No one else was in sight, none of the children, and certainly no one else in the neighborhood. They wouldn't want anything to do with such an event.

"Lyn! Kaen!" called Phoebe as she saw us. "Hel—" She was cut off as the stubble-cheeked man holding her gave her a backhanded rap across the head.

"Hey!" I shouted. "Let them go!"

Kaen came up beside me and turned to say something to Mandrie. I was too focused on the horrifying scene to pay attention to his words.

The leader turned to look at me, and Lentha coughed up blood behind him. "Well, looky here—more of the brats!" he said through a gap-toothed grin, shaking a bag of jingling copper and gold coins. Lentha's stash of money. "Your little friend here was trying to go back inside, but it's a bit dangerous in there, so I had the boys restrain her along with this old hag. Ain't that right, missy?"

I gritted my teeth and began to stalk toward them. I was strong; maybe Kaen and I could take them on. . . .

But then I saw the lead man do something strange, calling a flame into being with his right hand. Just like that. My blood chilled, and I stopped in my tracks. So that was how they had burnt it so fast. *Magic. . . .*

"You . . . monsters," I spat. I looked toward the flaming building, half collapsing from the structural damage already, and wiped tears from my eyes. There was no way any of the children were still alive in there. I couldn't hear their screams.

Kaen put a hand on my shoulder and addressed the thieves. "Put them down right now and back off! We have the city watch right on our tails. They'll be here any moment." His voice cracked, but it was a commendable effort at sounding threatening.

The fire mage laughed. But before he could speak, one of his men pointed the other direction and all eyes looked to see the city watch approaching at a run. The uniformed men shouted and began chasing the thieves, who scattered away. Someone must have seen the smoke and called for them.

The thieves cursed and dropped Phoebe and Lentha as they fled, and Phoebe immediately dashed to Lentha's side, wincing at her own bruises as she held her caretaker gingerly. "Mum, Mum! Lentha! Stay with me."

Kaen and I approached hastily and knelt down beside the grey-haired woman. Her face was beaten and bloodied, and she looked close to death. "Oh, Lentha . . ." I whispered.

Phoebe gazed up at us with tear-stained eyes, her dull brown hair in tangles. Her hooked nose, one of her distinctive features, twitched as she tried to keep it from running. Blood leaked from one nostril. "They demanded money. When she wouldn't give it, they . . . they . . ." She cut off, sobbing.

Lentha finally stirred, pulling back her greyed head to mumble something incoherent. I caught only the word "children." And then her body went limp.

Just then, one of the last of the city watch came up to us, his bronze scale armor clinking with each step. "Sorry to run, but the mage soldiers will be here any minute to douse the fires, and they'll give you any medical attention you need."

He was off before we could protest, and we were left with our dead foster mother in the courtyard of the burning orphanage. *Mage soldiers. . . .* Lord Kalceron's elite forces were the last thing I wanted to see. Lentha had always taught us to avoid mage soldiers, in fact all magi, whenever possible. I shivered and looked back toward the building, saying nothing. I wanted so badly to go and check, just to see if somehow, some way . . .

I made an illogical move to get up and run for the orphanage, but Kaen grabbed my arm. His face, normally so strong and resolute, looked hollow in the flickering light of the flames. His dark curls were plastered to his forehead with sweat and ash. With trembling lips, he said, "Lyn, they're dead. So is—so is Lentha."

Phoebe lay wailing over Lentha's body. I felt like doing just the same. My throat was raw and scratchy, bearing a lump that I couldn't swallow down. But I didn't pull out of Kaen's grip.

Slowly, Mandrie approached from behind us. I looked to see her small eleven-year-old figure beside us, clutching one arm to the other across her stomach. "Kaen," she whimpered, "Lyn, I'm scared. This is like a bad dream. I thought . . ."

I lurched to my feet and ran to embrace her, pulling the distraught girl to face away from the dead body of our caretaker. "I'm so sorry, Mandrie."

From behind me, Kaen said, "We should be going."

I nodded, turning to see two mage soldiers approaching from the street to the south. They were unmistakable in their ornately-graven silver armor, bearing blue capes and horsehair plumes: water mage soldiers. I had only ever caught glimpses as a child. Two more of the blue-cloaked men approached from behind them just as the first two ran up and started putting out the fires. The mage soldier in the far back locked eyes with me and nudged his companion, pointing and saying something. A chill ran down my spine, and my heart began to beat faster.

Kaen was leading Phoebe away, but I hissed at him to hurry and pulled Mandrie with me. "We have to go now!"

None of them questioned. We hurried back down the street we'd come from. Kaen looked back and whispered, "Everyone hide!" He pulled Mandrie and me down behind a wooden garbage bin. "How did they get here so fast? Are you sure they're after us, Lyn?"

I gave a nervous shrug, nearly gagging at the putrid smell of the refuse in the container. Breath coming quickly, I peeked over the top and saw the water magi dousing the flames while more mage soldiers clad in red and gold capes—other divisions, specializing in different elements—prowled the scene. They would find us in no time. "They're looking for something," I whispered back, "And I think it's us. Whatever they want, it won't be good if they catch us. We have to go, or they will soon."

Kaen looked out past the dumpster and swore. "More of them are coming. We'll just have to make a break for it. Come on!"

Mandrie scrambled out first, running for the street corner while Phoebe and Kaen followed on her heels. I followed, trying to keep an eye on the soldiers. They came closer and closer until . . .

They saw us. "You there, stop!" shouted one of the two. "You, with the white hair!"

The words sent a chill down my spine. I panicked and sprinted for the corner, where Kaen and Mandrie were. "Go, go!" I hissed to them, looking behind me to see the soldiers chasing us. I thought I saw a civilian or two staring at us from windows, but I was too focused on getting away from Lord Kalceron's men. We weaved down side streets toward the worse section of town, following Kaen's lead. I knew we'd be able to shake them there. The only issue would be Mandrie, who was not as fast, and Phoebe, who seemed to be hampered by the beating the thieves had given her.

"Over here!" I said quickly, pointing down another alley. "Go! I'll distract them. I'll meet you up at the nearest hideout!"

Kaen reluctantly pulled Mandrie and Phoebe down the alley with him, while I scrambled up on a nearby box and leaped for the overhanging roof. Using my gift of inhuman strength, I pulled myself up. As the mage soldiers came through, I shouted down to them, "Hey! You'll never catch us!"

One of the magi, a gold-caped woman, stopped and pointed as she looked up. "There she is! They've taken to the rooftops, Captain."

I ran in the direction of Kaen and my other friends, sprinting over the slate roof as fast as I could. I came to the edge of the first roof and took a flying leap, landing on the other side nimbly as a cat. The mage soldiers had rounded the street corner and were now firing firebolts and lightning my way, shouting for me to stop. *They're out of their minds—are they trying to kill me?*

I took off, leading them farther away. Whether they were actually trying to hit me or simply intimidate me, my decoy plan was working.

Gathering my energy, I bounded across the street to my left and scraped my way up the slope of the roof and over to the other side, sliding to dodge another firebolt. I braked, getting my feet beneath me as I slid, and then managed to leap once more across the street.

I landed with my feet on a windowsill and my fingers over the lip of the roof. The jerk of my weight brought a jolt of pain from my shoulders and elbows. Gritting my teeth, I forced my limbs to do the impossible as I leaped with my feet, pulled with my arms, and swung myself up and over the edge, landing in a crouch on the rooftop. Sometimes it paid to have inhuman strength. Someday I would find out why I possessed it, and very soon I would feel the tiring after-effects of it.

I heard their voices and the clang of their silver boots on paving stones even as I caught my breath and my bearings. Looking around to see the mage soldiers approaching from both sides, I made a split-second decision and dashed to my right, parallel to the street. I leaped from one housetop to the next, following the street, before swinging around to my left, following the slope of the roof. I followed the roofline in this direction, away from where I knew our closest hideout lay.

The mage soldiers were still on my tail, fortunately, although they had to be wondering by now why they were only chasing one of us. Had they split up? I stopped suddenly, stooping down to rip off a slate shingle from the roof below, then leaned back sharply as another firebolt sailed over my head, fired by one of the red-caped mage soldiers. An angry reprimand followed from one of the other ones—had he aimed too close? I peeked over and chucked the heavy shingle plate at my pursuers as they ran toward me. The shingle shattered, stalling them momentarily, and I began running again. It didn't buy me any time in my escape from the magi; I was just trying to keep them preoccupied with me.

It was time to lose them.

I took a deep breath and leapt across the street. I ran straight up the slope of the roof, slid down the other side and vaulted across the street. Pedestrians below stared up in surprise, but I ignored them. I landed on the roof of a large shop, clambering up the side and traversing the complicated twists and turns of the roof before hopping onto the next building, and the next, and the next, down the street. Finally, as my breath began to come in gasps, I hopped off the last rooftop and dropped five paces to the cobblestone street below, rolling and coming up running.

Confident that I had shaken the mage soldiers at last, I made my way as quickly and quietly as I could toward the hideout, conscious that half the city might have just seen my escape antics. I ducked my head whenever I passed by a person as I ran. I was beginning to feel the exertion, and sweat was breaking out on my forehead.

At last, I made it back to the run-down section of the city. I sought out the abandoned warehouse and let myself in the back door, glancing both ways first to make sure that no one was watching. It was an old building with worn, wooden siding, and the plain wooden furnishings inside were covered in dust and cobwebs. Kaen, Phoebe and Mandrie stood near the back, and looked up with relief as I entered.

Mandrie was the first to greet me. "Lyn! Oh, I'm so glad you made it back safely!" She ran up and threw her arms around me, burying her brown curls in my chest.

I patted her back as I caught my breath, ruffling her hair affectionately. "Of course. I wouldn't let some measly mage soldiers catch me."

"Were you followed here?" Kaen's voice had a sharp edge to it.

I shook my head, gently pulling Mandrie off of me. "No, I threw them off a ways back. They could only chase me for so long."

Phoebe looked skeptical. "And how do you know they won't still find us here? How did you even get away from them?"

"I led them in the opposite direction by rooftop," I explained. "Then I doubled back and came here."

She nodded, satisfied, not asking how I was capable of performing such a feat. We all knew that I was agile and quick on my feet, but Kaen was the only one who knew that that extended to super-human feats that no normal Legaleian—that is to say, no human—could perform.

Mandrie looked back at Kaen. "Brother, what do we do now? Where are we going to stay?"

"Right here for now," he answered. "Although we have to make sure that our scent has been lost." He glanced my way. "Lyn? You up for going back out with me to scout the area?"

I took a deep breath in, nodding slowly, and wiped my sweaty brow. "Yeah, I'm fine." No sooner did I say this, however, than my knees buckled. I almost fell to the floor before Kaen caught me.

He grunted at my weight, muttering, "You don't look fine. Phoebe, maybe you ought to come instead. They didn't beat you up too badly, did they?"

She scoffed. "No, just some bruises. I'll come. Can't trust you to watch your own back." Sharp-tongued as ever.

I nodded weakly. "Thanks. Mandrie, can I have some food?" My stomach was trying to learn to talk back.

She scrambled up to fetch some from our meager supplies, bringing me back a piece of a hard loaf. "Here you go, Lynx!" She used her nickname for me, though her voice lacked its usual brightness.

I devoured the bread like a ravenous wolf, swallowing it in a few seconds. Almost immediately, it helped to replenish my energy. "I feel a little better now," I said. "You two go, and I'll stay and watch out for Mandrie."

Phoebe grunted an assent. "Kaen, we should go and talk to your boss. Do you think he'd be willing to pay you for your work up until now?"

Kaen and I had been at work with a local construction crew when Mandrie came to get us. We had begged leave from the master builder, insisting that the occasion was urgent. Despite the general outlook toward orphans in the city, fostered by harsh laws made by Lord Kalceron, Lerr Harcost was a fair man who asked few questions and paid anyone willing to work for him.

"I was just wondering that," Kaen said with a sigh. "I don't . . . I don't think I can keep working for him if we're going to be on the run for a while. We need to leave this sector of town entirely, as soon as we can."

I nodded. "You're right. We can't stay here. We can find work someplace else. Just see what he says. But be cautious out there.

"We will. We'll see you two later," he said as he pushed the door open and walked out, holding it open for Phoebe.

"Be careful," Mandrie called.

Phoebe glanced back at us briefly and then let the door swing shut as they departed.

I looked over at Mandrie, smiling as warmly as I could. "It's going to be all right. We'll make it."

She nodded slowly before seating herself with a thump on the floor, not bothering to smooth her skirts. "Oh, Lyn," she murmured, hanging her head. "But it's not all right. They're all dead. They're all gone. Lentha . . . Tommy . . . Fran . . ." Tears began to stream down her cheeks, and her little chest heaved with sobs.

"Mandrie . . . I'm sorry." I stooped down beside her and stroked her mousy brown curls. They were just like Kaen's, but, at only eleven years old, her hair was not as dark yet. "It will be all right." She leaned onto me, and I held her while she cried, rocking back and forth. Try though I may to be strong for her, I could feel my own tears welling up behind my eyes as my lip trembled, my chin and jaw feeling strangely tight.

I squeezed my eyes shut. *Why did this have to happen? Why?*

- Chapter 2 -

Taken

The ancients write of silver being scarce. A precious metal cast into coins and used as currency. This has confused many scholars and is one of many secrets we still have yet to unravel. There are theories, of course. Some say that we, like the Wellspring, came from another world. Others claim Legaleian culture was simply different back then, or that, once upon a time, silver was not so easily accessible on Mani's surface.
— From *Secrets of Mani*, by Sor the Lark

(Fynle 26, 997—Sunrise)

Kaen and Phoebe returned an hour later, bearing a pouch of coins and a sack of food purchased from the street market. "Here's some food," Kaen said with a sigh. "Master Harcost was *very* hesitant to give me our wages, but he eventually did." He shook the coin bag, causing the copper inside to jingle. "This is all we have to go on for now."

I nodded. "It will have to do."

We stayed in the second story of the abandoned building that night, where we cleaned up a bit before setting up our sleeping arrangements. We kept one person on watch at all times. Tomorrow, we would move—it was too risky to stay in one place too long, as we didn't know what the mage soldiers wanted with us, nor what might happen should they catch us.

Nothing good. That's what my gut told me.

The next day, the backstreets were abuzz with news of the big chase with the mage soldiers. Everywhere we went, people talked about it:

"Oh, they'll catch them for sure."

"I heard they're part of the Underground."

"They say it was one girl, with hair like the blazing Sun!"

With each passerby we came across, I grew more afraid of what they might say, or who might report us to the authorities. My friends gave me glances that varied between amused and annoyed. Were the mage soldiers still after me? And why? There was no way they knew about . . . no, only Kaen knew my secret. There was only my white hair, but surely that wasn't enough to . . .

Wait. *'You! With the white hair!'* I recalled the mage soldier from the day before who had said just that, and groaned inwardly as I realized Lord Kalceron may be after me specifically—that this might not just stem from his well-known hatred of orphans.

The streets were cluttered as we made our way through the lower Market District. Here, the once-great city of Nytaea was brightened up by storefronts and merchant stalls. Colorful ribbons, banners and other decorations festooned the timeless white of the aged stone buildings, crisscrossing the streets not far above head level. Carts, horses and pedestrians passed by every second, hiding us in their midst. The hustle and bustle always made this part of the city seem so much more alive than other sectors, but it was hard to even think with all the noise. Varying scents from the food vendors' stalls rose and fell as we passed them by.

Sol shone her usual brilliant white through the silver sky to the east, the last colors of dawn fading away at this point—being as it was the third day of the Sunlit Cycle, or Day Season. Each day, the white sun would rise to its zenith and eventually set, and we would enter the Sunless Cycle, or Night Season; then after another two weeks, it was back to the Sunlit Cycle. I know, it's confusing.

Clouds rolling by cast long, flickering shadows of dawn upon the streets and the tall buildings. The peaked roofs around us felt like one more hedge of protection against those searching for us, but over them all to the north loomed the Nytaean Palace, gleaming white in the sunlight. Home of Lord Kalceron, governor of our city-state, along with much of the nobility. Nytaea, despite being only one of thirteen provinces of the Kystrean empire, had always been known as one of the greatest. Over all twelve kings—excuse me, governors—reigned a supreme Archlord, who I could only assume was eviler yet than Lord Kalceron.

We were heading to our next hideout. Hopefully, we could rest there for another while. We had made the hideouts over the years in case something along these lines ever happened, something that forced us from our home.

"Kaen," I said as I kept pace just behind him, "What do you think those mage soldiers were after? I mean . . . they did point out my hair. . . ."

He said nothing for a moment, brushing past a couple of men as he walked. I mumbled a quick apology in his stead, while Phoebe and Mandrie followed behind. Then he answered, "I don't want to believe that. Either way, I hope we don't have to find out. Whatever it was, they were already on the lookout. We always knew we would have to move if anything happened to the orphanage, so . . . here we are, looking."

He pointedly didn't add, *'and to Lentha,'* I noticed.

Phoebe made a growling noise behind us, muttering something about how "those pigs" most likely got away after the arson. While I understood her frustration and anger, the best I could do was hope they had been caught by the city watch and brought to justice. It was out of our hands.

"Let's just focus on getting to the shelter for now, all right?" I proposed. I couldn't wait to be done with this city entirely. That was our aim, but it would take some planning, the right timing, and . . . well, probably a bit of luck.

We came to an intersection in the street ahead, and Kaen turned right, with the rest of us following after. Labeled "Farley Avenue," this street was narrower and less crowded, and led away from the Market District. In a few minutes, we turned onto another street, and a few turns later, we were heading into the eastern slums. Here, we might be in for some trouble. But that was why I had my favorite knife belted onto my thigh beneath my grey skirt; just in case.

Looking over my shoulder, I saw someone following us thirty paces back. It was a woman. She wore a wide-brimmed hat and a non-descript grey cloak cinched at her breastbone with a brass pin. But underneath the cloak and hat I caught the glint of silver armor. On her wrists were silver cuffs, and on her legs she wore silver greaves and tall boots. A mage soldier, possibly an officer. And yet disguised.

"Kaen," I hissed, "We've got a tail. A mage soldier, maybe an important one."

"Just look straight ahead and keep walking," he replied, not turning his head.

I felt my heartbeat quickening in my chest. We kept walking past the backstreet that led to our hideout, lest we show the mage our lair. She probably had backup waiting somewhere as well. I glanced furtively down the perpendicular streets and up at the buildings above, attempting to spot possible threats. I caught a few shadowy figures hiding, but they seemed to be the local no-goods curious about who we were.

"What's our plan?" whispered Phoebe from beside me. "How do we shake this soldier?"

"I'm sure she has others around nearby," I replied without turning my head. "I just wish I knew why she hasn't come out and attacked us yet."

"I don't like it," Kaen said. "We're going to have to split up. Phoebe, you take Mandrie and hide out on the next left, while Lyn and I distract them. Make a break for it when you see a chance."

Phoebe knew better than to protest when time was of the essence. "All right," she muttered.

Kaen led the way down the alley to the left, and Mandrie and Phoebe hid themselves behind some crates outside an abandoned building while Kaen and I sprinted for the next small intersection, preparing to wait for the mage soldier to turn the corner—at which point we would bolt, as though we were only two of four escaping that way.

The woman came at us suddenly from the street to our left, hurtling out of the dark with a blue, crackling energy in her hands. She rushed me, but I dodged nimbly out of the way just before she released the bolt of lightning. She skidded to a halt, surprised that I had been able to evade her magic. She then pulled out a thin, silver sword, the weapon of choice of Lord Kalceron's mage soldiers, and turned to Kaen.

I rolled up the right side of my skirt and pulled my knife from its sheath with a small *ssshk!*

Seeing an opening, I leaped in with my knife and thrust at her neck. She saw it coming, however, and turned at the last moment, and my knife only grazed her shoulder.

The mage cried out in pain, twisting to slice at me with her sword. I ducked, and Kaen slashed with his own knife, which glanced off of her armor instead of sinking into her ribs. The enchanted silver armor proved as strong as they said, hard enough to shrug off our bronze blades. She sprang back, throwing out a stunning pulse that stopped Kaen in his tracks.

Now a second mage soldier, a red-caped man, jumped into the fray in front of the woman, shouting threats at us. He swung his sword at me in a horizontal sweep, but I leapt right over it and rushed him, throwing him back into the female mage and then closing in with my dagger. I didn't have any more fighting skills than Kaen, but I was quick and very strong.

The man dodged to the side and hurled a firebolt at me, but I leaned backward to evade it. The woman, already recovered, jolted me with lightning magic, stiffening my body and causing me to drop my knife. I would have cried out, or at least grunted, but the pulse took my breath away. My teeth ached and my ears pounded with pain.

I recovered within a few seconds, though, and dodged to the left, leaving my knife on the ground. Instead, I smashed the man in the head with my elbow, driven by every ounce of force I had, and he crumpled to the ground, rolling limply. I turned to the woman in time to see Kaen diving for her—only to have her bat the knife out of his hands with her sword.

I stole the opportunity, kicking the mage woman with all my might. My foot drove into her shoulder and sent her reeling to fall back-first onto the cobblestones.

"Thanks," Kaen said.

I paid him no mind, leaping in one bound to where the woman lay struggling to catch her breath after the fall. I knelt, placing one knee heavily on her armored sternum and pinning her right arm with one hand. I raised my other arm, making a fist. I wanted so badly to smash her face into a new one, but we had to know what it was that they wanted with us.

The woman glared up at me, still gasping for air, wincing in pain as I pressed my knee harder against her chest. Only now did I notice the gold highlights on her outfit, denoting her elemental specialty. With her hat off, I was able to see her face more clearly, and I was struck by how much it reminded me of a fox. Sly and vulpine. "So you are a monster," she gasped, almost triumphantly.

"I just . . . I just want to know why you attacked us," I said through heavy breaths. My heart was still beating like a racehorse, adrenaline rushing through my veins like wildfire. These effects were most likely due to the fight having awakened a buried energy that didn't often make its way to the surface.

"I-I'll admit," the mage soldier sputtered through gritted teeth, "I didn't think it would come to this."

I hesitated, but I didn't lower my fist.

"Lyn, you can't trust her!" Kaen shouted from behind me.

I pressed down harder with my knee, causing the woman to grunt in pain, and raised my fist, clenching my fingers tighter.

"Stop," she croaked, "Or your—friends—die."

- Chapter 3 -

A Visitor in the Night

Nytaea, city of mage soldiers, was given over to a tyrant known as Lord Edrius Kalceron. The proud city was known for its wondrous architecture, a city of alabaster and silver marvels, but its future is dark as long as Lord Kalceron remains governor. Even in Archlord Domon's new empire of Kystrea, Nytaea stands to experience one of the worst falls from grace— indeed, the difference is already marked. As a High Mage, however, he is extraordinarily long-lived.
— From *Secrets of Mani*, by Sor the Lark

(Fynle 27, 997—Waxing Day)

I froze.

Sharing a look of horror with Kaen, who had come up to stand beside me, I released the pressure from the mage's chest. She gasped in a couple of breaths, and then spat, "You fools didn't think I had backup? That I wouldn't realize two of you were missing?" Then she twisted her neck to the side, shouting, "Hespian! Do you have them?"

"Of course. Easy as catchin' pigeons!" came a gruff male voice from my far right. I looked and saw the speaker at the head of the alleyway, a tall man in silver armor, standing over Phoebe's unconscious body with Mandrie in his tight grip. The decorations on his shoulder plates seemed to indicate a very high-ranking mage soldier. He picked up both girls and began hauling their limp forms toward us.

The woman smirked at us. "Might want to let me up. I can't say what the captain might do to your little friends. We knew we may not be able to bring you in, but Lord Kalceron wants his target."

I rose to my feet, withdrawing my knee from the woman's chest. I kept my knife out, unsure what she would try next. "What target?" I demanded. "What do you want with me? Let our friends go already."

"Oh, his little white-haired wench," replied the captain with a grin. "Can't say why, but he's been looking for you. Oddities like you are growing quite popular these days, apparently, and it's not our job to ask questions. But I'm sure you could be coaxed into coming on your own if it meant saving your pretty friends here."

Kaen growled from beside me. "Fiends. How could you stoop that low?"

"Well, when you want to cage a wild beast, you have to be cunning," Hespian reasoned. "Come, Lorta! Let us be away. He didn't exactly give us a time limit. Don't worry, friends, we'll keep the wenches in . . . possibly good accommodation, and we'll wait as long as we have to for you to show up."

The woman, Lorta, limped down the alleyway to her captain, who handed Mandrie over to her while he hoisted Phoebe's limp body up onto his shoulder. She struggled with the girl's weight, grunting at the wounds I'd given her.

"We won't let you get away with this!" I hissed through gritted teeth.

"Ah, but you have no choice," purred Lorta with a snarl clearly meant to mask her pain. And then she vanished, along with Mandrie.

Hespian waved his hand, preparing to perform the same trick of magic. "See you at the Palace, friends."

He vanished, leaving only Kaen and me standing there in the alley. Looking back, I saw that the third mage soldier was gone now as well. My elbow still throbbed from where I'd struck him.

Kaen clenched his hands into fists, stamping his boot on the stone pavement. "Curse those low-down wolves!" After a moment of heavy breathing, he asked, "What now? They just . . . made off with them." He made a frustrated hand gesture, as though admitting how obvious his comment was.

I stared at the ground, shrugging my shoulders helplessly. "I don't know. I . . ." I swayed weakly, suddenly overcome with an immense tiredness. I felt myself fall toward the ground as my vision went black.

"Lyn! Lyn!"

Someone was slapping me, shouting for me to wake up, but I didn't know who it was. I mumbled something incoherent and then snapped my eyes open with a start, finding Kaen bending over me, face directly in front of mine and hand raised as though to slap me again if needed.

"Huh?" I groaned heavily. "Kaen?"

He lowered his hand, taking a half step backward. "You scared me for a minute there, Lyn. You suddenly lost consciousness, and I had to carry you here. It's . . . you know, at least a little more out of the way."

I looked about myself, realizing that I lay slumped against the stone wall of a building in a back alleyway. I groaned, sitting up slowly and squinting against the bright, white sunlight that shone from the east. It had faded from soft orange to its natural white over the last day. The cloud coverage was already rolling in for the day, building in layers. I stretched my hand, which still tingled from the shock of Lorta's lightning magic. "How long was I out?" I couldn't recall ever blacking out before.

"Just a couple of minutes. You hungry?"

My stomach growled. "Yes. Very."

Kaen handed me some bread, which I wolfed down in a few heartbeats. I took a shaky breath. "All right. I feel . . . a bit better now." I stood up hesitantly, and Kaen took a few steps back to give me space to stretch out, but he looked ready to jump in and catch me should I tumble again. "Really, Kaen," I assured him. "I'm fine."

"If you say so." He took a deep breath, pausing for a moment before letting it back out. "But we need to figure out what to do now."

I nodded numbly. "I know . . ." I held a hand to my head. *Ugh, what a nightmare. Not only Lentha and all the little ones—now Mandrie and Phoebe are gone too.*

"Lyn, let's just worry about finding someplace to lie low for the night. It's going to be dusk soon."

I looked up at the sky above the buildings once more. With the day's clouds streaming in, the auroras began to glimmer, a mirage of blue and green playing off of the thickening layer. "You're right. I . . . I could use some sleep, I think."

We ended up taking refuge behind the back of an old shop in a dead-end alley, where an overhang provided shelter from any forthcoming rain. I told Kaen to let me take the first watch, but he refused, insisting that he would stay up himself before waking me for the second watch. I was more exhausted than I could ever remember being, so I didn't put up much fuss over it. I soon fell into a deep, dream-filled sleep.

I saw a young girl's face fading in and out of focus. I didn't know where I was or who was bugging me, but she was speaking my name.

"Lyn! Hello, Lyn." Her voice was young and childlike.

She was shaking me. "Stop," I moaned, squeezing my eyes shut tighter. "Please just let me sleep. . . ."

"But Lyn, you need to wake up! There are things I want to show you."

I shook my head slowly, feebly. "More sleep. . . ."

"Sleep?" the girl repeated. "Come on, just wake up! It's been ages, and all you can say is you want to sleep longer?"

"What did you just say?" I asked. I opened my eyes to see who it was, but the girl was already fading away. I caught only the faintest trace of her childlike appearance, complete with white hair, before my dream changed.

⁂

It felt like no time had passed when Kaen woke me gently, whispering, "Your watch now."

I roused myself with an effort and rubbed my eyes. I nodded numbly, visions of the little girl fading as I glanced around for the first time. I still felt tired, and the wall of any building was no comfortable place to sleep against. I let my friend lie down to sleep and forced myself to focus on not drifting off.

Looking upward, I saw the last vestiges of the auroras twinkling through the thinner parts of the clouds. This was how every night of the Sunlit Cycle went—the clouds rolled in, heavily dampening Sol's white light until morning, and the auroras began to twinkle within them. In the morning, the clouds would roll by once more, taking the auroras with them and revealing the white sun again. It was a beautiful display, though my favorite season of the Sol Cycle was still the Sunless Cycle, when the auroras became the world's light in place of Sol.

Another phenomenon that accompanied each Cycle was what we called constellations: star-like patterns that appeared on the cloud layer as Sol's light struck the Energy Field that surrounded Mani. At least, that's how I'd heard it explained. There were a few that appeared in the Sunlit Cycle, and a few others in the Night Season. Right now, the Sun Dancer constellation was glowing its brightest in Mani's night sky. It was vaguely shaped like a dancing girl, but I certainly wouldn't have thought of that on my—

A sound came from farther down the street. I tensed, suddenly on the alert. I glanced back at where Kaen slept, debating whether to wake him. If it was just a dog roaming around, however, I would feel bad. . . .

Slowly, I crept toward the noise. It was footsteps; I could distinguish that now. Soft footsteps, heading across our alleyway. I moved forward quietly until I could just make out the figure in the starlight.

It was a young woman, not even my age from what I could tell. Shocked, I stepped forward and said, "Excuse me—are you lost?" I could have kicked myself for my stupidity, but pity and instinct led me to say it. What if she was an orphan like me? Like all the others who had died in the last day? What if she needed help?

The girl gasped, nearly tripping in fright as she scurried back from me. "You . . . w-who are you? Get away from me!" She spoke in a hushed whisper that said she was still afraid to catch attention. It proved to not be loud enough to wake Kaen.

"I-I'm sorry," I said, stepping backward as well. "I should not have . . ." I didn't know what to say.

"Oh." The girl seemed to truly see me for the first time. "I shouldn't be wandering around this late. I didn't . . . Are you—do you live near here?" She stared at me warily, and I caught a better look at her face. It was youthful in appearance, but in reality, she was probably the same age as me. Maybe fourteen or fifteen. She was very pretty, with dainty, refined features and thin, dark eyebrows over scared blue eyes. Her shoulder-length hair was a glossy black, surely washed every morning . . .

I gasped. "You're . . ." She was clearly of noble blood. Of all the luck. I didn't know what to say now. I was about to speak when I caught sounds of movement from the way she had come. I groaned inwardly at the thought that this young lady of the court had brought footpads or worse to our hiding place. "Quick—go!" I hissed.

"Huh? What?" She looked confused, almost hurt, until I clarified:

"Thieves! You have to get back to the Palace!"

She followed my gaze, nodding nervously. "G-goodbye, then. Forgive me." She ran off the other way, back towards the center of the city where the Palace lay—confirming my assumptions of her nobility—and I found myself wondering why I was helping this girl. Without a word, I spun to face the thieves, belt knife out and in hand.

There were only two of them, tall but scrawny men with un-kempt beards and a knife and a cudgel between them. Not much of a threat, yet my hands still shook from nerves. I'd had enough fighting for one day, so I determined to try and scare them off instead of engaging. If I had any of my freakish strength left . . . I didn't need to use it now.

"Don't come any closer!" I snapped at them, slicing the air in front of me, and leaped at one of them, pushing him back with moderation so as to only knock him backward. The other one I threatened with my naked blade, and he fled with a curse, along with his companion. Never had I known how easy it was to scare off thieves.

It was at this moment that Kaen came up to me, having been awakened by the brief scuffle. "Lyn, what was that all about?"

"Footpads," I answered him. "I was careless and made too much noise sneaking about. You can go back to sleep."

Surprisingly, he did so, wandering back to his perch against the alley wall and slumping with his back to the bricks.

I spent the rest of the night awake on watch. I couldn't help but wonder if I could have helped to somehow scare off the bandits from the previous day. . . . But that man had been a fire mage, and had a half-dozen companions, not one or two; I knew that I could do nothing for my dead family now, but it didn't make it hurt any less.

The tears came now, and I huddled up to cry to myself, silent tears that wouldn't wake Kaen up. When I was done, I wiped my face off and tried to take my mind off of Lentha's beaten face by running through possible options Kaen and I could take this day, ways to get Mandrie and Phoebe back. I could only think of two possibilities. . . .

Finally, I deemed it close enough to cloudbreak to wake him from his sleep. "Kaen, get up!" I said, nudging him with my foot. "Kaen!"

"All right, all right," he mumbled, getting up and stretching. Our situation seemed to come back to him. "Oh, great auroras. We need a plan."

"I know." I shook my head in despair. "We *will* get them back, Kaen. But . . . should I just give myself up? What else is there to do?"

"I-I don't know," he replied. "We can't just turn you in! I won't allow that."

"But Mandrie is your little sister. You've always—"

"I know!" Kaen stamped his foot to emphasize his words. "I swore I'd always take care of her, and I'll go to any lengths to get her back. But if there's *any* way of avoiding just marching you up to the Palace gates and turning you in . . . we can find that way. I know it."

I bit my lip, trying to hold back the surge of emotions from the past day. "I'm sorry. We'll figure something out." I sighed, gazing down at the grey cobblestones of the Nytaean street. "Well . . . what if we break in and try to free them somehow?"

Kaen shook his head. "Won't work. We'd need a disguise, a ruse . . ." He frowned for a moment and then snapped his fingers. "Wait, that's it!"

- Chapter 4 -

Infiltrating the Palace

Silversmiths: a long-lost order of men who used magic to work silver into any shape imaginable and imbue it with incredible strength. It was they who forged the blades of old, which are wielded by mage soldiers and elite swordsmen today, capable of breaking lesser blades and absorbing most elemental magic. Men have tried and failed to create a blade of any worth with the soft metal apart from the Silversmiths. But alas, they died out in the late 800s, taking their secrets with them.
— From *Secrets of Mani*, by Sor the Lark

(Fynle 28, 997—Waxing Day)

So there we were, two hours later, marching right up to the Palace walls of Nytaea. My hair was the most normal and unassuming color of brown possible—walnut shell brown, to be specific. Hopefully, not too many would notice that it was dyed. Kaen and I had changed our clothes into slightly more decent, if costly, ones. "Look natural," he would say to me periodically, or, "Don't act nervous." Sure, right. How could I *not* be nervous now? Ugh, I would never willingly work at the Palace if it weren't our only option. Kaen and his brilliant ideas. . . .

The Nytaean Palace was a beautiful, stunningly complex structure that loomed over the entire city, easily the greatest attraction that greeted the eyes. The River Ardencaul ran underneath part of it and out the other side. The Palace was surrounded by a wall, with multiple guarded gate points allowing the nobility and their carriages access in and out. The four high towers of the Palace, however, were easily visible over the barrier, along with the inner walls and arched catwalks that ran between them.

We didn't approach the front gate but rather circled around to a smaller side gate. They would still be looking out for a white-haired girl, of course, but the guards didn't have much time for anyone else. We were waved through impatiently, after a line about seeking work at the Palace.

At the door, we were met by a black-and-green-liveried servant, who politely but disparagingly asked what our business was.

"Sir, we are looking for work here," I said, bobbing a small curtsy.

The steward gave a small *hmph!* and rubbed his chin thoughtfully. "Well, we are always in need of good help. I assume you are orphans?"

We both shook our heads frantically, but before we could deny it, he waved a dismissive hand. "It matters not to me. I will tell my superiors that you come from impoverished families to work for their debts. You will receive sufficient food, clothing and lodgings as long as you are here."

"Thank you, sir! You are too kind," said Kaen, bowing deeply.

"Yes, well, come on in. My name is Gorman Sedler, and I will escort you to the proper senior staff to instruct you." The steward waved us inside.

I shot Kaen a quick victory grin, and he winked back. We were in.

A quarter of an hour later, I was talking with a maid to whom Gorman had directed me. She looked to be some ten years my senior, blonde-haired and dressed in the customary Kalceron livery: black-skirted dress with green cuffs and deep-green highlights.

"Well, new girl, what's your name?" she asked in a husky voice.

"The name's Podda," I said hastily, trying my best not to act nervous or scared. This was the alias I had prearranged with Kaen, who would be going by Roger.

"Well, Podda, you'll be needing proper clothing. I'll take you to see Lina, and she'll get you all fixed up. The name's Betty, by the way. Come on." She waved for me to follow. She was a busy woman, but not too busy to show me the ropes of the maidservant's life. Firstly, she took me to see Lina, a girl not much older than myself who handled all of the crafting and mending of the maids' and servants' attire. She fitted me with a spare black-and-green dress. It fit me all right, but far from perfect—shoulders a hair too narrow and made for one a bit less flat-chested than me.

After this, Betty took me around and began to introduce me to the other female Palace staff, teaching me as we went. I was surprised to find that many of the girls there—few were older than Betty— were as cheery as she, though it soon came to light that that was mostly just a cover-up for their stressful lives as servants to a harsh overlord.

I had come at a good time, because one girl had recently been lashed to death on the governor's orders. One minor slip-up, and . . . it did not go well with them. Or so I gathered, at least. All the rumors I had heard as a child in the orphanage appeared to be true. The maids said he took the pretty ones for himself if he chanced upon any that he fancied. They didn't expound any further on that.

I supposed Kaen should have an easier time with the menservants. They were a lot harder to find, given the relative rarity of men in our world. Three or four to one, if I recalled correctly. Perhaps he would even move up, or rather, he would if he didn't lose his patience and botch it all by going for Kalceron's throat at first sight. This was not going to be a quick operation.

That night, I slept in one of three main sleeping rooms in the maids' quarters, bunked side by side with a girl named Teli, who was no older than Mandrie. Probably ten or eleven. The bunk beds were triple-decked, so two more slept beneath me and two more above. It was far from luxury, but in truth it was better than my life had been at Lentha's orphanage. The food was decent—that is to say, finer fare than I had eaten in quite a while. I slept well that night, despite the feeling that any one of my new companions would turn me in to the mage soldiers come morning.

They didn't. The next day was a very ordinary one by a maid's reckoning, and entailed more work. We got up before cloudbreak and washed, swept, dusted, cooked, and served breakfast to the lord's family and household; we then broke our fast, cleaned, mopped, scrubbed and cooked some more. . . . Such was our routine. We served meals to the residents of the Palace, only after which we would eat our own meals. This consisted of either cold leftovers of the delicious foods that the noblemen ate or a selection of meals we were allowed to cook for ourselves—using only the plainest ingredients.

Over the next few days, I learned a lot about being a maid. I learned to cook fancy meals—tantalized the whole time by delicious smells without getting to taste a bite—as well as how to wash and fold lordly clothing carefully and serve meals. A few days in, I even had to serve Lord Kalceron himself dinner, which was nerve-racking but . . . surprisingly uneventful.

I caught on quickly to the maids' routine, and before long I was accepted as one of their own. No one even slightly suspected their new maid of being the white-haired monster Lord Kalceron was seeking.

I never got a chance to sneak down to the dungeons and search for Phoebe and Mandrie—I didn't even know where the infamous Palace dungeons were, and for all I knew, the girls were locked in some random tower instead—but I resolved to find out just where they were being kept. Perhaps Kaen had found out more about it than me.

In my rounds, I would occasionally see the young noblewoman I had met in the street that one night, whom the maids referred to as simply, "Lady Mydia." Fortunately, she never recognized me.

Nearly two weeks after my induction as a maid, I witnessed the first real cruelty I had seen from Lord Kalceron. I was one of a half dozen girls assigned to serve the governor's family that night at their long, richly embroidered table. The young girl named Teli was also there, along with a handful of menservants I didn't recognize. The dining hall was elaborately decorated, with high-backed chairs carved in intricate patterns and windows trimmed in dark wood overlooking the western view of the Palace. A crackling fireplace lay at the far end, hung with drapery in the theme of House Kalceron, bearing the green dragon.

Lord Kalceron sat at the center of the table, black hair slicked back, dressed in fine apparel of black silk laced with the deep green of the Kalceron colors. It was only the second time I'd seen the man up close, and I felt my throat tightening before I even got near him. I was glad to be pushing a cart at the moment instead of serving. Teli, my young partner, served tea to the nobles at the near end of the table.

Nervously, I glanced about and surveyed the guests, trying to be discreet about it. I noted Lord Kalceron's partner seated to his immediate right, a thin, curvaceous woman who appeared to be in her late thirties. Her black hair was done up in a fashionable bun and pinned to keep it in place. Lady Lieda, his newest wife.

To his left side, however, sat the girl, Mydia, pecking politely at small portions of appetizers the other maids had brought in. As Teli and I approached her section of the table and I was able to hear more of the conversation, I caught Lord Kalceron making mention of her in his deep voice as "my lovely daughter." Suddenly, it clicked, and I felt a chill spread across my skin.

The princess did not look up, however, as Teli reached over and poured her a cup of tea. She simply nodded, accepting the beverage.

When Teli got to Lord Kalceron, she slipped up and dropped one of the cups on her platter near the governor, and he backhanded her viciously across the face. His family and guests pretended not to take notice, or maybe didn't care, but I saw Princess Mydia duck her head as she tried to hide a mortified expression.

Fortunately for me, no one noticed me amidst all this. All I could do was stare dumbly and try to keep anonymous as he quietly ordered his guards to take the girl out and whip her at the post. What could I do? Attack the governor of all Nytaea? His Authority was said to be fearsome, and I knew well that he had half a dozen mage soldiers stationed in the shadows around the room. If I tried to stop Teli's punishment, I would only make a scene and get myself killed. I let them drag her away, the injustice of it boiling inside me. Princess Mydia ran from the room, either as a small act of rebellion or to hide tears. I wasn't sure which—perhaps a combination of both.

The rest of the dinner was torture. My palms were so sweaty from nervousness that I nearly made the same mistake as poor Teli, and I was shaking by the time I and the other maids were done. "There was nothing you, or any of us, could do," Betty whispered to me as we hurried back to the kitchen with the dish trays. "It happens often; you just have to try and forget it."

But how could I? Such things should not happen. I couldn't understand how a human could so dispassionately call for such meaningless punishment on another. The servants whispered that his wife, Lieda, was just as cruel. Was all nobility this way, or just House Kalceron?

Teli returned that night, bleeding from numerous stripes down her back. We did our best to take care of her, knowing that she had to be back to work on the morrow. When I finally climbed into bed, I lay there—without a bunk companion—and stared up at the bunk above me with restless eyes, unable to sleep.

Eventually, after all of the others were surely asleep, my insomnia prompted me out of bed to pace and meander about aimlessly. I wasn't even sure why I was up, but for the nagging guilt that I couldn't shake. And yet my story was not all that different from these maids'. My shame and horror likely stemmed from having to witness Teli's treatment after only recently experiencing the brutal tragedy at the orphanage. . . .

I wandered out of the maidservants' quarters, unsure of where I was going. I knew it was against the rules to roam the Palace after the day's work was done. We lived strict lives. But, unheeding of the warnings I had received time after time, I made my way out into the vast corridors of the Palace. I had some knowledge of the Palace's layout at this point, but I had no particular destination in mind.

I turned a corner and stopped in the doorway as I came face-to-face with a shorter, slender woman in a sleek black dress. With shock, I recognized her as Lady Lieda. She glanced at me with cold, vulpine eyes, causing me to take an unconscious step backward. "My . . . my lady. I am sorry. I-I lost my way, and I was—"

"Save your breath," she murmured. "I don't believe you maggots are supposed to be crawling around at this time of night."

"I . . ." I curtsied as humbly and deeply as I could. "I apologize. I am new here, and I forget the rules as easily as I forget the layout of the Palace." I kept my head bowed.

The woman gave an amused snort. "Well, someone is quick with her tongue, now, isn't she? The pig can speak, perhaps well enough to save her own filthy hide." Her velvety voice dripped with venom. I glanced up worriedly as Lady Lieda leaned in and whispered in my ear, "Or perhaps I ought to just kill you now, hmm?"

"M-my lady . . ." Inside, my heart was beating wildly and my mind raced. Would she really do something as sudden and violent as that? And with what, her Authority? She was . . . I racked my brain desperately. I was pretty sure they said she was a thunder mage.

"Don't worry," she said after a moment. "I will let you go this time. I am not interested in the likes of you tonight. Should I catch you in my way again . . . I'll make it quiet but painful."

"Yes, my lady. Thank you."

"Now get out of my sight!" she hissed, baring her teeth like a wild animal.

I shied back and turned the other way, scurrying off toward the maids' quarters. *That woman is insane.* Who spoke that way to a mere serving girl? I was pretty certain this was the right way back . . .

Footsteps sounded behind me. I was near to the front doorway of the Palace, where bracketed torches illuminated the way. I glanced back anxiously, quietly cursing my absent-mindedness, but I saw no one in the relative darkness of the hallway. I didn't call out; that would be foolish. Instead, I hid behind an ornamental suit of armor, waiting to see if the mysterious person walked by or turned another way. The footsteps grew louder, until at last I saw a shadowy figure come into the torchlight. I nearly gasped as I recognized Princess Mydia, complete with a cloak and cape, which I had only seen her wear that night in the backstreets of Nytaea.

I must have moved, because I caused the suit of armor to rattle, catching Mydia's attention. I could have kicked myself. She started and called out softly, "Who's there?" as though afraid of someone catching her. Who, I wondered, the guards or her stepmother? Turning, she caught sight of me and started once more. "Who are you? You're . . . you're one of the maids. What are you doing out and about at this hour?"

"I . . ." I had nothing more to say for myself than I did the other night, but she must have recognized me now, because recollection showed on her face.

"Wait a minute!" she hissed, still in a whisper. "You're that urchin I saw in the city the other night! The one who saved me from the thieves."

"No. You've got it wrong," I protested quietly.

The princess narrowed her eyes in disbelief, lips drawing in an almost pouty way. "No, I know it's you!"

". . . Yes," I admitted with a sigh, massaging my forehead with my palm. I couldn't very well try to hide my identity now that she had recognized me. I lowered my hand and attempted to introduce myself. "I'm, ah—they call me Podda."

"Oh, I see," she said slowly. "But how . . . hmm, so you came here recently? To the Palace?"

Well, at least she wasn't quite as unperceptive as I'd thought. "That's right," I answered at length.

"Why . . . ?" Mydia's youthful face displayed confusion. Then she glanced over her shoulder, as though afraid that her witch of a stepmother might catch her. "But never mind that. I was just on my way somewhere. Want to come with me?"

My heart began to beat faster. This princess was inviting me to sneak outside of the Palace with her? "Where?" I asked hesitantly.

"Just outside. Here." She took my hand in hers and pulled me with her, and that was that. She led me away from the entrance, down a hallway to the left.

"We can't just go out the front door," she whispered back to me. "The guards will let me past any time of day—my father doesn't care—but if I had one of the maids with me, it would look strange."

"And . . . why are you taking me with you?" I asked from behind her.

She glanced back at me as she pulled me through the halls. "What, you wouldn't have followed me anyway?"

"Well . . ."

Mydia laughed. Then she ducked her head in abashment, lowering her voice. "That's okay. I kind of want to show you now. And, come to think of it, I'm pretty sure you were there when my father ordered that girl to be whipped earlier."

"Teli."

"I . . . I'm sorry about that. You see, I feel the same as you. I, too, am saddened every time my father shows injustice to his subjects. My father is . . . a very twisted man."

I was shocked to hear such words from his own daughter. "You sound like you don't care for him much," I remarked.

"I didn't say that, but . . . he's just a terrible man. Come with me." Mydia led me out a side door, which led into the beautiful Palace Gardens. The place was lit by lamplight here and there, casting an almost eerie glow about the gardens. "This is my favorite spot," she confided to me. "It reminds me of my mother."

I nodded, taking in the starlit scene. Plants and shrubs were arranged meticulously in circular patterns, branching outward from the courtyard where we stood. Their leaves were actually . . . green, not the usual silver and grey that Mani's soil tinted most plants. The last light of dusk was fading away, and the dark sky of the Sunless Cycle was sprinkled with myriads of beaming stars whose light illumined the garden in addition to the lamps. Flowers of all sorts were curled into themselves, awaiting the coming sunlight, though a few seemed to be the nocturnal kind. Some plants needed Sol's powerful light to fully function, while others could subsist easily off of the Night Auroras.

"Who was your mother?" I asked.

"Eivael Badon, by birth. She came from the city of Cryvad in the far west and married into House Kalceron. I'm Mydia, by the way." She blushed slightly, after saying such an obvious thing. "I suppose you already knew that. It's Podda, correct?"

"Yes . . . correct." She seemed not to hear the hesitation in my voice. I felt almost bad lying to her, but it was needful, and I could not trust her, however genuine she seemed. "Did your mother pass away, then?" I asked her.

"Eight years ago, yes. I was devastated, and my father . . . Father became ever more unstable and violent in his rule. Mother was the only thing keeping him sane, and now I fear for him and all of Nytaea. That old hag, Lieda, has only served to corrupt him further." She grimaced.

I was silent for a moment, listening to the faint night sounds of the Palace Gardens in the absence of Mydia's strained voice. "Why do you trust me so much, having known me for only a few minutes?" I asked her.

She seemed to stop and consider this for the first time. "Well . . . I guess I don't know. I suppose it's because you just seem like someone I can trust. Perhaps . . . someone I need right now."

I frowned. "What do you mean by that, Princess?"

"Oh, please, Podda," she said, waving a hand. "It's Mydia, not 'Princess.' It's just . . ." She rubbed her hands awkwardly, tears shimmering in her eyes, and suddenly blurted, "Please! Will you be my friend?"

I blinked. *That was sudden.* Her friend? The princess of Nytaea was asking me to be her personal friend? "Wh-what?"

"Please!" she begged me. "I mean, not really, just—I don't have anyone in the whole Palace to talk to except my handmaidens, and they're such a sullen lot. Ever since Mum passed away, I don't have anyone left." At this point, she was wringing her hands nervously, and tears seemed to be threatening to run down her face.

I was at a loss for words. What was she asking of me? To sneak out and talk in the Palace Gardens with her every night? To risk everything to make her feel less lonely? I had known loneliness my entire life. I mean, in a way. I had no blood family to speak of. If I could help her, I would, but . . . *It's like she's a child. A little child.*

"A-all right," I said, embracing her gently. "You can cry if you have to, you know." She did cry a little bit, before pulling back from me and wiping her face sheepishly.

"I feel silly," she complained. "Crying for no reason. You don't . . . feel like crying, too?"

"I . . . don't like to cry in front of others," I said. It was true, though I didn't always manage it.

"Oh." Mydia cleared her throat. She seemed a bit embarrassed and almost disappointed. "I should cry less." Then she sat down on an ornamental birdbath, gesturing for me to take the small bench across from her. "So, tell me something more about you. Where are you from? How did you come to work at the Palace? I'm sure I never saw you around before the night I met you in the street."

I sighed. I still couldn't tell her, tentative friends or not. I felt bad about it, but my friends' freedom, my life and possibly Kaen's, too, were on the line. However, I could tell her some things. "I was taken in at a young age by an old woman who ran an orphanage in the city. My mother, I was told, was a commoner who had a child with an unknown man . . . I don't know who my mother or father were, and neither did Lentha. My mother is probably dead by now, just like the rest of the children in my orphanage. And Lentha."

Mydia gasped, holding a gloved hand to her mouth. "I'm so sorry to hear that. I wish—I wish I could help somehow." She looked to the side, biting nervously at her lip. "Podda . . . would you be willing to come back tomorrow night? I've got a certain . . . errand to run. I'd like you to come."

I eyed her carefully. "Perhaps. Does this have anything to do with what you were out doing the other night?"

Mydia shook her head. "Not quite. That was an orphanage run."

I gaped. "An orphanage run? You . . . help out orphanages?"

The princess nodded. "When I can. I take food and money. Like I said, the guards don't care, and my father only cares about me occasionally, as his little trophy to show off to guests. If you come tomorrow, though, you'll see what it is."

I nodded slowly. "All right, then. But I should go for now."

"Oh. Right." Mydia got up from her birdbath seat. "I apologize for keeping you out so long, Podda. I hope you don't get in trouble on my account."

"I'll be fine. Goodnight, Mydia." With that, I left.

- Chapter 5 -

The Underground

Iron is another mystery. According to ancient histories, it was once used to achieve great things, and provided strength to many nations. But none have been able to figure out how, as the little iron that has been discovered in the ground seems mostly useless—heavy, brittle, prone to rust, and not much stronger than silver. Not to mention that it is so scarce that only a king could afford to buy a piece.
— From *Secrets of Mani*, by Sor the Lark

(Dri'Shal 13, 997—Night Season)

The next night, I snuck out in much the same way, finding the door to the Palace Gardens after a bit of trial and error—careful, of course, not to run into the psychotic queen, Lieda—and found the black-haired princess waiting for me, dressed in a somewhat more practical fashion, with an apron over a long-sleeved dress and thin leather boots. She perked up as she saw me approach. "Podda! You actually came!"

"Of course. I said I would." I took a deep breath to still my nerves. "Now, where are we headed?"

Mydia hesitated briefly, as though making a last-minute decision to tell me. "We are going to a meeting with the Underground."

It took me a second to process what she said. *"What?* And you're taking me along? You're just . . . telling me, a complete stranger? Do you know how much danger you just put yourself in?"

"I . . . have already decided to trust you, Podda."

I laughed in disbelief. "Are you this way with everyone?"

Mydia blushed again. "As I said, I don't really . . . have anyone else that I ever talk to. No one except for my handmaidens, ever since my mother died. What are you going to do, turn me in to my father, the one who's made the life of every orphan in this city a living hell? Besides, do you have any idea how hard it is to be alone?"

I almost said yes, but stopped myself in time. Truly, I didn't. I had Kaen, as well as Phoebe and Mandrie until their kidnapping. "Sorry. I suppose I don't quite," I conceded. "It must be terrible."

She sucked in a breath, then seemed to change course. "Why would you even want to get a job here as a servant, when my father has treated children like you so awfully?"

"I . . ." I didn't know what to say. I couldn't very well just go right out and tell her what we had planned in coming to the Palace, or even mention my connection with Kaen—Roger; I had to remember that—but it was hard to leave her at a loss when her sympathy seemed so genuine. "Prin—Mydia . . . is it all right, if I, ah, withhold that information? I just . . . can't tell you yet."

Mydia looked slightly hurt. "Well . . . why not?"

"Look, it's not like that. I'm—" I took a deep breath "—I am in grave danger here in the Palace. People I love are in danger as well. As an orphan, I'm not a legal citizen by your father's standards, and so I . . . can't say more. Is that all right?"

Mydia considered this and then nodded. "All right. I understand. I'll take you to the meeting anyway, though. Come on, we have to hurry." She grabbed my arm and towed me out through the Palace Gardens down toward the city.

We arrived at the building just as the Charioteer constellation was glowing its brightest in the sky. It was one of a few that appeared during the Night Season. The structure she brought me to was old and dilapidated, possibly one of the many abandoned warehouses in Nytaea, relics of the city's glory days. Those were long gone, as was the life of this building. The air was chill, but not like it would be later on in the Sunless Cycle.

Mydia took me inside—to my surprise, the broken door opened right up—and led me down multiple flights of steps. She had brought a lantern, fortunately, or else we would be in total darkness.

We came to a door deep underground, probably at least two stories down, and Mydia unlocked it with a key and opened it up to allow me in. I stopped instead and placed a hand on her small shoulder. "Wait. Are you sure it's wise to show me this place?"

She turned to face me, frowning. "You keep asking questions like that. You really don't want to meet any of my acquaintances in the Underground? To do something to help?"

"I thought you said you didn't have any friends," I pointed out.

"I . . ." she lowered her voice. "Acquaintances. I wouldn't call them my friends. Just come on, you'll see."

I relented, allowing her to show me inside. The room was fairly spacious but only dimly lit by a few lamps along the stone walls. The ceiling was low, and a sense of claustrophobia made me almost fearful of it crashing down on my head. In the center of the room stood a large, round table. Around it sat an odd assortment of people on chairs and stools.

I counted four men and one woman, not including Mydia and myself. The woman, I could tell, was of noble blood, even though she wore plain clothing and little to no makeup. Her white-blonde hair was tied up in a practical bun. I could recognize that posture, that regal composure, anywhere. Mydia introduced her as Gaela. The men ranged from fat to rail-thin, to tall, to . . . small and greasy-looking.

Respectively, they were Big Bart, Skinny Sam, Tall Tom and Little Lester. Fighting to contain a laugh, I assumed that these must be aliases used only in the Underground.

I, of course, was introduced to them by Mydia as her friend and guest, Podda. She pretended that I was only posing as a maid, which was more or less true anyway. I hadn't thought much of my current clothing, but they all seemed to take it as the clever disguise of someone entirely different.

"So," said the noblewoman, Gaela. "You're late again, Mydia. Your little friend is welcome here if you trust her, but punctuality is a virtue, nonetheless."

Mydia gave a prim curtsy. "I'm terribly sorry for the inconvenience I have caused. I didn't mean to be tardy."

"Ahem!" Big Bart broke in loudly. "Yes, well. That's all well and good, but we still have actual things to discuss before the night is done. You came in at just the right time, my dears."

"Indeed," said Skinny Sam in a nasally voice. "The last orphanage that was burned . . . and that fight between the mage soldiers and unknown rebels. What have you all to say?"

A long string of opinions and conspiracy theories followed, some of which made sense while others did not. I, for my part, held my peace for obvious reasons. I noticed as the meeting went on that Mydia was right—these people were her allies, but not necessarily entirely upright. Most of the men leaned heavily toward an anarchistic mindset, and Gaela, who was probably the most level-headed out of them all, was very quiet and mysterious, seeming to have an agenda of her own. She and Big Bart seemed to be the leaders here.

At one point, however, when they were getting overly rowdy, Gaela had to quiet them all down. She raised her voice surprisingly high and shouted, "Silence! You'll bring the city watch down on our heads! I won't have that. Now, we must discuss the recent happenings in the city, *preferably* without shouting out baseless threats and other nonsense. The entire world is not our enemy."

"Pathetic," I said with crossed arms after having enough of it. "You're a bunch of children. Orphans are dying out there, and this is what the Underground is doing about it?" I probably should have kept my mouth shut, but it was hard to at this point.

The room went quiet. Gaela just stared at me strangely, almost coldly. Big Bart, however, didn't want anything to do with me. "Hmph. What's this little rat here for again? Think you can order us around, can ya, little maid?" He got up from his seat and towered over me with his fat stomach thrust forward over the table.

I clenched my hands at my sides and said nothing. Difficult though it was, I knew I had to hold myself back. I couldn't take out my frustration on them, and most certainly could not reveal myself for . . . whatever I was. That could only end unfavorably for all.

Mydia saved me, however. "Bart, please! We can trust her."

The large man drew back and gave a great *hmph!*

The meeting went on like this for upwards of an hour. I was dead tired by the end of it, hardly able to keep my eyes open and my mouth from yawning. Mydia finally led me out of the subterranean shelter, visibly displeased with how the discussion had gone.

"Wild bunch," I commented mildly, letting out a yawn. "That, uh . . . Big Bart, he's a handful."

Mydia barked a laugh. "Yes. Well, I did say that they weren't what I'd call friends. But Bart actually isn't that bad. He doesn't take well to newcomers. He's more intelligent than he lets on, and he is very knowledgeable about the city and its inner workings. He has many economic ties to the industry here in Nytaea. But I still want to know who it was that the guards were after that day . . ."

I glanced at her as we walked back toward the Palace. "Really? Your father didn't mention anything?"

She shook her head. "No. He was after someone in particular, or so I gathered, at least a certain type of person, and . . . Hespian brought back some prisoners that afternoon."

My heart rate sped up at those words. "Hespian?" As soon as the name came out of my mouth, I bit my lip, wishing I hadn't reacted at all.

Mydia did not seem to notice the change in my tone of voice. "Yes, he is the captain of the Mage Guard."

Captain of the Mage Guard. So, the big fish had indeed been after me. To think that the coward of a man who kidnapped my friends was the leader of Lord Kalceron's forces. But I needed to know . . . "And who are these prisoners? Where did he take them?" I tried to keep the excitement out of my voice.

"I don't—I don't really know. Top secret. I only got a brief glimpse of them. They looked to be a couple of street urchins like you, both girls—probably orphans. I don't know their names, nor where Hespian has them imprisoned."

She didn't expound further, so I didn't say any more about it, seeing as that would be risky ground to tread upon. I did not want to connect myself to Mandrie and Phoebe in any way, even when speaking to Mydia, since I still couldn't *fully* trust her. We soon arrived at the Palace and she led me inside through the garden gate.

Inside, she turned to me, lowering her voice. "Will you be all right, going back at a late hour like this? Don't get caught. Do you know your way?"

"Don't worry about me," I told her. "I know my way around pretty well now."

"Right, right . . ." As I turned to go, she stopped me once more.

"Podda. Again, tomorrow night, maybe? Meet me here?"

I stopped, hesitating. Was this going to be a nightly thing? "You mean, going to the . . . warehouse again?"

"No, no. Just to talk, in the Palace Gardens. I want you to be my friend, remember?" She grinned, a playful twinkle in her eye. "Please?"

"A-all right. I'll think about it, Mydia." She seemed satisfied with this, smiling as she scampered off to her rooms. My mind raced despite my fatigue as I made my way back to the maidservants' quarters. Fortunately, no one seemed to have noticed my leaving; they were all sound asleep. I dropped into bed next to Hamia, my bunkmate for the week, and fell right to sleep.

- Chapter 6 -

The Princess's Handmaiden

Silver was adopted by the mage soldiers of Nytaea as the armor of choice because of its availability and reasonable protection. Other nations stick to leather or even lighter materials. Some magi have gone into battle wearing only the robes that they use to study scrolls. Advanced magical protection includes frost armor, an invention of a Lygelli water mage two generations back; spell-reinforced silver armor of the old Silversmiths (which only the most elite of the current mage soldiers are entrusted with); and heavy stone armor made of stonesung rock plates by earth magi in the far reaches of Torlega, beyond the Styrite Mountains.
— From *Secrets of Mani*, by Sor the Lark

(Dri'Shal 14, 997—Night Season)

I awoke the next morning to Hamia shaking my shoulders. "Podda, Podda—wake up."

"What, Kaen?" I mumbled sleepily.

"Huh? Oh, you're awake! It's time to get up, Podda." She left me to get out of bed, fetch a basin of water to wash with, change into my day's work clothing, and begin working. Such was the life of a maid.

All day, I could not keep my thoughts off of Mydia, the princess. Friend, huh? The princess's friend . . . I had no idea how this would to turn out, but she seemed like a good ally to have in the Palace. Perhaps she could secure me a better position in the Palace staff, or even spirit me inside the Underground. But what would either of those things help? If I could get closer to the Palace Dungeons, that would be one thing. I couldn't help but feel a sort of tense anxiety as I pictured how another casual conversation with Mydia in the gardens might go. I didn't really want to meet the Underground leaders again, but Mydia was all right. She seemed honest.

After a day of the dreadful agony of waiting, I was almost taken by surprise when the day drew to a close and we returned to the maids' quarters for bed. Mydia had glanced my way once when I was serving dinner, smiling slightly. That was all I had seen of her all day, though.

My heart beating wildly, I waited for Hamia to fall asleep—most of the maids knew how to fall asleep quickly, in order to conserve sleeping time—and then rose furtively to sneak outside the sleeping quarters and into the hallways. At one point, I had to stop as a guard crossed the hallway in front of me, bearing a creaky lantern. Then I proceeded out into the Palace Gardens by way of the secret side door Mydia had shown me.

Part of me wondered why I would ever be so foolish as to sneak out here, trusting her not to turn me in, just to please the princess, but I forced my misgivings down. And there she was, waiting for me just as she'd said. (On the same birdbath as the first night, I noted with some amusement.)

"Yay, you came!" she said gleefully, getting up and rushing over to hug me. Her eyes looked suspiciously misty.

"I came," I said quietly, patting her shoulder. I felt a tear drop off her cheek and onto my shoulder. *Are all princesses this emotional?*

"I didn't think you'd actually come," she moaned into my shoulder. But then she let me go and got a hold of herself, taking out a sparkling white handkerchief and dabbing at her eyes. "I'm sorry. I don't know what's wrong with me. How can you stand to be so lonely and *not* cry all the time?"

"I . . . guess I manage somehow," I said, trying to keep a straight face. As I'd told her the other night, I made a point to never cry where others could see me. Perhaps it was just pride.

Mydia sighed and went over to one of the flower bushes and ran her hand across the retracted blooms, mouth moving absently. Under her palm, the flowers opened and flared bright red. They stayed that way for a few moments after her hand passed on, and then closed back up again.

I stared in astonishment. "You can use magic? Or . . . Authority?" I wasn't sure of the correct terminology.

Mydia smiled. "Of a sort, yes. My mother had the same gift, but mine isn't quite strong enough that you'd call it Authority. Simple Coaction. Mother made these gardens, and she used to tend to them every day. The flowers flourished under her care."

"I wish I could use magic," I said wistfully, before realizing what had just escaped my lips. "I mean . . . Not really. I wouldn't want to be a mage. Besides, that's a silly thought, anyway." I giggled nervously and then coughed into a hand. Despite the warnings I'd heard all my childhood about staying away from magi, something had always captivated me about them.

Mydia didn't say anything more about it, probably so as not to make me feel bad. After a little while, we got to talking about other things. She was curious about what life had been like for me on the streets, so I told her a bit about living at the orphanage.

Mydia nodded, explaining that she had made it a habit to donate, not only to the Underground, but to orphanages and soup kitchens around the city, trying to help out the poor wherever she could. Her father and handmaidens never bothered to notice her disappearances at night, or at least they didn't care. If she was ever actually caught lending money out to his enemies, though . . . She had been doing it less and less now, she said, and instead devoting money to the Underground in hopes that they could help the people for her where she could not.

It went back and forth like this for some time, until Mydia pulled out her pocket watch—a luxury which no orphan or maid could ever afford—and exclaimed, "Oh, my! It's later than I thought. Well . . . tomorrow night, then?"

I nodded.

"All right, see you then." Mydia returned to her rooms, and I made my way back to the maids' quarters. Everyone was still asleep again, fortunately.

The days seemed to pass in a blur. Every day, I would wait impatiently for nightfall—in the Night Season, that means the time that the auroras dimmed and the world returned to its natural state of sunless darkness—to sneak out and see the princess. We would talk for an hour or more before returning to our beds to find some sleep. It was probably all right for her, but the shortened sleeping time began to take a serious toll on me. Whenever I looked in the washbasin, I saw a tired, haggard girl with rings under her eyes. We couldn't keep going like this, or I would mess up and drop a platter or something, only to find my head misplaced after Lord Kalceron got angry.

One night, I couldn't take it anymore. "Mydia," I said sleepily, "We just can't keep doing this. I'm afraid if I go on staying up late like this, I'll be in danger of falling asleep on the job."

Mydia's brow furrowed with concern. "Oh, really? Goodness, you do look awful. . . . I'm so sorry. I suppose the maids have to get up dreadfully early."

Here we go, I thought. *She's going to cry again for sure.* But she didn't.

"Actually, I've been thinking . . ." she mused.

"What?"

"I wonder if I could get you as my personal maidservant."

"Your . . . personal maidservant."

"Well, think about it, Podda. Wouldn't it be better? I wouldn't have to say much about it, nor acknowledge you as anyone but a servant in front of others, but we could talk all we want. It'd be great, Podda!"

I considered her proposition. It really would help me out a lot. I would have a bit more credibility than as an ordinary maid, so I might not lose my head if Lady Lieda stumbled upon me again. "I suppose it's worth a shot," I said hesitantly. "But would you even be able to do that?"

She waved a hand. "Easy. A little finagling here and there. No one would think it suspicious."

"But, don't you have other handmaidens?"

"Yes, but one, um . . . left recently, and isn't coming back, so . . ."

"There is an open position?"

"Yes. I'll see what I can do. Until then, go get some sleep."

Not for the first time, I wondered to myself why she thought of me as a friend. If she could use magic, then surely she could have defended herself against a couple of no-good thieves that night. Perhaps there really wasn't a reason.

I simply nodded. "Thank you, Mydia. Goodnight."

(Dri'Shal 16, 997—Night Season)

The next day went as usual. I woke up at the normal early hour, and tried all day to not look as tired as I was. It was just after dinner was served, while I was eating with the maids, that little Teli—who had, fortunately, healed by this time—informed me that someone had come asking for me. My first thought was that it must be one of Mydia's servants, but no. It was Kaen.

"Kaen!" I nearly threw my arms around his neck, so happy was I to see him finally. It wasn't like I had not passed him by on my errands, but I hadn't gotten the chance to stop and talk to him in a little while.

"Shhh!" He pulled me to one side, away from the doorway. "It's Roger, remember?"

"Oh, yes. Sorry. Have you found anything out, Roger?"

He shook his head regretfully. "No. I'm not getting anywhere yet. However . . ." He stepped back and gestured at his new apparel. "Ta-da." It took me a moment to see that he was now dressed in a spear soldier's garb, a crisp-looking, black tunic emblazoned with the green dragon of House Kalceron, complete with black breeches, boots and leather gauntlets to go with it. A belt with a green-painted buckle held the tunic fast around his waist.

"Kae—Roger! Did you get enlisted into the Armed Guard's ranks?"

"I did. Must have been my shining skill with plates and platters. Easily transferable to the spear, you know." He gave a tense laugh, and then shrugged. "No. They needed a few extra hands, apparently, and they thought I looked decent enough to draft. Hopefully, I'll be able to go places a servant can't. Guards like me have dungeon duty occasionally. I can't talk long, though."

"Me neither," I admitted. "I'm glad you got in. I, too, might be . . . moving up a little."

"How's that?"

"I'd rather not say yet, but . . . I hope I see you again soon.

Remember, don't be too far away."

"Same to you." With that, he left to go and do whatever business he had.

I went back inside the maids' quarters, and was greeted by Lina with a plate of leftover noodles. She handed it to me and brushed back a strand of golden hair. "Who was it? What'd he want, anyway?"

I shrugged. "Nothing, I guess. It was just a spear soldier sent to tell me to be more careful when I clean."

"Why would they send one of them?"

"I guess it was his room."

Lina laughed, and left me to find a place with my maid friends and eat my supper.

Not a half hour later, one of Princess Mydia's own handmaidens, dressed in fine clothing, called on me and informed me that I was wanted by the princess. The maids watching nearby were astonished, but I told them not to worry as I let the woman lead me away. She was one of the oldest maidservants I had seen here, easily into her middle years.

"Take heart, little Podda," she said to me in a stuffy, lofty tone for a servant. "You have been chosen to be one of Her Ladyship's handmaidens. My name is Chara, and I will instruct you in your new duties to the princess."

My heart sank a little at hearing that, but I went with her nonetheless to Mydia's rooms, which were all the way at the northern end of the Palace—the back—and up a long, spiraling tower staircase. I felt ready to drop by the time we got there, though that was mostly just from lack of sleep. Normally, my stamina rarely flagged. Finally, we arrived and I saw Mydia. Arrayed in a gorgeous gown of light green, midnight hair pinned up on the sides with pins of matching green color, she looked a regal young lady; my new mistress, no less.

She did a good job of not looking overly thrilled to see me, but I still caught a glimmer of excitement in her eyes. "So," she said, chin held high in a noble posture, "You've arrived. You've been recommended to be my next handmaiden. I hope you will do everything Chara and I tell you. Mind your place and serve me well, and you will have more luxuries than most of the other maids around the Palace."

Oh, classic. I'd been 'recommended'. How had she managed that one? "Anything I can do to serve, My Lady," I said submissively. Chara seemed satisfied with that reply, and Mydia nodded curtly.

And so began my tenure as Princess Mydia's personal servant. Imagine that: Kaen, drafted into the Armed Guard, and me, a handmaiden to Lord Kalceron's own daughter. What would I do now, even if we did find a way to break our friends out of prison? Where would we go to hide, after the princess herself knew me?

No, put those thoughts away, idiot girl. I knew I could have no second thoughts now. We were getting closer, and there was no backing down.

I was given over to Chara again, to be shown around the princess's vast suites in the tower and to learn my new duties as a maid. It turned out that Chara was more like the one who made sure the *other* handmaidens did their job. My new partner, Julia, was a wide-eyed brunette around the same age as me. I would take over most of her duties, while she cleaned the room and ran errands for Mydia. I was to awaken my lady in the morning, dress her, serve her meals that Chara and Julia brought from the kitchen, and bathe her every day (I sincerely hoped that she was capable of doing some of *that* herself). In reality, it would be much easier than my former job as a plain old maid. I would be fed better, too, so that was a plus.

At last, Chara left me alone with Mydia, taking Julia with her on some errand or another. Mydia shut the door firmly and let out a long sigh. "There. That's better. All right; bath time, servant."

"Is that a joke?" I asked hesitantly.

"Actually, no. Bath time is about this time every night. Don't worry; it won't be that bad. I can scrub myself, mostly; you basically just hand me all of the hideous scented soaps and perfumes, and we can chat at the same time. Bedtime will be soon after that."

I had to start my new duties at some point, so I grabbed the necessary things for her and followed her to the personal bathroom of her suite. Who needed a personal bathroom, anyway? Oh, well. Chara had told me the basics already, and like Mydia said, it really wasn't that bad. I was basically just her attendant.

As she steeped, she explained more about how my job as her handmaiden would work, how we would arrange things. Mydia offered to let me go to sleep before her, in my new personal servant's room adjoining hers. I did have to be up before her every morning in order to wake her up, but she said that we could reverse it at least for one night. Chara wouldn't know. We talked for perhaps half an hour while she soaked in her bubbly bath. I couldn't help but notice that she enjoyed it far more than she pretended, but I wasn't about to question the personal contradictions of a pampered noblewoman.

I handed the princess a towel to dry herself off, and then did up her black hair in a soft towel, just the way Chara had instructed me. Mydia only had to give me a few pointers. Then I helped her get into her nightgown, and finally accompanied her back to her bedroom. Here, she left me to go to my own bed—one much more comfortable than the bunks shared by the other maids—bidding me a good night.

I fell asleep almost immediately.

- Chapter 7 -

Candlelight

Children born with an affinity, or Aptitude, for an element or elements are called Adepts. Most children are tested at the age of eight by magi of their local council, for that is the age by which Aptitude is nigh-always apparent. Of course, many lowborn children go untested, sometimes for their whole lives, and in this fashion much talent is wasted across the world, for it is said that a child will lose most or all of his or her Aptitude by the time they reach full adulthood if it goes untapped. At this point, it can never be retrieved.
— From *Secrets of Mani*, by Sor the Lark

(Dri'Shal 17, 997—Night Season)

The clouds had already broken when Mydia woke me with a giggle, shaking my shoulders. "Psst! Chara will be up here soon. It's morning."

"All right. Sorry about that, My . . . lady." The name "Mydia" became the title "Milady" as I clumsily corrected myself mid-speech. I couldn't very well call her Mydia when Chara might hear.

With a groan, I swung my feet onto the floor and glanced about the room, taking in the wood-framed bed on which I'd slept, the cross-stitched wall hanging on the far wall, the lamp burning in the corner, and lastly . . . my liege lady, who stood there looking at me with impatient green eyes. Amusingly, she hadn't dressed herself; but of course, that *was* my duty. I arose and dressed myself before helping her to do the same.

Chara soon arrived in Mydia's dressing room, reminding me of my many strict duties to the princess in her impatient tone. Over the whole day, Mydia only had a few moments to spare when she could actually talk to me without prying ears listening in. That is, until nightfall, at which point the old maid left us alone to retire to her own room, below Mydia's main suite.

After a minute of idle chitchat, Mydia said, "So, Podda, I was thinking . . . You asked about my magic the other night."

I hesitated, wondering where this topic could be going. "Yes . . . I suppose I shouldn't have mentioned anything."

"No, no," she said quickly. "That's not it. You just seem to me . . . well, you seem a bit different. I wonder if you yourself have any Coactive abilities."

I frowned. "I don't know why you would think that. I'm just a lowborn orphan. I'm pretty sure I don't have any magical . . . talent. Coaction, synergy, whatever you call it." I laughed uncomfortably. What I didn't want to say was that I had something else entirely; whatever it actually was, I did not want the secret getting out.

"Synergy is just another word for Coaction," she clarified. "But . . . maybe you don't. You probably don't. It's just—like I said, you seem different."

"Different how?" I asked.

"Let's just try a test, Podda. Please, I really want to know. Have you ever been tested?"

I shook my head, deciding I was just paranoid about her somehow being on to my secret. "All . . . right. What do you want me to do?"

Mydia must have been considering this already, because she had an idea all laid out. First, she took me by the hands and tried to 'probe', as she called it, for a hint of magical affinity. She claimed that magi could often tell using this method if another had the talent. She found nothing, as I expected, but she decided to proceed with a few experiments anyway. She had me try to reach her mind telepathically, light a candle with my mind, and break a jar without touching it. Fortunately, that last one was as unsuccessful as the others, else Chara would have had a fit when she saw it.

It slowly occurred to me that Mydia was totally guessing. "It's a tricky process," she admitted with a sigh. "And very difficult to know for sure, especially since I'm not the most highly skilled mage. You have to try many methods to explore one's potential talents, as there are many branches of magic."

I remained unconvinced. Noting her apparent discouragement, I said, "Well, what did you expect? I knew I wasn't a mage."

She let it rest there for the night, but I could tell that she still, for whatever reason, suspected that I possessed Aptitude. I was only surer than ever that I didn't, but we got to talking about other things anyway. Then it was bath time, which went the same as the last night. Finally, I saw her to her bed, and then went to sleep myself.

The next morning, I managed to get up early enough—as I was supposed to—to awaken my liege lady. I dressed her properly and did her hair for the day, and then Julia brought in breakfast for her. Chara still wanted to show me how everything was done, and was always around *somewhere*, spying over my shoulder. I got to know Julia a bit, who seemed nice enough—that is to say, not very talkative but a drastic improvement in personality from Chara. I got the feeling that she, like many of the staff around the Palace, held some sort of grudge against Mydia despite her kindness and easygoing nature.

This surprised me, as the princess was always very good to the maids, but they associated her with her father, and with nobility in general, whom they hated and who despised them in turn. I did as well, and if it had not been for meeting Mydia, I would still have thought that all nobles were terrible people.

That night, I asked the princess why it was that she had brought up magic.

Mydia seemed hesitant to answer me at first, scratching at her black bangs. "I . . . suppose I can't very well keep it from you. All right, then. Podda, the fact is that you remind me of my brother."

"What!" I'd always known I was ugly.

"Just a bit. He was always there for me, my elder brother, looking out for me . . . the only brother I had by true blood. My father had other children, but Kallyn was his only trueborn heir."

"Kallyn?" I repeated. "I've never heard the name."

Mydia's eyes almost seemed to glaze over as she recalled memories of her past. "He was everything my father wasn't—tall, strong, eyes blue and kind. His hair was fair like Mother's, and he had her face, too. He was always the good prince, pleasing Father and doing good at the same time. He practically raised me when I was little. I only wish . . ." Mydia shook her head. "But no, he never came back."

Now my curiosity was aroused. "Back from where?"

"I don't know," she whispered. "If only I did. He simply left one day, saying that he was . . . going on a journey. He never told me anything about it. I only heard from Mother. It's been so long now that—well, probably most of my memories of him were things my mother told me of him." The tears came now, followed by the sobs. I let her cry, since this was a different situation. No one talked about this Prince Kallyn. Where could he have vanished to?

"Mydia, how long ago was this, when he left?"

Mydia stopped crying long enough to say, "It's been fifteen years? Yes, I think fifteen years since he left. Don't worry, I-I know he's never coming back. I'm not such a fool as to believe . . ." The crying started up again. The poor girl. Both her brother and her mother. I'd never had either, so I didn't know what it was like, but . . . perhaps she was more like me than I thought.

"I'm truly sorry," I said.

When she was finally done, Mydia wiped her eyes and face with a pristine handkerchief and then blew her nose into it loudly. "I thought I was over it years ago. But thank you, Podda. I feel better now, thanks to you."

There was a moment of silence, and then I asked her, "So, how come you don't have any other siblings, Mydia? Your father has another wife now, and multiple concubines. I would've thought . . ."

Mydia shook her head with a pained look. "I knew this was coming. He . . ." She looked away, biting her lip. "Mother was only able to have the two of us, but then he acquired concubines and his second wife, Lieda, after she died. But ever since his first son vanished, he had no interest in another heir, and so . . . he made them all drink poisons that killed the children before birth. If any were born, the midwives were told to drown them immediately. I think it was actually Lieda who convinced him. I tried to get some of them to stop, but they were too scared, of course."

Mydia looked like she was about to throw up, and I felt the same way. "That's horrible, Mydia," I said quietly. "I never knew. But . . . why on Mani would he not want another heir?"

She looked up, tears in her eyes. "He is a selfish man. He's older than you know, and I think he intends to live forever if he can. He doesn't ever want to give up Nytaea to anyone, even one of his own offspring."

"But he can't part with you," I observed.

She nodded. "Because I remind him of my mother. He doesn't want to admit it, but I'm like her replacement in his eyes. One who doesn't stand up to him or demand anything. He has his women for comfort, and I'm . . . his antique on the shelf." She gritted her teeth bitterly.

I said nothing for a while. "I'm sorry, Mydia."

She merely nodded again dully.

"What sort of Authority did your brother . . . Prince Kallyn . . . use?"

"Hmm?" The princess glanced up from her sorrow. "Oh, he had the most amazing Fire Authority. He was a High Mage. He used to twirl flames in the air and eat them, and light the sky with blue flames, and green, and red. He used to perform for the palace nobility in the Night Season."

"A High Mage . . ." I didn't know much about magic, but I knew that was a title reserved for only the most powerful of magi. "What about your own magic? Could you show me some more of it? You said it was more like your mother's, right?"

"Indeed; they call it green magic. Here." She went over to a hanging plant by the window, whose stem was silver but whose long leaves were green, and passed her hand over it. Her hand glowed and sparkled faintly, and the plant grew by a great amount. The stem over which she had raised her hand sprouted beautiful blooms along it, blooms that glowed and changed color, finally settling on a rich purple. They stayed that way, unlike the other flowers in the gardens.

"You can permanently change the plant?" I asked with surprise.

"Yes. My mother could do better. I'm not very good at it, though there is . . . something else I can do."

"What's that?"

"Here." She put a finger lightly on my face, and it glowed white.

I stepped back. "What did you just do to me?"

She giggled and held up a mirror for me to look into. I appeared at least two years younger, with a perfectly smooth, unblemished face. "I made you younger. The effects will wear off within a minute, but I think I could make it work for real if you let me. My father has the same ability."

"Really? Making people younger?"

"Not just other people. He uses it on himself all the time. That's why his body is only that of a thirty-some-year-old. He is a highly skilled illusionist, a master of the Perception and Reality branches. They don't call him Lord of Illusions for nothing, Podda. He can make all sorts of illusions, even tangible ones—he could conjure a whole fake world, if he wanted to."

Lord of Illusions. The title sounded only vaguely familiar to me, but chilling. I had noticed that Lord Kalceron seemed much too young. It was almost unnerving to look at him when serving meals. Fortunately, he frowned upon that anyway. "How old is he really, then?"

"I don't even know. He's a High Mage, so he's naturally long-lived . . . but I'd say well over a hundred years old."

"What! Then how old are you?" I accused lightly.

Mydia's eyes widened. "Hey! What, do you think I'd use magic on myself just to appear younger?"

"Well, how old *are* you?"

"I'll be twenty years old next month. And no illusions. Happy?" She stuck out her tongue at me.

"Yes." I paused. "You're really that old? I took you for barely more than a child." *Yet she did say her brother left fifteen years ago . . .* Had I been paying attention, I should have realized it then.

"Come now, I'm not that immature. I can't help that I have this baby face."

I gave the princess a skeptical look, folding my arms. "Well, I don't even know how old I am, so I guess I'm not one to talk, am I?"

"Oh? You don't know?"

I shook my head. "I was brought to the orphanage by my mother as a small child, they say. I . . . don't remember. I was probably around . . . two? So, I might be something like fifteen."

"Oh, really?" Mydia's expression was one of surprise. "You look nearly as old as me."

"I do?" I stared down at the floor, frowning. Feeling a bit foolish, I asked, "Mydia . . . do you have another candle?"

"Sure. Here's one." She reached into a dress pocket and handed me a candle just like the last night, and I took it in one hand. Maybe I hadn't tried hard enough before. . . .

Taking a deep, steadying breath, I tried with all my might to mentally light the wick. It didn't work. "Should have known," I grumbled. Vainly, I imagined a cute little flame in my hand, instead of the candle. Only . . . it wasn't in vain. A fire appeared in the palm of my hand, flickering uncertainly and causing Mydia to stumble back in surprise.

"You *can* do it. I knew you reminded me of my brother!"

I was just as shocked. I had been sure that no magical talent resided in me, but evidently I was wrong. Flaring the flame bigger, I took it and lit the candle with it, and then banished it away. My hand wasn't burnt at all from the heat.

"Podda! Do you know what this means?" whispered Mydia excitedly. "You're a synergist!"

It was true. If I really could wield magic, then I was a mage—or . . . synergist. Not a mage yet, I guess? I was a bit fuzzy on those details. It was hard to believe, but Mydia had been right after all. If she didn't look and sound so genuinely surprised, I would have thought her to be fooling with me using some manner of illusions. "So . . . what does this mean now, Mydia?"

"I don't know," she replied. "My father would want you to be trained as a mage soldier, but . . . you wouldn't want to join them. We'd probably best keep quiet about it until I can think of a way to get you some proper training. . . ."

I started. "N-no! Please, that's not necessary. I don't want him catching onto me!" My forehead was beginning to feel hot and sweaty with nervousness.

Mydia eyed me curiously. "Catching onto you? Oh, you must mean—"

"Never mind," I interrupted hastily. "Forget I said that."

The princess stopped and then nodded. "Sorry. I won't pry."

I chewed my lip, staring down at my hands and back to the flickering candle, mind reeling. What if that could work out . . . ? No. I didn't want to go to some school and get stuck in classes full of children on their way to the military. I especially didn't want to waste precious time before we could find Mandrie and Phoebe. "I just feel it's a bad idea."

"Very well," she replied. I glanced up to see a pensive look on the princess's face, and I realized she'd been thinking on the subject as well. "There is one thing, Podda. We could get someone more versed than me to give you some pointers—"

"No, please no!" I protested, waving my hands.

She sighed. "Right, you wouldn't want that. Well, regardless . . . have you heard of the Wandering Mage?"

I hesitated, shaking my head.

She raised her eyebrows. "Never? Rhidea, the Wandering Mage? She's supposed to be arriving in Nytaea soon to pay a visit to the Palace."

Now that I thought about it, I had heard whisperings about such a thing. "Is she pretty famous, then?"

Mydia laughed. "She's only the most well-known scholar in the land, and—" she held up a finger "—the most powerful mage in the last century."

I made a silent *'Oh'* with my mouth, nodding slowly. Hmm . . . if this Rhidea was such a well-known figure, then maybe her arrival would at least provide a distraction for us to work with.

- Chapter 8 -

The Wandering Mage

There are eight elemental affinities, or branches, representing the eight forces present on Mani: Water, Fire, Lightning, Wind, Earth, Perception, Reality and Silver. But Silver is its own special case, as it predates all others and is a far more powerful and rare gift. It was around long before the arrival of humans, and it seems that Silver has already grown bored of the tampering of humans, as was mentioned in Chapter Four, paragraph eight.

— From *Secrets of Mani*, by Sor the Lark

(Dri'Shal 19, 997—Night Season)

Everywhere I went after this, I began to hear rumors flying around the Palace about the visitor soon to be making an appearance. No one seemed to know anything about this Rhidea or why she was coming, just that there was double the preparation work for most of the staff.

My bubbly liege lady seemed unable to keep herself from going on about the woman. She said Rhidea had once held the position of high magister to King Fenwel of Nemental, despite being born in Nytaea. Mydia had only met her once in her life, and that was when she was a little girl. The Wandering Mage was usually abroad, all over the world, and hadn't returned to Nytaea in some time. Nytaea was home to one of the world's largest libraries, so that attractor was bound to bring the scholar back to the land of her birth at some point.

At any rate, the entire Palace was in an uproar over it all. I was glad that I was no longer a maid, for the frantic cleaning I was getting out of, but I almost wished that I were among the mage students, so that I could perhaps meet this esteemed Rhidea. Oh, well. Mydia would undoubtedly want to talk to her, so I would at least get to hear some of the tales she had. Perhaps I'd even get to see some of her Authority on display. Part of me knew that was unlikely, as frivolous use of magic didn't fit the description of a stuffy scholar.

Three days after my appointment as handmaiden, on a cold day nearing the end of the Sol Cycle, we were there at the gate when the sorceress came pushing her way through the crowded streets. I was surprised that she hadn't simply hired a litter and servants to carry it, or even a carriage. A small crowd of people eager to catch a glimpse of the famous mage gathered at the sides of the street under the lamplight. It was full nighttime now, meaning that Sol had made more than a half circuit since Kaen and I came to the Palace. The stars twinkled beautifully in the night, casting light to see by alongside the auroras.

The mage at last made it to the front gate, where we stood, and was greeted by Lord Kalceron himself with a deep bow. I tried to keep my jaw from dropping at his token of respect.

"Welcome, Cae Rhidea. I hope that you accept our hospitality for as long as you care to grace us with your presence, and that you will find the accommodations up to your standards." He said the words so magnanimously as to almost convince me that he cared about her comfort.

"Oh, come now, Edrius," Lady Rhidea replied in a deep feminine voice. "I'm sure your Palace is just as fit as it was last time to house a dusty old scholar like me. I thank you for your kind hospitality."

"Indeed," Lord Kalceron replied. "It has been a long time, friend." He stepped back and waved her forward. *Friend,* I mused, trying to understand the exchange.

At this point, Mydia rushed up and took Rhidea by the hand. "Come on, come on, I'll show you to your rooms . . . My Lady."

"Just call me Rhidea," the mage replied. Her voice was like rich honey, deep and smooth, and her hair was long and of a somber scarlet. She turned to the princess. "You must be Mydia? You were just a tiny, crying red thing when I saw you last. My, that was years ago."

"I wasn't—"

"Never mind, child. If it pleases your soul, I shall allow you to escort me to my rooms on the condition that you carry all of my luggage for me."

"Of course, My Lady! Wait, what? But . . ."

"A jest, my dear. I have only this satchel of books here, and I would not entrust it even to the princess of Nytaea. By the way, there are crowds watching."

"Oh. Right. Here, follow me." Mydia took Rhidea's arm once more and led her inside the Palace, leaving me to follow behind awkwardly. Being the invisible handmaiden came with its own unique frustrations.

"Ah, this place feels so familiar to me," Rhidea commented as we crossed the elaborate entry hall. "It seems an age since I've walked these white halls. It doesn't feel . . . quite the same as it did then. Colder, emptier. You know, dear, you look so much like your mother now. I . . . heard about her passing eight years back, and am truly sorry. Eivael was a dear friend to me."

"Thank you," Mydia murmured. "I think I am over it now."

Neither of them mentioned the late Prince Kallyn. There was little more talk until they reached the rooms in the northwestern section of the Palace that had been prepared for Rhidea. Once inside, the mage took stock of her accommodations—which were nearly as rich as Mydia's own—and almost closed the door in my face before pointing at me and asking Mydia, "Is your maid trustworthy?"

"Podda? Certainly."

"How certainly? I need to know."

"Very." Mydia's trust in me gave me the nerve to step in as Rhidea waved a hand for me to do so.

"Come on in then, Podda." As odd as all of this was, it got odder still when she addressed me, saying, "Forgive me for being wary. Such is the way of my life. Well met, Podda." She held out a hand, and I took it uncertainly, wondering why I mattered. A slow smile crept onto her face and then faded quickly. "Hah. Well met indeed."

"I . . . I'm just a servant, My Lady," I mumbled, trying to sound humble. My nervosity was not fake.

"No," Rhidea said flatly, "but nice try." She released her grip finally, and I retracted my hand, feeling slightly strange. She couldn't possibly have read my mind . . . could she have? I sincerely hoped that she was just fond of weird jokes, because I did not want to have my identity unmasked by a mage so high that she could address Lord Kalceron by his first name.

Fortunately, she gave me no more notice for the moment, her attention turning swiftly to Mydia. "I have a gift for you, Princess."

"Really?" Mydia's face was split wide by a distinctly childish grin.

"I promised your mother that I would give this to you when you were old enough to study it, and now, eight years late, you shall have it. Here." The mage pulled from her bag a thick leatherbound tome of moderate width and height. Handing it to Mydia, she said, "Take good care of it, and do not let it out of your possession for any length of time. It is an old book, full of the knowledge gained from lifetimes of study in the fundaments and workings of Coaction and Authority. Keep it with you and study it closely. I wish to hear from you about it before I leave."

"Oh, how long will you be staying?" Mydia asked.

"About three weeks," Rhidea replied. "Now go, you and your handmaiden. I wish to be alone, and for you to set about reading your mother's book."

"Very well. Will I have time to talk with you at some point?"

Rhidea laughed. "Of course. I'm hoping we'll get along just fine. But I have some studying of my own to do right now."

Mydia turned to go, opening the door to the rest of the west wing, and then stopped. "My mother . . . was she a scholar of magic like you?"

"Indeed, my dear. She was a good friend, as was your brother Kallyn."

"I never . . . I never knew." Mydia's face took on a faintly troubled look. "Well, I'll be going now. Have a nice stay, Rhidea."

"Thank you, child."

Mydia took her leave, and I followed her out.

"Podda," the princess said over her shoulder as we walked back toward her rooms to ready her for her luncheon. "What did she say when she took your hand?"

"She just said . . . wait, what do you mean?" I frowned. "You were there listening."

"She has some strange abilities, and one of those seems to be hiding her words from certain people. Some kind of Perception Authority."

"Oh, really? So then, at the gate earlier . . ."

"Right. I think that was a joke. I'm sure no one was listening. If you don't want to tell me, that's all right."

"No, no, it's not that . . . I just . . ." I sighed as we walked. "It was nothing important. I still don't know what to make of it. Perhaps I'll tell you another time."

"It's all right. You don't have to. You sound like you think you'll get in trouble or something." She laughed softly, as though that was a funny thought. Hadn't I already explained to her that people I loved were in danger? She must have forgotten. She could be so frustratingly fluff-headed at times.

Back in Mydia's rooms, I met up with Julia and helped the princess get dressed for lunch. One perk about being a personal handmaiden was that I got a break while my liege lady ate a formal meal with her father and the lords and ladies of the castle. But, for whatever reason, Rhidea stopped me as I was leaving, after I'd seen Mydia to her spot next to the mage at one of the long tables. "Meet me in my room after the meal, Miss Podda," she murmured.

"But . . . I'll need to see the princess back to her rooms then." I could tell, somehow, that our words were sealed by her Authority.

"Then drop by directly after that. You may go for now." She waved a dismissive hand.

I left with a small curtsy, going back to Mydia's rooms. There, I found Julia waiting with food from the kitchens. "Here," she said, "Have some. Plenty for both of us. They made lots of extra apple dumplings today."

I wasn't sure if she was serious, or if she had snitched them, but either way, no one would miss the dumplings on a hectic day like today. The cooks and maids had been working double time to prepare for the meal, so there would surely be plenty. I only felt a little bit bad.

"Julia," I asked her off-handedly, "How long have you been working at the Palace?"

She stopped munching for a moment. "You mean, when did I come here?"

"I guess."

"Let's see . . . I can't really remember. I think four or five years ago now."

"And how long have you been Mydia's handmaiden?"

"Almost two years, I'd say. Before you, it was a girl named Andra doing your part. Then I took over for a while until they moved you on up. Still not sure why that was, but the Palace works funny. And I'm glad that all I have to do now is bring food from the kitchens and stuff like that. Bathing princesses is no fun."

"Speaking of meals," I said, "where did Chara go?"

"Chara? I don't know. Probably just more errands; you know, all that boring stuff. Better her than me." Julia scrunched up her face.

I nodded. I didn't mind, personally, but to each her own. I finished eating and then went to see if Mydia was done with the meal. I had to wait around a little while before escorting her back to her rooms. Immediately after, I asked leave for a few minutes. Mydia, although confused as to why, bade me go, and settled herself down with a sigh to read her new book—as Rhidea had requested. I went with some trepidation to Rhidea's rooms.

She was waiting, seated at a desk they'd set up for her in the second room back, lit by candlelight. I suppose that would have been called her study. "So," she began, throwing back her long, red hair, "You intrigue me. What is your name again?"

I was silent for a moment, looking down at the floor. Something about her forward, authoritative way of speaking made me uncomfortable.

"Look me in the eye," Rhidea said sharply, causing me to jerk my gaze back up to her impassive face. "Thank you. Now, your name. I seem to have forgotten."

I stared at her face, so calm and yet so frightening, feeling little more than the burning desire to run away. Her amber eyes were like a devouring fire. "Podda. My name is Podda."

Rhidea sighed, tapping a finger on her desk. "Just tell me the truth. I don't even need skin contact to tell when someone is lying to my face."

"My lady . . . I don't under—" I cut off with a gulp as she fixed her icy stare on me once more. "I'm sorry. My name is Lyn."

"Thank you. Have a seat, Lyn." She gestured toward a battered chair on the other side of the desk. I took it and sat down across from her, trying not to slouch in my nervousness. How had she coerced me so easily into revealing my true name? It was as if she was in command of the entire conversation before it even started.

"My lady—" I began once more.

Rhidea cut me off with a wave of her hand. "Don't start with the formalities. Here in my office, that all drops away. I've never been one for such vain propriety. You see, this was once my office before I left for my studies decades ago and ended up staying in Nemental . . ." She took on a wistful look. "Lyn, you might call me the inquisitive type—I seek out mysteries. When I stumble across something to uncover, I can't help but investigate it."

"Like . . . my false name?" I asked tentatively, still unsure whether she was mad at me or not. The mage was markedly more relaxed already, but I couldn't read her any further.

"Precisely. You interest me. I care nothing for rank or class, particularly with my current mission in mind."

I almost asked what her mission was, but I stopped myself.

Rhidea smirked. "You're wondering what that mission is, child? Of course, I can't very well just tell you, a total stranger." She leaned over the table, lacing her long fingers together underneath her chin. "Who are you really? Answer me honestly, and I may just let you in on a few secrets of my own."

I thought about her question for a moment. A few secrets, huh? This woman was more puzzling than any person I'd ever met. And yet, at the same time, she seemed . . . genuine. She had already shown herself to be cunning as a whip; I probably couldn't hide anything from her even if I wanted to. Taking a shaky breath, I said, "All right."

Rhidea smiled. "That's my girl."

Her smile put me at ease enough to begin my explanation. "I grew up in a backstreet orphanage, my lady—I mean, Rhidea. The woman who ran it was the kindest person I've ever known, like a mother to me. And now . . . she's dead. Along with most of my foster family. I watched them burn." I gulped, chewing on my lip to keep it from trembling.

"I'm sorry," Rhidea said with surprising gentleness.

I nodded, taking a breath to hold back my emotions. "A-and two of my friends who were left were captured by mage soldiers soon afterward and brought to the Palace."

Rhidea nodded, frowning. "Captured by mage soldiers? Why would Kalceron want them?"

"Well . . . I'm honestly not quite sure, but—"

"They wanted you," she said flatly. "Is that it?"

I paused. "Yes. How did you guess?"

"I have my suspicions. The question is, why did Kalceron want you? Did they say? And furthermore, why didn't they just take you?" There was a certain predatory interest in Rhidea's fiery eyes.

"I . . ." I trailed off. I couldn't tell this woman my secret. The secret that I didn't even understand myself. I had never talked to anyone but Kaen about it. "I have an uncommon hair color—pure silver—and they said that they were looking for a girl with silver hair like mine. My friend Kaen and I fought off our attackers, but they snuck up behind our two friends and took them hostage, telling me to come to the Palace and turn myself in."

Rhidea rubbed her chin with her thumbs. "Silver hair. . . . And you and this Kaen are trained fighters?"

I blushed. "No. He can fight. But I was . . . somewhat hard to take in for other reasons. I think they decided it was simpler to just take the hostages."

"Then they're clearly fools or amateurs—unless you're really that dangerous. Tell me, child: what is it about you that makes you hard to capture? My interest is mostly academic, I assure you." She chuckled softly at my expression of fear.

I smiled despite myself. Then the smile melted from my face, and I swallowed nervously. *I have to tell her now.* "It's . . . something I was born with. It took me a while to realize other children didn't have the same body as me. I weigh twice what most girls my size do, and I'm just . . . very strong. I have to be careful, or else I can break things and hurt people around me." I hung my head. "I even injured Kaen one time, when we were little. I felt horrible. He broke three ribs. Lentha never even figured out what happened."

Rhidea was frowning with interest the whole way through my explanation. When I was done, she said, "Hold out your hand and leave it still." I did so, and she took it in her right palm, feeling the weight of it. She grunted in satisfaction. "I'm no expert, but I'd say your arm is certainly heavier than the average girl's by a good margin. How much do you weigh?"

I hesitated. "I haven't exactly had access to a scale like that, Rhidea. . . ."

The mage rose to her feet. "We'll find out, then." She motioned for me to get up, and then made her way around the table to me. "If you will allow me, Lyn, I'm going to pick you up."

I laughed. "Rhidea, that's crazy. There's no way you could—"

"Hold still, child." She put one hand behind my back and the other behind my legs, and suddenly my knees buckled and I felt a strange, weightless feeling as she picked my whole body up off the floor, which creaked with the transfer of weight. She hefted me up and down once, and then set me back on my feet.

I thumped back to the floor, awkwardly catching my footing as my full weight returned. "How did you . . . ?"

She stepped back, dusting off her hands and then shaking them out. "I'm a High Mage, silly girl. That was simple earth-based Coaction. I'd say you weigh just over two hundred fifty pounds. More than most men. Remarkable. I honestly didn't think you were being serious, my girl."

I scratched my head. "Um . . . well, it's not exactly something I'm proud of. Weighing as much as a horse, that is."

"The average horse weighs around a thousand pounds," she said off-handedly. "And you're not fat, so it's not something to be ashamed of."

Please tell me you don't know how heavy a horse is from similar experience. I didn't say the words, but I was tempted to. Feeling heat rising to my cheeks, I cleared my throat. "So, back to the topic at hand."

"Right, right." Rhidea took her place once more behind the table, motioning for me to sit. "I wish I had a safe way to test your strength, but . . . I'm inclined to believe that you're telling the truth about it. I'll have to devise a safe test of some sort. In any case, you have been honest with me, so I will provide a few answers for you, Lyn.

"Lord Edrius Kalceron is looking for a white-haired girl with unique attributes—and so am I. I came to Nytaea for two reasons. One of those reasons was my research into the magic of this world, a phenomenon that has been ongoing for decades now. The second is that I'd heard the same rumors as my old friend Kalceron, that a strange prize walked the streets here."

"Me," I breathed. "H-how did you know? How did *he* know?"

"Well . . . quite honestly, that's half the puzzle. I think Kalceron heard it from someone in his inner circle, who heard whisperings from years ago about this or that—I don't know the specifics, but something about a child who was brought here by a very strange character. That woman, presumably her mother, disappeared without a trace, or something happened to her. Perhaps she died."

There's something she's not telling me about it. Her explanation was too vague. But I simply nodded. "It's true. I assume she died. That was how I came to the orphanage, though. My mother brought me. But . . . you couldn't have known that I dyed my hair . . . or is it that obvious? Is it wearing off already?" I grabbed my ponytail and began frantically inspecting the end of it.

"Relax, child. I can tell it is beginning to fade in places, but of course I'm looking for it. No, I was on the lookout for anyone odd or suspicious, someone on the run—say, a girl with a fake name." She gave me a knowing stare. "But in any case, Kalceron and I are old acquaintances. We've had many . . . disagreements in the past. You said he has your two friends locked up somewhere right now?"

The question seemed to come out of nowhere. "Y-yes. I don't know where. I hope . . . I hope to rescue them, if I am able."

"I see. So, Miss Lyn, are you aware that you possess elemental Aptitude?"

I started. "You knew that too?"

"There were a few things that tipped me off. Someone with as high a level of Authority as me in the different branches of magic can tell. When I first shook your hand and looked into your eyes, I knew. Curiously enough, it seems you know as well."

So she could tell simply by skin contact. I looked aside. "Mydia and I . . . we've become friends of a sort recently. She prompted me to try out a few magical exercises for discovering Aptitude, and I just sort of . . . stumbled upon it."

"What branch?"

"Excuse me?"

"Do you know what branch of magic your Aptitude lies in?"

I grimaced. "Not really. I think fire? All I can do at the moment is make a small flame in my hand if I concentrate."

Rhidea nodded. "You're probably a fire synergist, then. Show me what you can do, child."

She guided me as I summoned my flame and flared it as bright as I could—roughly the size of a torch flame.

"Remarkable," she said as she saw my red flame. "For one so new. Fire magi tend to catch on fairly quickly, but after only a couple of days and no formal training . . ." She looked into my eyes. "Be very careful with this power. You do not yet know the dangers of controlling a flame. You think it temperamental, but you have no idea yet. When you practice, summon as small a flame as possible. It will help build your concentration and also prevent accidents from occurring. Don't try anything else. And of course, don't be discovered."

She sat back, waving for me to dismiss the flame, and sighed. "Well, now I've got my hands full. You may just be more than I bargained for."

I laughed. "Is that a compliment?"

Rhidea seemed to consider for a moment. "No." Taking a deep

breath, she sat up straight and said, "Let's make a deal, you and me. Quite a simple one, too—you help me, and I in turn will help you."

I froze, mind racing back and forth. She couldn't mean what I thought she did. . . . "My lady, how will I help you? I have nothing to offer."

"Sure you do. You are, quite possibly, the key to unlocking one of the greatest mysteries of all time, an answer I've been seeking for years now. But of course, you have your own mission. That is fair. Let's say . . . if you become my pupil and agree to aid in my quest, I shall help you to free your friends. How does that sound? Once we find a way to free them, I ask that you continue to train under me and help me in my search for truth in this world."

Truth . . . I considered for a moment. How did it sound? "Rhidea, that's . . . that's amazing! I can't believe you would actually help me like that. But I, um . . . I don't really know you, and . . ." I trailed off, biting my lip. "Can I trust you?"

Rhidea laughed. "You're only now asking that? You can trust me, child. I understand your position, but at the same time . . . you really have no choice but to trust me. You will see whether or not I'm as good as my word when we put our plan into action."

"Plan? You have a plan?"

"Goodness, no! I'll need time to think. But—" she gave me a con-spiratorial wink "—we'll keep in touch. Remember, you're my secret apprentice now."

A smile popped unbidden to my lips, and I dipped my head in appreciation. "Thank you, Lady Rhidea. Thank you so much."

"Don't grovel, my dear—it's unladylike. Leave me be for tonight. I'll do some thinking and reach out to you and Mydia tomorrow." I turned to go, and she called after me, "Lyn, one more thing. Not a word of this to anyone save Mydia. I trust you'll keep your silence."

"Yes, Rhidea." I shut the door behind me and left.

- Chapter 9 -

A Secret Place

. . . These electrical currents studied by lightning mage scholars have produced some . . . well, puns aside, their findings are remarkable but hardly more useful than what other magics have already achieved. Once again, we have old writings that talk of many uses, particularly man-made technology powered by its own electrical current. . . . Such marvels must have taken centuries of learning to produce. Really, though, it seems impractical in the first place, considering that most of this technology sounds like something that mid-level Coaction can easily beat out: any scholar wishing to produce heat could just hire a fire mage, and so on, not to mention the volatile Energy Field in the sky which can be channeled so easily without the help of a device. And of course, most metals found on Mani conduct only a fraction of the energy put into them, even silver and gold.

— From *Secrets of Mani*, by Sor the Lark

(Dri'Shal 20, 997—Night Season)

Back in Mydia's tower, I found the princess at her own desk, studying much like Rhidea, which was something I rarely saw her do at all. One would think that a princess would have all sorts of teachers around, tutoring her, but even her Coaction tutor was someone whom she only saw once a week.

"Mydia?" I asked. Julia had already left the room, and Chara had also departed after the lunch, so no one should overhear us.

She looked up quickly. "Oh. You're back. You've been a while. Where did you go, the gardens?"

Why on Mani would I wander off to the gardens? Me, a maid? "No, Lady Rhidea had asked me to come see her."

"Oh, really? What for?"

"Well . . ." I wanted to tell her everything right now, but she looked busy studying her book, which was something I did not want to discourage at all. Rhidea seemed to think it important that she study that book of hers. Instead, I changed the subject. "Just a chat. How is the book? What's it about?"

"Oh. Well, it's a history of magic. A very . . . interesting one."

I came over and put a hand on her shoulder, looking at the parchment pages with the eyes of an illiterate commoner. "Why do you think your mother wanted you to have it?"

"I don't know." Mydia sighed, and went back to reading the book. "I wish I did. It is rather intriguing, at least."

"I'm sure it's very educational," I joked. She didn't even seem to hear me. I left her to her studying and went to find something to do. On my way out, I passed Julia, who was acting as royal snack courier at the order of the princess, and convinced the girl to let me have a couple of fresh koiberry fritters. Then I went on my way, stuffing them in my mouth, to see if I could find my friend 'Roger'.

The Palace was busy this time of day, especially after the grand luncheon that had just ended, but so great was the bustle of activity that I was totally concealed. No one minded me, nor stopped me to ask where I was headed. Errands, they would assume. In reality, no one cared about the servants anyway.

I headed to the back of the Palace, where the barracks of the Armed Guard branched out from side to side. I asked around for

Roger, the new recruit, and was told the number of the room in which he could be found. Upon reaching it, I poked my head in and saw Kaen and four others lounging around, eating the last of their noonday meal. And like total slobs, no less. They let them bring food outside the mess hall and eat it in their rooms? Mydia would never do a thing like that.

Finally, I signaled his attention with a glance, and he quickly shoved the last of his food down and told his companions that he would be right back. Stepping outside, he demanded, "Lyn, what are you doing here?"

"Shhh! It's *Podda*."

"Oh, very funny. No, seriously. You haven't ever been assigned to clean my room before. Why now? Did something change?" He looked more closely at my servant's garb. "Oh, did you move up like you said? Where to?"

"I thought you wouldn't notice. I'm the princess's handmaiden now."

Kaen crossed his arms. "You'll have to do better than that, Podda."

"I'm being serious. And that's only half of it. But that's beside the point. Look, we have to talk sometime. We *really* have to talk." I lowered my voice. "Kaen, do you know the Palace Gardens?"

"Of course."

"Meet me there tonight, after the clouds roll in. I'll bring someone."

Kaen looked skeptical. "That's easier said than done. Lights out is—"

"It's about Mandrie and Phoebe. I've got a few leads. Surely, if anyone can, you can find a way to sneak out and meet me in the Palace Gardens tonight."

"Well, yes . . . I suppose. But this had better be good. Who is it you want me to see?"

"Just be there, all right?"

He nodded, rolling his eyes in annoyance. "I said I would. But I have to get back now. See you later."

"See you." I retraced my steps back to the Palace before anyone could intercept me and start asking questions. I hurried back to Mydia's rooms, careful to avoid getting in anyone's way. Even the princess's handmaiden wasn't out of danger of a cuff on the ear for bumping into a soldier or mage.

By the time I reached Mydia, my fatigue was starting to get to me. Chara was there, complaining and chastening her for something in her cheery and humble way, but I didn't care. "My lady, if it is not a bother to you, I'm very tired today and could use a short nap."

Mydia glanced at me. "That's fine, Podda; go ahead." She focused back on the grey-headed handmaiden. "Now, what were you saying about the sweets, Chara?"

Chara flung a grouchy glare my way and opened her mouth to utter an objection, but she promptly closed it and went back to instructing Mydia on how to maintain her royal figure. She had no power to tell me no when Mydia had already allowed it.

Ignoring them both, I went and laid myself down to rest. I got a solid two hours of sleep before waking at the sound of someone walking past. It was just Julia, but I should have been up already. I went back in to see Mydia, and found her reading her book once more. She had gotten a good way through and had placed markers in the pages at certain points. A sheet of parchment sat beside her, which she scribbled on infrequently. I wished for all the world that I could read, but I would be doing well just to scratch out my own name. Lentha had shown me a little bit more, but without the need to ever use it, the knowledge had simply faded away—which was rather strange, given how accurate my memory was about a lot of things.

"Mydia," I said, getting her attention. Chara was gone now, and so with Julia off on errands, it was just the two of us.

"Oh, you're up." Mydia looked up from her reading and yawned widely, rubbing her eyes and stretching her arms. "Oh my, I think I've been here for hours. I didn't know books on magic were this interesting."

"I thought you said it was just a history."

"Of magic." Mydia looked surprisingly excited, despite an amazing three hours spent studying a dusty old book. "It's fun, and I've been learning a lot. It's a difficult read, full of big words and penned in an old script . . . but my, this scholar knew what he was talking about. I don't know who he is, though—or . . . was. I suppose I'll have to ask Rhidea."

"Oh? It doesn't say his name anywhere in it?" I asked in surprise.

"Well, it does: Sor the Lark. But I have never heard the name before, and I'm assuming that's a pseudonym. Whoever this Sor was, he was obviously well read in just about every subject: history, Coaction, Authority, politics, cultures, lore . . . everything. Right now, I'm learning about the different classifications of Coaction, but it jumps around here and there . . . I'll have to read the whole thing before I have him all figured out."

"Tonight?" That would be quite the feat for the princess I knew.

"Auroras above, no!" she said with a laugh, placing a page holder in the book. Closing it up carefully, she rubbed her temples. "No, I need a break." She got up from her seat and stretched. "How about Coaction? Have you practiced at all since yesterday? I can't wait to see."

"Not . . . really," I said, although that wasn't technically true.

"Well, let's do it. Come on." Mydia closed the wooden door and locked it from the inside. "There. Nobody can bother us now."

"Chara has the key," I pointed out.

Mydia made a face. "Well, at least we'll have more warning. Come on, try it again—see if you can make another flame like yesterday."

I sighed and tried it. I visualized the flame springing to life in my hand, and it came after a short delay: a flickering flame the size of a large candle's. I tried to keep it safely in check, as Rhidea had warned me.

"Ooh, so pretty." The way Mydia stared at the flame, I almost thought she was going to reach out and touch it. "And we have no idea how powerful you are. I need to talk to Rhidea about you."

"Rhidea . . . already knows," I told her.

"What? How? Is she going to teach you herself or something?" Mydia seemed to like the thought of that.

I shook my head. "We talked about a few other things as well."

"Like what?" Mydia asked, eyes flicking downward to the flame still in my hand.

As I watched, the flame flickered out. Pesky little thing. Apparently, I couldn't just make it do what I wanted once I had it. Oh, well. "Mydia," I said slowly. "Could you come with me to the Palace Gardens tonight?"

She snorted. "Me, come with you?"

"My friend is going to meet me there," I said, trying to get her attention.

"Friend? I didn't know you had a friend."

"I know. I . . . I'm going to tell you everything. But later. Tonight, when he can be there."

"Wait, it's a he? Don't tell me . . . come on! Tell me, tell me! Who is it?"

I rolled my eyes. "Mydia, it's not like that. I'm trying to be serious here." I could never tell if she was going to act mature or childish.

"All right. Well, I trust you, so I suppose I can wait. How about the flame, can you make it again? It went out on you already."

I grimaced. "It wasn't behaving very well. Look, I'm kind of tired . . ." But she pushed me, so I tried it again, focusing my mind to visualize a flame in my hand. The flame finally popped up, and then another appeared unbidden in my left hand. Mydia actually took a step back.

"Wow . . ." she said breathlessly. "Just like Kallyn. Can you make them different colors, or make them spin in the air? Or . . . or . . ."

I tried some different experiments, per my liege lady's request, including changing the flames' color, size and shape, and spinning them . . . Every single trick ended in complete failure, except the last couple, which ended in failure *and* almost burnt down the entire room. Chara would have a fit if she saw. Forget her, Rhidea would've killed me.

However, it was at this time that Mydia revealed her true gifting to be in the water branch of magic—which was apparently both broad and useful, particularly when it came to quickly dousing stray flames. Her control of the substance was astonishing; she pulled moisture right out of the air and quenched the infant flames with precision.

As though nothing had happened, the princess began to test me to see if I had any other coactive talents, but nothing worked except the flame. She showed me how she created illusions of age difference and other such things using her secondary branch, Perception, but I was no good at it. I did get her to give me a magical hair-dying as Rhidea had asked. Mydia gasped as she saw the pale grey underneath, having never known that my hair was such a strange color. She tried to get it as close to the natural brown dye as she could.

We were just finishing up with the hair illusion when Chara arrived, banging on the door and demanding to know why it was locked, "*Milady.*" Rattling the key in the door, she opened it and Mydia jumped out at her, as though she had simply set up for a small practical joke. "Boo!"

"Oh! My goodness, milady! Don't scare me like that."

Mydia grinned. "What? It's fun."

"Not everything that's fun is beneficial, Your Ladyship" Chara admonished, recovering from her shock. I was trying to keep from laughing, but I think a small snort came out, because Chara glanced suspiciously my way with an ugly glare.

"Well, I brought your clean laundry, My Lady. Here you are." Chara brought some freshly laundered dresses over and hung them in the adjoining wardrobe room. On her way back, she saw the burnt patch on the carpet and gasped. "Milady! What happened? You dropped another candle? Just look at this. . . ."

The old maid insisted on sticking around to do some cleaning and then needlework, perhaps just to bug us or, more likely, to keep an eye on us and make sure we didn't start any more fires. Chara knew I was a favorite of Mydia's, even if she couldn't figure out why. Mydia took me over to her sunroom and shut that door instead. Here, we could overlook the nearby River Ardencaul while at the same time practicing magic. The view of vine-encrusted castle walls and the starlit sky above was both gorgeous and peaceful.

"You can't just make us invisible when she's around?" I asked her off-handedly.

Mydia shook her head. "That's not how Perception works. Not without powerful Authority, anyway. I can't make something look like nothing. If you held very still, I could make you look like the window behind you, but the effect would be ruined as soon as someone looked at you from a different angle."

I nodded. That made sense. Such a pity Coaction couldn't just work like the magic in the stories.

Mydia worked with me for almost an hour, attempting to coax out new Coactive abilities from inside of me (with a zero-percent success rate). She claimed to still be recharging from studying her book earlier, and had nothing better to do with her time.

Finally, we called an end to the experimentation in order to start getting Mydia ready for dinner before Chara came and made us. The evening dinner was to be even more splendid than earlier, or so I had heard. I hoped for the maids' and servants' sake that every night of Rhidea's stay would not be this big of a production. It was supposed to be a sort of 'welcome home' feast, and would last for hours. What would Julia and I do?

Returning to the wardrobe room, we found Julia, and she and I got Mydia all dressed and primped to look lovely before shipping her off to the dinner party.

Guests were already swarming the spacious dining hall when we arrived. Mydia, of course, was to sup with the other high nobility and Rhidea at the honored table in the front of the great hall. The High Mage gave me a small wink when she saw me, but that was all. Julia and I accompanied Mydia to her seat next to her father, and I held my breath as usual around Lord Kalceron. I don't think Julia liked being near him any more than I.

We withdrew quietly to the kitchens. Some of the cooks and maids gave the dark-haired girl a scowl, warning against snitching food as was her wont. But we just rolled up our sleeves and washed our hands to help out where we could. Julia wanted to bake things, but the cooks set her to readying plates and dishes to be laden with food and carried out to serve to the guests.

After a half hour, when things were winding down a little bit, we took our leave, snatching some goodies as we went. "Let's go to my favorite spot," Julia suggested.

"Where's that?"

"I'll show you." She led me toward the back of the Palace and out a small door. The city wall, which connected with many of the Palace's outreaching spires, loomed in front of us, closing us off in a box the size of a large room. Moss grew up this side of the wall as well as the stone faces of the Palace's interior walls around us. A stone trough was dug in the ground before the wall, running underneath to the sides and filled with flowing water, crystal clear as it reflected the stars of the night sky above.

"Julia . . . what is this place?" I had certainly never been here before, and was lost as to its function.

She shrugged. "I don't know. My guess is that no one else really knows about it. Nobody seems to, anyway. No idea what it was made for. You'd think they would have just conserved space in the Palace and not put it in here. Look." She turned around, and I followed her finger as she pointed up towards the inner walls of the Palace. "Up there is the princess's sunroom, way up there above the wall. But, because of the lip under all the windows, you can't even see this place from any of the rooms that look out at the wall."

I stared up, taking in the architecture and the starlit sky above. I made a mental note of the layout of the walls. "So you come here to relax?"

She nodded. "It's quiet. I've always come here when Mydia

doesn't need me. Maybe grab an apple tart if they have extras, then come out here to just . . . sit. And think."

"What do you think about?" It sounded like a dumb question as it came out of my mouth, but I was curious.

"Well . . . my family, mostly. About the days when I didn't have to work at the Palace. I dream of the day when I can be free."

"Wait, have to? What do you mean? You didn't come here of your own free will?"

Julia laughed bitterly. "Who would? I mean, don't get me wrong. I like the princess enough; she's not like they all say. If they pick you for her handmaiden or something, and you live as long and as usefully as Chara—and you manage to stay below the nobility's noses— you'll be all right, but . . . most of them come because they need money. Others have debts to House Kalceron, or their families did, and came to work it off. I . . ."

"That was you?" I asked, knowing the answer already.

She nodded. "Yes. My brother died when I was really young, and he was all that my father had. And . . . well, we had debts. Father sent me here to work them off. I had three more years, as of a year ago. It would be two years now, but . . ."

"Oh. What happened?"

Julia began to shake her head slowly, and then faster and harder, as though wishing she had not brought up bad memories. "Father was always on the sick side. Apparently, he took ill and died . . . right on my birthday. Three more years . . . that would have been all." Julia sat down on the stone step by the door, and I did likewise.

"What about your mother?" I had a bad feeling about this story.

"They killed her."

I nodded, speechless. It was not an uncommon story: The father was unable to pay his dues. The family was poor, and so the children were sold into bondage to work off the family's debt. The father took sick or was imprisoned, or anything like that. The mother was left to die, or was murdered in secret by Lord Kalceron's underlings. No one said any more. Such was the way of his cruelty. He needed no more widows. What did they do for his economy?

"That's horrible, Julia," I said softly. "I'm so sorry."

"You probably don't know what it's like. I'm not the only one, but . . . now I'm left as a permanent slave to Mydia. She doesn't even know—she thinks I'm just here to make money for my family, and why would I tell her?"

I was silent for a moment. "I actually . . . almost know what it's like. I was raised an orphan. I don't know where or to whom I was born, but my mother took pity on me. Instead of just smothering me as a baby, she spirited me away to a legal orphanage instead. A small one, run by a kind old woman. She raised me from a little child, like the mother I never had. And one day, bandits killed her. They killed everyone and burnt the orphanage down to the ground. Nearly all of my friends . . . everyone I'd ever known . . . gone."

"Wow," Julia said hoarsely. "That's rough. How can you stand it?"

"I don't know. Same as you, I guess." There was more to my story than just that, but I was not about to share it all.

"I wish . . ." Julia shook her head. "I wish I could get out of here and be rid of this place. I know they'd kill me if I tried to escape, though. This little spot is the farthest I've ever gotten." She barked a laugh. "I wish I could climb the ivy here and disappear over the wall."

I looked absently at the dense growth of green vines on the Palace wall. "Julia, I don't exactly have any more of a place to go back to than you, but . . . I'm going to get out. When I do . . . I'll take you with me."

A tear glimmered in her eye, breaking and falling down her cheek, despite her confused frown. "Really? But how?" Somehow, somewhere deep down, she almost seemed to believe I could do it. If she trusted me on some level, then I would do anything to make sure that trust was not misplaced.

"I'm not sure yet," I admitted.

- Chapter 10 -

Secrets Unburdened

Scholars debate over whether magic always existed on Mani. The Wellspring of Life feeds the Four Rivers, and also acts as the source of all elemental magic aside from Silver, the most elusive and primal of them all. But when did the Wellspring come to be? For it is commonly said that the Wellspring was a gift of the gods in ages past. If that is the case, then when did men come into existence? The gods must surely have created us after the Wellspring, for life could not exist apart from its sustenance.

— From *Secrets of Mani*, by Sor the Lark

(Dri'Shal 20, 997—Night Season)

We went and fetched Mydia after the feast. Three hours went by surprisingly fast when one had nothing to do. Chara had put us to work sewing in the meantime, so I was relieved when she came and told us that Mydia was done at the meal. Mydia said she had overeaten a bit and was stuffed full. However, she plunked herself down at her desk and took out her book to read once more.

Proud to see my liege lady so hard at work, I went and sought out Rhidea. I knew that she had stayed a bit after Mydia at the meal, but she was probably ready to go by now. And judging by that strange wink she'd given me . . . she wanted to see me again.

I knocked on her door. "Come in," came her muffled reply through the thick wood of the door. I opened it up and stepped inside. "Hello again, child," she greeted me, glancing up briefly from what she was doing—it appeared to be re-inking some sort of old manuscripts—to acknowledge me. How was she so busy already, changed out of her party dress this quickly?

"Hello, Rhidea. You wanted to see me again?"

"Of course—you're my new pupil after all," she said, putting away her work and getting right to the point. "Podda . . . or should I say Lyn? Lyn, we need to come up with a plan."

"A plan for . . . ?"

"Don't be silly. A plan for our partnership." Rhidea steepled her fingers under her chin. "I still have yet to talk to the princess about this, because I wanted to go over what we discussed last time and start from there. We have your training to discuss, and of course the matter of your friends who are still locked up somewhere in the Palace."

"And are we going to get Mydia in on it, too?"

"Yes, if you are all right with that."

I nodded. "I trust her."

"As do I. She is childlike and naïve, but has a good heart, and she seems like she knows how to keep a secret, despite her penchant for incessant talking."

"So, about this mage training . . ." I began hesitantly.

"I've got it all worked out. You and the princess will meet me in my office every morning for Coaction lessons—ostensibly only Mydia. I'm good at sealing words using Perception Authority, so unwanted listeners and interrupting maids shouldn't be a problem as long as we are cautious. Does that sound all right, child?"

I nodded.

The mage outlined a few more details before getting back to the matter of our breakout plan.

"I've heard some rumors," Rhidea began. "I'm sure Mydia has as well. A girl with white hair was seen leading mage soldiers in a chase across the whole city, and then bested two trained magi and escaped with an accomplice. Two hostage girls were kidnapped to try and lure her to Kalceron. I did at least talk to Captain Hespian about that. He's very stiff and would say nothing, but then again . . . I didn't press very hard. I could easily find a way to get your friend Kaen into the dungeons, with his being a soldier now, to see them—perhaps we could even sneak you in there—but breaking them out without casting obvious suspicion on all of us would be far more difficult. And I think Kalceron has the girls kept locked up tightly."

"So, basically . . . we're sunk."

"Child, remind me again how long you've known me?"

I blushed. "I'm sorry. I didn't mean it like that. You have been most kind in agreeing to help me. If you could find a way to free my friends, I would be indebted to you for life."

Rhidea waved a hand at that. "No need for apologies. Trust me, child—I'll do what I can for you. I'll admit that, if you were a simple handmaiden, I wouldn't be so quick to go to such pains for you, but don't worry. I'll figure something out."

I took my leave and headed back to find Mydia.

Later that evening, after the full nighttime cloud layer had come in, Mydia and I snuck out to meet Kaen. Julia and Chara were sleeping, assuming us both to be sound in our beds.

Kaen was there, just like he'd said he would be. "There you are, Lyn," he said impatiently. "I was beginning to wonder if you'd show up. And look, you brought the princess. Oh, this is getting better and better."

"This is the one you wanted me to meet?" Mydia asked uncertainly.

"Yes," I answered, with a meaningful glance at Kaen. "Mydia, this is Kaen. Kaen, Mydia."

"So, you really are the princess's personal attendant, huh?"

"You don't have to act quite so surprised, Kaen."

"Um . . . why am I here?" Mydia broke in. "Podda, he called you . . ."

"Yes, I know. My name's not Podda. I suppose you knew that much. Mydia, I'm going to tell you everything. And Kaen, just hush. You can help me explain. We can trust her."

He crossed his arms. "Sure. There you go—tell the royalty everything. Sure way to get yourself killed. But hey, who am I to talk?"

"Kaen, she funds the Underground."

Now he was listening. "Say what?"

"So, it's true," Mydia whispered. "You are the girl the mage soldiers were chasing that day. And those are your friends held in captivity right now."

We were all silent for a minute.

"We have a lot to discuss," I said. "A lot."

The whole story came out for Mydia. The name Podda was thrown out the window entirely—I felt bad for ever having to use an alias with her—and she learned all about my past. Kaen grudgingly realized that Mydia could be a big help in finding his sister, and slowly opened up to her. Then I told them about my visits with Rhidea, the Wandering Mage, and how Rhidea had found out my talents as a mage and wanted to train me personally. Kaen wouldn't believe that I could use magic at all until I showed him some of the few tricks I had learned. But almost harder for him to believe was that the Wandering Mage Rhidea was going to help us free Mandrie and Phoebe.

Next, Kaen filled us in on what he had been up to. "They hand-picked me out of the rank-and-file servants," he explained. "A soldier suddenly drew me aside and handed me a spear."

"Just like that?" I asked. "Is that how they normally recruit new soldiers?"

He nodded. "Like I said, they thought I looked like a decent choice. They have some interesting methods. They test young men like that to see how they react. Apparently, I have a natural aptitude for the spear and sword, so they named me a third sergeant after only one day's training, and soon promoted me to a First Sergeant of the watch."

"Were you able to get access to the dungeons?" I asked hopefully.

"Yes, actually. I made contact with the dungeon guards, and I've been down there a couple times now."

"And?"

He shook his head. "No sign of Phoebe or my sis. I did hear some whispers, though. . . . They were taken to an abandoned tower they call the prison tower."

Mydia gasped. "Not that place. That's where . . ." She gulped and cut off.

"Where what?" Kaen hissed.

"Where they take important prisoners for questioning," she finished in a hushed voice. "Torture."

Kaen froze in shock. "No . . . they wouldn't."

"Y-your friends are safe. Your sister is safe; I'm sure of it," Mydia added hastily. "I'm sure they wouldn't harm them. . . ."

"Then why would they take them there?" Kaen demanded through gritted teeth. He looked as though about to strangle the princess.

"Kaen, calm down," I said, placing a hand on his shoulder to placate him. "She's right, they probably haven't treated them too—"

He threw off my hand. "We don't know anything, Lyn! They wouldn't have taken them to such a place if they weren't intending them any harm. I just—this is my sister we're talking about here. I can't bear the thought of her in danger."

I glanced at Mydia, whose green eyes shone with tears, and then back at my distraught friend. "If they wanted information out of them, I'm sure they've spilled it all by now. But in any case, we can't break them out of there by talking and worrying. We need a plan. And that's where Lady Rhidea is going to help us."

At the mention of the High Mage, Kaen huffed and folded his arms. "Right. I'll believe you about that woman when I meet her myself."

After the discussion, which must certainly have lasted well over an hour, we bid Kaen farewell and returned to our rooms. "So . . . it's Lyn, huh?" Mydia asked me quietly as we went.

"Yes. I'm sorry I had to hide so much from you, but surely you can see why it was necessary."

"Oh, I do. Don't worry, Lyn; I forgive you. I knew there was more going on here than you felt comfortable saying."

"Thank you, although you really shouldn't call me Lyn in front of any others. If what you said is true about Mandrie and Phoebe, then they would have already at least told them my name."

"I understand. Podda it is, then."

"I'll be in bed soon," I said. "There's something else I want to do first."

Mydia shot me a worried glance. "What sort of thing? Aren't you pushing yourself at this point?"

We'll find out. In answer to her concern, I just shook my head and ducked down the stairs, bidding her a hasty goodnight over my shoulder. I made my way to Julia's secret hideout. My conversation with her earlier had given me an idea, and I wanted to test out my theory.

I stepped out into the small, round courtyard, squinting slightly in the dim light of the Night Auroras. I approached the vine-covered wall and, taking a deep breath, gathered my strength and began to climb it. I tested the ivy as I went, finding chinks in the stonework of the wall for footholds, but it really wasn't a hard climb, thanks to my natural strength and agility and a bit of my secret energy reserves. I soon found myself at the top of the wall, glancing down only to shiver at the sight of the ground some twenty paces below me, half-hidden in the murky, torchless darkness. I could deal with heights. I just . . . didn't like to.

Pulling myself up onto the wall, I surveyed the view, quickly locating the prison tower of which Kaen and Mydia had spoken. That was where those fiends were keeping Mandrie and Phoebe. . . . My heart burned with anger at the thought. But I couldn't go there tonight. I wasn't about to risk whatever help Rhidea could be by blowing my cover now. Looking behind me, I saw Mydia's rooms just above my level, at the top of the nearest tower. A hundred yards to the east lay Lord Kalceron's tower, the largest and fanciest of the four major towers of the castle. The wall on which I now perched would take me down a winding path to that tower—and how could I give up such an opportunity?

I crept toward the governor's tower, keeping my eyes peeled for the roving lights of the guards' torches, and also any windows of the castle looking out on where I was. I eventually came to the tower and began to climb it, brick by brick. There was no ivy here, but I was able to do it with a large initial leap and a few careful steps and handholds. Slowly, ever so slowly, I peeked my head over the top of a windowsill, scanning the candlelit room inside.

There was no one. I continued upwards, until I found a good foothold to lean in and peer through the next window up. I quickly drew my head back, however, after catching a glimpse of a figure in a black robe. It registered in my mind belatedly that the figure—a slight woman with long, black hair—was Lady Lieda.

My heart rate quickened. I stayed exactly where I was, listening. Peeking back over the sill, I saw that she was gone now, but I could hear her talking to another, the Lord of Nytaea himself.

". . . The princess."

"Yes," replied Lord Kalceron. He must have been standing just out of sight. "I'm well aware that she holds to the ideals of that woman." The venom in his words sent a shiver down my spine.

"No, no, I'm talking about her new handmaiden," Lieda murmured. "That homely girl, one of the newer maids."

"Pah! You think I pay any attention to those wenches?"

"Occasionally." There was a suggestive hint of jealousy in her tone. "But perhaps there are a few things in this palace that you should pay more attention to, my lord. There is something strange about that maid. I know it. And I think your daughter knows it as well."

"Hmph. Last I was aware, my daughter knows painfully little."

So Lieda is onto me . . . and she's trying to rat me out to her vile husband! I would have to be more careful from now on. I may not be safe no matter where I went.

After a moment, Lord Kalceron said, "So, are you saying you think she may be the girl I'm looking for, in disguise?"

"I don't know that. And it doesn't seem likely, but it's possible. Your useless Mage Guard haven't found any leads on her whereabouts, after all. I will keep tabs on her."

At this point, the conversation moved out of hearing range, and I was left hanging there, brain working furiously to process the information I'd just heard. Lieda suspected me, and even Lord Kalceron—whose disdain for the lower class was well known—was mulling it over. I knew I did not have long.

But for now, I needed sleep. I made my way carefully back across the wall tops, pausing above Julia's special spot. Mydia's sunroom window was just a few paces above. . . . The room where Chara and Julia were sleeping was underneath, so they wouldn't hear anything. Taking a running start, I leaped from the wall-top stones and grabbed the stone ledge. Using the last of my tired strength, I heaved myself up and dropped as quietly as I could manage into the sunroom. One minute of tiptoeing later, I snuck in beside Julia and Chara's beds and crashed in mine.

I savored the sleep as it took me.

❧❧

"Lyn."

The little voice came from an equally little girl who sat in front of me on a bed of white mist. I stood looking about, confused who had spoken, before registering that the girl was there. Did I know her from somewhere? Had I seen her before?

She was perhaps seven or eight years of age and fair of skin, with wispy white hair reaching just past her shoulders. Pure, radiant white like Sol. Her form was slender, and she sat in a casual kneeling posture wearing only a white knee-length gown. Why did she look so familiar?

"Hello, Lyn," she said again after a moment, eying me with a cool but curious gaze, as though waiting for something. "May I help you find something today?" Her voice was high-pitched, bearing the squeak of a young child.

I smiled nervously. "I, uh . . . I'm not sure. Who . . . ?"

The girl put a finger to her lips. "Shhh. Don't speak; you'll probably ruin it."

"But . . . I don't understand who you are or what you're asking."

The girl cocked her head, putting on that pouting face little girls use to get what they want. "Now you've done it. I knew it. Oh well, goodbye. I'll see you another time."

- Chapter 11 -

Mage Training

On the subject of Dark Magic, a theoretical transversion of the Wellspring's power . . . I honestly do not know who came up with the theory, but it has been whispered in dark corners of the mage world for some time now. The idea is simple: everything has an opposite—just look in the mirror, and you will see your own opposite. Mani's magic is the source of life itself . . . and the opposite of life is death. I shudder to think what may come of our world should a mage think to touch such a power, no matter what reason he may have, be it evil or altruistic.

— From *Secrets of Mani*, by Sor the Lark

(Dri'Shal 21, 997—Night Season)

"Lesson one," said Rhidea the Wandering Mage, "Coaction is dangerous."

I gulped, but I kept my chin up. I stole a glance out of the corner of my eye at Mydia, who seemed to be feeling a similarly warm, fuzzy feeling at our mentor's words.

The two of us sat on a scarlet rug in Rhidea's study upon folded knees, hands held relaxed on our laps just as the mage had carefully instructed us. She herself sat cross-legged in front of us, hands folded in front of her face with steepled fingers pointing between us. She wore a satin dress that matched her red décor and her crimson hair, which she had pinned back in a twist like a folding flame.

It had been decided that Rhidea was going to give private tutoring sessions to me and Mydia both while she stayed at the Palace. Once we had our rescue plan laid out and the time came, she would help us break Mandrie and Phoebe out of prison, and then I would become her personal apprentice. I was perhaps the most scared about that last part.

The princess and I did not speak, but instead waited to hear what would follow Rhidea's ominous words.

"Magic is a pervasive force of nature in our world," she continued. "It is wild, primal and beautiful. Coaction is only a tool used by synergists to harness the power of Mani's magic that is all around us. But always, always use caution when practicing this art. Do not fear the elements, but respect them. Don't ever trust yourself too much, or think that you know everything there is to know, because it will be that unknown, that unpredictable variable, that overlooked piece, that gets you into trouble. For instance, Lyn, your flames. They can burn you quite easily if you lose control."

I nodded. *Makes sense.*

Then followed the practical lesson. She taught us a few pointers and rules on basic Coaction, not letting Mydia out of it just because she already had basic Coactive training. Rhidea refused to let either of us practice any Coaction without first proving that we could master her discipline.

After the lesson was over, we dropped the formalities and relaxed a bit. I took this opportunity to ask her what her goal of study here at the Palace had been.

"Oh? Interested?" was her response. "I seek the source of a major problem facing Mani right now. At this point, I've been all over the continent of Argent in my search." The mage let out a small sigh before continuing:

"Magic, my friends, is dwindling from this world. It is said that magi once wielded the power of gods. Nowadays, I am one of the strongest magi in the world, but a mere hundred years ago, my strength was not all that uncommon. In fact—" She addressed Mydia. "Do you want to know why your father fears me so much?"

Mydia gave a small shake of her head. "I . . . didn't realize he did."

Conscious of the speech seal Rhidea had placed around us, I asked, "Why?"

"It is the same reason that he bows to Master Gendric of the Nytaean Academy: he fears power. And the reason is that he is not naturally as strong as he seems."

"But I thought he was the most powerful in all of Nytaea," said Mydia. "That's what they all say."

Rhidea shook her head. "No. None in his family have ever held the power that he does. Even his son, the late Prince Kallyn, was close but could not match the strength of his father. No, Edrius gets his power on loan from the Archlord."

"From the Archlord?" I repeated. "How does that even work?"

"Oh, there are ways. Kalceron possesses a secret well of power which Domon keeps constantly filled from his capital. It is the Archlord's way of keeping control in his thirteen city-states of Kystrea, by way of his governors, the Twelve Lords. Domon himself holds unimaginable strength, that of the great ancient warlocks. I still have not discovered how he came to possess it, but I have . . . fears. I suppose my next place to head should be the Capital, Ti'Vaeth . . . perhaps."

"You don't like the place?" asked Mydia.

Rhidea grimaced. "I never did. Trust me, if you had ever met the Archlord, you wouldn't want to come within a city's distance of him ever again." She gave no more reason than that, yet something about the far-off look in her expression, along with the intensity of it, told me that there was far more between her and Domon.

Soon our first lesson with Rhidea was concluded, and she bid us a good day with a charge to practice *carefully*. Also, Mydia was to teach me phonetics, laying the groundwork for me to learn to read. I wasn't looking forward to that. . . .

That evening, Mydia had Julia and me bring in extra scones and fruit, and we all ate and chatted together. Mydia and I both got along well with the girl, quiet though she was, and the three of us often made small talk whenever Chara wasn't around. Julia could tell that we had some secret between us, but she would never get us in trouble with Chara over it.

My life as a handmaiden was so comfortable that I almost forgot about Phoebe and Mandrie sometimes. Almost. It was the most luxuriously I'd ever lived, all things considered, but I constantly felt guilty for enjoying this new life while my longtime friends were in a prison tower, held against their will and possibly tortured half to death for all they knew about me. It was enough to make a girl sick.

Later that evening, I decided I needed to make something clear to Mydia. I approached her just as she was putting her mother's book down for the night. "You know I'm not going to be here for much longer, right?"

"Oh." She looked up. "What makes you suddenly bring that up? I mean, I know you want to rescue your friends and all. And then . . ." She scratched her chin. "Then I suppose you'll be going off with Rhidea?"

"Right. Honestly, I'm a little scared. I still don't know what I'll tell my friends. 'Sorry, I have to go look for some dusty old scrolls with a scary mage woman?' I can't even imagine what Phoebe would say. . . ." I chuckled at the thought.

"I will be very sad to see you go," Mydia whispered. "Julia will, too. Honestly . . . I'd stop you if I could."

I frowned.

"Stop you from going," she elaborated, looking both guilty and sorrowful. "Even . . . from rescuing your friends. It's a selfish thought, I know. I'm a terrible friend."

I crossed my arms. "You do realize why I came here in the first place, right? And surely you understand that I didn't mean to be here for anywhere near this long. Mydia, nearly a month—an entire month—has gone by, and my friends are still locked in that tower!"

"I-I don't know what to say, Lyn. I understand, and I feel bad—responsible, even—for it. I'm sorry." After a pause, she said, "You know you're going to have to break them out yourself, don't you? You, Rhidea, Kaen. There's not much I can do. I could try talking to my father, but . . ."

"No, don't bother," I told her tiredly. "You'll only put yourself under suspicion. Rhidea has promised to help me; we'll figure this out. I trust her." *And Julia trusts me*, I thought to myself. How was any of this going to work? We had to act quickly. My lessons with Rhidea would have to speed up if my Coaction was to be of any use in combat. But then what? I had no idea what would happen once we succeeded in breaking Mandrie and Phoebe out of the tower.

We talked for a long while after that, mostly about happier things, but it all felt a bit hollow. Afterward, I said goodbye to my friend the princess and went to see Kaen in the guards' barracks. In a place that was safe to talk—or so he said—I updated him on all the latest information I'd received.

"Lyn—Podda—Lyn!" he stammered. "Look; we have to do something. If what you say is true, this magical Rhidea is leaving in one week, assuming Lord Kalceron doesn't chase her out sooner. And I'm still not seeing any action."

"Kaen, calm down. She's here to search out clues in the library to a terrible crisis . . . or at least so she says. Point being: when she's done, she'll leave. When she leaves, she'll help us break them out."

Kaen thought about this. "All right, fair enough. And then what? Does she take you with her to train as her personal mage student? If so, what happens to me? To my sister and Phoebe? I am *not* staying on to work in Lord Kalceron's army."

"Kaen, I don't know what's going to happen, but if Rhidea keeps her word, she will make sure that we are taken care of. Some way, sometime, somehow. We just have to trust her, all right?"

He cocked his head to one side. "And you really do? You trust that withered old mage? That's a lot of faith."

"Yes, Kaen. I actually do."

He considered my words, running a hand absently through his dark curls. "All right, then. I want to talk with this mage. Isn't that fair?"

I nodded. "Well . . . yes. She's probably in the library now, or studying. . . . How about you try directly after supper tonight? She should be there. Tell her you're with Mydia and me."

"All right. Sounds good to me. Where are her rooms?"

I told him where to find Rhidea, and then returned to Mydia's rooms, an idea coming to mind. I knocked on the princess's closed door, and judging from her distracted response, she must have been studying that book of hers again. She had likely finished it already, and was just studying it further to please Rhidea. When I announced myself, her voice brightened up, and she bade me come in. I did so and closed the door behind me.

"My lady." I looked around and listened to make sure that no others were in the room. I wished I possessed Rhidea's speech-sealing magic. "Mydia, can you get me into the Underground again any time soon?"

She looked up from her book. "Oh. With the leaders?"

I nodded.

"Yes, but . . . not tonight, if that's what you're asking. It would have to be, hmm . . . whenever the next meeting is. Dri'Shal twenty-second—oh, actually that's tomorrow."

"Thank you. That should work. Do you think you could send for my friend Kaen as well?"

"So he can meet them?" she asked.

"Right. I've got an idea cooking."

Mydia smirked, causing her dimples to emerge. "Then I hope you're a good cook."

- Chapter 12 -

A New Plan

*Fire magi are often recognizable by their temperament alone—
impetuous, spontaneous and passionate. Not necessarily prone
to anger, but strong emotion. It's a trait of the affinity. I would
almost venture to say that a fire mage who lacks these qualities
is not entirely human.*
— From *Secrets of Mani,* by Sor the Lark

(Dri'Shal 22, 997—Night Season)

The next night, I met Mydia in the Palace Gardens. Kaen arrived shortly after me, dressed in a soldier's uniform with a warm coat overtop to keep the deep sunless chill at bay, a sword belted at his side just in case. I was relieved that Mydia had sent for him as I'd asked. We set off into the city, headed for the abandoned warehouse front.

Upon reaching it, we found only a pile of ashes and charred stones. I gasped at the sight, and Mydia let out a small cry of shock.

"This is the place?" Kaen asked. "Seems a bit more . . . destroyed than I was expecting. Recently destroyed."

"I-I can't believe—" Mydia began.

"This is it," I confirmed. "They must have just done this."

Kaen inspected the premises, pointing out a dead body, burnt either from the fire or from the Coactive flames that had started it. It was either Little Lester or Skinny Sam . . . I wasn't sure which, and I wasn't about to go up and try to find out. Mydia was almost gagging already.

Kaen went over and kicked the corpse onto its back. "Newly

dead," he said. "Judging by that and the smoldering fire, I'd say this happened just this morning. Do you recognize this man?"

Mydia wouldn't look, and instead started to cry, so I gritted my teeth and inspected the face, kneeling next to it. My stomach churned at the sight of the charred flesh, but I recognized the general features.

"He was the one they called Skinny Sam," I declared.

Mydia sobbed louder.

Kaen put a hand on her shoulder. "My Lady—princess or no, you can't wake the whole town like that. You hardly even knew him. He probably would have stabbed you in the back as soon as take your money, anyway."

"You're . . . you're probably right," she said, calming down a bit. She still wouldn't look anywhere near the body.

"What should we do now?" I asked.

Mydia looked at me solemnly, tears staining her face. "I-I don't know. Do you think . . . ?"

"You there! Stop!" an authoritative voice shouted from the shadows. "In the name of Lord Kalceron—"

It was a guard with a torch. Kaen was faster than I would have thought, his sword out of its sheath and flashing through the darkness before the guard had a chance to cry out. There was a grunt, and dark blood in the torchlight, and the guard thumped to the ground, dead. Kaen ground his boot on the torch as it fell out of the man's hands onto the ground, and the light was gone.

"So, they are still posting people here," Kaen muttered. "There will probably be more if we dally much longer."

"Hurry," I urged, "let's get back to the Palace."

"What do we do with the b-b-b—" Mydia whimpered.

"The body can stay there!" Kaen said harshly. "It wouldn't look any less suspicious to hide it now. Come on!"

We all made a sprint for the Palace, retracing the way we had come. We got back safely, stopping only once we were past the wall and in the Palace Gardens. Mydia wiped her brow. "Whew! That was . . . a bit too much for me." She seemed almost dazed, swaying on her feet as her knees shook from the fright.

"I'm so sorry about that," I told her. "Look, Mydia—don't come out here any nights in the future until this calms down. Kaen, you should get back to the barracks immediately, and return your sword wherever you found it, once you clean it off. Try to avoid suspicion for a few days. My plan is off, so it's all up to Rhidea now. Working with the Underground is a bust. We may have less time than I thought. . . ."

Mydia nodded.

Kaen bid me goodnight, returning to his room in the guard barracks.

(Dri'Shal 23, 997—Night Season)

The next morning, rumors were already spreading that a conspiracy had been uncovered against Lord Kalceron. There was debate in the Palace over whether that was a good or bad thing, though. I discovered, to my great relief, that it was largely about the discovery and burning of the Underground's main building—not the mysteriously dead guard. Until this point, most of the Palace staff had thought the Underground a mere story whispered by people who desired their heads to be chopped off.

That evening after our lessons with Rhidea, she informed us that an execution was planned two days hence, on the yearly Nytaean festival called The Lament of the King. This festival was held on the fifth dawn of the year, ever since the days of the Old Kings of the city-state of Nytaea, before the province came under the banner of the Archlord.

Here in Nytaea, dawn came four days earlier than in the capital, so that meant the festival would be held on the twenty-fifth day of Dri'Shal, the fourth month.

The rebels to be beheaded were Gaela and one whose description matched Big Bart. Why on this particular day, though? It boded ill. Rhidea's stay had been planned to end after the two-day feast, but now . . . those plans may have to change.

Rhidea did not appear to be frazzled by it, but she did seem just a bit more . . . tense. Circumstances were beginning to overlap, affecting many different people, escalating so quickly that our plans would surely get caught up in it all. "Something historic is going to transpire here in Nytaea," she predicted. "And we may just be a part of it."

A plan began to hatch as we discussed the events. We all agreed that the execution had to be stopped—if possible—and the prison break would go best if such a distraction took place at the same time.

"But I don't want Mydia to be in on the operation at all, for her own safety," Rhidea insisted, eying the princess. "And also to keep you out of suspicion, my dear."

"I agree," I said, hoping that we wouldn't need Mydia's help. Not for the first time, I was tempted to question why Rhidea even wanted to help us, though I already knew the answer: she loved Nytaea and Mydia; she had no love for Lord Kalceron. Perhaps she wasn't all that different from me.

"Hey!" Mydia complained. "I can still make illusions for you all."

"That could certainly be of use, child," Rhidea said. "As long as you're not in danger and can't be implicated in the uprising. Now, about your friends in the Underground . . . you said there were two left who escaped?"

Mydia nodded. "I think I know where they are hiding out. I'll contact them tomorrow night."

"And I will come with you," Rhidea added. "Lyn, perhaps you could scout out the prison tower tomorrow night? You said you found where it was."

I nodded. "All right. I'll see if I can get in. And . . . Mydia, I had an idea about who will replace me as handmaiden." I told her of a special girl who would make a fine handmaiden, and her face seemed to brighten just a bit.

In two days, on the twenty-fifth of Dri'Shal, we would spring the trap. Rhidea and Mydia would coordinate with the remaining rebel leaders and get them on board with the plan, so that they could raise up a few soldiers to help in rescuing Bart and Gaela.

The next night, while Mydia took Rhidea to meet with Tall Tom and Little Lester, I went to do my scouting. I stepped out onto the wide sill of Mydia's sunroom window and hopped down onto the wall above Julia's favorite spot. Why bother to climb the wall when I could just get on top of it from Mydia's tower?

The evening was dim without the auroras, as clouds obscured much of the starlight this night. The chill breeze whipped at my hair and skirts, attempting to nudge me toward a midnight plunge. Just like last time, looking down from this high wall was enough to make me queasy. But there on the south side of the palace . . .

The prison tower.

I dashed down the wall-top walkway before realizing I needed to jump down to the next section of the wall for best access to the tower. After looking both ways, I leapt with my superhuman strength onto the next fold of the wall, and then once more, arriving at the stretch of wall that connected to the spire. All the while, I tried to keep out of sight of the Palace Guard. Spires and towers on the wall did most of that for me, fortunately.

Eventually, I made it over to the 'abandoned' tower, and began inspecting the twenty-foot-wide structure for a way in. I ended up climbing up the side. I scurried around the back of it, using the existing ivy and my own finger strength to claw my way up the stonework. At last, I made it to the top, where I found a trapdoor leading downward.

My heart was beating at a horse's gallop, and my body wanted to drop from exhaustion already, but I forced myself to breathe and continue onward. I could sleep later. I did, however, pull out some of the food Mydia had sent me with, which helped a lot. It was mostly energy that I needed after bursts of exertion, more than rest.

A couple of floors down, I found the highest-level cells. No guards were in sight; perhaps they only guarded the lower levels. I searched around for a minute before spotting Mandrie and Phoebe, huddled together in a corner cell and asleep. I gasped at the sight: malnourished and haggard, hair and clothes a mess. They had been beaten and whipped, with bruises and scars visible on their arms and necks, and I knew that there must be many bruises underneath their dresses. Even Mandrie's cute little face was marked up horribly, cut and bleeding from recent wounds.

"Oh, Mandrie, Phoebe . . ." I whispered, horror and anger dissonating in my chest. "What did they do to you?"

Neither girl stirred.

"Mandrie, can you hear me? Phoebe?"

There was still no response.

"Mandrie!" I whispered fervently. "Phoebe, *wake up!*" I shook the bars of the cage as I said it.

". . . Huh?" Mandrie's eyes fluttered open, and she drew in a ragged breath. She stared at me in disbelief, her countenance dark and sad under her greasy brown curls. "L-Lyn? Is that . . . you?"

"Yes! Yes, it's me. Are you all right?"

"You . . . you came. Finally . . . it's been so long, Lyn. Where's Kaen? Where's my brother?" Mandrie turned and shook Phoebe awake. Phoebe gasped upon seeing me.

"Good, you're awake, too," I said. "Kaen is here at the Palace. We're going to get you out of here. Don't worry. You're going to be just fine."

"Oh . . . thank you," whispered Mandrie. "Th-they hurt us. Beat us. Those cruel men with the whips. Oh, it still stings. And I'm hungry, too. They hardly feed us anything in here." She let out two pitiful coughs. The sight of my longtime friends in such a poor state sent an emotional jolt through my heart like a stabbing pain.

"Hang in there, Mandrie," I encouraged her. "Here. I have some food for you two." I handed each of them some fresh bread and sausages through the bars.

"Sausage?" Phoebe mumbled. But she took it eagerly and wolfed it down like a hungry animal. "Where did you get all of this? It's still warm and everything."

"I stole it from the Palace." I didn't want to tell them yet about everything that I'd been doing at the Palace. My white lie seemed to satisfy them for the moment; the poor girls were in no state to be considering things too hard. "I'm so sorry we took this long to find you. We're going to get you out of here tomorrow morning at the festival, so don't worry. Everything will be just fine."

"Tomorrow? Really?" Mandrie croaked.

"Yes." I took her hands through the bars and squeezed them gently. "We'll get you out of here, just trust me. We have a plan."

"You really mean it, Lyn?"

"Yes. I swear it: I'll get you both out of here."

"Thank you," she whispered. "Oh, thank you, Lyn." Now the tears started to roll down her cheeks. "We'll wait till tomorrow."

"All right. I have to go now. Stay safe."

"Goodbye," she said, and went back to her corner to sleep. Phoebe stared after me, and then sighed and resigned herself to one more night just like Mandrie. Hoping their tormentors left them alone until I could come tomorrow, I left the way I had come. I climbed down the side of the tower, and quietly traversed the walls back to Mydia's tower.

"You found them?" she asked in a hushed voice as I climbed in the window.

I dropped softly to the floor and nodded, breathing heavily from all the exertion. "I told them to expect us in the morning. You talked with Tom and Lester?"

"Yes. They were already planning a rescue operation for Bart and Gaela. You should be all set. You'd best get some sleep, Lyn. You look dreadfully tired after all that."

"Very well," I said with a weary nod. We both tiptoed back to our own beds. We had to be up early on the morrow. The execution was to be held at cloudbreak—the first light of the next month, Firvaen—so I had to meet Rhidea and Kaen by the barracks before then. Each Cycle began with dawn in Ti'Vaeth, but Nytaea's latitude was four zones east of Ti'Vaeth, so we saw dawn four days early.

At cloudbreak. Tomorrow morning, it would all end—one way or another.

That night, I had another vivid dream.

I stood in that same place of white nothingness. It was like an endless sea of warm snow, with mists curling gently up, tickling my feet. I felt sure I'd been looking for something . . .

"Hello, Lyn!" came a bright voice. I turned and there she was, that same white girl. White was the best description I could think of, considering her white dress, white hair and pale skin.

"Hello again," I said slowly. "Do you . . . know what I was looking for?"

The girl looked up at me with big, bright eyes, an innocent look on her face. She shook her head with downturned lips and raised eyebrows. "No. I don't have a clue." She didn't mention what a silly question it was. "So," she said, face changing into a hopeful expression, "Is there anything I can help you with? Something else I can find for you?"

I frowned, rubbing my head. "No. I don't think so."

"Aw, that's too bad," said the girl with a sad sigh. "But I figured as much."

I scratched my lip, looking upwards at the blank sky of whiteness. Find something, find something . . . "Oh, wait," I said suddenly. "I'm looking for my friend Mandrie. Although I don't think you can help me with her."

She shook her head dejectedly. "Nope. Sorry."

"Then . . . what about my mother?"

White perked up, her eyes gleaming. "Your mother? I remember lots about her. Do you want to see her?"

"See her?" I asked. "You mean . . . she's alive?"

"I don't know. I mean, you don't know. You know?" She smiled up at me and blinked.

"Um . . . no."

"Oh, well! Here, let me show her to you." The girl grabbed me by the hand and began to tug me along. I gave way and followed her.

Suddenly, we were somewhere else: a barren, rocky land beneath a starry sky bright enough to see by. A woman stood clad in a dark dress upon a rock the size of a horse that jutted out of the ground. She had long, startlingly white hair. I tried to look around for the girl, but she was gone. In fact, I couldn't move at all, even my head. Whatever this vision was, I was experiencing it in a very detached way.

I realized belatedly that the woman was speaking: ". . . Gone. Why does it have to be this way?" She spoke so quietly that I wasn't sure if she was addressing someone or just speaking to herself. "We've come so far. We can't very well give up here."

My vision, or rather whoever it was whose eyes I was looking through, turned and then . . . rolled over. It was the oddest sensation. The woman continued to murmur quietly from where she was, until she suddenly gasped. "Lynchazel! Be careful!"

I heard frantic, running footsteps on the rocks, and then suddenly I was grasped by two large hands.

- Chapter 13 -

Insurgence

Lightning magi tend to be intelligent and cunning, quick of thought and quick of learning. Some have been known to be quite greedy for power, but it would be unfair to apply that stereotype across the board, as the only possible correlation is their thirst for growth and knowledge, which are not bad things—as long as they are tempered with self-control.
— From *Secrets of Mani,* by Sor the Lark

(Dri'Shal 25, 997—Dawn)

I gasped in momentary panic, jerking awake. I was in my bed. I felt about my body as though searching for the hands, but they weren't there. I let out a sigh and leaned back onto my pillow. Just another dream—albeit a strange one. That vision . . . it was like . . . like I was seeing a small baby or toddler's perspective.

And then it hit me: that was exactly what it was. That girl . . . White, or whatever her name was . . . she showed me a glimpse of my mother. But it was more like a vision of the past, a . . . memory. Was that really what my mother had looked like? And how could it possibly be real if I didn't remember her at all? Or was my own mind creating dreams born of wishful thinking?

I gave up the mental goose chase with a sigh and got out of bed. This was a day of far more pressing matters.

The hour was still early, but I got dressed and prepared anyway. It was time for action. I woke Mydia and informed her that I was going out for the preparations.

I met Rhidea and Kaen in one of the smaller outer courtyards.

There was some introduction and explanation, and then we got to it. "Remember, we're going out in style," Rhidea said. "I will go and free Gaela and Bartimaeus, making a scene of stopping the execution, while you two head to the prison tower and free your friends."

I nodded.

"What about the princess?" Kaen asked. "Is she going to . . . ?"

"I'm here," mumbled Mydia, who was just now approaching in her morning gown, hair a mess and yawning widely. "Now, what kind of illusions do you need?"

Rhidea looked from me to Mydia. "Nothing too elaborate. If we run into your father, they're unfortunately not going to matter anyway."

Mydia nodded and gave us all powerful illusions that masked our faces. "They'll be good for about an hour," she said before departing for her rooms.

"Let's make haste, then," Rhidea said.

I nodded as she set off, then turned to my friend. "All right, Kaen. Let's go."

He drew his sword, a fine, long blade that gleamed in the light. Where had he come across such a stately weapon? "I'm ready. Can't believe we're storming the Palace—from the inside, at that—but let's go."

Fortunately, at this early hour, the Palace was pretty quiet, so we didn't have to worry about running into servants or soldiers. Upon reaching the locked entrance that led to the tower, however, we ran into more security. "Halt!" called the guards, two men in leather and bronze armor.

We had discussed this beforehand: Rhidea had insisted that we refrain from violence, so we would try to dispatch as many guards as possible without killing them—after all, we didn't need innocent blood on our hands. Bearing this in mind, we rushed the two guardsmen.

I took the guard on the left, who threw up his spear in a defensive stance as I came close, while Kaen took on the guard on the right. I ducked in and grabbed my opponent's spear just below the head as he thrust, yanking him off-balance with my inhuman strength. After ripping the spear from his hands, I proceeded to crack him on the back of the head with the haft. Even through his light helm, the force was enough to knock him unconscious, and he crumpled to the ground.

Kaen and the other soldier still clashed to my right. Kaen was holding his own, parrying his opponent's spear while searching for an opportunity. I gave it to him by sliding in and kicking out the guard's leg. Kaen knocked the man's spear away with a backhanded swing, and then slammed his sword pommel-first into his temple.

Two down, but they wouldn't stay down for long. Kaen and I nodded to each other, and I bashed the doors in with a kick.

Inside the tower, we were met by more surprised guards and silver-armored mage soldiers. The room was well lit by torches that lined the walls, and had a flight of stairs circling upwards on the right. That was our goal. But standing in our way were three mage soldiers and three guards, with the guards on the right and magi on the left. I knew there would be no games here—if we couldn't take them out without killing them, then we would have to do so.

I dashed in before the magi could collect their wits, taking out the nearest with a giant leap and a kick to his chestplate. The silver plate dented inward and he tumbled backward and fell. It must have not been the spell-reinforced grade. I was already upon the next, raising my stolen spear to strike for his head with the flat of the blade.

This mage was quicker, erecting a split-second defensive shield out of ice. Had he formed it from water in the air? Clearly, he was a water mage specializing in ice, not that I was an expert in classifications. My spear crashed right through it nevertheless, but it was enough to stop most of the force, so that the spearhead only staggered him as it struck his helmet. The strain on my spear's haft threatened to snap it in two.

The third mage fired a bolt of lightning my way, and I was forced to duck to avoid it, backing up toward the gaping doorway. The second mage, recovering from his stagger, swung at me, a sword of ice materializing in his hand as he did so. This I blocked with my spear, shattering the ice, shortly before evading another bolt from the thunder mage. Now I had an opportunity to attack again. I leapt at the ice mage, thrusting for his throat with lightning speed and precision—my strength accounting for the speed, while the accuracy I'd have chalked up to luck. He wasn't able to dodge my quick attack, and the spear took him just under his chinstrap, and he fell. I grimaced, feeling sick as blood gushed from the fatal wound.

Glancing back briefly at Kaen, I saw that he was holding his own against the regular soldiers until I could get to them. Just as I looked back, however, I saw the first mage, who I had assumed to be out of commission from his head trauma, sit up and attempt to blast me with a firebolt. The thunder mage came at me as well, and I was forced to dodge between two attacks at once. My body reacted faster than I thought possible as I danced around the thunder mage, tripped his legs and rammed my spear between two plates of armor in his side. The haft broke off as I did so, and I ripped it free, moving to confront the remaining mage soldier, who was now up and rushing toward me, twin flames in hand.

Hefting my broken spear shaft, I leaped to the side and swung my shaft of wood in a two-handed arc, cracking the wood into the fire mage's silver helm with enough force to stop him in his tracks. The fires in his palms went out and he wavered briefly before toppling to the stone floor.

"Lyn!" I heard Kaen shout over the ringing of metal-on-metal. "A little . . . help here!"

I looked his way, taking in his predicament in a glance. He crossed swords with two soldiers at once, the other staying back with a heavy limp and blood running down his leg. Kaen himself had two separate cuts, one on his left arm and one on the other leg. His performance was quite shocking, and he held his own, although it was plain to see that he was reaching his limits.

I rushed in to help, pulling out a boot knife. As Kaen parried the farther guard's next attack, I sank my knife into the closer one's shoulder, yanking it back out with a spray of blood as the man cried out in pain, dropping his sword and clutching his shoulder as he turned to face me. I scooped up the sword as it dropped and whipped the blade around to knock the flat into his helmet.

I looked up just in time to see Kaen run his sword through the leather armor covering the other soldier's stomach. He dropped to the floor with a gurgle and a thump. And just like that, the room went silent, all except for the shuffling sound of the third guard attempting to flee out the door . . . Kaen caught him as he limped away, knocking him unconscious with his sword pommel. He looked back at me and shrugged guiltily. "Sorry, I know. Couldn't have him getting away."

I nodded distractedly, drawing in a big breath. "I'm just happy we're still alive. I . . . think I might have killed a couple of them. I'm not sure."

"No time to dwell on that, Lyn. That's for later. Let's see what's up these stairs now."

We proceeded up the circular flight of stairs, encountering more guards, and took care of them as they came. We went up floor after floor of abandoned cells, torture rooms, and more cells. No one was inside of them, fortunately. Apparently, Mandrie and Phoebe really were the only prisoners in the tower.

At last, we reached the floor of their cell. Kaen rushed over and banged on the silver bars. "Mandrie! Mandrie, it's me!"

"Oh, Kaen . . . you came!" Mandrie began to cry as she ran to see her long-lost brother. Phoebe didn't say anything, but surprise and relief were clear on her face. Then I helped out and wrenched the bars apart to let them out. Crafted of solid silver one inch thick, these cell bars were only made to keep regular people—perhaps even magi—out; not monsters like me.

Mandrie shied back, never having seen what I could do before.

"How did you do that?" Phoebe breathed in a spooked tone, the first thing she'd said so far.

"It's not important right now," I answered, "but we have a lot of catching up to do once this is all over. Don't ask too many questions; we need to get you out of here. Come on!"

We led the three of them down the tower stairs and out through the wrecked doorway into the Palace grounds. Mandrie and Phoebe had a hard time keeping up because of their weakened condition, but they made it. I escorted them to one of the side gates of the castle, where Rhidea and the rebel soldiers met us up, Big Bart and Gaela in tow. Tall Tom and Skinny Sam were not among their numbers. By now, soldiers were swarming everywhere, and alarm bells rang in my ears. "Rhidea," I said hurriedly. "Get them out now!"

"Where are you going?" she demanded.

"I'll be safe; don't worry. Just get them to safety, and I'll meet you up."

". . . All right. Hurry now, child!"

I did. Kaen tried to stop me, but I ignored him, turning around and sprinting full-out for Mydia's rooms. I took the winding stairs of her tower three and four at a time, using my hands to propel myself off the walls for further speed. Why did I have such a bad feeling about this?

I burst into her room to find Teli and Julia right there, with Chara nowhere in sight. Perfect, except that Mydia was not here either. "Julia, Teli," I said frantically. "Come quickly."

"What?" Julia responded nervously. "What's going on, Podda?"

"I'm getting you out of here," I told them. "Now come with me, both of you!"

They did, to their credit. As I turned to lead them out, I heard Chara's voice as she approached, huffing and puffing. "Hurry, this way! She's got to still be up here—"

Chara appeared in the doorway a moment later, leading two men in leather and bronze armor—more of the Palace Guard. Pushing the two girls behind me, I said, "What do you think you're doing?" in as calm a voice as I could manage. *I just knew that old hag was going to make trouble. . . .*

"You!" Chara hissed. Turning to the guards and backpedaling down the hallway, she cried, "There she is! Seize her! She's the intruder who was conspiring with the princess!"

The two men grunted their assent and brandished their weapons at me. *What is going on? This Palace has turned crazy!* "Hide yourselves!" I whispered to Julia and Teli, turning only briefly. Taking out my second boot knife, I dodged backward as the men rushed in to grab me. I swiped the guard on the right twice in quick succession with my knives and kicked the other one into the left side of the doorway. He grunted while the first guard cursed in pain, grabbing at his arm. I turned to Chara with a scathing look. I took the chance to grab the first guard, pivoting myself to his side and throwing him roughly against the wall. He caught my arm, but I bashed his elbow with my knee, and the shock of his head hitting the wall stunned him.

The other guard took out his sword and apparently threw aside his apprehension about hurting me, shouting a threat as he lunged for my chest. I ducked and shin-kicked his legs out from under him, slamming his shoulder as he fell in order to aid his fall. His head hit the wood-paneled floor with a loud crack.

Chara stared from the hallway, still backing up, covering her mouth with a hand. "How did . . . how . . . ?" Suddenly she turned to run down the stairs.

"Oh, no you don't," I growled angrily, springing over the unconscious guard's body to chase her down.

Soon, all three of them—Chara and the two guards—were bound and gagged using scraps of cloth that the two frightened handmaids helped me find, and I was leading the girls out by the back staircase.

We did not even make it out of the Palace before Rhidea met up with us. "Lyn! Oh, I see. The handmaids. But I assumed . . ."

"Mydia's missing."

"Missing? Since when?"

"She left a few minutes back," said Julia. "And then Chara went and told some of the guards, and they came, but . . . Podda took care of them!"

Rhidea pointed toward an exit. "Go. I'll find her. Get these two to safety; straight that way, you'll find the rubble of the building."

"What! The Underground's old hideout? They destroyed that!"

"Exactly. But the subterranean chamber is fine, and sufficiently ventilated. Hurry, child!"

I did, leaving Rhidea to search out Mydia's whereabouts. I would come back to help, once I got Teli and Julia to the others' hideaway. It turned out that the old stairs that led to the meeting chamber were indeed accessible. I left the two handmaidens in the care of Kaen and the others, and turned to sprint back toward the Palace.

I ran as fast as my legs could carry me and quickly arrived at the site of the execution that had been planned. Perhaps Mydia was here . . .

Known as the Palace Common, the courtyard Lord Kalceron had chosen for his gallows was the largest in the palace. Not only was the entire area total chaos, with nobles, soldiers and trained magi running everywhere, but I did not see Mydia amidst the crowd, nor one of her common illusions. Although, how would I be able to tell with the throngs of people and the mage soldiers vainly attempting to keep them safe? Armed men, both soldiers and rebels—yes, definitely rebel forces—swarmed all over the Palace, and bodies lay scattered about already. I had no idea it would come to this. . . .

The princess was nowhere to be found. She would either be hiding out somewhere or, more likely, with her father, but . . . Lord Kalceron and his guard were nowhere in sight, either. At one point, I saw Lady Lieda in passing, who looked my way with a sharp glare from across the hall. *Oh, great auroras. Not her.* I scrambled for somewhere to hide, trying not to lose myself in the halls.

Finally, I found myself at the door of Lord Kalceron's royal audience hall. My heart beat rapidly from both exertion and nerves. This was the one place I hadn't looked. As I listened at the door, I heard raised voices and tense conversation. Just as I went to open the oak doors, I heard a soft voice from behind me:

"Ah-ah-ahhh, not so fast."

I stiffened at Lady Lieda's voice. *How in blazes did she find me?* She must have been following me. I jerked around sharply to see the witch herself standing there in her signature jet-black dress, one hand on her hip and the other half raised in an admonishing gesture. Her lip tilted upward in an expression halfway between a smirk and a sneer.

"What do you want?" I demanded, more bravely than I felt. This woman always unsettled me.

"Why, is that any way to speak to the queen consort of Nytaea?"

"I don't have time for this! Mydia could be in danger!"

"Oh my." Lieda put a hand over her mouth in mock concern. "What a horrible thought. Listen, swine. Barging in there will get you nowhere. He will see easily through your disguise, and then he'll finally have his prize."

I opened my mouth to say something—a retort, perhaps even an observation on her unintentional rhyme—and promptly shut it. She was right, of course: he would see through Mydia's illusion. But I knew Lieda was probably stalling for time. I turned back to the audience hall door as though to push it open, but Lieda stopped me.

"He didn't believe me about you," she said.

I hesitated, waiting to hear what would come next.

"That you were the one he was looking for all along. But I think he'll know the moment you set foot in that room. You think you can stand up to a High Mage like Edrius Kalceron? He may be a fool, but he's a powerful fool."

If only Rhidea were here now, I thought. *She'd crush you and Kalceron together.* Where was she, anyway? Turning to face Lieda, I said, "So Mydia is in there. What does he want with her?"

"Her? Nothing. She is trash. He wants you."

I scrunched my eyebrows together in a scowl. "I'm sick of listening to you. I'm getting Mydia out of here."

Before Lieda could respond, the door behind her flew open and Rhidea strode in busily. Lieda cursed, backing away, as Rhidea took in the scene. "Well, well," mused my teacher. "Lady Lieda. Harassing my star pupil again, are we?"

Lieda blanched, still backing up. "N-no, milady. I was just—just on my way through and—"

"Well, whatever it is, I don't have time to hear it," Rhidea muttered, waving a hand. An invisible wave swept Lieda even as she tried to run, knocking her off her feet before another force flung her up into the air and held her there.

I watched in awe, never having seen Rhidea's Authority in action before. As I watched, she used her powers to rip chunks of stone from the walls of the hallway, fusing them together over the woman's ankles and wrists, and then slammed her to the floor, using the same technique to bind her to the stones. Lady Lieda tried to scream up until the point when her head hit the stones . . . she was unconscious then.

"That should hold for a while," Rhidea said with a sharp exhale. "Now, it's time to make an appearance."

I nodded and kicked in the oaken doors, sending them to slam against the inner walls and then shudder quietly. At the far end of the hall, Lord Kalceron sat on his great chair, talking with two familiar mage soldiers—Lorta and Hespian—who held between them a young woman with her head bowed:

Princess Mydia.

- Chapter 14 -

Kalceron

Magical Authority can be compared to an heir who is inheriting the well-managed estate of his father. The boy grows up with many restrictions, his word bearing little to no weight at first, for he is just a boy. As he grows up and earns his place, his word means more. If he abuses it, there are repercussions. The more his father trusts him, the more rope he is given to work with, until at last his father entrusts to him the key to the entire mansion and command of his servants and guard. His subjects will obey him in proportion to how genuine his inheritance is, and will love him or fear him according to how he treats them. They will begrudgingly obey or readily jump to do his bidding depending on how easily he earned his title. A master who has worked for his rightful position will command more loyalty, no? And one who abuses his power may someday find that he cannot maintain the grip of his own authority.
— From *Secrets of Mani*, by Sor the Lark

(Dri'Shal 25, 997—Dawn)

All words from those inside ceased, and all eyes turned on Rhidea and me. The hall was large and spacious, mostly bare except for tall stained-glass windows and silver pillars. Upon each pillar hung tapestries depicting ancient monarchs of Nytaea's past, with bracketed torches beneath them casting eerie light and conflicting shadows around the hall.

"What is the meaning of this?" roared Lord Kalceron, rising from his throne with anger written large upon his face. Despite the horrifying stories told of the man, he was little more than five-and-a-half feet tall, and he only maintained a certain level of intimidating appearance because he stood three steps up from the rest of the floor. That and the black cape that he seemed to wear perpetually, which had lain draped over the side of the throne and now slid with his rising.

Rhidea strode into the audience chamber, and I followed right on her heels. "Kalceron, Kalceron," she said admonishingly. "I think I should be the one asking you that."

They glared at each other from across the hall for a long moment, until Lord Kalceron made a hand gesture to the two mage soldiers and they nodded and moved Mydia, still struggling, out of the way.

"Hespian, Lorta," he said, "is that the girl whom you apprehended but failed to catch?"

He waved a hand in my direction, and I felt my illusion slip off like oil. I gasped, raising a hand to my face, pulling a lock of hair over my shoulder to see that it was indeed pale silver again.

Hespian frowned, looking at me in a new light. "Yes. That *is* her."

"You!" shrieked Lorta. "I swore to make you pay and I'll still follow through on that—"

"Enough," Kalceron declared. Addressing me, he said, "So, you are the mysterious, white-haired girl I've been searching for."

I shifted uncomfortably. "Why? Why did you want me? And can you please let Mydia go now?"

"Hmm . . . I'm not sure I can answer that question right now. But . . . Hespian, Lorta, let the girl go. I have no need of her information any longer, for the girl I desire has come right into my hands."

The mage captain and his underling let Mydia go finally, giving her a cue to stay put. She gave a small *hmph!* and crossed her arms, probably putting on a bold front in order to not break down crying. "Pigs," she grumbled.

Rhidea strode calmly down the aisle toward the throne, looking up at Lord Kalceron. "Edrius, why are you doing this? You used to be my friend, but now . . . every command you make serves your own self, applauding evil and outlawing good. Your motives are twisted so far from what they once were. I hardly recognize you anymore."

Hespian and Lorta stood by, calmly but awkwardly waiting to see what their lord's reaction would be. Mydia looked around as though seeking a good corner to run and hide in. I couldn't help feeling bad for her.

"Motives? You talk like you know me closely," Kalceron replied, stepping down from his throne and onto the ornate, narrow rug which lined the aisleway. "You've been gone for many a year. And you, my dear old friend . . . Cae Rhidea, you are stuck in the same rut you were when we last crossed paths. You never long for change— change from your stale old ways that fool Gendric taught you?" His voice dripped with venomous mockery.

Rhidea brought her head back, chin raised in a gesture of proud indignation. "Are you insulting our mentor? The greatest sage still alive today? You think yourself better?"

Kalceron scowled. "Don't throw those cheap lines at me! I used to respect the man, but he has grown a fool in his old age. You think I serve myself, but everything I do is for a higher purpose. Archlord Domon showed me a new path long ago. Now you, you could be great . . . but you wouldn't join us, now, would you?"

Now this is interesting. I hadn't heard about their connection before. It was curious to watch this spat between old colleagues in the magic community. As I stood, hanging back and watching, my mentor and my enemy came face-to-face and stopped, staring each other down. Rhidea was a couple inches taller than he, and her very presence gave off a . . . regality . . . that Kalceron could not match. He had the authority, but not the noble air of Rhidea. I felt a new respect for her rise within me. Was I going to witness a battle between the two strongest magi in Nytaea?

"No," Rhidea finally said flatly. "You know my word stays firm. Your Umbra Council can burn for all I care."

Kalceron smirked. "Very well, then. It looks like we have ourselves a duel here."

"With pleasure. Lyn! Take out the other two!" Striding toward the mage king, Rhidea pulled a silver blade out of thin air. She twirled it around, and it changed form, once, twice, before sweeping to clash against . . . something, a wave of darkness that came from Kalceron's hand. I didn't let my eyes linger, but instead dashed over to do as she said. Hespian and Lorta stepped away from Mydia to engage me. I blasted fire toward Lorta and watched her face change to a look of shock upon seeing that I could use Coaction now. She dodged it nimbly and proceeded to circle me, silver blade held out warily. "Well, well," she purred, "So you have some other secrets."

My eyes flicked from the cat-faced woman to Captain Hespian, who tried to flank me from the right, holding a wicked bronze dagger. Behind him, Mydia scampered back, and I gave her a nod to say, *Run away while you have the chance.*

I drew my bronze knives and glanced about me. No one else was in the hall but for Mydia, who crouched behind a pillar. If only Kaen were here. *Wait,* I realized, looking back briefly, *Rhidea and Lord Kalceron are . . . gone?* I could neither see nor hear them. But I also didn't have time to look. Instead, I spun and rushed for Hespian.

He was ready. The large man immediately took up a guarding

stance, readying a spell of some sort. I shot a firebolt at Hespian—one of the few tricks of fire Coaction that I actually knew—and then leaped upwards over his head. He predictably blocked the flames with a water spell, but I flew right over his defense and seized his helmeted head. Spinning my legs in the air, I threw the captain by his helmet to one side while I dropped to the ground in an ungraceful spray of skirts in the other direction. I landed just as heavily as he did, but recovered faster.

Lorta was upon me immediately. She lunged in for a low sword thrust, forcing me to roll toward the far wall. I sprang back to my feet, gritting my teeth at the new bruises I'd just acquired, and hopped back a couple of paces—toward Mydia. I wanted to keep them away from her at all costs. Lorta snarled characteristically and crept toward me. Given her lightning abilities that could shock and stun, I wanted to stay far out of her range.

Hespian was on his feet now, holding his head, having ripped off his helmet and tossed it aside. He was a large, stout man, and would not go down so easily.

Lorta went on the attack once more, stepping forward to swipe at me with her blade. I made a split-second decision and went for her legs, sweeping them out from under her. She caught the ground with a clank of her vambrace, and my boot caught her brutally in the chest on the horizontal back sweep, just underneath her left arm that supported her, and sent her tumbling twice.

I glanced away, grimacing for just a moment at the injuries I'd surely caused the woman—she deserved them, though—and nearly got my nose frozen off by an ice spell from Hespian. I leapt back, and he followed with a jab of his dagger and a simultaneous curse.

Instead of trying to get out of the way, this time I darted for his knife arm with my left hand, ignoring the dagger, and seized his wrist just below the knife. I twisted it open, jerking his arm outward as I did so, and Hespian dropped the dagger on the floor with a gasp of pain.

"Monster," he spat. "Are you asking to die?" Even as he said it and I held his arm, he tried to elicit another chain reaction of cold in the air, but I grabbed his right arm with my own right hand and ducked underneath his side, pulling his arm swiftly with me until it made a horrifying *crack!* He howled in pain, but I held it still as he fought.

On the floor, Lorta groaned, rolling over to hold her broken ribs with a hand. "You wretched child," she moaned. "How are you so . . ."

"Just stop!" I shouted at them. "I beat you. Leave Mydia alone and stop trying to kill me."

Hespian chuckled through his pain. "Heh. Lassie . . . maybe you don't understand the way orders work, but . . . you don't just disobey the Lord of Nytaea."

"Then what must I do?" I demanded. "Kill you?"

"Of course. Innocent brat."

Growling, I grabbed Hespian's other hand, pushed him to the floor with a foot on his back, and held him there by both arms. Cutting off part of his sleeve, I made a makeshift tie and bound his left arm to his legs. I made my way over to Lorta and subdued her, tying her arms and legs in a similar fashion. She spat curses at me the whole time amidst spasms of pain.

When I was done, I looked over at Mydia, who had come out from behind her pillar and was looking on with a sort of awe. "Lyn, you really . . . ? Wow, you're amazing."

"I'm stronger than these two gave me credit for, I guess," I said. "Now stay back, all right? Don't get in the way."

"Okay. But . . . what are you going to do?"

"I'm going to see what's going on with Rhidea and your father. How much do you know about his Authority? Where are they now?"

"It's . . . it must be his Hall of Mirrors," she whispered. "It's his greatest spell, using a blend of Perception and Reality Authority. He can take you there and mess with your mind in all sorts of ways. I can't imagine what it's like right now."

"But . . ." I looked back at where Rhidea and Kalceron had been mere minutes ago. The air was distorted in strange patterns that seemed to move and shift. "Are they still here?"

Mydia shook her head. "Sort of. Just . . . please, don't get in the way. I'm sure Lady Rhidea knows what she's doing, but . . ." she sank to her knees. "Father is so terrifying."

So is Rhidea, I thought wryly. Mydia hadn't been there to see the High Mage wrap up her stepmother in stone. I turned and began walking toward the air distortions at the center of the hall. "I'm going to see. Don't try to stop me."

I strode cautiously forward until the air shimmered just ahead. Rhidea was right here . . . no, here . . .

Suddenly, a bright light flashed in front of me, and I shied back as Lord Kalceron tumbled backward out of nowhere as though pushed by a great force. His black robes, torn and bloodied from a hundred different cuts, fluttered through the air, and he landed roughly with a grunt and a curse. A rip, a seam as it were, hung in the open air where he'd come from.

Rhidea followed a second after, leaping through the seam and floating to the ground. She also looked like she had been through a battle in Kalceron's conjured world, but she was nowhere nearly as heavily wounded as he. Her white skirts, partly singed and torn, fell slowly to the floor as she stalked toward her opponent, who scrambled backward. Above her, silvery streams trickled through the air, coalescing into a dozen blades of silver, each poised as though ready to strike on command.

"You think you've won this!" he shouted hysterically. "That you're better than me. You always did." Finding his feet, he rushed for his throne, as though it would help him.

Rhidea let him go, not bothering to stop him. I stood looking on uncertainly. Mydia approached slowly from the spot where she'd been. "Father? Please, just give up. Don't keep fighting like—"

Lord Kalceron spun on his heel, a look of pure hatred on his face. "Don't patronize me, wench! First your useless slut of a mother, and now you . . ." He winced briefly, putting a hand to his side, and then summoned a sword of black flames out of the air.

"Kalceron, I'm warning you," Rhidea said in a cold monotone, "Don't touch her."

Lord Kalceron paid no attention to her words, as though not hearing. He glared down at his daughter, who had stopped six feet from him, with the deepest disgust. "I should kill you now," he whispered in a raspy voice. "And you could join her and your brother in whatever paradise they're enjoying."

Mydia sank to her knees, seeming to melt as she stared up at her father. "Father . . . father, I never—I never knew you were such a heartless monster." She bowed her head and began to sob, but made no move to withdraw herself from her father's wrath.

I tensed. Rhidea took a step forward and pulled back her arm, holding her gleaming silver sword. Lord Kalceron drew back his sword, and I saw a flash of what would happen in the next second.

"No!" I shouted, rushing to save Mydia. I could never reach her in time. I saw the black flames lick from the sword as Kalceron swung it, and heard the whimper of my friend the princess, about to be slain by her father.

As I ran to her, pumping my legs as fast as they could go, a silver shape streaked across the hall like a whip, cracking as it grabbed Kalceron's right arm. He gave a cry of pain and dropped the sword, which vanished into smoke, as the whip was yanked, throwing him to the floor. The silver whip retracted swiftly as the governor tumbled down the stone steps, and I turned my head, shocked to see Rhidea pulling her whip back into the shape of a sword. Her many silver blades still hung in the air.

I skidded to a stop in front of the groaning form of my enemy, Lord Kalceron, and held my bronze knife up, ready to stab it into his chest. "You would've killed her just like that? Your own daughter!" I fumed.

Mydia turned her head to look at me with wide eyes, tears running down her cheeks. "Wait . . ." she mumbled. "Lyn, that's . . . he's just . . ."

"Stop," Rhidea called, stepping up to where I stood over Lord Kalceron. "Stay your hand, Lyn. This is our duel." To Kalceron, who was beginning to rise to his feet on shaky legs, she asked, "What do you have to say for yourself, Edrius? What can you offer to save your pitiful life?" Her lips turned downward and trembled as she said it.

Kalceron braced himself with a hand and glared up into her eyes, gritting his teeth against the pain of his injuries. "You take that tone w-with me, after all these years? In my own palace? Heh, like you're any better than me."

"Kalceron, what were you trying to take Lyn for? Why did your men hold her friends captive in a tower for nearly a month, tortured all the while?"

Rhidea waited, but he gave no response. "And why did you try to take your own daughter's life, after all of this?"

He only glared.

"WHY?" she roared.

That one word echoed in the large room, and for a few moments there was silence, but for the sound of Mydia's sobbing.

"Very well," Rhidea said, voice heavy with resignation and bitterness.

"Rhidea," I asked, "Can I finish him off now?"

"No. He initiated a duel, and I would not have your hands soiled with the blood of one so vile. Among us high magi, there is one way we deal with those who turn their backs on everything they've vowed . . . and we do it ourselves." She grabbed a handful of the king's black hair and yanked his head upwards. "You really have nothing to say?"

"Wait!" Mydia gasped, finally finding the strength to get up. She made to rush for Rhidea to stop her, but I intercepted her and caught her.

"No, Mydia. It has to be done."

"But . . . Father . . ." She looked over my shoulder to see Rhidea raising her silver blade over Kalceron's neck.

"Don't look, Mydia," I whispered, pulling her into a hug that kept her eyes from seeing. She fought me, squirming and pulling to no effect.

"Father . . . Father!"

I heard the sound of flesh shearing, and the thump of Lord Kalceron's head hitting the floor, followed by his body. Mydia screamed in my ears as I squeezed my eyes closed.

And then she fell limp, breathing slowly but heavily. I slackened my grip on her shoulders and glanced behind me to see the limp form of Lord Kalceron, blood creating a pool around his severed neck, and Rhidea standing over him with a bloodied silver sword.

She stepped back and said, "It's done. He's gone. But stand back."

I pulled Mydia up the stairs, and she followed dumbly. I sat her down at the top, in front of the throne, and turned her shoulders to the side, toward me. Crouching, I looked into her eyes, brushing her black bangs out of her eyes. "Mydia, it had to be done. I'm sorry."

She nodded, and I pulled her into another hug, looking back to see Rhidea pointing her sword down at Lord Kalceron's body. What was she . . . ?

A white flame licked up from his fallen corpse, and then spread into a blaze, engulfing his body, the blood on the floor, and the blood on her magical sword, billowing upward in a beautiful display of golden light. I let Mydia watch as the pyre blazed upward ten, fifteen feet in the air. Anywhere else inside, it might have been a fire hazard —if indeed it behaved like normal fire at all—but in this hall . . . it was just the right setting for the ceremony, a last rite in the middle of a large, cold throne room. The last memory of a tyrant king.

"Goodbye . . . father," Mydia choked. "Oh, I wish I could say I'll miss him." She squeezed her eyes shut in emotional pain. "I really do."

Rhidea put away her strange weapons of silver and dusted off her hands on her dress. The blades, which had hovered above her the entire time, fell and seemed to drip through the air to coalesce on the silver of the pillars and floor of the hall, as though they had come from there. Ascending the stairs, she came to Mydia's side and laid a hand on her head. "Mydia, I'm sorry. I know he wasn't much of a father, but it's still a horrible thing . . . one that had to happen. You will have your time to grieve, I assure you. Unfortunately, right now . . . well, right now, I need to go see to that witch, Lieda. Lyn, get Mydia somewhere safe and then find someone to do something with these two mongrels." She gestured to Hespian and Lorta, who were still sitting hunched over, bound and gagged beside a pillar.

I nodded, and the High Mage made her way out the door to deal with Lady Lieda, brushing past a stunned group of onlookers. Had they been there the whole time? Perhaps it was good that there were witnesses.

Helping Mydia to her feet, I said, "All right, Mydia. Let's go."

Two hours later, I stood on the balcony that overlooked the Palace Common, along with Kaen, Mydia and a few others. We were at the back, while Rhidea stood near the railing, in full view of hundreds upon hundreds of Palace staff, servants, cooks, soldiers, officers, magi and rebels.

"Citizens of Nytaea!" Rhidea said in a clear, authoritative voice, louder than I'd ever heard her speak before. "Today, you have witnessed an uprising unlike any seen in over a century here in Nytaea. Lord Kalceron was to have the leaders of the rebellion executed for treason here in this very courtyard, but we enacted a plan to save them, throwing the military forces into chaos and rescuing captives held in the infamous prison tower of the Palace—a gambit that paved the way for a full coup d'état. Lord Kalceron, your tyrant king, is dead, and his rule is done."

Murmurs began below, cries of, "But you're not even a Nytaean!" or, "Who are you, anyway?" and, "How can we know for certain?"

Rhidea continued, "I am Cae Rhidea, a High Mage, scholar of magical Authority, born here in Nytaea. They call me the Wandering Mage."

Additional murmurs arose, but more subdued and respectful.

"I came to this city after many years for the purpose of scholarly research, and was horrified to see the state of the once proud city-state of Nytaea. The people of Nytaea have suffered increasingly over the years due to direct and indirect cruelty from mismanagement at the hand of Edrius Kalceron. He was once my friend and colleague, but . . . he went past the point of no return, and he needed to be put down. I became connected with one among the rebellion who has supported them the longest. This young woman was almost murdered today by her own father when we confronted him. Meet your new queen regent, Mydia of House Kalceron."

Mydia stepped out nervously beside me. I gave her an affectionate pat on the shoulder and as warm a smile as I could muster. Truth be told, I was just glad that it was not me who had to speak.

Mydia strode forward like a timid angel, arrayed in regal robes of pure white. She stepped up beside Rhidea, and the mage put an arm around her shoulder. She whispered a few words in the girl's ear, and Mydia nodded, facing the crowd. With a deep breath, she said, "I . . . I am Mydia Kalceron. I will be your new queen for now. It has pained me all these years to see my father mistreat you so. But know that I personally helped to reach out to the needy and hurting, and I will be working with the leaders of the former underground rebellion along with those in authority, both military and political, to ensure that our government is rebuilt stronger than ever. Nytaea is seceding from the Kystrean Empire as of this day."

Cheering arose from below, bringing a smile to my lips. Looking at Kaen, I said, "I think she's doing it." He raised an eyebrow and shrugged in response, but I could tell he was impressed underneath his pretense of indifference.

"What happens to us now?" The question rose up from one of the men in the common below, and others murmured assent.

"What about us soldiers?"

"What about our houses?"

"What will the Archlord say?"

Rhidea cupped a hand over her mouth and shouted, "Silence! The queen is not yet finished." Quietly to Mydia, she added, "Go ahead, dear. You've got this."

Clearing her throat, the queen regent raised her voice once more and declared, "The military has been ordered to stand down and not oppose the rebels. As I said, we are working with many leaders to decide what will be the next direction for the country of Nytaea. For now, I am your Queen Regent. We will deal with the Archlord's re-action to our secession and succession as the time arises."

"My friends!" Rhidea added in her booming voice before the crowd could object. "This is not a time for fear or cowardice. There is nothing for us in the Empire. That has been clearly shown by lack of interest in our welfare on the part of both Archlord Domon and Lord Kalceron in the past decades. Nytaea was once its own nation, and can be once again. We have the strongest military of any of the states save for Ti'Vaeth, and are the originators and leaders in mage forces in the entire world. We are not weak. You can continue to fight the petty battles of the Empire, or stand strong and pledge your hearts to a new nation, a better one!"

At this, the crowd roared. Mydia turned, and I saw the anxious smile on her dimpled face. I gave her a thumbs-up. "Good job, Mydia."

Mydia bowed and thanked the audience, and then backed away from the railing. "Oh, that was nerve-racking," she breathed, holding a gloved hand to her breast. "I managed to remember most of my speech, at any rate . . . I just found it so hard to get my words out at first."

Rhidea approached us, standing beside the new queen. "Thank you, Mydia," she said. "You put on a bold face and delivered your message well. I'm sure the public will forgive your lack of oratory skills, especially considering what you just went through. Now we'll just have to figure out what will *actually* come of your government."

"Now do I get a nap?" Mydia asked. "I'm so dreadfully tired. I just . . . It's been a lot." In reality, I knew the new queen was in a state of shock, and would remain so for a little while. The full emotion of the situation had not hit her yet. The tears and grief would follow.

What she needed now was rest.

"Yes, Mydia," Rhidea said. "I'm sure you can have your nap. Podda, why don't you go ready her chambers?" She gave me a wink.

That night, I dreamed.

The girl showed me a different scene this time:

I was in a stormy place atop a high tower, and lightning flashed all around. Rain pelted the stones below. Mother was holding me, rocking me back and forth as she crouched on the ground. She sang me a sweet lullaby, making my eyes heavy. I tried to speak, to say something, but I couldn't form coherent language yet, and all that came out was a pitiful cry.

Mother stopped singing. "Now, now, dear. It will be all right. As soon as the storm passes, we'll—agh!"

A bright bolt of lightning flashed behind her, prompting her to shield me closely. The immediate thunder was deafening to my little ears. Mother began the lullaby once more before taking off, boots splashing on the rainwater, the little bundle that was me carried close to her chest. She dashed down a stairwell, and I could no longer see anything, only feel the jostling and jolting of her stride and the occasional small slip on the slick stone stairs. But she was strong, quick and agile, and I would've trusted her no matter what. Mother had me. I would be all right.

⁂

The End of Part One

- Interlude-

Rhidea

I trust this letter finds you well. We have not seen one another in quite some time. I wanted to tell you of a breakthrough I made recently that will interest you greatly . . . and also a terrible piece of news. First, the news . . . My son Kallyn has gone missing. And by that, I mean . . . he has decided to seek out the ancient place of our ancestry. I needn't explain more. We will talk soon, I'm sure. But . . . I don't know what to tell Mydia. The poor girl is so young. She loved Kallyn, and now she cries every night and asks me where he is. I know the truth, but I can't tell her.

—Eivael Kalceron

(Dri'Shal 25, 997—Dawn)

Cae Rhidea sank into her cushioned chair with a thump. She let out a ragged breath and then sucked in another, fuller breath, sitting up straight. It didn't matter that she was tired—she had work to do.

Rhidea was back in her study, where she liked to be. All the pomp and politics were done for now, and her mind could be free of that. Oh, how she hated dealing with people of importance. Rebel leaders, nobles feeling slighted, military figures . . . the list went on. She rested an elbow on her oaken desk, placing a hand to her forehead in a vain attempt to stop the headache that pulsed through her temple.

"Come on, Cae," she muttered, rubbing her temple absently. *Focus, mind, focus.* There was too much to be done to spend time at her desk distracted. Sorting out affairs with the Nytaean government was only a small part.

Her left hand scratched idly at an old wound on her hipbone. She'd smoothed out that limp a few decades back, so it didn't bother her much; it was just a restless tic. She eyed the scattered scrolls in the left-hand corner of her desk, the misplaced ink well and pen, a missing book. Where had she put that?

Finally, she had all her supplies gathered and her desk straightened out. *My, I'm such a mess sometimes.* That thought drifted off as she stared, blinking, at the scroll that she had most recently been poring over, which still lay open before her. An old thesis on pyrokinesis, one she'd penned years ago. She shook her head and rolled it back up, setting it carefully aside.

Opening a side drawer in her desk, she rummaged around before finding a precious memo that had been stored in there for years. It was from the long-missing prince Kallyn, Mydia's brother, written to their mother. Rhidea squeezed her eyes shut briefly, in pain both at her headache and at the thought that she was still hiding this from Mydia. The poor child.

She unwrinkled the scrap of parchment and read its contents for the twentieth time. The man didn't even know that his mother was dead.

She put the letter down with a sigh, her mind wandering back to that day thirteen years back, when the white-haired woman had shown up in the city. Rhidea had only happened to be there, only happened to catch her on her way back from the Palace. She had caught Rhidea's dress with a hand that looked so frail and yet had so much strength. The nameless woman had babbled incoherently, the few words that Rhidea could make out sounding like words of another language. And then . . . then she had given Rhidea the letter.

Rhidea frowned deeply. The letter . . . why? There must be a connection. If he had really gone to Gaea, then he must have sent her back. But why her? Why to Nytaea?

That day had been the catalyst for Rhidea's research into the world of Gaea. She and Kallyn—and of course his mother, Eivael—had studied it together on numerous occasions, but it was a matter of scholarly curiosity. History. Even, one might say, more like myth.

Back then, when she encountered that strange, otherworldly woman, she already knew that Kallyn had gone to seek out Gaea. They had assumed him dead. But the note, from none other than the prince himself, proved that he had found it.

Lyn was the final piece. Seeing that girl for the first time, seeing what she could do, her strange body composition, her white hair . . . it all made sense. But she would not tell Lyn, not yet.

Rhidea shook herself and put the note away, getting back to her studies. All in time, as Eivael had always said. All in time.

PART TWO

- Search -

- Chapter 15 -

Independence

Coaction, then, marks the building of that trust along the way. It is the allowance which the heir is given on a set basis. Use up too much of it frivolously, and he may find that it comes with additional requirements or restrictions the next time. Or perhaps the father is exceedingly wealthy, and that young man never has to work for it. . . . Such money is not worth as much when it comes down to it. Perhaps the son is no rich heir, but works diligently for what he has. He reaches adulthood and still must work all the more. He manages his money well, he learns from his experience and from others, and makes a good life, though he may never have women jumping to do his bidding. This is the man who does not have the talent but puts in enough effort to become an accomplished practitioner of Coaction—and eventually, Authority.
— From *Secrets of Mani*, by Sor the Lark

(Dri'Shal 26, 997—Sunrise)

The next day, we sat in the conference hall of the Royal Palace, in discussion with the leading figures in Nytaea, along with the rebel leaders. The hall was long and rectangular in shape, dominated by a long table.

There was Rhidea, presiding over the table; Princess Mydia, fidgeting in her chair with tearstains on her eyes; Marshal Lanthar, a burly man with a well-trimmed beard, sharply-uniformed, with arms crossed and face resolute; Keuda the royal secretary, wide-eyed and nervous as a new bride; and Bart and Gaela, the sole survivors of the

Underground's leaders. Tall Tom and Skinny Sam, whose names I had discovered were Tomas and Dossam respectively, had died in the skirmishes that had broken out at the hanging.

And then there were Kaen and me, sitting in awkwardly, not knowing what part we played. Master Gendric of the Mage Academy, being one of the most esteemed personages in the city, had been invited, but had declined the offer to be in on the making or remaking of a government, insisting it was neither his place nor calling. Rhidea spoke very highly of the man; perhaps I would get to meet him someday. In the back stood two mage soldiers holding a bedraggled Lady Lieda between them. She wore a lovely-looking gag that I had heard was some sort of magic-disabling device.

"All right, let's get started," called Marshal Lanthar in a booming voice, breaking up any lingering small talk amongst the group.

Rhidea cleared her throat and spoke up. "We have assembled here today with one purpose, and that is to decide the fate of the government of our beloved city-state of Nytaea."

A few murmurs sounded from around the room. Ignoring them, she continued:

"Lord Edrius Kalceron, the notorious tyrant, has perished this last night. His rule has been one of cruelty, his hand a grim, oppressive darkness upon the land. And we have an opportunity to change it. But dare we, and what will be the consequences if we choose to?"

And so began the discussion. It was a heated one, but Rhidea did an admirable job of maintaining order and keeping the focus on the serious matters at hand. She was a bastion of stability here, all traces of the dusty scholar thrown off. Marshal Lanthar suggested surrendering to the Archlord and letting him appoint new leadership, not because of a sense of allegiance so much as because it was the most obviously bloodless choice. I was surprised that our medaled military leader would suggest such a seemingly cowardly course of action. To this, multiple people pointed out how it would essentially be a death sentence for anyone involved in the coup in any way. I certainly didn't like the idea.

The secretary, Keuda, wanted to serve someone more honorable than Lord Kalceron, as long as that could be arranged with minimal bloodshed—though, being a woman of great care, she worded this sentiment with the utmost tact. Along with others, Keuda seemed to fear offending Mydia with comments aimed against the late tyrant.

Kaen spoke up at one point, saying that he never wanted anyone else to grow up in an orphanage knowing that their very lives were threatened by royal law, to which I and many others heartily agreed. Mydia said very little, probably having already used up most of her public speaking skills the previous day—not to mention the trauma she was still coping with.

I stood up from my seat at this point, asking, "What will the Archlord do if we let him arrange our new government? Would he appoint a moral man? We were our own city-state before—can't we be that again? What if we convince the neighboring lands, along with the Archlord, that we are strong by ourselves? If not, then we will be enslaved to another evil man!"

Rhidea nodded my way approvingly. "The child is right. We have the strongest magic in all of Kystrea, the best academy, one of the strongest standing militaries—" the Marshal nodded his agreement "—and a long history of independence before Lord Edrius Kalceron made his bargain one hundred years ago with the Archlord. We are strong."

Marshal Lanthar rubbed his forehead with his hands. "Strong, yes . . . but you're talking about a potential war with the most powerful man on the continent."

"We will never know unless we try," said Gaela. "Nothing is ever accomplished without some degree of faith. Our cause is right, so why back down?"

The council eventually came to an agreement that we, the ancient city-state of Nytaea, should move forward with seceding from the Archlord's rule. Lanthar would stay on as commander of all military forces, Keuda would stay on as royal secretary, but Lord Kalceron's position as governor would be given over to three separate people: Mydia, Bart and Gaela. Mydia would be the acting queen regent, that is to say until a male heir could be chosen, a relative of her choice as approved by the council or, if all else failed, to another suitable for the job. The idea was to please those in the Palace who were uneasy about the rule suddenly being taken from the line of House Kalceron.

The two Underground leaders would be called vice-regents. Bart, despite having a temper, was chosen due to his skill of leadership within the Underground. Gaela was chosen because she was also a leader in the same group, and also because she had noble blood (again, they sought to please those noblemen in the Palace and outside who would balk at a commoner running the country).

As for Rhidea, she offered to take a contingent to the neighboring kingdom of Nemental, which lay just east of the bordering province of Storklance, to ask for an alliance to aid in Nytaea's struggle for independence. Being a dual citizen of Nytaea and Nemental, that was easier for her to arrange than for others.

More discussion followed on what the new government would look like, among other, more minor details, but the meeting soon trailed off. I was honestly quite tired of it after sitting through nearly two hours of political ramblings—and I knew Kaen was as well. We soon made our way out, grabbing Mydia on the way. Rhidea was too busy handling larger matters to join us.

Phoebe and Mandrie met us just outside the door to the conference hall. "So, what did they decide?" Mandrie chirped. I smiled just to see her beautiful, childish smile. Mydia had patched her up with her own Coactive healing, along with Phoebe, and the two looked as good as ever now, although I knew the emotional scars of their imprisonment and mistreatment would linger as long as they lived. Phoebe, I feared, might never smile again.

"Nytaea will secede and declare independence," Kaen told them, stooping to hug his sister and tousle her hair. He looked at Phoebe with an odd expression. "We were wrong about them, Pheebs. Rhidea pulled it off and got them on our side."

"But we still need to survive the Empire," the dark-haired girl muttered, crossing her arms and turning her head. But I could tell that she was pleased to hear the news. I knew her too well to see only the pessimistic front.

"And we will be heading out with Rhidea to Randhorn," I informed them. "That is . . . if you want to come." I cocked a half-smile.

"Really?" Mandrie exclaimed, still beaming. "We get to travel with Lady Rhidea?"

"That's what I said. She is offering to take us and whoever else wants to come. But not too many in the party. We are going to ask King Fenwel for help in recreating an independent state."

Phoebe arched an eyebrow. "He would actually help our city? Uh . . . country?"

I shrugged.

"Lady Rhidea seems to think so," said Kaen. "She can be pretty persuasive; I'll give her that."

I laughed. "I thought you still didn't like Rhidea?"

"Well . . . I don't have a whole lot of trust in her, but I don't doubt her. Does that make sense?"

Mandrie blinked up at her big brother. "Nope. But she helped you two get us out of that dreadful tower, so . . . I think she's my best friend forever after that!" She flashed another dimpled grin. *What an irrepressible aura of happiness, even after all that's happened. Mandrie is truly a special child.* Ugh, now I was starting to think like Rhidea.

Mydia was to go with us to Randhorn, as she would be the official spokesperson among the new rulers, being the heir of House Kalceron. The final group was as follows: Rhidea, me, Kaen, Mydia, Julia and Teli (accompanying the queen as her handmaidens), Phoebe and Mandrie. The last two simply would not leave us, and Kaen and I did not want to leave them either.

Rhidea added two promising students of the Mage Academy to our mix: Cort Flanning, a young lightning mage of noble blood, and Syneria Tolruin, a water mage. Rhidea had wanted to bring along a couple advanced mage students to introduce to some of her colleagues at the Randhorn school, and Master Gendric had apparently recommended them highly. Cort was a snobbish blond boy who got under my skin before I knew it, while Syneria was a snooty blonde girl who . . . well, was quite similar. I could see why they seemed to be friends.

The next day, we headed eastward out of the Swan Gate. The breeze smelled of fresh grass and freedom, rustling the grey fields and silvery-leaved trees, but the bloody sun rising behind us, usually so pale, reminded me of the last Cycle's dawn, when everything I knew and loved burned and crumbled away. Since then, we'd broken into the Palace, made new allies, freed our friends, and displaced our longtime oppressor, Lord Kalceron . . . such a crazy month.

I would never forget Lentha and the children, my old life at the orphanage. But today marked a chance to help create a new life for us, and hopefully for many other orphans. Therefore, it was a day for joy and hope.

It felt strange to have the gate guards nod in our direction, to watch as the portcullis was raised for my very own group to pass through. I still felt like an orphan, a shadowy figure who raised suspicion everywhere I went, whom the government did not recognize as a legal citizen, able to be enslaved without anyone batting an eye. Hopefully, all that would change in the coming months. And hopefully, we could hold the new nation of Nytaea from the Archlord's grasp.

Most of our group was not used to riding, and so Rhidea let us stop in the late afternoon at a nearby village called Haversfleet. Ironically, the pampered once-princess Mydia was one of the better riders, as she had been taught by equestrian instructors at the Palace from a young age. The locals welcomed us nervously, word having already reached them about the coup in Nytaea. We kept our identity a secret from them with the help of a little illusion work from Mydia. None could tell Rhidea and Mydia from two other noblewomen. They had coin, so that was enough for the innkeeper.

The next day, we came into Storklance, the eastmost province of Kystrea.

Storklance did not welcome us. They did quite the opposite, in fact, sending soldiers and magi after us. Word had spread quickly, and they seemed downright unfriendly toward traitors of the Empire for some reason. Thus, we kept on, straight out of the realm of Kystrea and into Nemental, headed for Randhorn.

- Chapter 16 -

At Randhorn Court

Water is the very essence of life in our world. But in a most fascinating way, water is also the source of magic. Or one could say . . . magic is the source of water, and water the source of life. Evidence points toward there being no life here on Mani at all until the introduction of the Wellspring of Life.
— From *Secrets of Mani*, by Sor the Lark

(Firvaen 5, 997—Waning Day)
Within a week of riding, we came upon the capital of Nemental. Randhorn was a great city, but perhaps a little less great than I had been expecting. Despite being the king's capital city, it was no more impressive than Nytaea, with walls slightly shorter. The stones used to build it were of a sandy color, not gleaming white. I shouldn't have been surprised, as Nytaea had once been a prosperous nation of its own, but that was long ago, before the Archlord took over Kystrea.

Nemental was one of a few nations scattered at the edge of the Empire's grasp, ones which were never in the Kystrean Alliance before the Joining Wars or which Archlord Domon had simply never bothered with. Yan'Vala was hidden away in the rocky canyon lands to the north, so it didn't have much to offer. On the southwest coast, there were Lygellis and Torlega, which had also somehow escaped the Archlord's grasp.

Rhidea led us right up to the castle and had us leave our horses with a couple of young grooms at the stables. The rest of us were to stay put while Rhidea went in to request an audition with the King. She had taken but a few steps, however, before she turned on her heel with that look of having forgotten something. "Lyn, Mydia, come with me."

I looked to the queen and shrugged. She shrugged back, and we followed our mentor. A servant opened the ornate doors for us with a polite, "Lady Rhidea," and we entered an elaborate entry hall, somewhat similar in design to that of the Nytaean Palace but decorated differently, with more hanging plants and artwork and less gilded trim.

Another servant, noticeably surprised to see Rhidea's familiar face, informed her that he would show us to King Fenwel, who was open for petitions right now (and certainly for the legendary Wandering Mage, as he made sure to add). We let him guide us to the King's Hall, even though Rhidea could certainly have gotten us there just fine by memory. After all, it hadn't been that long since she'd been here, right? Had there been a falling out?

At length, we reached a set of large, oaken doors with brazen handles, one of which the servant opened for us. "Right this way," he said politely, waving us inside.

At the end of the long, spacious hall, under the farthest arches, there was situated a majestic throne, and upon the throne sat, presumably, King Fenwel. His hair was thick and white, like mine—though I had hurriedly gone back to dying it via Mydia's Perception Coaction after Lord Kalceron had dispelled it—and his long beard was the same color. He looked like a very noble, wise king, and my immediate instinct was to trust him. He was well-built, or at least looked to have been strong in his youth, though the years had clearly taken their toll on him, and if he had magic, he did not use it to make his visage any younger in appearance. Above all, he looked . . . tired, but he brightened when he saw who it was that had paid him a visit.

"Ah, it's you, child!" He seemed ecstatic to see the mage.

"Yes." Rhidea knelt, and the idea of her doing that for even a king was so peculiar that I instantly did likewise. Mydia knelt as well. "It has been a long time, my king."

"Yes, indeed. It is good to have you back, Rhidea." The King smiled. "I trust your search has gone somewhat positively these last years, to allow you to return once more to Randhorn?"

Well, it appears there was no falling-out, I noted.

"You assume correctly, King Fenwel . . . in part, at least. We shall have to talk more, but for now, allow me to introduce Queen Regent Mydia of Nytaea."

"Queen Regent," the king mused. "Hmm, so the rumors are true . . . If she is anything like her father, then I want her out of my castle. But if she takes after her mother more, than I think we should get along fine. My lady, how old are you?"

"Twenty years, my lord," she answered in a somewhat reticent voice. I could see that the mention of her father had brought back a shadow of sorrow.

"A grown woman, then, is that right? Well, my dear, I have but one question for you—do you like broiled mushrooms and ruta-bagas?"

The new queen looked understandably taken aback. "Together? I can't say that I do . . . Your Majesty."

King Fenwel laughed. "Good, good. That's very good, child, be-cause I don't either. What a horrible dish. At least you tell the truth. You must be all right. One would be surprised to hear how many claim to love broiled mushrooms and rutabagas when the question is posed to them." He pointed at me, then. "How about you? Do you like it?"

"I . . . uh . . . no, your majesty. Probably not."

"Good, good. You must be all right, too, then."

"The king has the same ability of Truthseeing that I have," Rhidea told us, "But stronger. He's only jesting about the rutabagas."

"Quite right, my friends," said the King. Addressing me, he asked, "Now, who are you?"

"They . . . called me . . ." I bit my lip, unsure of what to say for some reason. Finally, I cleared my throat and answered, "Lyn. Lyn of Nytaea, Your Majesty."

"Lyn? Well, that is a pretty name, now, isn't it?" His reaction was the same as Rhidea's had been.

"She is an orphan from Nytaea," Rhidea informed him.

"Is that right? Well met, child."

"Yes, my lord."

The King looked at Mydia. "I am sorry for your loss, truly. And especially for that of your mother and brother years back. I knew them quite well."

Mydia seemed surprised to hear that. Had he known them before her time?

"Thank you," Mydia said hoarsely. "But . . . he wasn't much of a father. He never loved me. Kallyn, maybe, although even for him . . . I don't think that my father could find any love in his heart."

"Who was it that finally killed him?" King Fenwel asked Rhidea. "My sources didn't say."

"I did," the Wandering Mage replied. "He challenged me to a duel. Before we were even done, he turned on his own daughter. I executed him in the ancient fashion of magi."

Fenwel shook his head sadly. "He would truly try to harm his own trueborn child? How saddening. The world is a dark place, I am afraid. Well, Rhidea, how many more have you in your company?"

"Just seven more, my lord."

He raised his eyebrows. "Is that all? A pity. I suppose you were busy tidying up from all the chaos. I trust you didn't cause such insurgencies in every place you visited?"

Rhidea smiled. "No, my lord. Fortunately not. It was mostly for the girl, Lyn, whose friends had been imprisoned as hostages to lure her to the Palace, to Kalceron."

"Oh?" The white-haired king laughed drily. "You overthrew a tyrant and caused all that ruckus just for her? Why did he want her so badly?"

Rhidea glanced between me and the king. "She is . . . a most interesting specimen; relevant to my mission, in fact. Perhaps we could speak more on this later?"

"Yes, yes. Please, let everyone get situated. I will have rooms prepared for all of your friends. I'll tell the cooks to make an extra big dinner tonight. We shall celebrate!"

"Celebrate what, sire?" Rhidea asked, tongue-in-cheek.

"Do we need a reason?" He waved a hand in the air as he searched for a reason with meaning to it. "The . . . the Wandering Mage has come back to Randhorn! And with fine guests in tow, no less! There you go—reason enough. Now go soak in a hot bath or something. You know—hospitality. My castle is your castle."

"As you wish, my lord." Rhidea led us out of the King's Hall with a half-smile, and we returned to fetch the others. The servants informed us that they would escort us to some pre-readied rooms.

Kaen and Cort Flanning settled with sharing a room, and Phoebe and Mandrie stayed with Teli and Julia, while I got to share Mydia's fancy one and Rhidea reclaimed what was apparently her old room. I couldn't help but wonder if she had a home in every country across the continent. Syneria, the snooty scholar girl, was an object of some jealousy, as she got to stay in her own room amongst the Randhorn scholars.

Mydia had offered to let Julia and Teli go free from her service if they wished, but they both agreed to stay on. Julia had thanked me profusely for managing to pull off what she'd thought impossible by freeing her from her indentured servitude to House Kalceron. The ironic part was that, though our rescue operation had ended with her and Teli being freed from the castle, their freedom lay in the afterthought that was the regime change—for Mydia laid down new rules regarding Palace servants—not in their being physically set free.

Kaen and Mandrie were just happy to be together after all that time of separation. She and Phoebe were recovering well thanks to Mydia's healing.

That night, King Fenwel held a great feast in our honor, inviting many of the nobility in the city. It was actually a happy occasion, unlike what I had seen of those held at Lord Kalceron's Palace. There was more to a joyful feast than good food and some stringed instruments. I suppose it helped when the king himself seemed genuinely pleased to have us. It was . . . amazing.

After dinner, there was some discussion—mostly light stuff, with no big secrets or details shared about the recent events at Nytaea. Many of the nobles were curious, but they knew better than to pressure the Wandering Mage. Rhidea told some stories of the places she had seen and the castles and palaces that she had visited. People ooh-ed and ahh-ed when she told of the beautiful foreign cities, and booed when she called any place more beautiful than Randhorn. Then the other dinner guests began to trickle out. I got to meet some of them as they left, but most of the names passed right over my head.

Once most of the dinner guests had left, all except for King Fenwel's most trusted advisors, we got down to brass tacks. In discussion of the prospective alliance, we learned a bit more about the reason behind Rhidea's long absence from Randhorn after becoming high magister. Apparently, she was indeed still high magister, at least in technicality, despite her having been away from her office for a long spell. All of the court officials tread lightly around her, and even called her, "My Lady" and other such titles. I knew from my own experience, watching her slay the great Lord Kalceron, that she was a very powerful mage, but her reputation was widespread from one end of the continent to the other.

Rhidea had left with King Fenwel's blessing to search the world for clues to the mysterious recent waning of Mani's magic, and had lastly come to the city of her birth, Nytaea, in her hunt. She and King Fenwel had studied books of old stories, practically legend, which spoke of the origins of our world.

"And Gaea," the king added soberly, to the confusion of most of those present.

I glanced around at my companions, searching for a hint of familiarity with the word, and settled on staring distrustfully at Rhidea.

"That would be the name of an ancient land," she said, fixing a meaningful gaze on us. "Some say Gaea is our place of origin, while others call it a myth."

"A mythical . . . continent?" Mydia asked.

Rhidea shook her head. "No. Scholars have never been certain, but presumably it is an entirely different world. Human history on Argent began only one thousand years ago, after all, so it would make sense if we somehow came from another world before that."

"Right," I said, "but how would we just *come* here?"

The king laughed. "If only we knew that."

There wasn't much more said on the topic, to my frustration. I wasn't certain I believed any of it. After the discussion, we all trickled away from the table to find our way to our rooms again. I slept very well that night (a luxurious featherbed helped with that).

The next day was our big tour of King Fenwel's court. Imagine that—me being *shown* around a castle as an honored guest. I had been all over the Nytaean Palace in my short career as a maid, to be sure, but that was different from the life that I now led. I was a low-born girl off the streets. I had thought myself to be living in luxury as a handmaiden to Princess Mydia, but now I was free and had it almost as well as she herself.

The queen and I finally had time to talk as near-equals, chatting ofttimes for hours. Kaen joined in as well, along with Mandrie, Phoebe and the two royal handmaidens. Mydia became a sort of adopted sister to us. Mandrie and Teli got along great, although Phoebe mostly kept to herself, pretending she didn't like it here when Mydia wasn't looking. Phoebe and Julia seemed to share similar dispositions. Julia and the two younger girls were both shocked and intrigued to hear all that we had been doing behind the scenes at the Palace. Even Mydia had been largely in the dark for most of the time of our friendship at the Palace, and Julia had hardly known anything at all about me.

Cort and Syneria got over their stuffiness and became more talkative. They warmed up surprisingly quickly to us, though they soon found the castle's resident magi to be of more similar tastes.

Not long after our arrival at Randhorn, I was alone with the blonde mage and Mydia when a new topic came up. "So . . . have you given any more thought to Ethas, Mydia?" Syneria asked.

I looked quizzically at my new queen.

Mydia snorted, not the derisive sort but rather in a way that said she had forgotten about something. "Not . . . enough, probably. But I am thinking he's the best choice."

"Mydia," I said in mock indignation, "Is there something you're not telling me?"

Both women looked at each other and laughed, faces reddening slightly. "Not like that, trust me," Mydia replied, waving her hands. "Syneria's the one who's marrying into his family. Ethas Gandel just happens to be my best choice for regent at the moment. He's a distant cousin of mine."

I nodded, turning to Syneria. "You're engaged already? You look like, what, sixteen?"

She raised her chin. "Sixteen and a half. But no, I'm not the one getting married! Why do you think I'm out here in Randhorn, if not to avoid the eligible bachelors?"

It was my turn to laugh.

"It's my elder sister, Aldyr Tolruin," she said.

"Ah." That made more sense.

To be honest, I didn't feel as though I fit in with any of the scholars. Sure, they all wanted to meet me, to get to know Rhidea's new star pupil, and I did seem to have great Aptitude in the fire branch, but . . . all they wanted to do the rest of the day was study. I couldn't hold myself still now that I had freedom, not to mention my reading skills were still only a step above abysmal. I made myself study when Rhidea said to, slogging through an assigned book while keeping to our daily lessons (and literacy lessons with Mydia). Whenever I asked about Gaea, Rhidea would say dismissively, "All in time, child."

I basically split my life in half at this point, dividing it between making Rhidea proud with my studies, and trying as hard as I could to avoid them—which I did by running around the castle and climbing towers when no one was looking, and asking Kaen to show me how to handle a weapon. He had learned quite well the way of the sword and the spear, and had quickly risen to taking finer instruction on different sorts of combat. (He had also, he admitted, stolen that lovely blade he'd been carrying around, but Mydia gave him official permission to keep it.) The training translated very nicely to using my abnormal strength efficiently. He taught me how to punch so that the knuckle bones did not get crushed, how to kick with the ball or heel of the foot, and quick defenses to common attacks with various weapons, and with none at all.

I truly enjoyed all of the time spent at Randhorn Castle, and I almost wish now that it could have gone on longer, because it was so peaceful. . . . At any rate, even there at Randhorn, as I said, I was reading up on the workings of our world, its magic, and the slow disappearance thereof.

I couldn't shake the feeling that something was going to happen. I didn't want to accept that I was a part of it all, yet instinct told me I was.

On the tenth of Firvaen, Rhidea and King Fenwel summoned Mydia and me. We had been chatting, but now stopped and went to see them, only to find Kaen already there. *What is going on?*

"There you are," Rhidea said in a tone that had no brightness in it. She got down to business quickly. "It is time to talk about Gaea."

Ah. . . . "Finally," I muttered wryly.

Rhidea flicked a glance my way. "Indeed. Our world is falling apart, expiring . . . dying. We need to do something."

"Rhidea has it right," agreed Fenwel. "We have deemed it time to stop putting off what must be done."

"Which is?" I asked. Kaen and Mydia kept silent, taken aback by

Rhidea's sudden announcement.

"We must find the Wellspring of Life," said Rhidea.

"Wellspring of . . ." Kaen glanced my way confusedly.

"The legendary source of all magic on Mani," I said. "Right, Rhidea?" I had read about it in a book.

"That is correct. The source of all magic *and* life here on the face of Mani." The red-haired mage held up a long finger for emphasis. "Said to have been placed there by the creator himself. It lies far to the west, in Ti'Vaeth, the capital of Kystrea."

"The Wellspring of Life," Mydia murmured.

Rhidea nodded, as though the queen's words had been a question of its existence. "Without it there would be no life on Mani. Its power is weakening, and Mani is dying as a result. We need to discover the reason for that."

Kaen frowned. "Why? What does this 'Wellspring' actually do? Is it a literal well? Like a water well?"

"Yes. The Well is the only source of water on the entire face of Mani. From it spring the Four Rivers: Yartel, Gantz, Rudaens and Ardencaul. The Wellspring gushes up and feeds the rivers continuously. Without the Well, there would be no water on Mani, and thus no life. Its streams have lessened, affecting many different areas of life across the world, resulting in food shortages and crop failures, sickness. . . . But the Wellspring is also the first source of magic on Mani. Without it, it is said that magic would cease to be. And its power is waning."

"But wouldn't that just affect water magic?" asked Kaen.

"Nay," said King Fenwel. "Water is indeed the greatest element, but all elements can only be manipulated, whether by Coaction or Authority, by the power of the Wellspring."

"So . . ." I fingered my silver ponytail, staring thoughtfully down at the floor. "The origin of magic and life here on Mani must have taken place at the same time. They're tied together."

"That makes sense," said Mydia. "If the Wellspring was placed on Mani by a higher force through magic, then said magic would surely affect the whole world."

Rhidea nodded approvingly. "Precisely, my dear. It changed our entire world. Or at least . . . so the ancient scholars seem to have believed. No one knows for sure."

"That's what it said in my mother's book," said Mydia.

"So . . . you mentioned *finding* the Wellspring," I said carefully. "But, as you said, it's in—"

I cut off as King Fenwel chuckled.

Rhidea grimaced. "It's not that simple. The fountain that springs up in Ti'Vaeth is hard to miss—in fact, any polestone will point you right to it—but the actual opening of the Well . . . I have never found the entrance to it. Mostly because Domon keeps his palace heavily guarded and one must get into the deepest underbelly of the Hall of Eternity, at the center of the Ti'Vaeth Citadel, to find it. But I know that it is somewhere deep beneath the Capital City, walled in by the Hall of Eternity."

"So we're going to Ti'Vaeth?" Mydia asked in hushed excitement.

Rhidea smirked. "We? You are soon to be resuming control of a kingdom, my dear child."

Mydia opened her mouth and paused. She was about to speak when Rhidea continued.

"Oh, that reminds me." Rhidea turned to her liege lord. "Have we finished all of the preparations?"

The aged king nodded. "Yes, Rhidea. I will send Christoff with a battalion of one hundred spear soldiers to supplement Nytaea's troops and bolster the defense forces in return for Nytaean spices. We've arranged the necessary . . ." He began to rattle off a long list of political, economic and military details cited in a treaty document, which Rhidea and Mydia pored over with him.

Kaen and I looked at each other with bored expressions. *Political stuff,* I mouthed to him, eliciting a small smile.

Before long, the meeting was adjourned, and we were introduced to Lieutenant Christoff, a man of middling height and a proud bearing whom the king trusted. He was to travel with us back to Nytaea and station his troops there.

The next morning, we would set out.

- Chapter 17 -

Official Business

I believe that there is much more to it than this. What causes the auroras to shine in the night sky and the clouds to obscure the sun in the Sunlit Cycle? What causes our regular days, when Sol herself makes her rounds only once per month? Such things are so normal that most do not even question them, but all these things . . . these too are magic.
— From *Secrets of Mani*, by Sor the Lark

(Firvaen 11, 997—Night Season)

King Fenwel bid us farewell from his castle, where he was bound by his duty to his people. Kaen, Mydia, Rhidea, and the four other girls and I set out from Randhorn Castle for Nytaea, followed by Lieutenant Christoff's battalion. Since his soldiers were on foot and we were on horses, we lost them pretty soon, but they would catch up within a week. They would be going a more roundabout way as well, taking a detour to the north so as to cross as little Storklancian territory as possible. (Seeing as our neighbors had been so accommodating to us.)

Cort and Syneria had decided to stay on in Randhorn for a while. Rhidea begrudgingly allowed it, conceding that the Randhorn school was an excellent place to study as a sort of break from the Nytaean Academy.

Rhidea continued to teach me Coaction each night. We had our own little tutoring sessions. Mydia would usually be in on it as well, and sometimes Kaen would come over to watch us as we sat away from the fire, practicing spells or learning dry pieces of knowledge about Coaction in general—in fact, this was most of it. Learning the nuances of the art. Since Coaction was a two-way exchange, it had many rules to follow. If not, the art could be very dangerous. Coaction essentially meant sparking a change in the surrounding atmosphere, prompting the magical makeup of nature to respond in turn via the Wellspring's power, which then produced the desired effect.

Authority, which I could not perform yet, was the higher art of exerting one's will upon the surrounding elements, commanding the elements to do one's bidding. It was much more powerful as well as reliable—if one had the necessary requirements for it. Rhidea still kept these requirements in the dark, probably so that I would not go out and try to command nature as I wanted.

(Firvaen 18, 997—Night Season)
We arrived in Nytaea within the week. Sol was hidden well beyond the western horizon, for it was the Night Season, so the auroras were our light, the stars our guide. In another week, dawn would break and the Sunlit Cycle would begin. As confusing as it can be, the term 'day' means two different things on Mani, as it applies to the times of the four-week Sol Cycle—otherwise known as a month—as well as each individual day.

We met up with Bart and Gaela and Marshal Lanthar upon arrival in the white city, relaying what was going on over a splendid lunch put on by the Palace staff. It was good to eat familiar Nytaean cuisine after the good but foreign fare of Randhorn.

It was at this point that we were informed of the arrival of an imperial emissary from Ti'Vaeth, who had deposited a threatening letter from the Archlord himself. This was something we had been expecting, of course.

"What did it say?" asked Mydia tentatively.

Gaela unfolded the letter. "There's a lot of pomp and nonsense here, but the important part reads: '*I am giving a period of thirty days for Nytaea to give up all pretense of rebellion and surrender to her Lord. After that, there will be neither parley nor quarter, and a full invasion of Nytaea shall commence, until every man, woman and child is subject once more to the throne of Ti'Vaeth or lies dead in the streets. You choose.'*"

The noblewoman closed up the letter and handed it to Rhidea, who was already reaching for it with a frown.

"But . . . we've got some hope now," Mydia said uncertainly. And she began to relate what we'd been arranging with King Fenwel. We caught them up on all the details of the alliance, which was very positive so far, and told them of the troops Fenwel had sent with Christoff, and then briefed them on the journey which we must soon embark on to Ti'Vaeth. Rhidea left out a few of the details on that part, saying that it was somewhat of a secret mission.

We got a short reprieve from our travels, resting well that night, but I knew that we had to depart on the morrow. I was given a guest bed at the Palace—a guest bed!—upon which I laid, staring blankly at the ceiling, trying to sleep. What would Ti'Vaeth be like? Greater than Nytaea or Randhorn, if Rhidea's stories were true. The Veiled City, the birthplace of magic. I was both nervous and excited.

Finally, I fell asleep.

(Firvaen 19, 997—Night Season)

I awoke with the feeling that someone was missing. That girl—what was her name again? White? No, that was my own nickname for her. If she had a name, I didn't know it. Had I caught a glimpse of her in the night?

I shook my head, climbing out of my comfortable bed and changing into more formal attire given me by Mydia. It was a light grey dress with a cross-laced back—such a pain—mid-length skirts, and a blue sash around the waist. A comely thing, and fairly comfortable as well. The two qualities did not usually come together. My hair I braided down my back.

Looking out through the window of my guest room, I saw that a fair drizzle was trickling down from hazy, low-hanging clouds, which obscured much of the day's light from the auroras and stars. A pity that we had to travel in this weather.

Downstairs, I found Phoebe and Mandrie in the dining hall, already getting breakfast. In fact, they were helping the maids to prepare it, like good girls. Kaen wandered in shortly thereafter, looking as bleary and disheveled as on those long-ago mornings at the orphanage. Mydia still wouldn't be up for a while. . . . Queen Regent though she may be, she was still a princess. Her duties demanded much more of her, but it was a hard adjustment for the dainty young woman.

After we had all eaten, we set about preparing for the journey to Ti'Vaeth. Afterward Rhidea, Kaen, Mydia and I would depart for Ti'Vaeth, leaving Phoebe to look after Mandrie. Phoebe would have been fine on the journey—she was tough—but we couldn't risk Mandrie. Phoebe also had that orphanage she wanted to start. Mydia was pretty frail as they went, but she also possessed magic, such as healing. That set her apart. We would need all the specialized party members that we could get. However, Julia and Teli would be staying at the Palace, since this journey was considered too pressing—and too dangerous—to bring unnecessary companions.

For this reason—and because her advisors wouldn't let her go without them—we took along Mydia's newly-appointed Queensguard, which consisted of a mage soldier named Kath and two swordsmen, Inno and Ruel. Kaen was happy to have some men along for a change. He grumbled left and right about being surrounded by women, and honestly . . . I didn't blame him. It was a shame that the world was the way it was, with roughly three girls being born to each manchild. This is what had eventually led to women being inducted into the ranks of the mage soldiers, and even on rarer occasion the spear soldiers and swordsmen as well, although women were not naturally inclined toward that. They were simply considered, well . . . expendable.

Ethas Gandel, Mydia's long-lost cousin, did indeed agree to act on her behalf while she was away. A cunning man a bit too tall and thin to be a nobleman, he seemed more responsible than most. Frankly, he seemed to look down on most humans, but he treated Mydia with respect. Our trip would be a long one, so hopefully he didn't run the country too badly—and didn't try to hold onto his power when it was requested of him. . . . If he proved a good ruler, Mydia planned to make him the next king in her place.

We set out from the East Gate that afternoon. We were traveling by horse once more, fortunately (and unfortunately, said my sore backside). We got about three leagues from the city before stopping to rest for the day.

Kath and I bonded fairly quickly. He was a fellow fire synergist, so we had that in common. Kath was middle-aged and agreeable, but apparently just short enough that a lot of jokes went over his head. He claimed to not have much coactive talent, but he had years of experience and his skills were far higher than mine. (And yes, Rhidea still called him 'child.')

Inno and Ruel, veteran soldiers formerly stationed on the Yan'Vala border, sparred with Kaen every night after we stopped to make camp on the roadside. They were specialists in the sword, Kaen's weapon of choice, and both acknowledged his raw talent with the blade. That didn't mean they went easy on him, however.

Despite having less of my friends along to talk to, the Queens-guard made traveling quite enjoyable—which was good, because we were in for a long trip.

- Chapter 18 -

On the Road to Ti'Vaeth

The imbalance of male to female births, a phenomenon which affects our entire world today, was first recorded somewhere between the years 560 and 590. This was shortly after the height of Mani's old order of magi (520–580), and so one could make the logical assumption that the waning of the Old Order of magi had something to do with the decline of male births. But, as with any such data, correlation should never be taken as conclusive evidence. If only we had such evidence. . . .
— From *Secrets of Mani*, by Sor the Lark

(Firvaen 22, 997—Night Season)

Three days into our journey, we came into the province of Fircas and soon stopped at our first village. We had passed two others already, opting to keep going straight on the Imperial Highway to make as good time as possible (ignoring complaints from Mydia).

The village was called Andeir, and it was really more of a town, set right on the highway but with houses sprawling farther to the sides, small paths connecting them to the highway. Many houses were of earthen brick and shingled with slate, although there was no magic-assisted architecture as in Nytaea. Lit by the auroras of the Sunless Cycle, the landscape was beautiful, with rolling hills and pastures full of grey prairie grass and sheep, terraced gardens, and Gumba trees spreading their white leaves here and there. Farmland lay to either side on the fringes of the village, and beyond that stretched dense forest.

We needed a few supplies. Since we were traveling as light as possible, we were keeping few rations and other supplies on hand, buying them where we could, when we needed them—which was now.

Kaen pulled up his mount, pulling the reins smoothly with one hand. He was getting a hold on this riding thing. "That's the town, Rhidea?" he asked, looking over at the red-haired mage.

She nodded. "Andeir. We'll stop here."

"Finally a real town, eh?" said Inno. "Maybe we'll get a good night's sleep." He winked at his companion, Ruel.

"Surely we can rest at the inn one night, Lady Rhidea?" Mydia asked, flopping forward to lean on her horse's neck, panting as though exhausted from a month-long journey.

"That was my plan," Rhidea muttered. "If the residents aren't scared to death of the Archlord's threats and actually let us in."

"One way to find out," I said, spurring my mount on. He was a gelding named Redring. Don't ask me why, because he was grey.

We descended the hill toward Andeir. A few of the local children looked up at us as we approached. Some of them scattered, some shouted. A woman looked our way and scowled, taking her children and going inside the house with them. Not a good sign for the public relations here.

Two burly men stood in leathern armor, one on either side of the road by the arched village gate which read . . . I actually couldn't tell what it said—it was in High Legaleian. They lounged against the posts nonchalantly, as though not eying us warily, probably getting paid to keep out troublemakers from Nytaea. The broadswords slung at their side were awfully big and quite prominent.

Rude of them to post guards, of course, when the Imperial Highway led straight through the town.

"Hoy, there," called the one.

The other soldier nodded curtly. "Travelers."

Rhidea pulled up her reins, and the rest of us followed suit. "Are we allowed into the town?" she asked calmly.

The man on the right shifted his cross-armed stance. "Any peaceful travelers are allowed through . . . depending on whence you come and what your purpose is. And you've got a right retinue of armed guards with ya."

"We have protection, yes."

"A mage soldier, eh?" said the guard on the left. "Magi and soldiers. Ya come from Nytaea or thereabouts?" His brows were narrowed with suspicion. Both soldiers looked more tense than they meant to let on, clearly ready to call for backup at a moment's notice (even though that wouldn't be much good against multiple trained magi).

"We are headed for Ti'Vaeth from Nemental," Rhidea explained. "I am a wandering mage, and these here, accompanied by soldiers we picked up along the way, are my companion magi." A true story. Not the whole thing, but not a lie either. *Well played, Rhidea. . . .*

The guards looked from Rhidea to the rest of us. "A wandering mage, or . . . *the* Wandering Mage?" asked the man on the left.

"That is of no consequence. We mean no ill to the town of Andeir. And if you do not let us in, we will continue a different way—"

"No, no, go on. We won't stop ya." The guards seemed to have made up their mind. They waved us in.

We passed through the archway into Andeir, while the soldiers muttered something under their breath about 'those pesky magi, throwing their weight around.'

Still, wise of them not to anger Rhidea. Very wise.

We stopped by the marketplace in town and traded some gold

for foodstuffs for the journey: jerky, wineskins, dried fruits. Inno and Ruel took Kaen and browsed through the local bronzesmith's assortment of weapons, probably with no intention of buying anything. (Nytaea did already have some of the best smiths around.)

The locals seemed to warm up to us after a bit, and Mydia began to attract small children like a Polestone. They could tell there was something lovable and loving in her, or maybe just that she was a softie and would let them get away with playing around, tugging at her skirts and teasing her. Their mothers began to gather them away and scold them as soon as they noticed, however. Mydia looked a bit disappointed.

We spent the night at the inn, enjoying some music and all the local specialties (though Fircasian cuisine was not exceedingly special), meeting some of the town's residents, before hitting the hay. We rented two rooms for the night, one for the men and one for the women. For all her coin, Rhidea seemed to frown on excess spending.

(Firvaen 23, 997—Night Season)
I slept well that night, waking in the morning without any dreams. Everyone seemed to feel well rested after a proper sleep. We ate an early breakfast there at the inn, and then departed for the rest of our trip shortly after the auroras came out for the day. It would be about two more weeks until Ti'Vaeth. We were not pushing our horses all that hard, traveling about five leagues per day. Each day carried the same routine: break camp, break fast, ride, stop for lunch, ride, stop to make camp for the night, practice Coaction with Rhidea (or swordplay, for the swordsmen), and sleep. We stopped at villages and towns along the way every few days, always avoiding the biggest towns and cities because, well . . . we didn't need extra trouble, and that would be where to find it in these times. Many side roads pro-

vided alternate routes.

We encountered few monsters along the road. We didn't really expect to, since the stationed armies and magi of Kystrea did a pretty good job of keeping the country clear. There was so much civilization, and so many soldiers per capita, that we had eradicated most of the monsters which used to prowl the areas. We did run across a large, dark shadow in the forest one night, however, causing more than one in our party to panic. Rhidea simply lit a warding lamp and had Inno stake out a couple of extra torches. We always kept someone on guard, regardless of the immediate threat, due to the potential for bandits, hostile soldiers and monsters. Each night we staked out four torches at the perimeter of our camp. We never strayed too far into the forest or off the beaten path.

That said, I never found out what that black shape was that I saw that *one* night . . . but I could swear it was there, and it was large.

We encountered many travelers along the Imperial Highway. Most would pass us by with no more than a nod or a murmur of greeting. Some were probably afraid of our well-armed group. Others probably thought we would bring trouble upon them if they interacted with us. And of course, some were just unfriendly.

But a few of the travelers we met would stop and talk to us. We would ask them how things fared in Fircas, or whatever province we were currently in, or what word there was from Ti'Vaeth.

One night, Kaen came up with an idea. He came over to me by the campfire after most of the others were asleep in their bedrolls. "Hey, Lyn, I've got a proposition."

I rolled my eyes. "Okay."

"It's a good one, really." I gave him a patient look, and he went on, "So, what if we started up a little act to make some extra coin in the towns? Starring you?"

"You mean causing a spectacle. Kaen, this sounds like a bad idea . . ."

"No, no, that's the whole point. Say we set up a little game—three copper pieces to the man who can best our champion in an arm-wrestling match, with one piece paid to try. Then we spring it on them! We tell them that we're having this random girl wrestle them. I mean, you may be big-boned, but you're still a girl, so it will be surprising."

I bit back a retort at his description of me—which was true anyway—and actually considered his idea. "Now, that would be fun. But Rhidea would never let us make a show like that . . . plus, the new soldiers don't know anything about me yet."

"Oh. . . ." Kaen scratched his head, clearly struggling to justify his idea. "They've traveled with us long enough, and . . . well, we can probably trust them. They'll find out soon enough anyway."

I nodded slowly. "I'll talk to Rhidea tomorrow. I know Mydia would get a kick out of it . . . but for now, I'm just so tired. I have to sleep."

"Right, of course." He left me to find my own place, picking his way carefully to where the men were camped.

(Firvaen 26, 997—Night Season)
The next day, we came upon another town.

Here, we would try out Kaen's idea.

We entered the town just like normal. It was on the larger side of the towns we had visited, a place called Snowbell. Our plan was to start up our little game in the market square. If things went badly, we would bolt westward out of town before too many soldiers arrived. If things went well, we could make a good bit of coin. . . . I was pretty sure we had only convinced Rhidea because she was curious to gauge my powers' limits better.

In the market, we found a mage named Alfred who agreed to oversee a competition to make sure no magic was involved (this kind of thing was not an uncommon use of a Perception mage's talents; they were known to be far better than others at telling when magic was being used). We paid him three pieces of copper, which seemed a satisfactory amount to the man.

A few burly men came over to us after we announced the arm-wrestling challenge. We set up two chairs around a heavy wooden table and one of the big-armed, burly men plunked himself down on the other side after paying one copper piece to Kaen. "So, where's my opponent?" he asked, scanning the men among us. Most likely trying to gauge whether it was one of the smaller or larger men who would be our champion—sometimes size isn't everything, after all.

Our two soldiers and Kath looked at each other uncertainly. We hadn't exactly told them much about what was going on.

I took my seat across from the large man. "Hello."

He scowled, then laughed a hearty laugh. "You jest! All right, lass, you've stepped up, so I won't go easy."

We locked arms, my hand fitting snugly in his meaty palm, and looked each other in the eye. The mage, Alfred, looked on intently, probably seeing now why we'd asked for his assistance, and Kaen called, "Ready, set, go!"

I wrenched immediately, quick as I could think, slamming my opponent's hand into the table's surface with a heavy *thud!* He cursed, yanking his hand back and shaking it out. "What sorcery is this!?"

"None," said Alfred plainly. "It was a fair game." I could see interest on his face. Surely he was wondering, along with many others, what sort of trick I had used. I couldn't help but smirk, just a little bit. This was going to be fun. I hadn't used any of my hidden reservoir of strength, nor even my full natural strength.

"Anyone else?" Kaen asked, looking around. "Just one copper piece to try your luck."

At this point, there was much murmuring among the men around. Their pride spiked, and we got many more contestants.

The next one sat down across from me, and we locked hands, waiting on Kaen's call. My opponent fought me immediately, and he had good form, but I wrenched his arm down as well without tapping my reservoir of strength. The last time I had used speed, this time brute force, but failing that, a bit of my stored energy was plenty to beat any of these men. Unless there happened to be a ranking arm-wrestling champion here in town.

There was not. Kaen continued to collect copper coins without ever paying out a single one, and I continued to win match after match, growing slowly more tired. Finally, as soldiers began to gather and tempers flared increasingly, I decided to shift the notoriety over to another, losing on purpose to a giant mountain of a man. Honestly, he may have beaten me anyway, given how tired I was at that point.

The townsfolk cheered as we paid out the three copper pieces to him, and suddenly all the attention was on him. Now all the other contestants wanted to try their hand against him. I felt bad, as he would probably lose to one of them.

We slipped out quietly, heading to a smaller inn on the west side of town (close to the exit—just, you know, in case). Here we stayed until the morning of the next day.

Kaen was now fifty-one copper pieces richer . . . and I wanted my share.

- Chapter 19 -

Training

It was not too long after the birth rate's change became widely known and obvious that the people of Argent began to accept it as the new norm. Over the next century, cultures accepted the larger pool of women in varying ways: baby girls drowned or cast away from birth in some places, while in others the excess female population was put to forced labor. Across the world polygamy became commonplace, for the fact was undeniable that more women meant more breeding, more potential children and thus more potential males.
— From *Secrets of Mani*, by Sor the Lark

(Firvaen 28, 997—Night Season)

We pulled these same stunts in the next town of Lorcost. I was beginning to like it. It had taken a bit of explaining before Inno, Ruel and Kath understood and trusted me. They knew that there was something special about me, and they knew the stories of Kaen and me infiltrating the Palace in order to break out our friends from the inside.

Each night after the arm-wrestling, it seemed I had another dream with that girl, showing me visions of . . . well, not really much. Old memories of Kaen and my other friends, mostly. And Lentha. I wondered if it was my exhaustion that brought on the dreams, or the expenditure of whatever fueled my eerie strength.

Sadly, Rhidea put a stop to it after the third town, saying that I should learn to make money more honestly—and also, we were beginning to draw more widespread attention. Mydia and I stuck to our nightly Coaction practice with Rhidea. She wasn't going to let us get out of that, no matter how tired we were. Kath would often join Rhidea to give us pointers, although his pertained more to me, as he had more practical knowledge of using Coaction in combat or other dangerous situations. And of course, he was a fire mage like me.

Over the course of the trip, I grew in my control of fire Coaction. I had very little in the way of Authority, but according to Rhidea, I was getting close to my first command. One night when Kath was busy with the soldiers, Rhidea finally let Mydia and me in on one of her secrets that she guarded closely.

This secret was her three treasures, some of which I had glimpsed before but none of which I had actually seen in use. They were magical artifacts forged by strong magi long ago: A nondescript copper coin that returned to her hand upon a snap of the fingers, a small, pinecone-shaped silver trinket imbued with a restorative energy that drew from the earth to heal wounds and other injuries slowly, and lastly a whitish gemstone that gave its bearer the power of instant transportation. This last one, which Rhidea called a Reality Stone, interested me the most.

"It is a gift from a friend long ago," she explained. "I prize it very highly. It grants a high level of Authority in the art of Reality. If you hold it and imbue it with energy, the stone allows you to instantly teleport up to a distance of one hundred yards to any place in sight."

"You have Authority over Reality already, though, don't you?" I asked.

"I do. But this is far simpler oftentimes. I can only use it twice in succession, though. Then it needs to . . . cool down, you might say. If you promise to be careful, I will let you try it out. Here, hold it just like this . . ."

After giving me a couple of pointers, she nodded, and I focused energy into the device and decided on a point in the close distance, and next I knew, I was there. It was the most unsettling experience I'd had in a while, but the wonder of it brought a smile to my lips. I had just leaped through space using an ancient magical artifact. . . .

I asked my teacher afterward if the mage soldiers back at Nytaea had used similar stones when they teleported. "Yes," she said in answer, voice thoughtful. "That is the most likely explanation."

I loved our little practice sessions. Some were fun little discoveries like this, while others included me almost burning down the forest whilst Rhidea yelled at me and Mydia gathered water from around us to douse it—so . . . something interesting. Rhidea taught me to "work with" the flames instead of just letting them run rampant, and in time I built enough control to apply heat to the smallest point, for instance the innards of a lock (not, she added, that self-respecting magi went about breaking into locked places, but it could come in handy in that way and many others).

Mydia learned to use her newly-attained Water Authority to assess bodily problems in a person and better heal them. Cuts and bruises were the extent of her healing abilities, but Rhidea said they could grow far stronger. She also improved her ability to "speak" to plant life, asking it to grow, bend or change to help her out. She managed to wrap Rhidea up in grass and weeds one time before her teacher politely requested to be let go. The girl giggled like it was the funniest thing she'd ever seen.

Kaen and the others began including me in their sparring sessions. Mydia practiced her tree-shaping Authority by crafting us wooden practice swords. Inno and Ruel were, of course, a bit leery of the monstrous strength that I had displayed in our arm-wrestling shenanigans, but I made sure to temper my strength and avoid tapping into that reserve that I always kept on hand. Kaen said that it would be good practice for my control as well.

I picked it up reasonably well. I lacked the deftness and hand-eye coordination that Kaen had, but I was quick on my feet and precise enough to practice what they taught me and master it at a steady rate. Any one of them could best me in a duel—sword to sword, by the rules, skill for skill. That was why, when it came to a real fight, I never played fair. When Kaen and I had fought the mage soldiers and spearmen at the Nytaean Palace, I had made sure to dispatch my opponents in whatever way was quickest, as long as it didn't mean needless death.

Mydia would simply watch and laugh whenever I got myself cornered by Kaen or one of the two soldiers. And she wondered why I fell asleep so quickly every night. . . .

(Norvaen 12, 997—Waning Day)
At long last, on the twelfth day of the sixth month of the year, we approached Ti'Vaeth. Here at the center of Argent, that meant the sun hung midway between its zenith and the far horizon. Three weeks of journeying, finally at an end.

Ti'Vaeth was more breathtaking than I had ever heard. It was for good reason that it was known as the "Birthplace of Magic." First, we led our horses through the Veil—a giant, twisting, roiling wall of water—which was the first visible landmark we had seen as we approached. It was wet, but did not have the force that I had assumed it would. Neither was the noise of it overwhelming.

Soon, we were out—or in, rather—and I found myself gasping alongside my companions. Before us stretched a road made from sparkling blue stones, leading all the way down a long slope that ended abruptly at Lake Lucia. Around the glittering lake hung the tallest waterfalls I had ever seen. And upon that lake, across a multi-arched bridge, on an island called Kysedon, sat the city of Ti'Vaeth, crowned in gold by the great citadel upon a smoothly-rounded hill.

All around us, the land was richly fertile, and all manner of plants grew amidst a lush savannah of grasses. It was . . . green. The grass was not grey but vivid green here. So much green, as though the thrum of life overpowered the subterranean silver that tinged most life on Mani. Towering Cyvil trees shaded the area with frondlike leaves—tinged with silver only on the tips—and Kystrean Gazelles grazed upon it. Mist hung everywhere in the air, and the temperature was of a perfect warmth.

But perhaps the centerpiece of the whole scene was the Sky Funnel, the great geyser that sprang up from the Wellspring of Life deep underneath Ti'Vaeth. It seemed to pierce right through the center of the citadel. The geyser reached all the way up to the sky, streaking out and spraying in all directions. The water from it was drawn by its ancient magic upward and outward in an arc, streaming along the Veil that protected Ti'Vaeth, coming down in the sheets that made up the Veil.

"Impressed yet?" Rhidea asked over the sound of falling water. She waved us onward, remounting her horse. We followed her along the road, overcome by the sheer beauty around us, dripping as we went. As we grew closer to Lake Lucia, we got a better look at the Sky Funnel and the golden city that spread underneath it on the Isle of Kysedon. We rode down the smooth decline and over the bridge toward the capital city of Kystrea:

Ti'Vaeth, the Veiled City.

- Chapter 20 -

The Veiled City

Of course, none of these things addressed the problem. In fact, throughout history it is as though people forgot increasingly about the disparate proportions, despite those proportions creeping slowly farther and farther apart. One-to-two has long been the estimated ratio, and yet today medics and midwives say that it is barely one in four—though the imperial census tends to be silent on the matter.
— From *Secrets of Mani*, by Sor the Lark

(Norvaen 12, 997—Waning Day)

Silver-armored mage soldiers stopped us at the gate to the bridge. A few words from Rhidea got us through with little issue, though. The bridge spanned nearly a mile across the water, and the beauty of the lake and the city before us awed me the whole way as we rode across.

At last, we reached the city gates on the far side. More guard check-ins here, and then we were in. Inside, Ti'Vaeth was just as beautiful as outside. The roads were paved in the same faintly-blue stones, while rooftops made of copper plates glinted in the sunlight. Most houses and buildings had tall, arched windows and prominent overhanging roofs. Nytaea was an impressive city, to be certain, but I begrudgingly had to admit that Ti'Vaeth was far more striking. Even without the breathtaking setting surrounding it, Ti'Vaeth's display of architectural design and elegance was second to none.

The city bustled with life, carts and pedestrians and mounted nobles swarming around here and there. For all its liveliness, however, there was a . . . tension . . . in the air. It was faint; was it the uncertainty about the Wellspring? People in these parts surely knew more about it than in the outer reaches like Nytaea. Glancing upward, I saw the Sky funnel looming and swirling above the citadel, a bit too close for comfort. It droned steadily in the background. What was it like before this "dwindling?" The lake, was it usually higher?

Soldiers passed us by on either side of the street, along with magi and mage soldiers. As we approached the inner city, ascending a low grade towards the citadel on the central hill, the buildings became taller and more ornate while more and more guardsmen were stationed outside larger keeps and mansions.

Finally, we arrived at the wall of the citadel of the Archlord. Its crenelated top was easily a dozen paces up. Rhidea hailed one of the mage soldiers who guarded the gate and asked about an audience with the Archlord. She was rewarded by a dry, well-practiced response to the effect of having to wait a few days for the request to be processed, bla bla bla. . . . After a bit of convincing, Rhidea persuaded them that she was the Wandering Mage, at which point one of the guards bowed, mumbled an apology, and ran to report that the Wandering Mage was here.

Soon, a high-ranking mage soldier came out to the gate and greeted Rhidea with a gracious bow. "Lady Cae Rhidea," he murmured. "It is an honor that you have graced us with your presence once more. Archlord Domon is busy. I am afraid he will be unable to meet with you this evening."

She huffed. "Well, if that's all the better he can do, then I'll leave him to his business for now."

Turning her mount, she started back in the opposite direction, and the rest of us followed closely. She took us back toward the lower levels of town, a much less opulent sector. Here, we eventually came to a small inn called the Sleepy Dragon. I wasn't exactly sure what a dragon was, aside from the heraldic symbol used by the Kalceron family, but hey, it was a place to stay, and it was a bit nicer than the few inns we'd stayed at on the way here. The food was very good, featuring lots of fruits and vegetables in both sweet and savory dishes. Dinner included a large salad, something I was not too accustomed to but enjoyed nonetheless. Apparently, meat was not a big part of the cuisine here.

At the seventh hour, Rhidea went back to the Palace alone. No one went with her, for she said it was best that only she go. I didn't question her, even though Mydia and I ordinarily got to accompany her wherever she went. The main reason, however, was that we had all come from Nytaea, and we did not yet know how the Archlord would receive such guests. . . .

She came back two hours later with an expression clouded by annoyance and anger. "That selfish pig!" she cried. "He is so unreasonable, miserable and . . . rrrgh! Sorry, sorry. I'm not upset. I'm not upset. . . ."

I had never seen the mage so stirred up. She looked like she wanted to kick something.

Mydia ran up and hugged her. "Lady Rhidea, it will be all right." It was just the way Mandrie would comfort someone.

Rhidea sighed. Then, smiling, she patted Mydia's hair and said, "Yes it will, dear." She proceeded to back up and recount what had happened. She relaxed a bit as she went. At the last, she summarized: "So, he plans to take back Nytaea from the new government struggling to run it, and he will not show us the Wellspring. He has forbidden access to either one."

"Then we'll just have to break through and get there anyway," Kaen said resolutely.

"Or learn what we can here in the city, then make our move," I suggested.

Rhidea nodded. "Yes, probably the best course of action. He may change his mind. Or we may discover all we need to know. We can find a way into the Imperial Archives."

The irritation, despite her words, had not diminished from her face.

(Norvaen 13, 997—Waning Day)

The next morning, after a restful sleep at the Sleepy Dragon, we set about our new goal. We split up into two groups, with Kaen and the soldiers going out into the streets to talk with the locals, while the women—Mydia, Rhidea and I—spoke with officials of the Citadel about getting inside the Archives. Within a short while, we had convinced the keepers of the Archives to allow us access.

The Imperial Archives was an impressive structure, though one would not know it from the outside, tucked away as it was in the midst of the Citadel. Inside, it was a massive three-room complex featuring a domed ceiling six spans high painted with murals. Multiple levels of walkways spiraled around floor-to-ceiling shelves of scrolls and books. The other two rooms branched off, with more regular shapes and ceilings rising to a lower level, one wing on the left and one on the right. Still not as scholastically rich as Nytaea's library, according to Rhidea, but larger and much more visually impressive.

We were let in through an exterior door by a scholarly contact of Rhidea's named Rodessa—a nervous young woman not much older than myself. Apparently, she indirectly owed Rhidea a favor. I spent a minute just staring in awe at the beautiful design of the Archives—Mydia and I both—until Rhidea gave us a pointed look and cleared her throat, reminding us of our purpose.

"This way, my good scholars," said the library attendant. "I can show you to the historical sections."

"Perfect!" Mydia said brightly, and then gave a bashful look to Rhidea and a shrug to me.

I wondered why we wanted to look through old, dusty histories in the first place; I would've thought that we'd just go straight for anything on the Wellspring of Magic here in Ti'Vaeth. But Rhidea must know what she was doing, right?

"Specifically, histories of magic, Rodessa," Rhidea said as we passed into the historical archives.

The attendant paused for a brief moment. "Histories of magic, got it." I could tell that she wanted to question the mage further, but of course this was the Wandering Mage, Rhidea of Randhorn. . . .

We ended up with a few ancient scrolls, poring through them for hours. Rhidea had already been through much of this library, she said, but this time we were researching specifically how to get into the Well without the Archlord's attention. Of course, that wasn't explicitly mentioned anywhere, so it took some digging.

From here, we worked our way over to documents on the Archlord's palace, the Hall of Eternity, and how it was built. This would be helpful for once we got inside it. The Hall of Eternity, which housed the Sky Funnel, would not be an easy egg to crack, as it was nestled in the very center of the citadel.

Two hours later, my brain felt like a plow horse after a long day of work. Mydia was complaining about much the same thing, and Rhidea looked up, sighing. "All right, all right, you may go now. Good work, students."

"Yay!" Mydia stood up from her chair, immediately putting a hand over her mouth as she realized how loud her voice was. She whispered an apology, and then proceeded to stretch.

"Rhidea, you're staying here longer?" I asked as I rose.

She half glanced up, eyes still on her roll of text. "Yes. I'm sure you girls can stay out of trouble for a little while until I'm done?"

"Yes, Lady Rhidea!" Mydia whispered, dropping a curtsy.

With a murmur of assent, I followed Mydia out. Rodessa politely led us out of the Archives, and then we exited the whole fortified Citadel, and soon we were out on the city streets, overlooking the lower sectors of Ti'Vaeth. *Such a sprawling city. . . .* The bronze of the rooftops gleamed and glittered in the sunlight, which had been progressing toward the western horizon for a few days now. "So, we're staying out of trouble . . . right, Mydia?" I grinned mischievously at her.

She grinned back. "Of course! Why do you ask?"

"The others probably aren't back yet, either. Want to explore the city?"

"You bet I do!" she replied. She checked her pocket watch, noting the time.

We set off aimlessly down the next main street on the left (no back streets, thank you), heading northward and slightly downhill. The streets of Ti'Vaeth and their intersections were not perpendicular, despite most of the uphill–downhill streets going straight up to the center of the city. Some wound their way up, and the side streets crisscrossed at all angles. Mydia skipped gaily, and I followed a bit more warily.

She stopped skipping, jumping back with a yelp, as a squad of mage soldiers passed in front of us at an intersection. "M-mage soldiers!" she hissed.

I grabbed hold of the back of her dress. "Mydia!" I whispered. "Calm down, it's fine."

We stood and watched as they crossed, and then continued on

our way. They didn't even glance our way. I took the lead this time. "Do you know much about the city?" I asked the queen, turning to her.

She shook her head, obsidian hair glittering in the evening light as it waved. "No, not a thing. Why do you think I wanted to explore?" Then she pointed toward a tall statue one block down from us. "Ooh! Let's go see that!"

I nodded, and we hurried downhill to the square where the statue stood presiding over the middle. It was about four paces tall, and stood on a knee-high pedestal atop a shallow fountain pool. It looked to be crafted of solid copper, its form that of an important-looking soldier from a past era, uniform and armor forming both a sturdy and stately look.

"Hmm, he seems familiar," Mydia murmured. Stepping forward, she peered at the plaque on the pedestal. "Trevias Lhordes . . . oh, I know him! I learned about this man in my history classes—the general who brought an end to the Styrite wars two centuries past. Feared and respected for his great tactical prowess."

"He looks . . . very angry," I observed, peering at the statue's face. I soon went back to scanning the square, eyeing the dozen or so people gathered around and the passersby bustling to and fro.

I don't like this place. I couldn't quite place why I felt that way, but . . .

"Mydia, let's be on our way," I murmured, starting toward the opposite side of the square.

She turned and followed after me, close on my heels. I was glad that she did, because the last thing I wanted was to have to track down a lost queen in a city this big. What had begun as a fun jaunt would quickly become a stressful endeavor for me.

We came across a few more mage soldiers, some rough-looking

characters and giant carriages, but no one accosted us or tried to kidnap my friend, thank my lucky stars. (I've long suspected I don't have any lucky stars, but that's beside the point.) We stopped to grab a snack at a booth. The woman there was selling imported southern fruit bowls—foreign fruits like bananas and pineapples, chopped and sliced with coconut shavings on top. It was delicious.

Presently, Mydia checked her pocket watch again and found the time to be 6:30. We scurried back to the inn, where we found with some relief that Rhidea was not back yet. She would have tanned our hides for staying out so long. (Although we did at least manage to stay out of trouble, eh?) Kaen and the others were already back, with nothing new to report from their end. Except that Kaen said they encountered one of the elite assassins of the Archlord, known as the Dalim. They sounded frightening from his description: shadowy figures who wore many layers of clothing and seemed to radiate danger.

Tomorrow would likely be a similarly dull day of research, reconnaissance and desperately banging our heads together for a way to get into the Well. It would be Night in only two more days . . . perhaps that could actually work to our benefit, giving us more cover to try to sneak into the Well.

Rhidea came back after another hour, looking mentally drained. She shook her head before we could ask about her findings, slumping down into a chair. After a moment, she resumed her regular, proper posture and smoothed back her fiery red hair. "Nothing, children. I'm afraid we're getting nowhere so far. But all we can do is keep trying."

We ate a filling dinner of Ti'Vaeth cuisine and then hit the hay for the night. Before bed, however, I pulled Rhidea aside. "Could I go with Kaen and the others tomorrow?" I asked.

"Oh," she said with a frown. "Why do you ask?"

"Well, I just thought I may be of more use in other areas. I just—I'm not cut out for all this scholar stuff."

"Yet."

I tilted my head from side to side, trying to come up with a response. Then I paused and sighed. "Actually, I had some . . . crazy ideas." In a low voice, I outlined a plan I'd been tossing around, and she cocked an eyebrow in response.

"Well, well . . . that again. Sounds dangerous, child. Be careful."

"So you'll let me go?" I asked.

"Yes. As for how you will get in . . ."

"Well, see, that's the thing—" I began, but she cut me off.

"Let me guess: you're wanting to borrow this?" Rhidea produced her white teleportation artifact, the one that allowed a person to access Reality Authority in a limited sense.

I hesitated, eyeing the artifact. "Yes. That's my plan."

Rhidea sighed and reached out her left hand, which held the device. "I really have to train you in the arts of Reality. If only I had thirty years on my hands. . . ."

I reached for the Reality Stone, but she drew it back. "You promise you will be *careful?*"

I nodded innocently.

"Very well." She handed it over.

The next morning, after the clouds had cleared, I found Kaen and pulled him aside to explain my plan. "Are you game?"

He shook his head. "You're crazy, Lyn, but that's what I like about you. I'm in."

(Norvaen 14, 997—Waning Day)

An hour later, we crouched atop a copper rooftop, underneath one of six bell towers in the city. The wind ruffled my false-brown hair and blew in moist, tangy lake air from the west. From under the long shadow of the bell tower, we surveyed the Citadel, whose wall lay just in front of us.

"So what's our plan now?" Kaen asked, fingering his sword scabbard. "Nytaea all over again?"

"Hopefully not that whole fiasco," I muttered. "But Rhidea's taught me a few things . . . and we have this." I held up the white jewel in my hand. Then, taking hold of his hands, I closed my eyes and concentrated. A ripple passed through the gemstone in my hands, through my body and his, and the air around us. Another ripple, and another, and then we stood on the wall of the Citadel. A *whoosh!* accompanied our landing, along with a surprising but brief disoriented feeling.

Kaen caught his balance clumsily, and I steadied him with a hand.

"Oh, that was . . ." He held a hand to his head. "Very strange. One way to solve a problem, but . . . please don't do that again."

"You'll be all right, Kaen."

"Yes, well." He adjusted his sword belt and looked left and right, watching the guards' torches pass by in crossing patterns along the walls. "Let's be going."

The walls of the Citadel had bridges and arches which spanned the gap between the outer and inner walls. We had to get from here to there without the guards seeing us. So we began to stealthily make our way down the walkway toward the next guard station turret. There, we hid behind a wall as the nearest guard came out our way, ducking in after he was gone. We turned to the right and headed out onto the arch. I made the mistake of looking down and saw the courtyard sixty feet below. Shaking my head with a gulp, I kept going.

We crept along like this, avoiding the guardsmen and staying out of the torchlight. At least at this time of the Sunlit Cycle, nearing sunset, we had a bit of extra cover. Our goal was to get as far as we could into the Citadel without having to take out any guardsmen. And I really, really didn't want to have to kill any of them.

At the inner wall, we paused once more, surveying the premises. "Can you teleport us in any closer now?" Kaen asked me in a hushed whisper.

I shook my head. "I think I only have the power for one more . . . and I want to save that for a sticky situation."

"You're expecting one?"

I gave him a look.

He grinned. "I'm kidding. I always expect trouble when you're involved."

Climbing down and to our left led us out to a catwalk that could normally only be accessed via a staircase inside the nearest spire. Fortunately, Kaen was a daredevil and I had my mysterious strength to boost my confidence. We dashed in a low crouch across the catwalk to the first of the great towers of the Inner Citadel. The library we had visited before was in the Outer Citadel. The Inner Citadel was gargantuan, far bigger than the Nytaean Palace. Inside this second wall, however, stood six towers with archways stretching between them and many important buildings beneath. And in the center of the city, rising far above all, surrounding the gushing geyser. . . .

"There it is," I murmured as we crouched near the tower.

"The Hall of Eternity," Kaen finished. "It's a long way off, though."

"Then let's get a move on." I led the way, leaping off the catwalk and landing on a building ten feet below and fifteen feet out. It was quite a jump, but I managed it with ease. "Can you make it, Kaen?" I asked.

He nodded, making a "back up" gesture, and took a running leap, rolling as he hit the roof tiles. He gave me a thumbs-up after a moment. "How's that? You think I'm weaker than you or something?"

I cocked a wry smile. Then we were off again, running over the rooftops and around the main courtyard. Around here, it seemed that no one really watched the roofs, although we still kept an eye on the guardsmen up on the walls. We hopped over a couple more gaps between roofs, climbed where necessary, and eventually made it to the Archlord's great palace, the Hall of Eternity. It was a massive, multi-tiered spire jutting up fifty paces into the air, surrounding the great Sky Funnel. Therein lay the Wellspring of Life, if everyone was telling the truth. Guarded closely by the Archlord.

And so we began to climb the palace. We made it over the first wall without too much trouble, helping each other out when necessary, and then found the best point to climb the next wall. The Hall of Eternity had a series of walls, each one higher than the last. The whole Hall formed a ring shape, leaving a large amount of space for the Inner Hall, which contained the Well.

Finally, we reached the top and looked out over a circular space nearly a hundred paces across, reaching far below to the . . . no, all the way *into* the ground, from the looks of it. It was a dizzying drop, causing Kaen and me to shy away as we saw it.

"Wow," Kaen breathed. "That's quite the pit." It was impossible to even see what lay at the bottom, or where the floor was. But rising out of it was a single stone pipe enclosing the gushing Sky Funnel.

Looking upwards, I gazed at the awe-inspiring geyser, which now roared with the sound of a thousand rushing rivers, so close were we to it. The very air seemed to vibrate with the intensity of it.

No wonder the Archlord had his whole palace walled off from it—the noise would be quite the distraction otherwise.

A soft *thud* of feet sounded from our left, and we spun, Kaen drawing his sword, only to see Rhidea alighting on the stonework of the wall.

"Hello, children," she said evenly. "You can put away your sword, boy."

He sheathed it, looking slightly abashed but still startled. "Next time, milady, perhaps you could give us advance warning of your joining us."

"Well, that would be no fun at all," she said with raised eyebrows. "Just call me your extra security. You'll probably need it." She surveyed the view, upwards and downwards. "Ah, but what a sight! I've never been here before, though my curiosity has nearly gotten the better of me on more than one occasion. But, well, I've never been this desperate. This might just pay off. I must say, it's surprising that the two of you were not caught already."

"Oh, come now, teacher," I muttered, rolling my eyes. Then I frowned. *It's a good thing the rush of that great geyser is so loud, otherwise we would all be heard by now.*

"So what is your plan now?" Rhidea asked.

"We . . . weren't sure," Kaen admitted. "We didn't plan this far ahead because we didn't know what this supposed Well even looked like."

The mage nodded, staring down into the black, abyssal hole. After a moment, she said, "Stay put."

Then she jumped off.

- Chapter 21 -

The Hall of Eternity

. . . As for my discovery, it was a few months back. It's still a working idea, nothing concrete. I was working with Thames and Jinna in the experiment room under the North Tower, and we discovered that the unstable state that a Reality mage can inflict upon an object can actually be supercharged using electricity. The result is . . . well, it just kind of explodes into a mess. But I think if we get it right . . . it could theoretically vaporize the entire (small) object without a trace. I know, I know, we'll be careful.

— Your friend, Eivael Kalceron

(Norvaen 14, 997—Waning Day)

"Wait! Lady Rhidea!" Kaen shouted.

"Shhh!" I put a hand over Kaen's mouth, pulling him back from the edge as I did so. "I'm sure she'll be fine. She's Rhidea."

The mage dove head-first through the air, crimson skirts and flaming hair rippling behind her. Then, as we watched, she spread her arms and slowed her descent greatly. Using some kind of magic— probably Wind Authority, with which I was not familiar—she glided in a circular pattern, slowly dropping out of our sight until her blurry form vanished in the darkness. No sound or visual signal came from below, until . . .

A light. A white flame. It illuminated the mage, who stood a dizzying distance below in the blackness, looking up at us. She waved a bug-sized hand, motioning us downward.

Kaen and I looked at each other with fear. Taking a big gulp, I gathered my resolve and jumped. I felt my stomach turn somersaults and my heart flutter, while my hair whipped upwards past me in the rush of air. My skirts billowed upwards, because I jumped feet first (I wasn't as crazy as my teacher). Looking down, I saw Rhidea and her flame rushing up to meet me, until suddenly my fall was abbreviated as gravity . . . reversed to stop me, finally allowing my feet to gently land on the ground.

Rhidea lowered a hand and my weight returned. "Well done, my pupil," she smirked. "You just did a very daring thing indeed. You're almost as crazy as I."

"Almost," I muttered. "What kind of Authority is that, anyway?"

"Earth. My strong suit."

I nodded, gazing around at the floor of the huge cistern. Black stones, shiny and moist, formed an interlocking pattern in the ground. Looking back up, I waved at Kaen and watched as he, too, leapt from the great height into the darkness. After a few moments, Rhidea reached up her hand and guided his fall as well, reversing the gravity around him and setting him gently on the ground.

He caught his balance as she dropped the field, and then shuddered. "Please don't make me do that ever again," he pleaded.

Rhidea smiled, and then tousled his hair. "No promises, boy."

Then we set off into the darkness. Rhidea's pale flame guided us, dancing in her hand and piercing the thick, wet darkness ahead. The air was cool and misty. Rhidea led us to the center, where we approached the great stack that contained the rushing water of the Sky Funnel. Placing a hand against it revealed the cold dampness and faint rumbling coming from within the black stones. The pipe was perhaps ten paces across, and I would have wagered the stones were thick, and of course magically reinforced.

There were no openings anywhere on it. We searched for doors, but it was entirely sealed shut.

Next, we searched around the outer perimeter of the pit. It turned out that there were large tunnels carved in the sides at intervals, some leading downward while others ended abruptly. "Ancient Ortheian design," Rhidea muttered upon seeing them. "We're below the palace here, so all of this was built far before the so-called Hall of Eternity."

"How did they even build it?" Kaen asked. "Any of this? Magic?"

Rhidea nodded. "Magic and hard labor. As for these tunnels . . . I cannot say."

"Please tell me we're not going to explore each and every one of those now," I protested.

Rhidea gave me a glance, face half lit by her artificial white light. "There appear to be six open tunnels leading down into the Palace's underbelly. We can at least look inside one or two and get an idea of what the inside is like. Back at the inn, we can formulate a plan based on what we find."

Kaen groaned. "All right, but we're sticking together."

We picked a random tunnel and started with it. Rhidea knelt at the tunnel's mouth and drew a few lines into the stone floor just outside the door using a finger. She stood back up, leaving a five-pointed star burnt into the stone.

"Is that some kind of . . ." Kaen began.

Rhidea gave him a flat look. "It's a mark. Nothing special, no spell. Just to mark which one we've been in, because they all look identical. Now this—" she pulled the end of a silver string from her dress "—is something a bit more magical."

"Wait . . . Rhidea, you have more magical artifacts you haven't told me about?" I asked, almost hurt.

The mage snorted. "You thought I'd divulge all my secrets? It's actually a pretty simple design." She dropped the end of the string onto the ground by the star, and it stayed as though held by an anchor. "You'll see. Now, let's go."

We turned and entered the yawning door. I summoned a hand flame to add to Rhidea's own white light. As we walked, the passageway began to slope downward into the ground. The illuminated stone walls and floors were carved from the same black stone, a type I didn't recognize. Every so often, however, we would see a vein of pure silver arching over the tunnel, like the roots of a giant tree, forming around the tunnel. Roots . . . I had read about how the bones of Mani were said to be made entirely of silver at a certain level. We must be deep underground right now.

I shivered, glancing down at the thin silver string that Rhidea was leaving behind us. As it dropped to the ground, it stayed put, always having just enough slack, just enough weight, so as to not pull from its line on the ground. The tunnel split two ways, and Rhidea led us to the left after a brief hesitation. The string did not pull with us or cinch against the corner, but stayed limply where the trail lay.

When we reached a dead end, Rhidea drew a mark on one wall and began to wind the string, careful to keep it away from our feet, and it retracted smoothly and then trailed behind us just as smoothly as we took the other path that had led to the right. As she had said, the silver string was a simple tool, and yet a wondrous piece of magical artisanship.

We wandered through an increasingly complex labyrinth of tunnels, picking our way carefully through each option and marking where we had been.

"So, how did you know it'd be a maze in here?" I asked at one point.

Rhidea grunted quietly. "Just a feeling. After all, there were multiple tunnels to start from, so I figured it would be a headache finding the Well in here. Who knows if they all lead to the Well or not? We may wander through this whole cavern and not find it."

Finally, Rhidea stopped. "We should head back for now. I will speak with Kath and Mydia about finding our way through these tunnels, and perhaps . . ." She trailed off and shook her head. "Well, we shall see." She cut the string and laid it down on the ground. "There. We can always get right back here."

We simply retraced our steps back out of the tunnels, following the glint of the silver string, until we reached the mouth of the tunnel.

"Now, what about that string?" Kaen asked. "Wouldn't somebody see it if they happened upon that tunnel while we're gone?"

"What string?" Rhidea said, waving a hand over the silver line; it vanished before our eyes. "It will reappear when we come back."

I nodded, impressed. The Wandering Mage always had another trick, didn't she?

- Chapter 22 -

Mysteries of the Labyrinth

In the year 890, High Mage Domon of Ti'Vaeth rose up against the king of Ti'Vaeth, Glenidar, and challenged him to a duel. There are many claims to his reasons, most of them having to do with injustice against his noble family, but historians agree that he cornered Glenidar politically in a way that he could not refuse. Glenidar was an accomplished mage in his own right, of the water branch, but was no match for the ruthless bearer of earth magic.

— From *Secrets of Mani*, by Sor the Lark

(Norvaen 14, 997—Waning Day)

Rhidea performed the last necessary teleport back, and a short while later we were down in the shadowy, twilit streets of Ti'Vaeth. She looked exhausted at that point, having used up most of her own power in addition to the artifact, and we practically had to drag her back to the Sleepy Dragon.

We all slept well that night. Surprisingly, as exhausted as I was, I had no dreams of White.

(Norvaen 15, 997—Waning Day)

The next morning was a groggy one for me. Even Rhidea slept in late. Coaction took a lot out of a mage, so both Rhidea and I were drained bodily and mentally from the previous day's exertion. She looked like a walking nightmare, hair a mess and eyes dark and ringed. "Hello, children . . . good morning," she moaned, closing her eyes briefly and then reopening them. "Oh, I need more sleep after that."

Mydia and the others had no idea what had transpired the previous night, so we gave them a rough report of our exploits in the enemy territory of the Inner Citadel and the tunnels that twisted below the Hall of Eternity, a maze that guarded the Wellspring of Life. The queen was, of course, very worried, but also jealous that she had missed out on "so much fun!" She could never make up her mind how to feel about a thing, of course.

That day, we constructed our plan. Rhidea called everyone together and declared that we knew enough to go on. This was mostly due to the fact that we had already found the Well, or rather, had gotten close . . . so we had something to go on. The issues we needed to address were as follows:

- How to get into the tunnels above the Wellspring again.
- How to distract the Archlord's men, and hopefully the Archlord as well, to divert their attention from our actual doings.
- How to find our way through the tunnels.
- How to get inside the Well (It was said to be sealed with an ancient seal).
- What to do while inside.

So we chipped away at all these points, brainstorming ideas. We all agreed that whatever seal was on the Well must be broken, no matter what it took. The problem was . . . how?

We decided to come back to that one later. Rhidea seemed confident enough that brute force would work if all else failed. The distraction was a big one we needed to focus on. We wouldn't be so lucky with avoiding attention twice. The Wellspring itself would be heavily guarded, and we needed something to occupy the forces of the Archlord.

Finding our way through the tunnels would really just be a mat-ter of time. With a bit of magic and a reasonably intelligent plan—and of course the power of sticking together—we would get through.

Finally, we had a strategy outlined. We would go back tomor-row. We would execute the plan much like the coup at Nytaea. Disguise, distract, break in, extract. Hopefully, things went a bit smoother. There would be no taking over the government here. No indeed, we could not handle Ti'Vaeth like that. Our only purpose was to get inside the Well and find out what was going on—what the Archlord was hiding. The man himself said he didn't care, so . . . we did, and we were going to get to the bottom of it.

Kaen, Mydia and the two soldiers were to handle the distraction. (Kaen was willing to take care of Mydia after some coaxing from me, but he didn't like it.)

Rhidea, Kath and I would go for the Well. But we had a backup plan. We would go the same exact way as before, but if we couldn't end up getting to it, we would extract and go in through the palace. That was, of course, only a last resort, because going through the Hall of Eternity would be very dangerous. And without being seen . . . next to impossible. It would not be a silent mission in that case.

My team would use Mydia's illusions, nearly-full shadows and as little magic as possible to get from the inn to the inner sanctum of the Hall of Eternity. I hoped Kaen and the others would be all right, and that he wouldn't be . . . well, Kaen. Reckless was his middle name, after all. He was supposed to start the distractions after we would already be inside the tunnels above the Well. That way we had time. But he was intelligent, and we had a good . . . well, okay, a decent plan.

We had already tried to sneak into the Citadel, of course, but that was Kaen and I, without Rhidea's aid. This time, we would use

Rhidea's superior Authority to get in much quicker.

(Norvaen 15, 997—Sunset)
We set off in the early morning hours. The night was dark, and the sun was beginning to set, so we had excellent cover. Sure, the guardsmen had torches everywhere, but what good were torches when the intruders had magic? No one expected a faithful mage soldier or a rogue mage and student to be trying to get in . . . well, actually, they probably did. It made me a bit uneasy, how low the security appeared to be.

We made it past the first Citadel wall with ease, Rhidea using her Earth Authority to help us climb it, and proceeded onward, across the courtyard and alleys and over fancy gabled roofs of important government buildings, heading toward the second wall. We climbed this one with a mix of my natural aptitude for the thing and Rhidea's gravity Authority, and then we were in the Inner Citadel.

Here, Rhidea warped us straight up to the top of the Hall of Eternity. We gazed down once more upon the gaping hole that went straight down to the stone floor some two hundred feet below. Rhidea leapt first, and Kath and I followed after. Neither one of us had the Authority in earth magic to do as Rhidea did, so she stopped our fall for us. It was a very unnerving feeling to have her do it, but what a miraculous ability. . . . Not for the first time, I was grateful to have such a powerful mage on my side.

We then searched for a doorway. "Remember," Rhidea said to us now, "This time, we will go in separately. Kath, you already know spells of guidance. Lyn, I will set a tracking spell on you and then we will enter the caves." She set the guiding spell on me, which would apparently lead me toward the others no matter where I went, and then we found the closest three cavern entrances, marking them and then entering. We left the one we had explored the previous night with the invisible string, deciding to come back to it if all the others returned no results.

It was just as unsettling a place as before, dimly lit by eerie, sporadic torchlight from the ceiling. I had a flame in hand (I was good with flames, remember?) to light my way, so I didn't mind. But I was glad for Rhidea's spell, without which I would never have entered such a place. *Kaen should be causing an uproar right about now. . . .* Hopefully, we found the actual Well in time.

The passage twisted and turned in front of me, never still, until my sense of direction was completely lost. All I could tell was that I was going progressively downward. I hummed old lullabies to myself as I went. Kaen wasn't here to complain about how off-pitch I was.

A shudder went forth from below me, and I heard a loud screech a moment later. A shiver ran down my spine in reply to this.

I felt another shudder, this time from deeper below, and a long, low moaning sound echoed forth from down the tunnel, making my arm hairs stand on end. "What in the . . . ?" Perhaps it was the door to the Well. I couldn't know, so I just proceeded further in.

In a moment, however, I felt a tug on the invisible string of magic that tied me back to the entrance. Someone had found the door. Whew. That saved me from having to find out what was down this tunnel. I turned around and hurriedly retraced my steps. It was much quicker to go back out via a single path than to wander about downward, and so in five minutes' time I found myself at the entrance, looking Rhidea in the face. Kath was by her side. "Did you find it?" I asked.

Kath nodded.

"Indeed," Rhidea confirmed. "Kath stumbled upon it on his second tunnel. Let us make haste!"

I glanced up briefly before ducking inside the cave, listening to the distant sound of horns and alarms. Hopefully, Kaen and Mydia were safe.

Then I followed Rhidea and the mage soldier underground. Our path twisted and turned along with the tunnels as Kath led us back along his route. It was only a few minutes before he said, "Here it is." At the end of the tunnel, the tunnel walls became more of a hallway, rough stone transitioning into stonework lining walls and floors. We ascended a flight of stairs that curved sharply to the right, and then were faced with a door of glimmering silver. It emanated a cold . . . energy. *This is it.*

Kath stepped aside to let Rhidea approach the silver door. She put a hand on it and concentrated, then stopped and listened.

I spun, looking the other way. "That's the guards."

Rhidea transferred energy into the door and it rumbled and began to open as the footsteps and shouting grew louder. And then I recognized the voices. It was our friends . . . probably being chased.

The door slowly continued to rise. Kaen and his three companions burst through the corridor and into sight at the bottom of the stairs, just as the door was opening wide enough to slip under.

"Hurry, hurry!" cried Mydia, lifting her skirts as she dashed to keep up with the men. "They're close on our tail!"

Rhidea stopped us, stepping in first and looking down into the darkness. "I'll go first." The mage ducked inside, palm flame glimmering, and then waved us inside. "Come on, quickly."

I was one of the last to enter. I kept looking backward, until I saw the torchlight of the guardsmen coming. They were going to catch us. "Rhidea!" I shouted. "They've already caught up to us!"

"It's all right," she answered, "we can—" She cut off as her flame went out.

- Chapter 23 -

Tales of the Exile

The fount of water that spurts from the Wellspring is different from the actual well from which the magic comes. It is hidden deep below Ti'Vaeth. Unless the depths of the Wellspring are uncovered once more and the Archlord allows scholars to see inside of it, to see what is actually in that ancient placed whence magic bloomed . . . we may never know its true secrets.
— From *Secrets of Mani,* by Sor the Lark

(Norvaen 15, 997—Sunset)

"Hellsbreath!" Rhidea cursed. "The Well is canceling my Authority."

Mydia, Kath and the soldiers ducked inside, and I jumped through the doorway right after Kaen (who was the only one with an actual torch aside from Ruel), as the door began to shut upon itself. The soldiers who had caught up first desperately chased us inside, until the door shut too far for any more to get in. I tried to force them off, kicking the first guard and knocking him back into his friends. There was at least a half dozen of them, each armored and outfitted with swords, spears and crossbows.

As I retreated down the stairs, however, I began to feel my strength leaving me. Not my innate bodily strength, but that surging energy that enabled me to perform superhuman feats and enhanced my reflexes and speed. I felt . . . tired. *Is this how normal people feel all the time?* Gritting my teeth, I turned and hurried after the others. "Kaen," I gasped as I caught up to him. "My abilities are vanishing in here, just like my magic."

"Well, then we'll just have to fight our way out somehow. 'Bout time we got to save you magi the old-fashioned way."

We took the stairs as fast as possible. Rhidea and the torch-bearers led the way, a whole floor below us, the torchlight flickering on the walls around us. Behind me, I heard mumbles of uncertainty, followed by the sound of shouting and soldiers' boots on stone as they charged in after us. "After the desecrators!" bellowed one of them.

Desecrators. Perhaps that was what we were. But we had to know what was down here. We had to find the secret of the magic of our world, lest it vanish out of our hands forever. Turning my head as I went, I said, "We need to be here! Just leave us in peace."

"Not if the Archlord has anything to say about it." The lead soldier stopped and aimed his crossbow at us.

"Kaen, get down!" I yanked him down as I ducked, and the bolt scraped the wall above and behind my head.

The man cursed and pointed toward the door at the top of the stairs. "You, guard the door! Remember your orders!"

I glanced up as the rear guard stood his place by the door. It closed completely, sending a heavy *thump* reverberating through the tall chamber and echoing downward. Now we were trapped, with no magic to open up the door again.

"You'll die in here one way or the other," said the captain. "We all will. We are trained to follow our orders to the letter, whether it costs us or not."

"He's lying," Kaen muttered.

"Forget about it, Lyn!" came Rhidea's voice from below. "Just hurry."

I followed Kaen down the steps toward the others below, dodging a couple more crossbow bolts from those guards who had a clear shot. I looked back angrily. "Give up, why don't you! What do you all gain from hunting us further?”

"That is not for us to know," answered the leader. "But none are allowed to intrude upon the Well except for the Archlord himself and his personal retinue."

"And that makes you all special?"

"No," the man called back after a short pause. "That is why we will die here as well."

At this point, Kaen growled in front of me, stopped, and pushed me along in front of him. "I'll teach him a lesson."

"Kaen!" After a brief hesitation, I turned around, backing down only a couple of steps as I watched what would happen. What worried me was that another guard farther up had a crossbow as well . . . I hesitated, still backing down the stairs.

Kaen rushed the lead guardsman, torch in left hand and sword in right, swiping the crossbow from his hands with his sword blade—it tumbled down to clang against the stairs below, and seemed to never stop falling—even as the man went to draw his own shortsword. "Defend yourself!"

The man kicked at Kaen, forcing him to hop back two stairs to avoid his foot, and snapped his fingers, signaling the rearguard to shoot a bolt at him.

"No!" I saw it coming and rushed up to grab my friend, yanking him back just in time to avoid fire.

"Thanks," he muttered.

I let him go. Then I reached down to pull out one of two belt knives—I kept two, with a dagger in each boot and a fifth strapped to my thigh—and flicked it at the man with the crossbow still in hand. I missed both the crossbow and his hand, as I had never been a terribly good knife shot, but it did the trick. He cursed and dropped the weapon, grabbing at the new puncture wound in his chest. I grimaced, realizing it had been a hair's breadth from a fatal shot.

Kaen fought with the captain, dancing up and down the stairs, their swords flinging sparks in the darkness as they rang steel on steel. The other four guardsmen had no access to the fight, and were stuck uselessly in the middle. Kaen seemed to have the advantage in skill and weaponry, but his opponent had the high ground, a distinct advantage in itself. "Not going to just give up, huh?" Kaen taunted.

"Not this easily," the man grunted. He kicked again, causing Kaen to fall back, and then swung horizontally at his head.

Kaen blocked the attack. "Then I guess it's the hard way."

I made sure to stay back, so as not to trip Kaen or get in his way. His duel with the guardsman seemed surprisingly even-matched, and I was nervous over who would win. I glanced downward, seeing Mydia and the others two floors below (if one called a full circle of stairs a floor).

"Come on, Kaen." I retreated down the steps, and he backed up after me, still crossing swords with his opponent. Eventually, he turned and ran after me, and we made for the rest of the crew, dashing as fast as our legs would take us.

"Hey!" yelled the guard captain. "We weren't finished! Come back here!" And they gave chase.

"Why must they insist on trying to kill us?" Kaen half-growled, half-sighed. "Such idiotic loyalty."

"Well, they're worth their pay, I suppose," I replied. "At least we got their crossbows away from them."

I said this no sooner than a dagger came out of the darkness above and grazed my leathern leggings. "Ugh, would you *stop* that?" I shouted. I turned and rushed back up the stairs toward the guards.

"It's that kicking girl again," muttered one of the guardsmen, presumably the one I had previously kicked.

Drawing my dagger with my left hand, sword in right, I squared off against the same captain Kaen had fought. "Tell your men to back down," I said, "or else."

He cocked his head to the side. "Oh yeah? That all you've got, 'or else?'"

I rolled my eyes. "It's getting old."

"Well, I ordinarily don't like to fight women, but seeing as how I have orders to kill you all anyway, I suppose I'm obliged to." He swung his sword at me.

I evaded and swiped my long blade at him. "What's your name, Captain?"

"Corporal." He parried and jabbed at my chest.

"Captain Corporal." I deflected with my sword and jabbed with my knife.

Annoyance flashed across his face. "Corporal Harold." He caught my dagger with his sword hilt and swept a boot at my legs.

"Well, Harold, you're quite good with a blade."

He snorted. "You're a chatty one. I don't take swordsmanship compliments from women. That'd be like—" He took another swipe at my defenses "—taking handwriting tips from a milkmaid."

I paused briefly, almost allowing myself to be caught off-guard. "What a ridiculous thing to say."

"She's a bit better with a sword than a milkmaid," Kaen called from below. "I taught her myself." There was a note of pride in his voice.

Harold snorted once more. "I see that, boy. I, for one, don't know many milkmaids. Now, shut up. I'm trying to focus."

I managed to keep up with Corporal Harold just barely, thanks to my natural agility, but I really missed my extra physical enhancements. One never knew what one had until it was gone, and right now was that moment. "Look," I grunted, my arms aching, "Can't we just resolve this peacefully?"

"Afraid not." He took advantage of a stumble that I made and rammed my sword with his as my arm was held over the edge. My sword flew out of my hand to clang against the opposite side of the shaft, eliciting a cry from below, and I staggered on the edge before falling after my sword.

"Agh! Kaen, help!" I cried, but there was no time. I tumbled from the stairs head-first. I couldn't reach the other side. I heard Kaen yell my name as I fell, amidst the rushing of air past my ears, and then a shriek from Mydia. Flights of stairs whished past me, one after another. I saw them rushing by as I looked upwards, my back toward the pit below.

At the bottom, I hit a pool of water with a painful crack, squeezing my eyes shut as I plunged toward the bottom. Dazed but still awake, I blew bubbles out of my mouth as I struggled to make my way up to the surface, but it was no use. I continued to sink despite my efforts, my momentum and weight dragging me down, until my feet touched the gooey bottom of the pool. Frantically, I kicked off the bottom with all the strength I had left, propelling myself upward until my hands grasped the knobby stone of the side and I was able to claw my way to the surface.

I gasped air into my lungs, blinking water and dirt out of my eyes and clutching the stone floor that surrounded the pool for dear life. Pain arced through my back, the sting of hitting a surface of water at such a speed. I knew I was lucky to be alive. I peered into the darkness around me, but I couldn't see much of anything. Shakily, I pulled myself out of the water, cringing at my stinging skin and bruised muscles.

"Never want to do that again . . ." I breathed. Realizing that the others were calling out in desperation, I craned my neck upwards and shouted, "I'm—I'm all right! Rhidea? Mydia?"

"Lyn!" Mydia's voice came from not too far up the stairs. I could see the torchlight where they were. "We'll be there in a minute! Kaen's still holding the guards back. Well, I think they're . . ." Whatever she said after that was lost to me.

I sat down and put my back against a large pillar, exhaling in relief. Leaning my head back, I took a few breaths and tried to will away the pain. My stomach was all messed up as well, abdominal muscles clenched tightly. I wasn't sure how far I'd fallen, but it must have been at least thirty paces. I knew that if I weren't in this strange well, my inherent physical boons would have helped to guard me, but everything came now just as it did for anyone else. . . .

It hurt to be human.

Mydia, Kath, and the others arrived shortly after, their torches illuminating my surroundings. Looking up, I forced a smile and called, "It was a long fall, but this pool saved me. I'll . . . be fine."

Rhidea looked at the black pool, which measured about ten paces across. Now that I could see the room clearly, I realized that this bottom section was, contradictorily, much larger than the limited diameter of the stairway shaft. In fact, the whole well must fan out as it went down. . . . Such a curious place. "That water . . ." Rhidea said. "This must be it. The Well."

"This?" Mydia mumbled. "This little puddle? What's . . . wrong with it?"

It was only once she mentioned it that I saw the black goop splattered about on the floor, oozing from cracks in the stones, dripping into the pool . . . dark slime covered the ornate pillars and seemed to coat the far circular wall of the room as well. It was hard to tell in the dim light. The air smelled dank and foul.

"It's Domon," Rhidea said. "I know it. He has been tampering with the Well off and on, and I believe that it is how he has created his own Dark Magic."

"Dark Magic . . ." I muttered. I had heard her speak of it before, and I was pretty sure that Lord Kalceron had used the very same type of magic back in the Nytaean Palace, while fighting Rhidea.

Just then, Kaen came down the stairs, leading Harold and the other soldiers. "I think I convinced them to come peacefully," he said.

Kaen actually used . . . diplomacy?

"You!" I shouted, starting toward the corporal. But my bruises screamed in agony, and Rhidea grabbed my arm. "Sorry," I mumbled in embarrassment.

"I didn't exactly mean to . . ." Harold began.

"Oh, save it. Kaen, bring your torches over here."

With the extra light, we began to inspect the nearest pillars and then the wall behind them. There were eight pillars in all, each about double the thickness of my waist and reaching twelve feet to the sloped ceiling above. The stairs landed between two of the pillars, the stone merging with the floor and wall, cutting off the full circle of the bottom chamber. The pillars were ornately carved with strange creatures, fruits and flowers, delicate yet exuding a sense of power—but covered in dried rivulets of black goop and marred by stains. The perimeter of the wall seemed to be all one large, tiled mosaic, also half covered in the same goopy stains.

"We'll clean it off," Rhidea said, less a suggestion and more a command. "Those not bearing torches, use your swords to clean all this mess off. We need to see this mural."

We hacked and peeled the goop off of the mural. Then we used spare pieces of our own clothing for rags, dipping them in water and scrubbing the mural as the Wandering Mage said. I was reminded as I cleaned of my time spent in Lord Kalceron's employ as a maid . . . An almost dreamlike time in my life, looking back on it now, and one that I would never forget. Within a quarter of an hour we had cleared, if not completely cleaned, the entire span of the mosaic.

The mural had a long line of ornate letters engraved along the bottom, which Rhidea identified as High Legaleian. She began trying to decipher the writing, and then gave up with a huff. "In a bit. Let us focus on the picture first." The mosaic was divided at the point where the stairs reached the floor of the chamber, giving an obvious beginning and ending point. Starting at the far left, we gathered around as Rhidea pored over the pictographic story on the wall, musing as she went.

The artwork looked old, but not ancient as I expected—not prehistoric. It could have been painted by a famous artist of the last century. Well, maybe the last few centuries. It told a sweeping tale starting with a round world—mostly blue, which I found very odd— amidst a bed of stars, with golden rays shining from the sun, and a smaller world . . . orbiting it? This one was yellow. Presumably, the blue world was Gaea, but we couldn't say for the other. From this yellow world, a silver dragon came, whose meaning we could only guess at, and a war ensued. Men fought with the dragon, and then with fellow men.

Amidst the confused mutterings and contemplative musings of our group, Kaen gave a snort. "Imagine that: humans fighting each other."

Alongside many of the pictograms, some underneath or just above, ran small lines of script completely different from the sweep- ing, curly High Legaleian script, more jagged with a certain intense geometry to it. Presumably, it was a Gaean language. And . . . the writing felt familiar to me. Almost.

"Rhidea, you're sure these two languages aren't telling the same story?" Mydia asked.

The High Mage shook her head. "It could be, but I doubt it. They seem to be names, or possibly descriptions, while the Legaleian letters at the bottom spell out a continuous message."

I frowned, trying to recall any meaning I could from the other-worldly captions accompanying the pictures. Nothing. If there was any true recognition in my memory, it was locked deep.

Continuing on in the mural, a group of people, likely magi, seemingly used their powers to . . . create a world? This one was silver, obviously Mani. They were either making a new one, or changing an existing world to support life, which would match up with our stories of the Wellspring being brought to Mani, creating life on our world. There was an indication of a mass exodus of people from the large, blue world to this new silver one, depicting a magical bridge of sorts. A few more images illustrated the pilgrims' journey across this new world, fighting with monsters and discovering what seemed to be the power of Silver magic.

Lastly, it seemed to show a sort of religious reverence for the Wellspring. The people had kept it safe, but not hidden. Presumably, that lasted up until or near Domon's rise to power. Rhidea could not say. As interesting as the mural was, we could do little more than theorize on the meaning of the various parts without being able to read both scripts printed on it.

"The great . . . exile," Rhidea read slowly, tracing the bottom words with a slender finger. Her mouth moved silently as she walked the length of the mural over again, translating the High Legaleian at an agonizing rate. Finally, she stopped, looking as though running the entire message through her head to discern its meaning.

"What does it *say*, Rhidea?" Mydia asked impatiently.

"It says . . . 'The Great Exile. May it never be necessary again.' The rest appears to be a poem of some sort:

> *"'To take the bait a world away,*
> *A Wellspring hid amongst the grey.*
> *We wait, remember, for the day,*
> *For one millennium we stay.'"*

As she finished, I felt that same prickling sense of familiarity, as though I should recall something within the poem. Or perhaps it was just that feeling of disquiet.

"That . . . is certainly foreboding," Mydia said quietly. "A millennium? It's the year 997."

"And, uh, the whole 'bait' thing," Kaen pointed out. "Don't like that. What would they have been trying to bait, that dragon?"

"Don't remember ever seeing any silver dragons here, though," Inno pointed out.

Rhidea turned to me with a pensive expression. "Lyn, you don't happen to . . . recognize anything about this artwork, do you? Or the Gaean writing?"

My eyes flicked nervously from side to side. "Why are you asking me?"

She sighed impatiently. "That should be obvious, child."

"I . . . no, I don't." I didn't mention the strange feeling I'd had, however. "I don't know if we'll be able to figure anything else out right now."

A cough came from my left, and I turned to see Corporal Harold. "The, um, the young lady is right," he said. "There's nothing more to gain from staring at the mosaic, as fascinating as it may be."

"Well," said Rhidea with a tone of resignation and annoyance, "there is one who can certainly answer our questions: the Archlord. And he has a *lot* of answering to do. We need to find a way out of here."

"Actually," the Corporal said slowly, "there might be a way."

- Chapter 24 -

Domon

*Soon after Domon took his throne, he named himself Archlord
and began pressuring the surrounding city-states of Kystrea to
join with him in uniting all of Kystrea. The first few joined
thinking that they could get something out of the arrangement
themselves, before realizing that he wanted an unequal share of
the power. Domon was cunning, and pitted one king against
another to eventually force them all into submission. Thus
began the Joining Wars.*
— From *Secrets of Mani*, by Sor the Lark

(Norvaen 15, 997—Sunset)

We worked everything out in the end. Mydia came up with the plan,
in fact. It involved willing surrender and a bit of cooperation on the
part of the very guardsmen who had chased us down and tried to
capture us.

First, we had to escape the Well chamber. We managed to force
the door open with the help of the outside guardsmen, who heard us
banging on it. Afterward, Harold and his men dragged us through the
underbelly of the Hall of Eternity, up the many levels of the palace,
and back to their superiors, who then took us straight to the
Archlord himself. What better way to see our beloved emperor than
to allow ourselves to be captured?

The guardsmen led us, hands bound and mouths gagged with
magic-dampeners, all the way up through the main floors of the Hall
of Eternity, until we came to Domon's personal tower. The doors to
his room at the top were of solid stone, and swung inward on magic

automation as soon as the guards announced themselves and Domon's deep voice came from inside, bidding them to bring us in.

Inside, the circular room was lavish and trimmed with gold all around. Numerous lamps shone, casting light from multiple different angles. Domon himself sat on a gilded seat with a high back embedded with emeralds and amethysts. He sat with back straight and arms crossed, golden hair slicked back to trail down his neck. He was of average weight and just above average height, and yet he cut an imposing figure on his throne. His eyes were hard and unyielding.

"So, you brought the guests . . ." he muttered, rubbing the well-trimmed facial hair on his chin. He smiled as his eyes lit upon Rhidea, as though she hadn't been standing front and center already. "Ah, there's an old face. I wonder, do we know each other, sweetheart?"

She said nothing, but only glowered with head bowed. I knew it was a glower, even though her expression was not easy to make out at that angle.

"My Lord, we found them by the well," Harold explained, "We waited for them to enter and then apprehended them while their magic was down." There was a strong hint of pride in his voice. He really wasn't a bad actor.

"Hmm. Yes, I see." He waved a hand at the guardsmen. "You may leave us now. I'm not worried about the intruders."

"But Milord!"

"That is an order, corporal. Stand by outside the door with your men."

The guardsmen left, led by the corporal.

"Now." The Archlord clapped his hands. "What to do with my little intruders . . . ? We'll start with you, High Mage." He pointed at Rhidea. "I knew you would be back, yet somehow you managed to slip inside the Hall of Eternity without any of my men knowing. What all did you find down there, hmm? Besides a sudden severance of your Authority?"

The Wandering Mage looked up at him, still silent, for the magic dampener also prevented our speech.

Kaen, Mydia and the Queensguard stood to our sides. The tension in the air seemed palpable as Rhidea stared down the ruler of Kystrea, who gazed back imperiously from his high-backed seat. Time seemed to hang in the air as we waited.

Domon finally sighed. "Speak." He waved a hand dismissively, and the magic dampener disintegrated and fell from her mouth.

Rhidea breathed in and said, "We found . . . secrets, which you have been keeping hidden."

"Most of which are meant to be kept hidden down there," Domon said. "Do you think that Well was meant to be revealed to the world?" He spread his hands in a decidedly imperious gesture. A small smile crept to his lips, indicating, *You didn't learn anything anyway.*

"We saw enough that it needs to be revealed," replied Rhidea. "The corruption, the mural. I ask that you come clean and tell us what you've been doing."

"Oh? You must have figured me out. Why, you *clever* little pup." I couldn't tell how serious the Archlord was being. "I assume you speak of the Dark Magic I have created. My finest achievement, I must say . . ."

Surprisingly, he continued, "You really wish to know what I've been working on here in Ti'Vaeth? Why, I've a plethora of reasons to want the ultimate power, but I am no narrow-sighted fool like Kalceron was. I only worked with him because he was useful to me. Along with a few other tools.

"The Umbra Council," Rhidea said flatly. "I know all about it."

Domon raised his eyebrows, sitting up slightly straighter in his throne. "Is that so? We have been quite secretive, but of course the great Wandering Mage would have sniffed out such a thing. We seek a higher goal than you know—higher than you can imagine. We seek a new world. To unite all of Mani with the strength to stand against another, greater force."

Rhidea seemed to hesitate. I didn't say anything either, waiting for him to elaborate more.

Mydia spoke up now. "You're talking about Gaea?"

The Archlord eyed her with a small, lopsided smile. "Perhaps. So you do know a bit." Then his face grew grim. "I am not the selfish tyrant you think I am. I am not Edrius Kalceron, a ruler consumed by his own lust for money and power. I seek to *save* this world."

"Save it, Domon?" Rhidea asked. "Or break it?"

The Archlord scowled, and then dipped his head. "I am aware of the cost. I have drawn from the same Wellspring whence comes all the magic in Mani, twisting it into something else, something darker. The black substance in the Well chamber is a by-product of that. The world will not break, but the magic that sustains it . . . who is to say? But you must understand that there is a force out there that wants to crush us, and I will not allow that to happen. They *will* come, and I *will* be ready."

I frowned. "But—"

Rhidea cut me off with a raised hand.

Domon stood up, prompting us to take a step or two backward. "I do not have time for this," he said. "This talk is pointless. Perhaps if you wish to prove yourselves correct, you should show your determination through a test of strength. Just like heroes in an old tale; I'd be more than happy to play the villain." He held out his hands, gathering small black clouds between them with electricity like miniature lightning running between both hands. I flinched at the display.

"Wait," Rhidea told us, putting out her hands to either side in a warding gesture. "Domon, we really cannot talk this through?"

"We can. I'm simply bored with that. We shan't get anywhere."

"Then I have a proposition."

He frowned. "I am not joking, mage. You cannot defeat me."

"No, not a duel of Authority. I'm thinking of a simple test of strength, as you said. But against her." She pointed to me, and I felt a sinking feeling in my chest. At the same time, it was a feeling of hope—anything was better than getting zapped to dust by the Archlord's Dark Magic.

Domon sized me up with a dark but subtly curious look. "What . . . kind of test?"

"An arm-wrestling match," Rhidea said brightly.

The Archlord froze, bewilderment in his eyes. But I could tell he was considering it, processing why someone like Rhidea would ask such a seemingly silly request. He didn't drop his Authority, but he didn't act, either.

"You're quite serious?" he asked Rhidea, who nodded. Then he turned his gaze on me. "Well, consider me sufficiently intrigued." He dropped his lightning spell, which sparked and disappeared, and stepped down from where his throne sat, down to our level. He came directly in front of Rhidea, looking her in the eye, and I saw that they were nearly head for head. He was an inch or so taller. "And what if I win?" he asked. "I'm sure you're willing to bet something on this, no?"

"If you win, we shall turn around and walk straight out of Ti'Vaeth. We shall leave you alone, and you can commence your attack on Nytaea or whatever you wish."

Domon raised his eyebrows again. "Well, well. I believe those things are mine to give or take anyway, but you know what? Just to make things interesting. . . ." He looked at me with a predatory stare. "I accept. And in return, if the girl wins, then . . . I'd do fairly anything you asked. I will call off the attack and draw up an alliance with you."

I had to work to keep from gaping. Had he just said what I thought? Was this man bipolar? I glanced at the others, and they seemed just as shocked. Was he really that confidant? Surely he knew that Rhidea had reasons for picking me as our champion. Did he somehow suspect why?

Within a few minutes, the Archlord had a table readied by his servants, solid and just the right width, and we sat one on each side. He looked a bit more regal—you know, emperor-like—than me, but he didn't intimidate me. Not this time. We had decided that magic was allowed, so long as it did not directly affect the opponent or anyone else in the room. I didn't know any Coaction that could help me win an arm-wrestling match, so this basically just meant that he could use whatever he wanted to crush me.

And yet I didn't think he wanted to simply crush me and exult in beating a teenaged girl . . . I got the impression that he was testing me. Might Domon actually have an inkling of who I was? I put the thought out of my head. All in time, as Rhidea would say.

One of Domon's retainers, who was overseeing the match, said, "Begin," and we did so. I shoved as hard as my bodily strength would allow, but he already had some . . . earth magic? Yes, earth magic in place to disallow me to push him. Gravity magic, much like Rhidea used. It made sense. This pull from his magic made sure my hand barely moved his, though my squeezing probably hurt his hand. I made sure not to just put all my strength into grip.

Instead, I twisted my wrist, getting my hand into a higher, more dominant position with more leverage. Simultaneously, I pulled with my biceps, drawing his hand toward my shoulder, also giving myself more leverage. I could see intense concentration on his face, but also a look of shock.

I smiled slightly, and then I broke the barrier that held my strength and tapped into that superhuman reserve hidden deep inside. With a growl, I forced his hand backward, fighting against the Authority he was using to fight me. And I was winning. His face screwed up in effort, disbelief and rage, but I brought his hand down to the table with a last cry and a burst of strength. I tried not to crush it *too* much, but he still gasped in pain.

Domon retracted his hand immediately, shaking it and rubbing at his wrist. "You . . . you *beat* me. And I was using Authority." The way he said the word clearly implied that 'supreme' should have preceded it. He narrowed his eyes at me, face still a red mask of pain and exertion. Then he turned his gaze on Rhidea. "I knew you were awfully cocky, witch." His eyes flicked back to me. "You win, girl. How did you do it?"

I tried to keep my face as neutral as possible. "I'll tell you that . . ."

"When you tell us what you did to the Wellspring," Rhidea finished, triumph clear on her face.

Domon sat back on his stool with a growl and a glare. He crossed his lordly arms and stared down toward his stomach. His right index finger tapped rapidly on his opposite elbow, until at last he looked up, face having cleared a bit. "Very well; come with me."

- Chapter 25 -

The Treaty

Lastly of all went Nytaea, home of the mage soldiers. They had the strongest military of all other states, and did not take kindly to their freedom being taken. But they were no match for the combined might of the other twelve states joined together. Finally, after the last of the Joining Wars, Nytaea came under control of Archlord Domon and he set up Edrius Kalceron as her ruler. Satisfied, Domon called an end to his economic and military wars and began setting his new empire in order. Truth be told, he has not been a harsh emperor since. It remains unclear why Domon wanted all of Kystrea so badly. . . .
— From *Secrets of Mani*, by Sor the Lark

(Norvaen 15, 997—Sunset)

A short time later, Kaen, Rhidea, Mydia and I sat in one of the Archlord's private audience rooms, seated around a half-round table. Two imperial guards stood watch outside, along with Inno, Ruel and Kath. It wasn't that we didn't trust those three, they just weren't fully a part of our mission and we wanted Domon to feel like he could have a private discussion with us.

Domon sat regally but with a somewhat . . . resigned air. His head was slightly bowed, clasped hands clenched a little too much. His chair was on the flat side of the table, its back away from the door, and it was tall and just that little bit grander than ours. That little bit made all the difference sometimes, but not today.

"So, as promised," he said tiredly, "I'll give you the whole story. But where to begin? One hundred years ago, I forged this empire of

Kystrea under one banner. Thirteen, and yet one. The other warlords I made rulers of the other twelve city-states, while I remained in absolute control of Ti'Vaeth and its surrounding lands.

"Then I began to search for the key to Authority. For nine hundred years, our people had possessed magic, yet we knew so little about it. Most of the ancient texts say that it was a gift to humankind by the gods of long ago, but a gift for what? And why? Who are these gods? At that point, the Wellspring was not such a well-guarded secret. Just forbidden. The water pouring forth from the Well was far stronger then, and possessed a thick, vibrant power." Domon sounded wistful as he said it. Then he continued:

"I forced my way into the Well, against all advice from advisors. There, I found a wealth of knowledge. The deeper I dove into it, the more I discovered. It appears you've seen the mural? The High Legaleian was easy, but eventually I was able to puzzle out some of the Gaean writing as well. There are also other snippets from ancient Legaleian writers left on the pillars.

"One thousand years ago, we came from a world called Gaea. This world, Mani, is not our home—it is the exile. An exile from something I still do not understand. But it had to do with the evil force depicted as a dragon, which came from the golden world—a "moon" as the pillar writings called it. It would seem that the living force we call Silver overtook this "moon" shortly before, or in preparation for, our exile here.

"The Wellspring was originally given by a powerful being, a god or gods, perhaps someone from Gaea. I know not, but it seems the Wellspring was transported from Gaea to Mani somehow, and it was what made life possible here on Mani. But its power has been waning ever since its arrival, a well-documented phenomenon that corresponds with the increasingly unbalanced birth rates of boys and girls.

"To summarize, we had two issues: our Wellspring was failing, and a force from another world posed a large, potentially existential threat to Mani. I gathered together a group of inner advisors over the last century. Edrius Kalceron was one of them, but . . . he was consumed in the end by his own greed. We gathered under one purpose—the salvation of Mani."

"The Umbra Council," I whispered. "That's what you were after?" Somehow, that didn't make them seem any better.

He nodded soberly. "We wanted to guard the secrets of Mani while also guarding Mani itself from this threat."

"Of course," Rhidea said smoothly, taking my opportunity to respond. "And from there, Domon?"

The Archlord paused just long enough to convey his annoyance at being prompted. "Well, we plotted for years in the shadows, a coalition of rulers, few though there were of us. Meanwhile, I harnessed the power of the Well to create a Dark Magic that is far more potent than most of the natural forces of life here on Mani. Remember that, without magic, our world would have no life at all. Now, the power that our world does have was clearly limited, but we saw fit to make use of this limited power in order to better protect Mani from the coming threat."

"Which is?" Rhidea prompted with a hand motion. "Is there an actual monster coming to attack us? Are the Gaeans themselves going to invade? Is there a way for them to access this world directly?"

He pursed his lips. "The writings spoke of a malignant force from the other world that seeks to wipe us out. It seems our ancestors did something to anger this evil, and one day it will catch up to us. The ancient Legaleians wrote of a . . . doorway . . . on the other side of the world. A gate from our world to another, presumably Gaea."

"The . . . other side of the world?" Mydia repeated.

"Yes," said her teacher. "Far beyond the Sea of Emptiness." She leaned forward. "And this other world, Domon, what do you know of it?"

He grimaced. "Too little. I know our people originate from Gaea, but also that another people dwell there, possessing a power that we do not. Whether they and the evil that seeks to destroy us are one, I do not know, nor whether they possess magic or not, but they likely have the capacity to wipe us off the face of Mani. There are numerous materials such as iron mentioned in the old texts, ones that do not even exist on Mani, and given the pathetic amount of advancement the average Legaleian scholars attempt to make in our technology . . . I think it's safe to say that their technology and weaponry are far advanced beyond our own."

Rhidea furrowed her brow in thought, appearing displeased at his words. "You may be right. The question that remains is what to do about it? You seek salvation from within, while we seek to restore balance by making a voyage to Gaea to understand the problems facing Mani and create a solution."

"Indeed," said the Archlord. "Perhaps I was rash to not listen to you before now. But . . . there is something I must know first: is this girl is from Gaea?"

My breath caught briefly. I'd known it was coming, but there was nothing like that moment where your powerful enemy suddenly finds out your deepest secret—particularly one like that.

"That is . . . our going theory," Rhidea said slowly.

Domon squinted his eyes at me. "So, what are your powers like? Did you really fight my Authority with only brute strength? You, a mere twig barely grown?"

My face reddened slightly, not because what he said was an insult. Perhaps it was just the attention on me. "I did," I said in a strangled voice. Then I coughed and continued, "I was born this way. I'm . . . strong, at least stronger than I look, and . . . when I really need it, it's like I have a secret well of power that I can draw upon. It gives me incredible strength in return for great fatigue and hunger soon after."

"Fascinating. And when did you discover that you were different? Did you hide this from others as a girl?"

I nodded. "I've known since I was little. My hair is also normally white without dye or illusions, and it gives me away pretty quickly."

Domon's face showed surprise, indicating he hadn't thought that I might be wearing an illusion. But, evidently believing me, he didn't seek to remove it now.

"I found her in the Nytaean Palace," Rhidea explained. "It is a long story, but Lyn and her friend here had a personal goal, someone they wanted to rescue from the prisons. I helped them, and it spiraled out of hand. The rebellion happened that day, and it all went to chaos."

Well put, I thought to myself. No need to tell the Archlord exactly how big a hand we'd had in orchestrating it all.

Domon simply nodded, taking in this information. "So, you know my story and I know yours. Now is the part where we strike an accord, yes?"

Rhidea nodded, preparing to speak, but I interrupted:

"Wait. What about the poem?"

Rhidea and Domon both frowned at me, and I recited word-for-word the ancient poem inscribed below the mosaic:

> *'To take the bait a world away,*
> *A Wellspring hid amongst the grey.*
> *We wait, remember, for the day,*

For one millennium we stay.'

"If . . ." I swallowed. "If the bait has to do with these monsters, or whatever is out to get us, and that was our cause for migrating to Mani, then what does it mean about one millennium? It's the year 997 right now."

Rhidea gave me a speechless look before turning to the Archlord. "Domon?"

He licked his lips. "I have a theory on that. A few, but one that I think is more likely, and it ties into the Umbra Council's plans. The Wellspring could have been given to Mani with the intent to take it back after a thousand years, or it could be a reference to the lifespan of the Wellspring—that it is projected to shut down after one thousand years."

"Which would make sense, since we've been losing magical strength on Mani for centuries already," said Rhidea.

Domon nodded. "But I think it is more likely a reference to an accord made between the Legaleians and the other people of Gaea. To the effect that we can come back after one thousand years, because the danger should be over. A thousand-year banishment."

"But you don't think the danger is over," I said.

"Correct. I do not trust the people of this other world. I would rather prepare and wait it out until the thousand years have passed and see what comes. Which is why . . ." He sighed. "Which is why your plan is a good one. We can work together to find Gaea, and then see what is actually going on. And yes, we can make an accord sparing Nytaea from military invasion."

Rhidea snorted. "I fail to understand how it never occurred to you that our goals are so similar. But in order to move things forward . . . we will volunteer to venture out across the world and find this gate. If you will work with us, Archlord Domon, I think we can discover what we are both looking for: a true and lasting solution to the plight of Mani, both domestic and foreign."

The golden-haired emperor drummed his fingers on the surface of his desk, nodding his head. I could tell that he didn't like ceding his plans to anyone. He liked power. That was why he had been ready to have us all executed just for discovering his plans. "Very well. Had I known you were so foolhardy, I may have offered my help to you sooner. I'll send you off, but only with my support."

"Excellent," Rhidea said. "Now we just have to discuss an agreement between the Kystrean Empire and Nytaea. Mydia, heiress of House Kalceron, will be Nytaea's representative. . . ."

After a long session of planning and a subsequent meeting with some of Domon's highest advisors, we had a pact mostly outlined. He would send us off with an elite soldier as well as a few magical trinkets of his own creation (which we would see on the morrow).

As for me, I was exhausted from my exertion of power during my match with Domon. I had used the very utmost of my strength, and even that short burst was enough to take the wind out of my sail. Whether it arrived immediately after or a few hours later, the backlash always came. One of the servants whom the Archlord had assigned to us pointed me toward a place with a bed to lie down, and I dropped onto the mat without a care to strip off more than my dirty boots.

"Lyn, it's been a while."

I turned to see her there, right beside me: White, the dream girl. She lay on her side in the silvery field, one arm propping up her chin, picking at some little flowers that grew amongst the pale grass. She looked from the flowers to my face, almost bashfully but more like . . . yes, I knew that emotion: she felt neglected . . . rejected.

I was kneeling beside her, wearing a long gown of pure white. "I'm sorry," I said awkwardly. "I mean, I can't really just—control it. I dream when I dream. You're . . . still not going to tell me who you are, are you?"

She shook her head in a pouty way.

I sighed. "Nor why I keep having these dreams? White?"

White looked up, a frown wrinkling her perfect, childlike face. "White?" she repeated. "That's new."

"Well, you're . . ." I gestured to the girl, her skin, her hair, her cute little pasty-white dress. "You're, you know, just sort of . . . white."

She giggled. "Yes, but so are you, silly!"

I looked down at my own white dress and then pulled a long lock of my hair into view, seeing that is shone brilliant silvery-white in my dream—no dyes, no illusions.

"Well, you can call me whatever you want," the girl chirped. "I'll always be here to help you out when you need it." She rose to her feet.

"Wait!" I protested. "You're not going to show me anything to-night?"

"A memory? Just say the word, Lynx, and I'll fetch you one."

Lynx . . . "I-I don't know," I said sadly. "I'm not the one with the memories. I can't—"

"Yes, you are!" The girl said indignantly. "You really don't get it. Well, whatever. I'll see you next time, Lyn!" With that, she turned and skipped off.

"Wait—" I began, but it was no good. The girl disappeared into the distance, leaving me in the field of waving grass.

(Norvaen 16, 997—Dusk)

The next morning, we stood ready to embark on a riverboat at the southern pier of Ti'Vaeth. We would be taking the vessel down the Ardencaul to Nytaea. I still didn't fully understand how it worked, but apparently earth magi had long ago dug out long channels from the lake to each of the Four Rivers, creating a direct path from Ti'Vaeth to most provinces of Kystrea, as well as the outlier kingdoms like Nemental and Lygellis. The water from the Wellspring rained down and also sprung up from underneath, both filling the lake and supplying the water of the rivers and their tributaries.

When the Archlord said he would send help with us, though, I hadn't expected him to mean an assassin bodyguard. Kymhar was a tall man, wiry and wearing so many extra layers of clothing that he looked like he'd be overheating in it. His face was like a mask, expressionless as Mydia's childish paintings, and he had a . . . presence about him. Or a lack thereof. He seemed to exude danger. He carried at least a dozen sharp objects on him, ranging from his curved, single-edged sword to daggers, to a strange type of throwing knife which Kaen called a kunai. His shoulder-length black hair was tied in two places, one above the other.

He was one of the Archlord's best assassins, known collectively as the Dalim. He was tasked with accompanying us to the edge of the world and beyond.

Another gift from the Archlord was a nondescript leather bag containing three orbs of Dark Magic. He said to use them only in a pinch. Our discussion with the Archlord had led to some eye-opening, and surprisingly satisfying, conclusions. We now carried with us a list of stipulations from Archlord Domon to the city-state of Nytaea, a tentative proposal including the conditional promise to call back his armies and not invade. Some of these things would be made public while others, such as our own personal, updated quest, were to be kept to only the most trusted acquaintances of ours and the new leaders of Nytaea. Domon had agreed to "Hold off and see what may become of this fledgling nation—if they agree to work with me."

We couldn't have hoped for a better resolution. I almost felt foolish for the ways we had tried to get into the Well, going under Domon's nose, before I remembered that he had not been willing to parley with Rhidea or hand over information until after we had proven that we were not only motivated enough to go through all that work to sneak in, but that we had . . . me, the very proof of his life's work, in our party. So I supposed the arm-wrestling paid off.

Sol was buried far behind us, already beyond the western horizon. It cast a glowing silhouette over the lake, creating a shimmering tapestry of color on Lake Lucia's surface as the light played on the surface of the water, reflecting off the misty dome that surrounded Ti'Vaeth. Mydia, as usual, was the first to break the silence:

"Beautiful, isn't it?"

We all looked to the princess—or, well, queen—as though she were not supposed to have spoken. I nodded slowly.

The captain of the riverboat called out and a bell rung. "That's our cue," said Kaen. "Let's be off."

The End of Part Two

Mani

- Interlude-

The Umbra Council

We, the Umbra of the Moon, shall remake this world. We shall work in the darkness to create a new day, a new Mani, and a new order. We shall forge an unbreakable world, untouchable by the shadow that looms afar, whether it take ten years or another thousand. This we swear, by the blood of Mani.
— *Pact of the Umbra,* paragraph one

(Norvaen 16, 997—Dusk)

Archlord Domon watched the party leave and then departed with his retainers for the Ti'Vaeth Citadel. He talked with them as they went, keeping the appearance of interest in such topics as the joust that Lord Humphret's son was having that day.

Inside, his mind was working—working on something else. He was always thinking, always planning, even when he spoke with others, when he made judgments on petty border disputes, even as he slept oftentimes. Today, Domon could think of nothing other than what would come of his alliance with Nytaea. . . .

All that time, and they did *have the girl,* he thought. Perhaps Kalceron had been worth something, setting the events in action that would eventually end in the girl coming out into the open. But he never would have imagined they'd bring her here, of all places. Hopefully they would be able to accomplish their goal and make it all the way to the Gate on the other side . . . Domon had a lot riding on that one thing.

Later that evening, the Archlord bid his retainers good day at the palace and withdrew from his audience hall for his inner chambers, which lay directly behind. If they needed him, they would call, but this was the time of day when he had no duties pressing him, and he disliked company.

Besides, there would be company enough soon.

Shoes off and dressed down, he took a seat in his high-backed reading chair near the already-crackling fire in the hearth. He let out a contented sigh. With no scrolls to read right now, he simply pondered the pact he had just made.

Those Nytaeans . . . it galled him to have to cede such a thing as liberty to those rebels, although in truth he could have still flatly refused. But they had pointed out flaws in his plans and matters of great importance regarding Mani and his thousand-year deadline, and he needed someone competent to help him in this new task. It was potentially worth almost anything in the world. But would it be enough to stop the Silver Beast?

Absently, he rubbed at his right arm, massaging the sore muscles from his exercise the previous day. That silly romp had actually been quite fun minus the torque that girl had and the bruises on his knuckles from the solid wood table and the collision therewith. Such raw behemoth strength . . . he could only imagine what power the Gaians truly possessed. If only he had been able to meet her mother before she died. There was a secret there that Rhidea had been keeping close to her chest.

Domon reached out and pulled an emerald orb off his desk, just the size to fit nicely into the palm. It was one of his treasures, perfectly matching one that he had sent with Kymhar. It was no great secret, just a tool to communicate with his favored servant and check up on their progress. The orbs had been crafted by Domon himself, for his specialty lay in imbuing objects with power from various sources. With his range of Authority, and a bit of Dark Magic, he was able to experiment and invent all manner of useful devices. Many magi seemed to think magic a tool sufficient in itself, not worth bothering to experiment with and try new things. Idiots, all of them. Rhidea was one of the few with any real talent—she always had been, she and that Kallyn Kalceron. . . .

Domon rubbed the emerald absently. In a few minutes, the Umbra Council would reconvene and discuss the new happenings, but he wouldn't tell them everything. Not just yet. Lhiard would be curious, and Lieda . . . well, he would see if she even made it or not.

Domon got up from his seat and changed into his dark attire for the monthly Umbra Council. Approaching the back wall of his room, he slid his hand along the side of a bookshelf and used a small bit of Coaction to slide the lock. He then shoved the shelf to the side. It slid on oiled rollers, revealing the path to his meeting hall.

He stepped inside, passing through a doorway into an octagonal chamber dominated by a central table, made of stone raised directly out of the floor by earth magic. A stone chair stood right beside him, and eight candles sustained by magic lit the room from the eight corners of the table. Two other magi stood around the room, leaders of Kystrea whom he greeted with small nods: Kyal, Lord of the province of Imdek, and Lhiard, Lord of Uphel. Within a minute, Lord Tyiv of Dotham—an upper-class noble, not a governor—arrived, and shortly afterward . . . there she was.

Lady Lieda teleported in, holding her own crystal. She murmured an apology for her tardiness, noticing that she was the last one there.

"So, you made it, Lieda," came Lhiard's high-pitched voice from across the room. "Looks like that makes all five of us, then. We all know who will never be coming back now."

Lieda didn't so much as flinch at the mention of her late husband. Of course, Domon knew that she had despised him for a while. If only she knew what a pathetic hound dog she was, licking at the heels of those higher . . .

The Archlord clapped his hands. "Let's begin, then. We have some news to discuss. You see, a pact was formed just yesterday between me and Nytaea. This pact will allow them to keep their freedom and secede from the Empire of Kystrea." Gasps followed his announcement, but he held up a hand to silence the four. "However, I only agreed to it on the condition that a certain party of magi from the city-state partner with me—with us—in fulfilling our goal of uniting the world."

No need to tell them that he had been backed into it.

"And how, my lord, can they possibly help us achieve that?" came the raspy voice of Lord Tyiv.

Domon looked toward the smaller man. "The Wandering Mage herself is among those who pledged their help. I believe that they can cross the Great Chasm and find the Gate for us. Of course, I'm sending them off with one of my best retainers, skilled in espionage and stealth among other things, and he will be keeping tabs on their journey's progress and making sure that things go smoothly."

"My Lord," Kyal said in a worried tone. "This is truly worth giving over one of our kingdoms, one of the oldest and most powerful?"

One of my *kingdoms,* Domon thought. But he didn't say this. Instead, he simply nodded and said, "Yes, it is."

PART THREE

- Journey -

- Chapter 26 -
Reunion

My dear friend Rhidea,

I have decided to put away my Coactive Theory studies for a while. Possibly forever. Jinna . . . she died recently—because of me. Thames was blaming himself, but I know it was my fault. We were trifling with things that ought not be touched, and now a friend is dead because of it. Magic is a dangerous force, and not to be trifled with. I wish you and your colleagues the best, but I am done. I hope to see you soon, regardless. Also . . . please don't believe what you might hear about my illness. I don't know why Edrius was telling people I was so close to death, because I'm already getting better. It's not life-threatening, and I'll be back to full strength soon.

— Eivael Kalceron

Manidor 5, 989

(Norvaen 23, 997—Night Season)

One week later, we were back in Nytaea. The boat ride was far faster than taking the road by horseback, as horses could not travel round the clock.

It was the middle of the Sunless Cycle, yet at the third hour of the day, visibility would still be decent if not for the rain pouring down upon the ivory city, rendering all but ten paces ahead completely invisible. The only color came from the orange glow of the torches mounted upon the Palace parapet, battling the rain, slathered so thickly with pitch that it dripped on the cobblestones below.

I stood on the second tier of the Palace parapet, hands on the crenelated stone battlement that ringed the wall, gazing out into the rain. Kaen stood beside me, arms crossed. "You almost ready for the meeting?" he asked.

"Yeah. I'll be in soon." I sighed. "It's been a long, crazy trip, Kaen. It's good to be back, but this rain . . . ugh, what a day."

"But that's not what has you like this. I know you, Lyn. You've been in a funk lately, ever since Ti'Vaeth. Maybe before."

I hung my head. "You're right. I'm not really upset or anything, though. Just . . . I don't know how to explain it. My world, and my place in it, seems to change with every Sol Cycle, every *day*. And these visions in my dreams . . . I still don't know what they are." It wasn't entirely true, as I had a very good idea of what they were, just . . . not why I had them or what they meant.

My friend was silent for a moment as the rain continued to pour down. We were getting soaked thoroughly. Hopefully we didn't catch a cold from this. It was not a cold rain, not the kind that chilled you to the bone and made you want to curl up and die like on some days, especially in the cold Night Season.

Kaen took up the same leaning position as me. "You really think they mean something? That they're not just, you know, a manifestation of your own fears, or stories you've heard? A way of—of coping with your past? Our past?"

I shook my head. "No." I still hadn't explained them in detail to Kaen, or anyone other than Rhidea. I told her everything important. Almost everything. I trusted Kaen with my life, and had for years, but certain things made him uncomfortable. Authority, political games, talk of other worlds . . . perhaps he struggled to grasp such subjects, and didn't like to try.

White always asked me the same question over and over: *Well, what do you want me to show you?* By now, I remembered most things about those dreams even outside of them. And still they mystified me.

I didn't explain any more. Even though I probably should have. "I appreciate your concern," I said softly.

Kaen was silent for a minute. "Lyn," he said at last, looking at me and blinking rain out of his eye, "we still have some unfinished business to attend to, don't we?"

My heart began to beat more rapidly, and I shivered slightly—not just from the rain. *He has to bring this up now.* I squeezed my eyes shut. I didn't want to face it right now. "I thought we weren't going to—"

"You said we would talk about it when we got back," he interrupted. "So here we are. I already talked to Phoebe about it. And she still insists on coming."

"I know." I knew she would. She had a real dark side, just like Kaen. Only while his was a quick-flash anger, one that crouched inside and waited for a chance to spring, hers was that cold, ever-present looming of a wrong that would never be forgotten, the kind that only a woman could have. Her thirst for repayment would never be quenched until she saw justice administered upon the thieves that had killed Lentha, killed our whole orphanage.

Vengeance. We needed vengeance. I still wasn't certain on the whole matter. I knew all too well where Phoebe stood, though Mandrie would beg us not to go if she found out about it. That was why . . . well, that was why she would always remain the little sister of the group.

I felt unsettled about the whole business. It didn't make me feel right. And yet at the same time, it *seemed* right. It was right, it had to be. But what would Rhidea say? I hadn't told her of our plan, partly because she had already promised to inform the authorities about the thieving band and put a bounty on their heads.

We would see it done ourselves. Just the three of us. I knew that we could do it. And quench my soul in the thickest oil, but I would do it. I *would.* "Kaen, I will. I'll go with you."

"Really?" He seemed almost surprised. "I thought you weren't sure about whether it was right or not?"

I shook my head slowly. "I'm still not. But let's get it over with before I change my mind."

He hesitated, and then nodded sharply. "All right. Two days from now. I'll let Phoebe know."

I was done wrestling with these things. *Let's just get it done and over with,* I told myself.

The meeting with Mydia's cabinet was long and boring, as I'd known it would be.

I finally made it out of the conference chamber, trailing behind Kaen. He was commonly included in such meetings, and occasionally Phoebe, even though they had no high birth, political experience or other such clout. They were part of my group, and I was trusted by Mydia and Rhidea, so it got them in. Ironically, we all hated such things. Politics, schemes . . . mind games. In my case, it was mostly just boredom. I could follow along with most of what was said. Kaen, too, was great with strategy and critical thinking. He spoke up once in a while to add an important detail that helped the governors . . . well, sometimes they just plowed over him, but it *could* have helped. But he and Phoebe couldn't stand Gaela or Big Bart. It was hard to blame them on that point.

Mydia managed to squeeze out of the conference room a bit later and catch up to me. She took me by the arm, and I turned to look at her. She had on a beautiful green dress and her queenly tiara. She almost looked like she fit the thing. Almost. The tiara, that is, not the dress. Mydia remained Queen Regent. I didn't understand it completely, but the government was still somewhat amorphous.

Everyone was relieved to hear, however, that there would be no war between Nytaea and the far more powerful empire of Kystrea, of which we had been a part until recently. It wouldn't have been much of a war, more a bug-stomping. A rebellion to squash. Just one of thirteen to put down. But we would have gone down fighting. Nytaea was easily the largest and strongest of the thirteen—but had few experienced leaders, and twelve versus one made for terrible odds.

Bart and Gaela had done well in Mydia and Rhidea's absence. Keuda's experience as a state secretary and Lanthar's military knowledge had seen the city-state well prepared (as well as possible) for the expected invasion and working smoothly. New soldiers were being trained. Kaen was offered the position of corporal, but he turned it down, as he had already chosen to set out with us. I was half surprised that Phoebe didn't try to take the spot, as ferocious and ambitious as she was. She was going to stay and look after Mandrie for us. She always tried to pretend she didn't have a motherly side, and yet it came out so naturally.

Kaen and I were relieved to see the girl for the first time in a month. Mandrie always seemed to brighten a room just by being in it. She stood in the hallway now, a brilliant smile on her face. I knew she still bore emotional scars from her imprisonment in the tower, but she was recovering remarkably well. "Lyn!" she chirped. "I've been waiting this whole time with Phoebe. She said I couldn't go in, so I stayed here."

I smiled and scooped her into an embrace, ruffling her hair as I always did. "Thanks."

She grinned. "It wasn't that bad. Are we still going out for lunch in the city?"

Kaen rolled his eyes. "Yes, we're still going out. Come on, Myd . . . ah, Your Majesty. You're paying, remember?"

The queen held up her money pouch. "Of course. What do you think I have all this money for?"

We were soon strolling through the rain-glossed streets of the alabaster city in search of a reputable restaurant—trailed all the while by Mydia's persistent Queensguard. The rain had subsided and the stars shown amongst the auroras in the sunless sky.

It felt like old times, yet now we acted as high-society snobs, searching for a sit-down restaurant instead of just a bakery selling something to eat. We were eating for the social activity of it, not for mere sustenance. Well . . . I was pretty hungry. Mydia would be paying a pretty penny just to feed Kaen and me. We could eat a bear just between the two of us. It didn't really matter if I was using my strength or not: my metabolism chewed through anything I gave it. Mydia and Phoebe were always jealous, but they didn't understand the *hunger*.

The establishment that we chose was a well-respected one frequented by anyone of middle-to-high class, bearing a cute overhang and a carved wooden door. The Pleasant Pastry. Inside, the dining room had a low-hanging ceiling with wagon-wheel lanterns suspended from crisscrossing beams. The lantern light cast a warm glow on the place, augmenting the aurora light that seeped in through the open windows at the front. We sat at a table near the front, proceeding to order a large plate of rolls and butter and a roast turkey to share. Kaen and I got a beef roast as well. Meat of any kind was a luxury we orphans had never been able to afford, particularly choice cuts.

Mydia wore one of her usual disguises, that of a thin noblewoman a few years her senior, bearing unremarkable features—yet I caught a few knowing glances and nods from the present nobility that indicated it might be a bit too common by now. Of course, if they had noticed the Queensguard waiting just outside the door, that would have been a dead giveaway as well.

Our conversation was mostly light, with a lot of laughter. Phoebe and Kaen had accepted Mydia as one of our group, and Mandrie treated her like just one more older sister. Kaen seemed to feel a bit uncomfortable in our group, being outnumbered four to one by gender, but it was the more familial kind of discomfort that a boy might show growing up in a family with eight sisters (not too uncommon on Mani, remember). Mydia and Mandrie were the only ones in our group who were anything resembling ladylike, or . . . girlish. Whichever one it was. I was probably supposed to know the difference.

Afterward, we went to see the orphanage that Phoebe had helped to start. It lay on the western side of town, a repurposed warehouse purchased with grant money straight from the Nytaean royal treasury. I had been overjoyed to hear of the matter. This was only one of three new orphanages. Inside, a stocky young woman in a matronly dress greeted us warmly. "Phoebe! You brought your friends like you said." She put her hands on her hips and looked the four of us up and down. "Well, I'm Berta. Come on in."

We did so, following Berta. Immediately inside, a couple of young noses poked out, a girl and a boy, bringing a smile to my lips. As she showed us around the place, some dozen children running about the different rooms, I felt a growing sense of sorrow building within my chest, weighing me down, contrasting with the bright happiness that should have dominated. The two emotions, strong as warhorses, struggled against each other.

Looking to my side, I saw that Mandrie seemed to be feeling the same conflicting emotions, albeit a little differently. They were the childlike emotions of one torn from her childhood, as opposed to my own . . . different ones. *Ugh.* I couldn't make sense of it, yet I couldn't help but shake my head and grimace a bit, lips trembling, eyes misting up. I never got emotional like this. I'd been trying so hard to ignore that day . . .

Kaen took hold of my shoulder. "Lyn, are you all right? You look awful."

I nodded. Then I shook my head slowly, backing up, drawing complaints from a couple of the children. "No. I feel . . . I don't know. It's just a bit too much for me. It hasn't been long since . . . you know . . ."

"Just hang in there. Remember, this is a beautiful thing. Try not to associate it with the past. She's making a new start here."

I nodded. "Thanks. You're right. I think—" I wiped my eyes "— I'll be all right." I felt so stupid for crying.

We made our way back over to the others, and a little girl approached me tentatively. "Are you sad, Miss White Hair?"

I smiled despite myself. Dropping to my knees, I took the girl's tiny hand in my own two hands and said, "Yes, child. I am. But I'm also so very happy, and sometimes you have to balance both of those in the best way."

The girl nodded as though she understood, and then shook her head. "I don't understand, but . . . you're really pretty." Then she cracked a winning smile.

My smile deepened, tears running down my cheeks, and I scooped the girl up in a hug, careful not to crush her small frame. She squealed in delight, and I spun her around. The other children swarmed around me, some reaching their arms up for a similar ride.

Berta smiled. "They seem to like you, Lyn."

"Careful around her," Phoebe warned them with mock rebuke. "She's secretly a monster. Cracked many a man twice her size over the head and threw a couple from the Palace."

The children giggled.

I supposed it was a funny story to hear, despite being nearly accurate. I ignored Phoebe's jibes, however, lest I spoil the moment by my reactions.

A short time later, we left the orphanage, leaving a package with Berta. Contributions to the children: clothing and food. Then we headed back to the Palace.

- Chapter 27 -

Vengeance

Beware the end of the earth, for none come back who fall from Darsor's fell cliffs. The Silver Beast, the scourge of Mani, swallows them whole. Long has he prowled in the ancient abyss, seeking souls to devour.
— From *The Collected Lore of Mani*
Property of the Grand Library of Redufiel

(Norvaen 23, 997—Night Season)

I met Kaen and Phoebe by the West Gate at twenty-two hours. "There you are, Lyn," Kaen said. "Are you sure you're ready?"

"Yes," I replied. "What about you? You're sure your information was correct?"

He nodded. "It's them. I'm sure of it. Fire mage running a small gang of violent thieves. Last seen in the Balrun Sector."

I was silent for a moment. Kaen had many contacts in the city, and while I might not trust them all, I did trust his judgment. Taking a deep breath, I said, "Okay. Let's go."

"Right, let's," added Phoebe.

And we were off. We made our way down the streets, checking for lights and pedestrians. I couldn't quite believe that we were actually doing this. . . . Was I doing the right thing in agreeing to the mission? It reminded me of two months prior, when we were running from the mage soldiers, or of the old times when we would sneak out at night and look for trouble. We always managed to find a way out of it, but there were a few sticky situations, mostly involving us trespassing where we shouldn't have been and getting chased down by hired thugs or noblemen's guards.

Now, there was less fear of being caught by guardsmen or the city watch, but we still didn't want to alert anyone. We would let the policing captains know afterward, once we'd caught the thieves.

Overhead, the stars twinkled ever so faintly, for it was only a lightly hazy night. But it was still deep in the Sunless Cycle, so we were partially hidden by the ambient shadows. We kept just close enough to the torchlight or candlelit windows to see by, but just far enough away to stay hidden from view.

"We're almost to the Balrun Sector," Phoebe hissed at some point.

Already? She always was fantastic with directions. I could swear she had a mental map of the entire city clear in her head. And I was supposed to be the one with the great memory . . . at least according to my dream friend, White.

The buildings here were mostly low-standing shanties. Balrun was a fishing and transport district. Boats came in nearby, and docks spread over to the right side a block away, along the Ardencaul. Burly guards stood watch at warehouse doors. Lots of places to steal supplies, if one were a thieving band capable and inclined to do so. One specific warehouse, according to Kaen's sources, would be the target for the robbers. We took up cover behind a nearby building, waiting and watching. Kaen knelt behind one wall with a view out over the docks to both sides, Phoebe stayed farther down the street, and I climbed high atop the next-door building. Each of us would watch the others' backs whilst keeping an eye out for the thieves.

An hour passed, and I was just starting to think that they may not show, when suddenly a figure darted toward the side street. Kaen was looking the other way, so I gave the pre-arranged low bird call to alert my friend. Kaen turned his head, tracking the man's furtive movements, and then tackled him, clasping a hand over his mouth and choking him out. He dragged him under the front steps of the building and waited for the next. A similar event happened again, and then he had a stash of two unconscious bodies, bound and gagged.

I leapt down from the second story roof to the first at this point. Then I crept around the rooftop, making my way down the street parallel to the docks. I gave the second bird whistle as I spotted more of the thief crew. I hopped to the ground behind them and knocked them both out with a couple of strikes to the side of the neck. Knife hand just between the ear and the neck, just as Kymhar had taught me.

For the first time, I appreciated the assassin's training he'd given us on the return trip from Ti'Vaeth. I proceeded to bind, gag and hide the bodies behind the building, and then dashed in a half-crouch, circling the building counter-clockwise. More were coming in from the right at the next intersection, calling out for their comrades, and I waited thirty feet from the corner, letting them go past. Phoebe would be right up ahead on the left. I couldn't risk another birdcall with the thieves so close, so I trusted that she wouldn't be found or hurt. Then I crept up closer to the corner and poked my head out to the right.

The fire mage was coming.

He was flanked by two guards armed with heavy bronze long-swords. They looked like they knew how to use them. Probably the most well-paid of the lot. I could take them, but I couldn't say exactly how skilled or powerful the mage was.

I gave the third birdcall. Kaen would rush over and help Phoebe take out and bind up the remaining frontrunners. While I couldn't speak too much for her own combat abilities, Kaen was excellent, and well-armed. None of them would be getting out of there, dead or alive.

I stepped out into the street. "Hello, murderer," I said.

The fire mage stopped, halting his guards. "And who might you be?" he asked. A small flame appeared in his hand, illuminating his face and my figure as well. The man was tall, with flowing, shoulder-length red hair, and bore a thin rapier, which he drew smoothly but rapidly. He surely noted my white hair first, bound though it was in a practical ponytail. "Ah, yes. Yes, I remember you, girl. If I recall correctly, hmm . . . there was a bounty out for your pretty head. Thought about turning you in to Kalceron myself. I'm sure he would have rewarded me handsomely." He slowly circled me as he spoke, his men spreading out behind him.

I snorted. "Not likely. The reward, yes, but taking me in? No."

"I don't recall you winning any fights against my group the first time," the man noted. "And where are your friends? The ugly girl and the antsy boy?"

"Oh, Kaen? He has been training with swordmasters at the Palace, ever since we personally disposed of Lord Kalceron."

He chuckled. "Funny. I've heard many a story about how all that happened. Some talk of a girl with white hair, others say the princess plotted to murder her own father and take his throne. But you know what I think? I think you're nothing more than a girl with a cocky attitude who needs to be put down like the rest of her precious family. The world doesn't want you anyway."

I scowled, trying to suppress the hot emotions. This man was trying to rile me. He was toying with me, confident that he could take me out with ease. Probably confident that even his two cronies could take me out. "Well," I said as evenly as I could, "You should be more careful with your words, fire mage. You never know who may—" I summoned a flame in my left hand "—surprise you."

He raised his eyebrows in satisfying surprise. "Well, well. Ain't this a shock. Hmm. Get 'er, boys."

The two brutes hefted their longswords and rushed at me, their roughshod feet scraping against the cobblestones of the narrow street. I backed up and waited till I could practically smell their breath, and then I acted. I ducked under the first guard's swing, my bronze sword and left hand touching the ground as I low-kicked the second man's feet out from under him. He toppled to the ground with a curse, nearly dropping his sword. He was dazed as his head cracked against the pavement stones.

I faced the first guard, who was swinging at me once more with his three-and-a-half-foot blade. I brought my own bronze blade up just in time to block it, parrying another blow, then another. I was glad for Kaen and Inno's training, though I was nowhere near as good as them. Fortunately, I didn't have to rely too much on my raw skill. However, I kept the ringleader in view, or at least . . . blast, where had that rat gotten to? I silently cursed my carelessness.

I fought off the first guardsmen, using some of my hidden energy to get inside his defenses and land an uppercut on his chin. Then I bound and gagged them both.

Now to find that mage . . .

I dashed off toward the target building to find Phoebe and Kaen unharmed. They had overwhelmed and subdued all of the men, although I couldn't tell if the one on the end was alive or not. . . . I tried not to think about it as I said, "The leader, the fire mage—I lost him!"

"Oh, I'm over here, sweetheart," he called from the shadows.

I illuminated the alley with a summoned flame and saw the fire mage once again, twenty paces in, near the intersection with the street I had previously been fighting in.

Kaen drew his sword, baring a dark silver blade polished to a mirror finish. I wasn't sure if he'd named it yet or not. "You foul piece of dung! Come here, so I can slit your throat."

The thief lord grinned a wicked, maniacal grin. "Well, that's right nice, but I can't just let ya do that."

"If you run," Phoebe said calmly, "Lyn here will chase you down in a matter of seconds."

"Oh yes?" The man took a couple steps forward. "Well, that sounds like fun, but I've got a little thing here called Coaction. Fire synergy. White-hair, where did you come across the ability to use Coaction so soon, hmm?"

I gave no response, but only gripped my sword hilt tighter.

Kaen put out a hand in front of me. "You'll have to get through me first, dastard."

Foolish, I thought.

"Foolish boy," said the man. I barely had time to call out before he blasted a burst of fire straight at Kaen. He was clearly shocked to see Kaen come out of his defensive stance a moment later, completely unscathed. His dark-toned blade glowed a faint red which dimmed slowly as we watched.

Impressive. I had doubted the sword's abilities.

The man finally got angry. "Fine," he snarled. "I'll fight whoever wants to. Come at me and we'll settle this little score the fair way."

"Lyn," Phoebe murmured to me, "we have to do something. You know he doesn't really mean fair. But we don't know the extent of his powers or training, and we certainly don't want him burning down half the city, particularly since you have, erm, similar powers."

I nodded. "Phoebe, stay behind Kaen. Do *not* get hit by a fire blast. Kaen, keep him distracted." With that, I extinguished my flame and leaped away as quickly as I could, so as to confuse the bandit leader. I heard him curse as he summoned a brighter light. Meanwhile, I scrambled up the side of a building, my inhuman strength lending me enhanced climbing abilities as usual. For this reason, vertical maneuvers were a specialty of mine. I ran as softly as I could across the slate rooftop. It sloped gently to one side, the side facing away from the thief—toward the docks. Above, the partially obscured stars tried and failed to light my path, but my nimble feet picked out the way.

Peeking out over the roof's gutter gave me a glimpse of my quarry. He was only a dozen feet away now, looking from side to side and up at the rooftops for me. I pulled back quickly, hoping he hadn't seen me. And then the roof exploded underneath my feet. I leaped over the hole with a quiet yelp, dashing past the second of his fire blasts. Flames were already beginning to lick up where they hit. Before long, we'd have a large-scale structure fire on our hands. Great. How had this man led such a tight-knit, focused and successful thieving band for this long with a half-present mind?

"Come on out, monster!" he called from below. "You know you are the same as me on the inside. A deranged animal waiting to be put down. I can help with that."

I leapt down in front of the man and began to drive him backward with my sword. The alley echoed with the harsh clang of bronze on bronze. I could practically feel the dents and chips forming with each strike. Anything to distract him from creating any more unnecessary property damage. I could feel the heat from the flames of the building from all the way over here. He was good, far more skilled with his thin blade than those men I'd fought just moments earlier. Far better than Corporal Harold back at the Hall of Eternity.

"Monster?" I growled. "You have no idea."

He laughed maniacally as we scraped sword against sword. "Oh, I think I might. I've heard about ya. You're not exactly the same as me, because you're also a monster on the outside, not just the inside. But Fraid the cutthroat don't care. Fraid the murderer, the thief. Once upon a time, mayhap . . ."

Kaen made it to us, but I motioned him back as I kicked free of my engagement with the crazed killer. His sword work was such that it was difficult to find an opening to get in close and use my strength. Fraid. Yes, that name had come up when we were searching for him and his band. "Fraid," I said coldly. "Where did *you* learn Coaction? Who taught you?"

He cackled through quickened breaths, remaining in his stance while watching Kaen and me warily but not attacking for the moment. "Don't know. That Fraid is a different man. I knew him once, and I know him no longer, because he is not me. The man who taught me, he's long dead. I killed him with a knife in the back." He laughed again, and Kaen and I closed in on him.

Kaen stepped up and attacked Fraid again with a backhanded strike to the head, which he of course blocked. "You will die, worm," Kaen spat. "Such a pathetic excuse for a man." He kept at the thief, harrying him with strike upon strike, dodging backward whenever Fraid's own blade got too close.

Fraid's skill was remarkable. For all his mania, his mastery of the blade was grounded in countless hours of practice. Kaen might have had the edge of talent and creativity, but his opponent had more experience with the blade. Glancing around, I saw that Phoebe had gone, presumably to call someone to put out the fire with water from the docks.

Looking back to Kaen, I saw that Fraid was still trading blows with him, but I knew that he would remember his magic soon, find an opening, and then my friend would be charcoal, just like the others from my orphanage. The thought churned my stomach. I would not let this happen again. I didn't truly want to kill him, especially since the city watch would undoubtedly be here soon. An idea slowly sprang to mind.

I crept around to the side, watching for an opening in the fight. *Clang! Clang!* There: I used the utmost of my speed to swipe my sword in and bat Fraid's sword right out of his hand. He cried out in pain and surprise as the force of my blow flung his arm backward, possibly breaking the joint. I gave him no time to recover, leaping in with a kick that sent him sprawling to the ground.

Kaen, who had pulled back immediately as I attacked, brushed the sweat out of his eyes. "I didn't need any help."

"Oh, yes you did."

Kaen ignored me and hopped over to where the red-haired man lay clutching his wounded arm. Standing over the groaning thief, he placed one boot on his chest, sword point at Fraid's throat.

"Kaen!" I shouted, rushing over. "Hold on."

My friend looked over at me. "Why? He's a deranged murderer who needs to be put down. Just like he said."

"I know, but . . ."

"You said you were in for this mission!" he hissed angrily. "And now you're trying to plead for his life?"

Fraid sputtered a wretched laugh from his position on the ground. "This is so rich. I love it. Even you, boy, I see it in your eyes. It's not that you're too righteous, you're just a coward."

I knew otherwise. *Oh, Kaen. . . . Don't do this to my friend.*

Suddenly, I heard voices behind me. Phoebe had returned, and with her . . . help. In more than one way.

Gripping Kaen's wrist tightly, I whispered, "Just wait."

He tried to yank his wrist free, but I held it too tightly. "Don't try and stop me, Lyn," he growled.

"No, I *will* stop you. There's a monster in all of us, Kaen. And yours is calling. Don't answer it. That's . . . that's what he did."

Kaen froze. Fraid grinned up at him. Kaen made an anguished face and then stood up, pulling his boot and sword from the man, looking up at me and nodding. I let go of my friend's wrist as Phoebe led a group of watchmen and dockworkers with buckets ready to take in all the thieves. They were already finding them, collecting the bound outlaws like children on a treasure hunt. She led the dockworkers straight to the fire on this street, and they began throwing what seemed a measly amount of water onto it. Only now did I realize that we were all standing amidst a flaming danger zone. The watchmen, however, had a water mage trained in fighting fires, who made quick work of it while we all moved out. Steam began to hiss and spread everywhere, mingling with the smoke.

The watchmen tied the thief lord Fraid securely and led him off, heeding our warning that he was a trained fire synergist, and the three of us showed the men where all the remaining thieves lay scattered around the area.

The guard captain thanked us profusely for our help, but also questioned why a group of youths such as us were out at this hour and how we found them. "We just happened across them," Phoebe lied, eliciting a shrug from the man.

"Well, I'm not going to question you too much since you helped out the city a great deal. This is the thieving band that's been evading capture since long before Kalceron was ousted."

We headed home, exhausted but satisfied. I was relieved that it had gone so well. Kaen took my arm, however, partway back to the

Palace. "Hey, why did you stop me back there?"

I frowned, looking at him as I walked. "I told you. I didn't want you doing something out of hatred."

Kaen looked down. "I-I know. But . . . ugh, then why did we go out there tonight? It ended well, but now I almost feel like we did something really wrong."

"It wasn't wrong," Phoebe said. "It was . . . the right thing to do." Then she sighed. "Okay, maybe our motives could have been more benevolent.

"If we had killed Fraid," I explained softly, "killed him in anger, without letting the law prosecute him, then it would have just been a successful murder mission. We wanted justice. We got it. Rhidea would say that to kill a man to satisfy your own thirst for vengeance is an act of self-gratification, one that has nothing to do with law or justice."

The other two were quiet for a minute, then Kaen spoke up. "Thank you for stopping me, then."

I clasped him on the shoulder, taking Phoebe's smaller shoulder with my other hand. "Of course. We are friends."

- Chapter 28 -

Tectonic Levitation

I didn't ask to be the Mother—I never wanted it. Given the choice, I would never have willingly volunteered. To be worshiped by all of Gaea, imprisoned in that terrible place, and later hunted by the Senate. The thought that this fate may one day be pressed upon my own child weighs on my soul, but . . . it is our only chance. One day, she must learn. One day, she will return and learn the truth of the broken world that was left to her. The buried secrets behind the Mother Project, the threat of the Cydenges, and the nightmare that is Gaea. Lynchazel . . . oh, Lynchazel.
— From Lynchazel's Vault, Svenhal 15, 2323

(Norvaen 23, 997—Night Season)

That night, I met White once again in my dreams.

She was more cheerful this time, and took me to see a memory of my life at the orphanage.

Lentha was there, her brown hair streaked with a touch of grey from her middle years, as well as little Tommy and the rest of the children. The day was a Sunlit one, and radiant white light streamed in through the windows that faced the street as I washed dishes with Phoebe. We were around nine or ten years of age, our hair pinned up in matching ponytails. The children were playing, and Phoebe and I were conversing back and forth with Lentha.

It was odd, that feeling of detachment that I felt as my own body moved and talked of its own volition. It was just some silly banter about one of the neighbor boys and his latest stunt that had gotten him in trouble, but I . . . remembered the conversation. How had I forgotten it?

"Now, Lyn," Lentha said presently from across the room as she wiped the table, "I don't want you running off and getting into trouble, either. I trust you'll be a good girl this week."

My ten-year-old self jerked slightly at that, heat rising to my cheeks. I had only meant to catch the little cat, not break down that man's door. Sometimes I got going too fast for my own good, but was that really my fault . . . ? Yes, I supposed it was.

Phoebe gave me a small nudge as she wiped a silver plate with her rag. "Well, are you gonna?"

"Of course!" My voice came out not only high and childlike but almost strangled from guilt. I heard Lentha chuckle from behind me.

I grabbed another cup from the pan of water we were working in and, clearing my throat, tried to change the subject to something less embarrassing than accidents and boys.

The memory went on like this for another minute, after which it began to slip away. My detachment from my ten-year-old self grew larger, until the scene vanished and my dreams changed to something else entirely.

(Norvaen 24, 997—Night Season)

The next day, I felt like I couldn't look anyone in the face, particularly Mandrie and Mydia. We didn't tell either of them of the incident with Fraid and his band, even though they'd surely hear of it at some point. I stayed in a partitioned guest room near the Queen's tower (her very same tower) in the Palace with Phoebe and Mandrie, while Kaen had gone to stay with Inno and Ruel in the soldiers' barracks.

We stood once more in the upper council chamber, which had

been nicknamed the strategy room for now. The meeting was a usual occurrence these days, especially for Rhidea and Mydia. Today's topic was twofold: how to respond to the Archlord on his proposition, and how to go about finding this gateway to the other world.

Bart, Gaela, Mydia and Marshal Lanthar all agreed that the Archlord's proposal was fair. That sentiment was unanimous, as everyone was relieved that Domon had been so accommodating in the end. Granted, it was mostly due to our mission and promise to cooperate with him on his quest. I still felt like we had slightly different goals regarding that, but for now at least, we were aligned. Ethas Gandel, Mydia's regent, was also present, but seemed hesitant to cast a vote with her present. I couldn't tell what he thought of the deal.

Then we began to explain the details regarding the Archlord's mission and our hunt for Gaea. Another world, far away from Mani. And we were going to find it. Rhidea would head the expedition, the same group as we took to Ti'Vaeth. Again, Mydia insisted on coming despite the rest of us trying to object, and had already arranged it with Lord Gandel. I had to admit, she had been quite useful during our previous journey. Her illusions and powers of healing were invaluable.

Mydia was already getting all manner of flak for her month-long disappearance, and this one would be longer, so Ethas' agreement to continue in her place was one step toward keeping the officials happy. With effort, she convinced her Queensguard to stay and protect Ethas instead, as it didn't make sense to inflate our group so much this time, and he would soon be the king anyway. If she somehow didn't return from our trip, then . . . well, it was official.

Wait . . . that means that stuck-up Syneria is going to be directly related to a queen, I realized.

We would have obstacles. The first and most obvious one would be the great chasm called the Sea of Emptiness. The Archlord said that the gateway we sought would be on the other side, and Rhidea agreed. It made a sort of sense to me—no one seemed to know what lay over the endless Sea of Emptiness. If there was a world past there . . . well, then that must be where we needed to go.

"The Isle of Scathii."

It was Gaela who spoke. We all turned to look at her, Rhidea nodding.

"Scathii," the regal noblewoman repeated. "One of the sky islands to the east, further from the shore. The locals are not said to be very accommodating, but knowledgeable—surely they know some secrets about the Sea if anyone does."

"It is the logical place to start," Rhidea said. "I have never thought to search among them, because I never sought to go beyond the Great Chasm."

"Why do you call it a chasm?" Kaen asked, shaking his head. "It doesn't make any sense. You're saying there's more land on the eastern side, past the islands?"

Rhidea thought for a moment. "Possibly only in the east . . . Or in all directions."

I shook my head in disbelief. It was still hard to believe that our world could be so big. The entire world as we knew it, the continent of Argent, took upwards of two months to traverse in whole, even on horseback. Over three thousand miles. And there was more?

We left at dawn on the next day, the first light of the Sunlit Cycle. It was good to see the sun once again. *Randhorn, here we come.*

(San'Hal 3, 997—Zenith)

The old stone castle of Randhorn was a familiar sight by now. The great stone walls greeted us with that same timeless implacability. The guards standing watch atop the walls pointed upon seeing us and the gatemen stood taller as we rode up. "Lady Rhidea!" said the man on the left, saluting. "Lady Mydia!"

"It's Queen Mydia," I said as we rode past them.

"My apologies," the man murmured, causing a smile to spring to my lips.

We rode onward toward the court of King Fenwel, where we left our horses with the stablemen. The king himself came out to greet us, raising his arms, a warm smile on his aged face. "Welcome," he called. "Welcome, friends."

"My lord," Rhidea said, stepping up to embrace her liege. Then Mydia ran up and hugged him, and he patted her hair fondly. He was one of those people who could exude a great strength at the same time as an equally great kindness.

"I assume that you and your entourage come bringing news?" asked the grey-headed king.

"News we have," Rhidea affirmed. "And more."

"Come in, come in," said Fenwel, turning and waving us toward the large oaken doors. "We can speak inside."

He led us through hallways, past stairwells and into the deeper parts of the Palace, past uniformed servants and ornate decorations. Tapestries depicting ancient legends lined some walls.

Eventually, we came to one of his audience chambers, a smaller one than the one used for when he held court every week. The interior decorative theme was dark, but not depressingly so. A couple of windows were at the back, taller ones with drapes half open, allowing Sol's white light to pour through. We all took seats and got down to business.

"The Wellspring," Fenwel said, his face growing serious. "Did you find it?"

Rhidea took a breath. "Yes. We found it. And then we made a deal with Archlord Domon."

The king shook his head. "So, it's as the messengers said. I heard briefly of it. I cannot believe that snake is actually willing to let Nytaea off so easily. But . . . I have only heard vague reports. Tell me the details."

We explained in great detail, leaving out nothing of importance from the king. Fenwel took it all in with a somber face and a lot of nodding and "hmm . . ."

"And that is what we had in mind as we set out from Nytaea once more," Rhidea finished. "One way or another, we are not returning for a while. We will cross that chasm and find what lies beyond."

Fenwel stroked his grey beard. "My scholars speak of the theory that the world of Mani is actually round, not flat. Well, round*ed*. I don't understand it myself."

"The idea, my lord, is that instead of the earth underneath our feet being one flat plane with gravity pulling downward directionally, the earth is actually conformed to a smooth, round curve, with gravity pulling toward a center far below."

Fenwel nodded at the explanation, as though it made sense.

"My head," Kaen groaned. "My head, it just . . ." He turned to Mydia. "What on Mani did she just say?"

"Um . . . I think it was something to do with gravity—"

"Never mind, I don't want to know. I'll just ignore the rest of this conversation."

I snorted at the background banter. Most of my attention was on

Rhidea and Fenwel's discussion. I was trying to follow it, as was Mydia.

"But the Sea of Emptiness," I pointed out. "It encompasses Mani completely. There can't be any round sphere, because the whole continent floats."

"Mmm, that's only if Grivnel's thesis on tectonic levitation is correct," said my teacher. "There is no currently known way to pierce the fog of the great abyss or survey the cliffs of Mani farther than a few hundred feet downward. They could be straight cliff faces reaching down to a certain depth, or they could be the edges of a great floating continent, as Master Grivnel proposed. Who is to say but those who have plunged to their deaths trying?"

Silence hung for a few seconds following her last remark.

"Um, but we're not planning on falling to our deaths, are we?" Mydia asked with nervous humor.

"Not particularly, my dear. I mean, if it ends up being a viable way of achieving our goal, then by all means."

Mydia gulped. I knew that she wasn't greatly fond of heights. How *was* she going to cope with the traversal of the great chasm, however we decided to do that?

Looking around at our confused group, Rhidea sighed. "How about I demonstrate?" She cast about and found a decoration on a nearby windowsill, which she retrieved. It was a bronze globe with engravings around its length, standing on a thin pedestal. "My lord, I assure you this will come to no harm."

Rhidea moved a hand over the bronze sculpture, which was around the size of one of her hands, and its surface began to change.

Mydia nodded and said quietly, "Perception Coaction."

When Rhidea was finished, she presented the globe to us, and its surface appeared to be silver, split by a furrow that ran its entire length. Thus, it now consisted of two bowl-shaped halves, juxtaposed and held near each other as though by some strange manner of polestone. On the top half, curved though it was, I could make out Ti'Vaeth and Lake Lucia, the Four Rivers, and other landmarks. . . .

"Is that really what you think it looks like?" Kaen asked skeptically.

"It's what I'm certain it looks like," she returned. "It's the only way we could have the time zones that we do. Why should the sun rise six days earlier here in Randhorn than in Ti'Vaeth? Sol would have to be circling a sphere." She demonstrated this by creating a brilliant white light that orbited her mock planet, casting light over its surface. As the light moved toward and then over the other side of Argent's depiction, the angle of the continent caused the light to appear far earlier in some places than others.

"Twenty-eight days it takes Sol to make her rounds," she said. "This is the only way it makes sense."

I nodded slowly. "When you put it like that . . . it actually does."

Kymhar watched in silent fascination, saying nothing.

"Back to the topic at hand, Rhidea," said King Fenwel. "Will you enlist the aid of my scholars here at the castle? How long will you be able to tarry before leaving?"

"Technically, my king, you are still in charge of the mission."

The king barked a laugh. "And technically you are a dusty old scholar from a city recently overthrown by, well, you. Small details."

The king's light-hearted humor brought a smile to my lips. King Fenwel had a certain genuine air that one would not expect from a king, and it was very refreshing.

Rhidea cleared her throat with the utmost dignity and grace. "Yes, we will need your staff's help. We will be staying as long as the preparations take, hopefully no longer than a week." She went to return her round sculpture, which reverted to its original state.

The discussion concluded soon after that, and before long Rhidea and Mydia were hunting down the king's scholars and philosophers to enlist their aid and assign them some tasks. I actually didn't know all of her plans, because she hadn't shared them in great detail yet. But if there was one thing I knew about that wonderful, terrible woman, it was that she was *never* without a plan.

- Chapter 29 -
Twilight Voyage

The waning of magic on Mani, on the other hand, is just as little spoken of, even in the Kystrean Mage Councils. Countless stories are told of feats that none in recent years have been able to perform using even the highest Authority. And many scribes have written over the last three centuries of the fact that with each generation, magic seems to slowly ebb away. Quietly, imperceptibly—like a woman's hair whose length is robbed of just a mite every year, beneath her notice. Or a road to the nearest village that lengthens every year, though an old man not notice his walk from the farm growing longer and longer

. . . .

— From *Secrets of Mani,* by Sor the Lark

(San'Hal 3, 997—Zenith)

I eventually left them to their studies to search for Cort Flanning and Syneria Tolruin, the two mage scholars that Rhidea had brought with us to Randhorn three months back. Though I soon found out that Syneria was out on field study in the nearby town of Faliday. That left the blond menace, Cort. Why wasn't that rascal helping Rhidea already?

I found him in one of the studies near the scroll archives. He looked up as I arrived, and then brushed back a long lock of fine gold hair. "And what do you want?" he asked nonchalantly.

"Cort! Is that any way to treat an old friend?"

"Um, but you're not old. I have old friends, but they're mostly among the scholars." He paused for a moment and then sighed. "All right, all right. I'm just messing with you. I'm glad you all got back safely."

I considered slapping the young man, but then I got a hold of my feminine impulses and remembered that, with my strength, I might accidentally hurt him. "Good to see you, too," is all I said.

He showed me what he'd been working on—some scientific research regarding air currents, something that Rhidea had set him on. After about five minutes of trying to understand it, I gave up and headed outside to find a good tower to climb.

(San'Hal 9, 997—Sunset)

Six days later, at the tail end of the Sunlit Cycle, Rhidea entered the rooms where Mydia and I were staying and announced: "Our preparations are complete. We are ready to head out to Scathii."

Mydia looked up from her desk where she studied her mother's book, *Secrets of Mani.* "We're finally ready? You mean to leave this morning?"

The High Mage nodded. Her face, impassive as ever, looked so . . . old as she stood there in the doorway, leaning one hand on the oak trim. The lines of age on her face, usually so faint, stood out more, belying the face of an almost ancient woman, wiser than I could ever hope to be. How old was she, anyway? She looked so tired. "I had my colleagues working on a few bits of research for the trip."

She waved a few sheets of parchment in her free hand. "But now it's ready. As ready as it can be. We don't have much time to waste," she added, before turning to walk away.

My queen and I looked at each other. "You heard her," she said unexcitedly.

We packed up our things and made preparations to depart for

the eastern coast. We met Kaen by the Palace entrance, where Cae Rhidea stood holding a large leather bag, talking with King Fenwel. As we strode up, she gave the King one last bow, and then slung the pack over her shoulder and turned half around to face us. "Let's be off."

We said our goodbyes to the wonderful King Fenwel and followed after Lady Rhidea. Mydia whispered in my ear as we went, "How does she do it, Lyn? Looking so . . . cool? Stately, yet mature."

I chuckled softly. *Queen research?* "I have no idea, Mydia. She's Cae Rhidea, so I'm not sure she's really a regular human like us."

The mage turned her head as she led us down the East Road. "What are we whispering about, girls?"

"Your old age," I said evenly.

Our teacher gave a snort. "Well, that's not so bad. Not something I'm ashamed of. Age is wisdom, after all."

"Not all folks get wiser with age," Kaen pointed out. "Some never learn."

"That is true. But those ones usually don't live that long in any case."

"Fair point." Kaen squinted up at her as he walked. "Huh. Maybe you're wiser than I thought."

Another snort, this time from Mydia.

We arrived at the coast an hour and a half later, as the coast of the continent was little more than a five-mile hike from Randhorn. Sol lit us from behind, creeping closer toward the horizon as we crested the last hill and got our first view of the coast. I couldn't help but gasp; nothing I had heard could prepare me for the sight. Grass of the palest green, no longer grey, stretched a half mile in front of us, down a gentle slope to an abrupt edge where the world dropped off.

And beyond . . . beyond lay the great expanse.

The Sea of Emptiness.

Grey fog rose up from the depths, blending with the horizon, and rising above that were the majestic sky islands. They were scattered across the horizon, floating chunks of grey rock topped with more grass and buildings here and there. Sky ferries moved back and forth between them from station to station. One such station lay at the bottom of the hill before us. The East Road, which was more of a well-worn path now, led right down to it.

"Welcome," Rhidea said grandly, gesturing toward the vast drop-off and the island-dotted sky beyond, "to the Sea of Emptiness." Then she admitted, "Actually, I have only been here once, and it was long before any of you were born. I hardly remember the place. My, what a sight." She stood admiring the view along with us for a minute, before proceeding down the long hill. "Come on. Let's see about getting ourselves a ferry out to the islands."

It was a gate town of sorts. We entered on the East Road and strode in nonchalantly. Some of the buildings looked to be residential houses while others were warehouses, shops and other businesses. The local workers mostly lived on the Sky Islands, apparently, and took the ferries to and from home. I couldn't wait to see how these ferries worked. I was pretty sure that Rhidea's plan for crossing the chasm had something to do with those ferries and hovering ships which were able to traverse the open air. Marvelous technology, that.

The street terminated at a section labeled "Docking." Indeed, there were docks stretching a hundred yards to either side, with their skyships, small and large, moored here and there. A couple of the smaller ferries were just coming in from the nearest island, which was one of the biggest. I heard a couple of the workers call it Noduin.

Rhidea stopped and asked one of the dockworkers about passage to Noduin, but they all but turned her away. Irritated, she set about searching for the man in charge. Kaen used this chance to show his way with people, especially workers of this type, and proceeded to coax some helpful advice out of one of the swarthy men.

"Ye looks loike outsiders to me," said the sky sailor. "But if you go through the roight channels, ye can find passage to wherever you'd loike." He pointed at a run-down shack on the far-right side of the docks. "Old Carth knows people."

We found the man in the shack as promised, an old man who looked like he got washed, wrung out and hung up to dry repeatedly. He sat drinking a pint of ale in an old wicker chair. "Whaddya want?" he called grumpily from the back of the cabin.

"Passage," Kaen said. "Passage to Noduin."

"What fer? Ye don't look like locals ta me. Nor do ye look like yer in the cargo business." He lifted his head back and squinted at us. "Highfalutin folk, eh? Well, if ye want passage, you've come to the right place, because Old Carth doesn't ask many questions. Do ye have coin?"

Kaen looked to me, and I tilted my head to one side briefly. "Enough."

Old Carth gave a grunt. "A'ight then. Follow me."

We met up with Rhidea outside, and in short order, Old Carth's men were readying a ferry for us. "How?" she asked in some frustration.

I grinned and pointed at Kaen.

"I have my ways," he said. "I guess your old-timer persuasion skills just don't cut it sometimes."

We paid up to Old Carth, and one of his men motioned for us to board the small wooden boat. It was perhaps fifteen feet long and six feet wide, with a thin, light hull made up of leather-overlaid boards with bracers running in between at intervals and long fins sticking out of the sides almost like wings. We all stared wide-eyed at it, watching it rock gently from side to side. The ferryman laughed. "Don't worry," he said in his accented voice, though his was lighter than that of the other men we'd talked to. "She's quite safe. Last person who fell and died off my boat was a man called Ferriman, and that was years ago." His face was completely straight. When he saw that his words weren't helping us, he added, "That was because he was a fool and leaned out over the side. You're supposed to stay in the boat."

We stared at him for a minute, and he added, "He was also drunk."

Mydia gulped audibly. "How far down is it?"

"Mighty far. We think it's infinite. Most folks think you will just keep falling and falling, though some think there's a bottom where you'll eventually just splat like a large fruit."

The Queen winced, turning her head and squeezing her eyes and mouth shut in one of the most painful grimaces I'd ever seen. "Th-that's . . . that's not the image I needed right now."

Rhidea climbed stoically into the boat, stiffly but steadily. The boatman took her hand in a gentlemanly way and helped her to her seat toward the front of the boat. She crossed her legs and looked at the rest of us with forced relaxation. "It's . . . not so bad."

Kaen went next, and then me, and lastly Mydia. The boatman helped each of us to our seats, seating Mydia right up against Kaen in a comical scene. He looked as uncomfortable as I'd ever seen him, almost strangely so, as she clutched his arm for support.

I realized suddenly that the boatman was speaking to us.

"—The railing, because you can't rely on it too much. Just stay still in your seat and you'll be perfectly safe. It will be about fifteen minutes to Noduin."

Rhidea's attention was fixed very tightly on the man as he started the boat moving, her discomfort giving way to fascination. It seemed to hover completely on its own. The sailor used a long oar to shove off after untying the ropes that held the craft to the dock, and we were moving. Then he went back to the front of the boat and said, "We're off."

- Chapter 30 -

The Sky Islands

Authority is not so much a science as it is an art. Nor is it so much an art as it is a right. But more than a right, it is a gift. The gift is not so uncommon, but Authority itself must be sparked, kindled and—most importantly—worked for. Needless to say, it is complicated. But who would ever have expected the power to command nature itself to be easy?
— From *Secrets of Mani*, by Sor the Lark

(San'Hal 9, 997—Sunset)

Feln the boatman did absolutely nothing. He just stood with hands clasped, and yet the boat began to pick up speed. I felt a breeze blowing inexplicably in the direction that we were going, in addition to the steady, warm updraft which drifted up from the chasm itself. A glance to either side showed me that the wind seemed to lift the fin-like wings, propelling the little boat.

I looked to Rhidea to see her thinking the same as I was: this man was a wind mage. As I paid more attention to the boat, the wind and the boatman, I grew more and more sure that that was how he was moving it. To Rhidea, I'm sure it was obvious, being such an experienced mage.

Rhidea did not mention it, and so I didn't either. We would figure out how to utilize this information once we reached Scathii and learned more.

I watched the "shore" leave us, growing more distant. The rock face faded and vanished after just a hundred yards into the thick, grey mist of the Sea. Grey flakes of an ash-like material floated in the air. Was that what actually obscured the bottom? Ahead of us loomed the island of Noduin like a great fortress.

"So, where are you headed?" the man asked, turning to look at Rhidea. "I'm assuming Noduin is not your final destination?"

She considered for a moment, and then replied honestly, "We are on our way to the Isle of Scathii."

The man nodded. "You wouldn't be the first wanting to see the secret island of the wind sailors. Folks have all sorts of reasons to visit there, though most don't make it out for this reason or that. As you've already found out, it's hard to find anyone willing to take strangers out past the shore, even to Noduin. I can find you one of my friends who can take you farther, but you're on your own after that. We aren't going to be able to get you to Scathii."

"We understand," Rhidea said politely. "But as they say, where there is a will there is a way. Our quest is very important to us, as well as to others."

The man nodded again. "I see. My name is Feln, by the way. You see, our people may technically be part of the nation of Nemental, but we consider ourselves to be our own people. These are our lands. We control all travel to and from the Sky Islands and are the sole provider of wool in the whole world. If King Fenwel, bless his kind heart, ever tried to force us into submission, well . . . the Islanders could easily escape beyond reach. It would not be the most pleasant existence, but we are technically self-sufficient."

"I've never thought of that," Mydia said, her voice still sounding nervous from the flying experience.

"Worry not," Rhidea said, "King Fenwel would not try to force the Islanders like that. He would have specified your destruction as part of our mission in that case."

Feln froze momentarily, tensing up. "The King sent you?"

"Yes," she answered, prompting a nod from Feln. "But it's not about trade, laws or any such thing. We are here for more scholarly reasons. I was merely jesting about destruction."

He nodded again, looking a little more relaxed. "Well, you seem like harmless enough folks. Remember, I'm one of Old Carth's men, and I don't say anything about anybody, strange or not, mysterious or not."

At this point, we were about halfway across the span from the shore to Noduin. Every time I looked down, I still got a dizzy spell and felt almost sick to my stomach. It was now that Mydia chirped, "So, you're a wind mage, aren't you?"

I put a hand to my forehead. "Mydia . . ." I mumbled her name so quietly that nobody would have heard.

Feln turned, frowning. The boat rocked and stuttered slightly in its course. "Aren't you perceptive, little mage? Hmm." He looked at Rhidea and me. "Are you all magi?"

"Are all the ferrymen magi?" I returned.

"Well, now I'm only more curious what your mission is at Scathii. And I'm sure you're all very curious about how we get these boats to move. Most newcomers are curious, but you folks have hidden your curiosity very purposefully."

"We meant no rudeness," Rhidea said. "We did not want to appear to be opportunists come to steal your secrets."

"And are you?"

"No."

Feln's expression softened. "Then we should be all right. Others are much more uptight than me, especially those who work for different masters. As you can imagine, however, I cannot just divulge secrets of so great importance to outsiders. If the Council of Scathii were to deem you worthy, they may entrust those secrets to you. But that is highly, highly unlikely."

"Thank you for the warning, sir," Mydia said, bowing her head slightly. I nudged her, giving her a look to remind her that she should act more like a queen—a tactful queen. Her only response was a small shake of her head. *No,* it seemed to say, *I will not act like a queen all the time, my subject.*

Feln didn't say more on the topic the rest of the trip. We arrived in a few minutes at the western docks of Noduin and the boatman let us out one-by-one after mooring it to the pier. Mydia looked overjoyed to be back on land, albeit floating land, although I had to catch her as she tottered on her feet.

"Careful, there, Myds," Kaen said, though he himself looked a little shaky. She shot him a quick glare, mouthing the new nickname he'd used.

"Thank you, Master Feln," Rhidea said smoothly. "We are in your debt."

"My pleasure, good lady." He dipped a formal bow. "I'll show you to my acquaintance here on Noduin. Now, will you be needing a pickup to take you back to the mainland in a while?"

Rhidea glanced between the four of us briefly. "No. I think not."

He frowned.

"Don't worry," I assured him. "We'll work something out."

He shook his head. "I'm not even going to ask. Your business is your own, travelers, and I will trust you to not get yourselves in over your heads. Come with me."

He led us into the bustling town that was Noduin. It was where most of the trade went on between the Sky Islands and mainland traders. Feln explained as we went that the people of the various inhabited sky islands sent their crops and merchandise here, and from Noduin it was exported by skyship to the mainland, and vice versa. Incoming wares were distributed as ordered by the various islands. There was a residential district on Noduin, but it was mostly made up of wealthier trading families.

Feln's friend turned out to be a greasy-looking (but trustworthy, as Feln assured us calmly) short fellow with straggly black hair. He had a nasally, high-pitched voice that squeaked as he said, "Ahoy there, jumbucks!"

I didn't know what a jumbuck was, but I couldn't help but think how different all of these men were, considering how well they seemed to know each other.

His name was Shanagel (he said it like "finagle"). That didn't help.

"Shanagel is an old friend," said Feln. "He will get you closer to Scathii, as quickly and safely as any. Farewell, and may your travels be blessed by the warm winds of summer."

"That's right, mates," squeaked Shanagel. "You're in right good hands. Now hurry-hurry, let's be off'n. 'Fore the clouds roll in."

I rolled my eyes and glanced at Kaen. He raised his eyebrows questioningly, and I mouthed the words, *He's annoying*. He smirked, nodding with an askant glance at the short man.

We followed after Shanagel, and he led us to his boat, which was just as small as the one that Feln had piloted. This one had a different pattern of wings (fins, or whatever they were) on the side, painted strange colors. Again, I looked over the great ledge, this one more sheer (in fact, the islands tapered inward as they went down, having a roundish bottom).

We left the town behind us as we drifted toward the next island, Nomu, which lay just to the southeast of Noduin, its near cliff lit by the low sun. We chatted a bit with Shanagel, but I didn't listen to much of it. I was nervous about getting to the Isle of Scathii. From Nomu, we would be able to get there . . . if someone was willing to take us to the secluded island. Well, the biggest hurdle would still be finding a way to travel all the way across the Sea of Emptiness.

The great expanse made me feel . . . queasy. The dizzying drop into the unknown depths was as frightening a fate as I'd ever faced, and it was also just . . . eerie. What was down there? No one knew. All I knew was that every time I chanced a look downward, I regretted it. So I kept my eyes on the approaching island.

". . . And there's these giant beerds on the island. Huge, lunkin' things, the biggest beerdies you ever saw! Great black things. Scary, Oi tells ya."

"Giant black birds?" Mydia gasped. "That does sound quite scary."

"Aye! Aye! I tell ya, I tell ya . . ." The strange man waffled on, but I tuned him out.

Eventually, we landed at Nomu Island and said farewell to Shanagel.

"Ahh," Kaen breathed. "Good to be back on land. Uh, land . . . ish? Land away from land? I'm getting overwhelmed by these strange magical boat rides."

Mydia laughed, although it was a nervous laugh born of relief. "I still feel like I'm going to hurl."

Rhidea, for her part, seemed unfazed aside from the initial discomfort she'd exhibited upon getting into the first sky boat. When questioned, she simply replied, "I'm used to traversing the air through abnormal means using my magic. I've gotten quite clever with the art by now. But the worst is yet to come, young ones."

I turned, looking back over the western horizon. I couldn't help a soft gasp of amazement. "What a view . . ." The setting sun lay half hidden by the hill near the shore of the mainland, smoldering with a lazy light-red hue and dripping pastel colors onto the fields of pale green. It refracted off the atmosphere in the Sea of Emptiness and filtered through in odd ways at the same time. Overhead spread a beautiful gradient ranging from orange to pink to magenta. No stars shone yet. It would be another two days at least until they were visible. Hopefully we would be on another continent already and would not have to span the great chasm of the world by starlight.

"Lyn? Come on." Kaen nudged my shoulder, and I shook myself.

"Oh. All right." I followed after the other three, and we made our way through the docking bay of Nomu Island. Once out of the district, I saw that the buildings gave way to rich pasturelands with various animals, with wooden fences separating individual farms.

"Oh, how cute!" Mydia cried. "They have little sheep farms here!"

"Of course," Kaen said. "How did you think they managed to export all these things if they didn't raise anything of their own? Huh. Sheep, though. So that's what they look like . . ." He stared at the wooly white animals as we passed them by.

Nomu was nearly as large as Noduin but nowhere near as densely populated. Most of the land here was used for efficient but small-scale farming, each plot probably managed by just one family. On the southeast side was a small trade market which dealt largely with the people of Scathii.

Upon reaching this establishment, we met with a lot of furtive and untrusting glances and few words. So the people really were untrusting of strangers. We talked with some of them and got evasive answers that amounted to: no, I won't take you to Scathii.

Finally, Rhidea gave up and called out in a loud voice, "People of the Market! Traders, merchants, captains and citizens! I am the

Wandering Mage, Cae Rhidea, and I come on behalf of King Fenwel of Randhorn."

A hush fell over the few dozen people in the crowd. People stopped what they were doing, and many faces turned to look at the mage, who stood tall with one hand raised in a reaching pose.

"Who's that?" called a young child before his mother clamped a hand over his mouth. "Hush, Benny. That's someone very important and very, *very* dangerous." The mother's voice grew ever quieter as she spoke, though I could just barely make out the words.

Finally, two men strode up to us, one in a red coat and the other in blue. "Good day, Madam," said the one in red, bowing politely. "We are the senior tradesmasters present here today. What is your business, if we may ask? And how can you prove that you are indeed who you say you are?"

Rhidea pursed her lips. "The business of my companions and me is our own, but it is of the utmost importance. As for proof, well . . . many of the simplest ways to prove my own identity would likely result in a minor disaster. Are you all right with that, my good men?"

The man in red blanched slightly. "Uh-um . . ."

The man in blue cleared his throat. "Lady, we mean no disrespect. We simply want to verify—"

"I trust this will do, then." Rhidea proffered a small slip of parchment and held out her left-hand bracelet, upon both of which were the King's own insignia.

"The royal emblem of Randhorn!" said the man in blue. "Truly, there is no mistaking it."

"Our apologies, Madam," said the man in red, giving an even deeper bow. "While we may not see eye-to-eye on all fronts, the people of the Sky Islands recognize the royal authority of Nemental and seek to please King Fenwel as much as is reasonable. What do you require of us?"

"Passage to the Isle of Scathii."

The men looked around nervously.

"What for?" asked the man in blue.

"You asked what I require, not *why* I require it." Rhidea's words were cutting, nearly producing a flinch in the men. "Can it be arranged? I know they are a secretive people, that they keep to themselves and do not like to have visitors, but it is important to us and to the king of Nemental. And it is quite possibly vital to our world at large."

The man in blue raised an eyebrow. "The world at large, hmm? So . . . what you are saying is that this quest of yours is of great import to many different parties. We may be able to arrange a ship to take you to Scathii, if—*if*—you can produce for us a treasure from the mainland of a fitting price."

Kaen scowled. "What kind of money-grubbing . . . ?"

Rhidea raised a hand to the side, touching his chest in a warding gesture. "Patience, Kaen." She looked the man in the eye. "A treasure? That is all?"

"Yes."

"We are . . . commonly swayed by items of great importance to other people," explained the other man. "It is like an advance deposit of trust."

More like a way to swindle people who look rich, I thought with annoyance.

"Well, then here." The mage produced a curved horn of solid silver, bearing a spiral pattern. "A horn from an Anteleth of the Plains of Nandaer."

The men grew wide-eyed. "An Anteleth horn?" The man in red reached gleefully for the item, then paused, looking up at the tall mage. "May I?" She nodded, and he took it. The two men inspected the piece, nodding and whispering to each other, and then said, "Very well. This is a fitting treasure from the mainland. We will grant what you ask."

A cheer rose up from one of the nearby merchants, eliciting a glare from the two tradesmasters. The man quickly turned back to his work, abashed. Apparently, some ears were still listening in on our conversation.

We followed the two merchant leaders to a group of Sky Sailors, who looked up as we neared.

"Men! Who will take these four travelers to the Isle of Scathii? They have made a bargain for safe passage to the island."

This got mixed reactions from the sailors, ranging from impressed to offended to politely uninterested. One of them spoke up, a large, burly man with black hair and a full beard. "You've informed them that there will be extra charges involved?"

The man in red coughed and nudged his companion, who said, "Of course!" He pointed a meaningful look at Rhidea, who sighed.

"We can manage whatever fee you may throw at us."

The black-bearded man almost seemed taken aback. "Hmm. Whatever fee . . . ?"

"Whatever *reasonable* fee," I spoke up. I tried to look as imposing as possible, crossing my arms and assuming the same pose as Kaen. Belatedly, I added, "Sir."

The man laughed. "Well, I'll take you. When do you need to head out?"

We looked at one another. "As soon as you can manage, sir," Mydia said politely.

"In one hour, then," the big-chested man said earnestly. "As soon as my crew has packed up from the sale."

An hour later, we were boarding the *Listening Gale*, the pride of the large captain—who had belatedly introduced himself as Charta. This was a *ship*, a real ship! Two decks high and forty feet long, decked in wood with a metal prow and guards on the front and back, the *Listening Gale* was unlike any vessel I'd ever set foot on. I'd seen the large wind-sailing ships from a distance and in passing, but it was different to see one up close and set foot on it. The ship had a mast in the center like the ships that had been used on the lake at Ti'Vaeth, sporting two massive sails. Wings spread out on either side of the ship in a vaguely triangular pattern, narrower in the front and reaching over a dozen feet out to either side near the back end.

We boarded the ship between two of these long wings which drooped over the dock. At the rear of the ship was affixed a long fin—called the tail by the sailors—which angled backward to either side horizontally like that of a river porpoise. It was fixed to a triangular vertical piece, shooting off from either side and tapering at the back end. It angled slightly upward, but could be adjusted as needed. Apparently, it was to hold the back end downward so that the ship didn't simply swoop in vertical loops. Now that was a horrible thought.

Mydia was excited but also terrified as she boarded the ship in front of me. At her request, Kaen, who walked up the plank in front of her, held her hand awkwardly and then helped her up the last bit. Captain Charta gave him a manly punch on the shoulder and winked. I nearly groaned.

After the plank was drawn up, the captain began bellowing various orders to his crew. It turned out that this huge ship was actually driven by pedal power, with six different crew members pumping pedals that drove silver shafts, which in turn drove circular fans positioned at the rear of the ship. These could be seen from the back, and all of them started up soon after the orders went out. We cast off, and the giant ship began humming its way through the sky, toward Scathii.

Only . . . I couldn't *see* Scathii.

I cast about, searching for one of the crew to ask about the mysterious place. Scanning the far horizon, all I could see was the grey haze all about us, tinged with other colors from the sunset. Sol's rays melted into the sky in an indistinct horizon. There were a couple more sky islands out this far, but they were off to either side, none in the direction we were heading. Was the island really just that far away?

I settled on asking my teacher. "Rhidea, where *is* Scathii? Is it so far away that we can't even see it yet?"

The scholar frowned. "I do not actually know. The sailors say that it takes about an hour to travel there by ship."

"Wow. That is far for such a big ship."

Rhidea shook her head. "Not really. Six fans drive this ship, but no wind magic like the Ferries so far as I've seen. They probably have some mechanism helping to keep it aloft, but that is all. I'm sure it is not any faster than those small vessels. Honestly, I suspect that the island is hidden partially under the cover of the grey haze that permeates this place. We have been heading in a gentle downward course, or haven't you noticed?"

"Huh. I didn't." I scratched my chin, head tilted upward as I stared out over the tall bow of the ship. The triangular, interlocking wings vibrated on the wind, rocking the deck gently. Hidden in the grey layer . . . well, it wasn't grey in the fading cast of Sol's colorful light, but . . . could she be right? What an odd place to live. I sighed and resigned myself to waiting.

- Chapter 31 -

The Hidden Isle

Water magi, on the other hand, tend to be people of wisdom and empathy—merciful, thoughtful and supportive of others. Water magi are held in high esteem, as it is seen as the greatest of all branches. Inexplicably, or perhaps ironically, water magi tend to be women, although in a world of predominantly women, that is not saying much.
— From *Secrets of Mani*, by Sor the Lark

(San'Hal 9, 997—Sunset)

Rhidea was right. As we drew nearer to the island, moving slowly but steadily downward, the floating landmass seemed to appear out of nowhere, fading from the mists. The Isle of Scathii. The sunset painted it the strangest shade of violet, the vibrant colors in the misty air mixing to create a new hue. As we approached to land, that hue resolved into a steadier grey, and then more specific colors. Dark slate-colored rocks cropped the edge of the island. Silvery grass grew farther toward the center. Coniferous trees grew along the southern edge of the island, needles a dark green that faded to silver.

We docked in a small bay nearby a few other ships and some smaller craft I did not recognize. The *Listening Gale* coasted to a stop at the pier and the men began hopping ashore to tie down the boat and lower the gangplank.

"Welcome!" bellowed Captain Charta, coming up to clap Kaen and me on the shoulder with one huge hand each. Then in a lower voice, he said, "It's probably a once-in-a-lifetime chance to see the Hidden Isle of Scathii for you travelers. You got lucky with the tradesmasters." He looked to Rhidea. "Now, about that gold. I don't do this just out of the kindness of my heart, you know. There was something in it for me. Twelve copper pence and we'll call it done."

The mage held up her coin pouch, left hand pausing as she inserted it into the bag. "Ten."

"All right, all right. We'll go with eleven," he conceded grudgingly. "Since you've been such good passengers."

She paid out the eleven small pieces of copper and then shook hands with the large man. "A pleasure, Captain Charta," she said formally.

He gave a hearty smile and an equally hearty salute. "Of course, my lady. Are you going to be needing a quick return trip as well? Should we stick around and wait a day or two?"

Rhidea shook her head. "No, thank you. That won't be necessary."

"Well, then. Farewell, travelers, and . . . make sure you mind your manners while you're on this island. Wouldn't want to upset the locals too much. After all, you're a long way from the mainland now."

"We understand," Rhidea replied smoothly.

"Oh, and one more piece of advice," said Charta. "Whatever your business is here, you're going to end up going through the elders. If you try to skirt around their authority, they will find out and they will not be happy. They are very . . . old-fashioned and traditional, though, so don't get your hopes up too high. They may just turn you away and boot you out."

"We'll keep it in mind," Mydia said from beside me. "Thank you very much, sir."

We parted ways with the trading crew and headed into the island. Scathii was small, perhaps a mile in diameter and home to one little, tight-knit village, also called by the same name. This village was situated straight ahead, left of the grove of evergreens by a sparkling pond. It was odd how the ash-like particles in the air played with the light, giving a similar distortion effect to faraway sights as that of the whole island when we were approaching it, except that from this angle it mostly made things look grey. Here, we were just beneath the reach of the setting sun.

"So . . . I take it the locals aren't very welcoming?" Mydia asked tentatively. "Wait! Where are we going to stay the night? What if they don't give us a place to stay?"

"It will be all right," Rhidea said calmly.

"Princess," Kaen added in a low voice.

Mydia gave him a weak punch to the ribs as she walked beside him. "That's 'Queen'."

"Then act like it," he said, and then went on to change his voice as though to imitate the queen. "Oh, thank you very much, sir." He batted his eyelashes for effect. "Fifteen copper pieces for you, sir."

Mydia stopped for a moment, as though unsure how to react. Then she giggled and kept walking.

This time I groaned. "Cut it out, children."

Both heads turned immediately forward. Rhidea, at the lead, just pretended to ignore the banter. She was used to it by now.

The village was little more than a few houses lumped together with a quaint wooden fence and an open double gate. A couple of mottled sheep lay by the gate and lifted their heads to bleat when we came by.

As we came closer and passed through the gate, I saw that a few people milled about in what was obviously the village square. We approached them to inquire about where to find the village elders, and were told that some of them could be found in the Arbiters' Hall, a tall, peak-roofed building at the western end of town. On our way, we passed a couple of children playing in the yard. Cutest little kids, too . . .

Rhidea strode right up the steps to the Arbiters' Hall and knocked on the simple wooden door. An aged voice came from inside, "Who is it?" Soon, a greying middle-aged man poked his head out the door. "Oh. Oh." He seemed to take in the fact that she was someone of importance, not to mention a stranger. "Who are you?"

"I am the Wandering Mage, Rhidea," she said. "My companions and I have come on behalf of King Fenwel of Nemental to seek a favor from the people of Scathii."

"Oh, dear," the man breathed. "Come on in. And we will . . . talk."

"So . . . no, we won't help you," said Hermas, one of the five village elders. He was a bald man of at least eighty years, the oldest of all five elders.

We sat on a blanketed floor around a fireplace, across from the four elders present tonight. The inside of the Hall was quite cozy, its plank walls draped with various furs and quilts. The elders had been courteous enough, particularly the man who had first greeted us— who had introduced himself as Ben—but were very reluctant to listen to us at all, let alone heed our request.

Rhidea sighed and rubbed her temples. I could tell exactly what she was thinking: *This will be a long evening.*

(San'Hal 10, 997—Dusk)
We ended up staying the night at the Village Inn and Eatery. In the morning, we set about talking to whatever townspeople were willing to speak with us. At one point while Mydia was with Rhidea and our

assassin friend, Kaen and I ran across a young boy of perhaps twelve or thirteen years, not quite at that age of a boy's growth spurt into a man's size. He had sandy blond hair and bright, keen eyes. He was also quite friendly, returning a bright, "Hullo!" when I greeted him. He ran up to us and asked, "Are you the strangers my uncle was talkin' about?"

"Probably," I said with a sidelong glance to Kaen. "We're quite strange, after all."

The boy laughed out loud like it was the funniest joke he'd heard in a while. "I think you're pretty. I mean—pretty nice. You're nice. Who's the tall man?" He gestured to Kaen.

I gave Kaen another look and mouthed the word *man* in a disbelieving way, eliciting only a raise of his eyebrows. To the boy, I said, "That's my friend Kaen. And I'm Lyn. We're from Nytaea. What's your name, boy?"

He sniffed, crossing his arms and turning half away. "I'm almost a man." Then he grinned and said, "Name's Oliver." He stuck out his twiggy hand, and I shook it gingerly. "Nice to meet ya, Lyn. You have big hands."

I felt my face heat up a bit despite myself. "Excuse me?"

"Well, you do! You have big shoulders, too. You're just kind of . . . big looking. Bigger than you actually are." Now it was Oliver's turn to blush. "Sorry, that probably sounds kinda rude . . . I'm not very good with words, mate. Er . . . madam."

Kaen and I just laughed. I reached out and ruffled the boy's blond hair. "I like you, Oliver. Where do you live?"

"Oh!" He turned and pointed across the village, bouncing slightly on his feet as he did so. "See that house with the windmill waaaaaay over there?"

We nodded, following the point of his finger.

"Well, it's not that one. It's that little one beyond it; past the fence. That's my uncle Ben's place. I stay with him. My parents work on Isle Noduin during the Off Season."

"Both of them?" Kaen asked. "I'm surprised they'd leave you alone, Oliver."

"Nah, they, uh, they're fine with it. But I'm not alone. I like my Uncle Ben! Even if he is a stuffy fuddy-duddy most of the time." Oliver made a pouting face. "He doesn't let me go gliding very often. And I love gliding."

I perked up at that. "Gliding?"

"Yeah! And he's got his own whole wood shop, so I get to use it to make whatever I want. Like my inventions. I make gliders— wanna see?"

"Sure," I said hesitantly, trying to mask my excitement. "Your uncle won't mind?"

"Well . . . he can't really say anything about inviting strangers over right now, because he's out of town, too. Heheh. He left this morning, and won't be back till tomorrow."

Kaen shrugged and said, "We're interested in anything to do with flying, so . . ."

Oliver took us over to the little house he had pointed out, which was small but had an attached workshop of almost the same size. Boards were stacked beside it. The blond-haired boy went to this building and unlatched the double door, pulling it open to reveal an assortment of wooden tables, saw-horses and frames placed here and there. Wooden planks leaned up against the far wall. And on one of the tables sat a contraption made from wood and leather, roughly eight feet in length, with triangular wings, one folded up and the other only half-together.

"Here she is," said the boy, walking over to his project. "I call 'er the Gyrfalcon. My latest glider model.”

“Would you look at that,” Kaen breathed, hovering behind the boy. “This is impressive. The wings fold out and snap into place in order to catch the air and let you hover for a little while?”

“Right. In normal places, you could glide for hundreds of feet on one of these. See, I have older models over here.” He gestured to one wall, which had multiple designs with wings folded up and bound, leaning against the corner. “This one should hopefully be sturdier. That’s what my uncle is always worried about. He doesn’t mind me making them, ’cause it keeps me busy, but he gets nervous every time I talk about actually testing them out. Anyway, here in the Sky Islands, I know some tricks.” He grinned, pointing upward. “Up-drafts.”

I frowned. “You mean air currents that blow upward?”

“Yep! The air around here is warm. Some spots are warmer than others. Kind of random where the warm spots will come up from the Sea, but if you can predict them right, you can tell where they’ll be and make out ones that are already blowing. An updraft or two’ll let you gain quite a bit of altitude, although the sweet spot is usually in the same height where we are now, below the rest of the Sky Islands. The air gets cooler up there and it’s harder to fly.”

“So you’re saying you can actually fly with one of these,” Kaen said. “For an extended period of time.”

The boy rubbed his chin. “Pretty much. But it’s tricky.”

“So, Oliver,” I said, “Would you care to come and have lunch with us? We have two other companions, scholars who are interested in flying and would love to meet you. And since your uncle’s still away . . .”

“Well, ’course I know what my Uncle Ben would say,” he huffed. “But he doesn’t rightly have to know.”

"Are there others around here who study this sort of thing?" I asked him. "Anyone more knowledgeable on the flying machines around here?"

"Eh . . . I don't really think so, mate. Unless you're talking about the great big sailing ships. I'm kind of my own experimental . . . inventor." Oliver grinned.

"Well, you're awfully full of yourself," Kaen said. "Come on, kid. Where's a good place to eat around here?" And then to me, "Where did our friends run off to this time?"

I shrugged, and we set off to find them.

"You make flying inventions?" Mydia asked incredulously. "Wow. You're, what, ten?"

"Thirteen. Almost." Oliver sat next to Kaen, across from Rhidea, Mydia and me, kicking his feet like, well . . . a child. We were in the Village Eatery, waiting for our food to cook. Rhidea was making a splurge on the boy, getting him the most delicious-looking thing on the menu. Of course, he didn't know she was loaded with royal coin.

As I watched, Oliver ducked his blond head and whispered to Kaen in a voice that we could all hear, pointing semi-discreetly at Mydia: "She's really pretty!"

Kymhar, who sat on Oliver's other side, glanced down impassively at the boy, and Mydia herself blushed almost imperceptibly, ducking to cover an amused grin.

Rhidea cleared her throat. "Oliver, as I'm sure Lyn and Kaen here have told you, we are searching for a way to traverse the Sea of Emptiness."

"She said you're interested in flying, madam," he said politely. "Didn't say nothing about sailing around on the Sea."

"Not just sailing around," she said, and then gave us a small shrug that seemed to say, '*might as well be direct*'. "We want to cross the Sea of Emptiness."

Oliver ran the words over silently, as though trying to process what she meant. "You mean like . . . the other side of the world? There's . . . there's more land out there? Everyone says the Sea is endless." He seemed excited by the possibility.

Rhidea shook her head. "We believe there to be another continent on the other side. That this Sea is no more than a very large chasm. No one has charted the Sea to an edge—this does not mean that there isn't one."

The boy nodded, an attentive look on his face that spoke of intelligence beyond his years, and then rubbed his lower lip with a thumb. "So . . . you're travelers, come from the mainland to find something out here. Out there. You lot think there's more land across the sea, and there's something you want on that land, eh? I reckon you're somebody important, then, madam?"

"Call me Lady Rhidea. But yes, you're pretty close, child."

"Rhidea. Miss Rhidea, where are you from?" he gestured to the rest of us. "Nemental?"

"She is," Mydia said. "Most of us come from Nytaea, but we left from Randhorn."

His eyes lit up. "Randhorn? Did you see the king?"

Rhidea glanced at Mydia briefly. "I am retainer to King Fenwel. And this is Mydia, Queen of Nytaea."

The boy's jaw dropped. "Blimey! I *knew* ya were important people! Wait, Nytaea has a Queen now? Huh. So . . . heheh, you must be on a pretty top-secret mission, then, is that right? And you're really just gonna trust a wee boy with your secret?"

"Well, if you can help us in any way, lad, then it's worth it."

"Oh, that's right. Flying. . . . Well, I make gliders. See, the air around here, blowing up from the deeps, it's warm, right?" Oliver began to explain some of the science of the chasm, as well as how he designed his little fliers.

Rhidea brought out a scroll with experimental blueprints scrawled on different sections of it. "Here are some plans." She began pointing out different ideas to the boy, who perked up immediately and listened with rapt attention. From what I'd seen so far, Oliver was likely smarter than me, despite his scrawny, youthful appearance and childish mannerisms.

Oliver's mouth formed a silent *'Oh'* as he studied the scroll. He asked questions and Rhidea and Mydia replied (they were most of the brains behind all of this stuff).

Before long, we agreed to ask Oliver's uncle the next day about helping us out with our project.

We stayed overnight at the same inn and then came back to find Oliver and his uncle at the house. Oliver had obviously told him about us and our far-fetched plans, because the man stood at the door with beefy arms crossed, a disapproving look on his face. "So it's the crazy travelers," he said with a grunt.

He was also one of the elders that we had met the other night. Ben, one of the quieter ones. Somehow I hadn't put together that he must be the same Ben we had talked to.

We were a bit uncertain what to say to his welcome, but Kaen broke the silence. "Sir, your nephew was very kind to us, and . . . we really need to make this work somehow."

"If there's somewhere better to go to . . ." Mydia began, but the middle-aged man cut her off.

"Nah, nah. Come on in, travelers. You're all daft, but it doesn't mean I won't help you out. Seems I underestimated your tenacity the other night. The name's Ben, by the way. You can call me Uncle Ben if you like, because it seems I'm everyone's uncle around here any-way."

He showed us around the house, which was more spacious and well-decorated than I'd expected, and treated us to some piping-hot tea from the cook stove. Then he sat down to talk with us. We told him pretty much the same stuff as we had Oliver, and he took it with mostly grunts and down-turned lips of consideration.

"Well, you're definitely right crazy," he said at length. "Not tak-ing that one back. But if what you say about the magic of Mani is true . . . then this fool's errand may be pretty important after all. And here I thought old King Fenwel was just on about nothing lately . . ."

"You heard something about his research?" Rhidea asked with some surprise.

"Well, sure. Word travels fast in the Sky Islands where the right folks are concerned. Since I'm on the Scathii Council, I hear a thing or two now and then. They've always said Fenwel's the type to take interest in things that most others don't, and of course let's not forget your own reputation, my lady—" he dipped his head in a brief show of respect to Rhidea "—but lately they say he's been pulling some long strings. Helping Nytaea secede, and something more . . . covert. I'm guessing that's what this would be." He spread his hands around the room at our mismatched group of five.

"You're not wrong," Rhidea said. "The covertness was mostly be-cause we knew that we had to go behind the Archlord's back for the large part, although now that's not so big a deal. He is our . . . tempo-rary ally, shall we say? Tentative ally, let's go with that." She glanced briefly at Kymhar. "Domon is helping us in our journey, as our goals happen to align."

"So what do you want of me, then?" Ben asked.

"We want to build a sky ship," Rhidea said. "We have plans, and you and Oliver have the keys to making them work. We will pay for your services and any required materials, and then we will depart over the chasm to find the hidden continent."

Ben rubbed his chin. "Chasm . . . Well, then. Hmph. I guess so. But remember, boy, you are not to get any big ideas about all this adventuring stuff. I can't have you gallivanting with a rag-tag group of strangers."

"R-right, sir." Oliver swallowed and tried to look innocent, as though he had not even entertained such thoughts.

What a little troublemaker, I thought. Though there was something else in his reaction to his uncle's words, something I couldn't place.

"So," said Kymhar in his gravelly voice from across the room, causing everyone to turn and look at him as though suddenly realizing he was there, "this means we have work to do."

- Chapter 32 -

Flight Testing

The magic of Mani is a wild, untamable thing, and so the magi who attempt to tame it put themselves at risk in doing so. Any Coaction tires us out, of course—the greater the use, the more the fatigue—and attempting a feat of Coaction that one has not mastered yet, or is out of his or her branch of expertise, shocks the body, much like intense exposure to heat or cold will, often triggering severe fatigue, headaches, and vomiting.
— From *Secrets of Mani*, by Sor the Lark

(San'Hal 13, 997—Night Season)

Two days later, we had a prototype ready to go. Oliver's parents were set to return in one day's time, or so the boy had said, but we would probably not even see them if things went well. Kaen volunteered to test the machine. Its design was relatively simple, close to the ones that Oliver had built.

By now, it was full nighttime, but the auroras lit up the long yard behind Uncle Ben's house just fine. Kaen went up onto the roof and took off, diving straight into the air in a show of defiance against gravity. The wings caught the wind and held him up, and he drifted to the ground in an awkward but somewhat controlled spiral before tumbling the last few feet to the ground. The glider did not get damaged, fortunately.

Rhidea went next. She belted on the contraption over her utilitarian dress and tested her limited ground mobility while wearing it. Nodding to herself, she took a deep breath and then ran off the building as well. She wasn't quite as graceful as Kaen, but I saw the look of concentration on her face as she adapted with difficulty to the odd, unintuitive controls of the flier. Then her descent stopped completely as, evidently, she began using her gravity manipulation abilities to test out her magical control of the ship. She flew parallel with the ground for nearly a hundred feet, faltering only briefly, before letting it go and alighting on the ground. Mydia and I ran to help her out of the gear.

"Well?" asked Mydia. "How did it go?"

"You saw yourself," she said. "I was able to keep it aloft easily for a while, though it was mentally taxing due to the odd physics involved. Handling will take some getting used to for anyone, of course. . . . All in all, I'd say it's a success."

Oliver grinned and gave her a thumbs-up.

"But the real test has yet to come." She gestured to the wide-open expanse of the Sea of Emptiness which spanned the dark horizon just a hundred yards away.

"M'lady," Oliver broke in now, distanced as he currently was from his uncle, "I should tell ya again, I've got . . . doubts about how well you'll be able to use the flier over the open Sea without certain skills. Er, abilities."

She glanced over at his uncle, one hundred-odd feet away. "You never mentioned exactly what those were, boy. I assumed you were just trying to make yourself out to be as useful as possible, in hopes that we'd take you along with us when we left."

The boy reddened a bit. "Well . . . that may be, ma'am. A bit. But you see, I'm . . . I'm a wind mage. There're lots of us here on the island."

The Wandering Mage's eyes narrowed. "So, it's true."

"Yeah . . . we try to keep it secret as possible. That's the key to making a lot of the sky ships work. And that's how I can use my gliders so well over the open air. The updrafts aren't a magical boost that just anyone can make use of. You have to harness 'em."

Ah . . . I thought. So that's the key.

Rhidea nodded once more. "I see. I am no wind mage, but I can manipulate gravity, and I think that ability will allow me to circumvent most of those problems."

"Right . . . but I'm not so sure, my lady. Y'see, the farther you get from any big landmass, I think your Authority is going to grow weaker and weaker. Because it's earth-based, right?"

She hesitated. "Sort of. I have never had the opportunity to test it off-shore."

"So . . . you'll need a wind mage to harness the power of the wind and keep you afloat!"

Rhidea gave him a stare, and he grinned back sheepishly. "Heheh."

"No," she said flatly. "We're not going to go against your uncle or your parents' wishes by letting you steal away with us. We can find another wind mage if we must."

"But . . ."

"We cannot risk the life of a child, boy."

He clamped his jaws shut and swallowed. "Yes'm."

"Lyn, Mydia," said the High Mage, "We will do some more experimentation. We still have the hot air idea if this doesn't work. But we have to see about taking two in one glider, and we have to test out those hot spots that Oliver speaks of. . . ."

"Rhidea! You're insane!" I shouted over the rush of air. I was diving nearly straight down, head-first, after Rhidea, who flew the other glider ten paces in front of and below me, strapped together with Mydia. Rhidea was on top, controlling the glider, with Mydia strapped below her. The skirts of both women flapped madly behind them, restricted though they were by the purposefully-chosen style.

I had leapt from the cliff mere seconds after the two, Mydia's screams of terror and excitement in front of me and my own heart pounding blood through my ears in an audible, frenzied rhythm.

"I know!" shrieked the queen. "I didn't volunteer for thi—" The wind took the words, and possibly the breath, right from her mouth. I veered slightly to the right, twisting to the side and adjusting the wings with me, just in case I would need to dodge if they braked suddenly. But they continued to plummet, pulling out only gently before making a wide swoop that brought the glider up steeply. I followed, approaching the mistiest level of the chasm. The wings of the glider rattled and creaked, straining at the mad force of the arc. From the sound of her, Mydia seemed to be on the verge of puking all over us.

"Sorry!" I could just barely make out the words trailing from Rhidea.

I gritted my teeth and took the upward curve at a gentler degree, or at least I tried to. I had very little practice at this glider. Most of the control lay in turning and tilting one's own body in the right directions. We had arranged for Rhidea to carry the extra passenger because I was nearly as heavy as both of them put together. (No, I am not fat. We've been over this.)

According to Rhidea, she would be staying well within range for her gravity Authority to save us should these gliders shred themselves to bits—although of course at this point, if they hadn't already, they should hold up. That was largely the purpose of this little escapade—to test the craftsmanship and safety of Oliver's inventions.

A quick glance behind showed me a terrifying picture of the rocky cliffside which ran down into the unfathomable mists. I had to reorient myself after glancing back. Up ahead, in front of Rhidea, I could make out one of the air disturbances that Oliver had talked about; hot air streams swirling up from the mists below. Rhidea and Mydia caught it just as their upward swoop was beginning to level off, and the wings lifted as they began to whirl upward with the updraft. And then they were out of it, left to their own. Mydia was making some kind of nervous racket about them never returning to the island at all.

As I approached the updraft, I prepared to test out one of our theories: would my Flame Authority be of any use over air? I spread my palms, willing the air to heat up underneath me. I unleashed a weak but long burst of fire just as I came into the air current, and I felt the heat bolster my wings to drive the glider upwards. It took effort to keep myself from tipping, and I made my glider swoop into a tight curve in order to keep as close to the updraft as possible. In this way, I managed to get a large boost to my height and exited the "chimney" with extra vertical speed. Extra, but not by much.

I saw the Isle of Scathii as I circled back once more, straightening out my flight to glide towards the cliff. But it was just above me. At the brink of the land, I could make out the ant-sized forms of Oliver and Kaen waving their hands madly. Almost enough height, but not quite.

Below me, Rhidea had pulled their glider back into the chimney and seemed to be getting some lift this time. Perhaps now she was using her gravity Authority to try and minimize their weight and let the draft carry them higher. It might work . . . but I had to focus.

The curved cliffs of Scathii approached ahead. I wasn't going to try anything to fancy. I planned to climb right up the side. Kaen and Kymhar would have the ropes ready to toss over for me anyway. If only . . .

There came a sudden *snap* from my right wing. The end of it broke and began to dangle, sending me into a twirling tailspin straight for the cliff. I cried out and struggled to right myself and stop the spin, but all I could do was check it a little. I lost more altitude as the cliffs rushed to greet me. Up above, amidst the dizzying spinning, I glimpsed a rope being thrown out hastily for me, but it wouldn't reach down this far . . .

I crashed sidelong into the stone of the island, breaking the left wing of my glider into an L shape and crushing my ribs, hip and head painfully. My ears immediately began to ring and my vision swam as I shouted, slipping against the stone, falling . . .

I threw out my hands and scrabbled desperately against the jagged stone, slicing my hands. I managed to get a hold and stop myself, but my weight was nearly jerked from my grip by my own velocity. My neck whipped back and I thanked my unknown mother and father for my strong, resilient body, without which I'd be hopeless at this point. I shook my head, trying to clear the fog of pain as I gripped the rock with adrenaline-fueled fingers. Looking back, I saw Rhidea and Mydia gliding toward me, shouting desperately.

"No!" I yelled back. "Just get back up—I'll manage!" I knew I could make it somehow, and did not want them risking their own necks as well. Gritting my teeth, I looked upward, searching out my next handhold. I took it, dragging my glider's broken wings with me, trying not to scrape my wounds against the rock, trying but failing to ignore the scream of bruised, possibly broken ribs in my chest. I hauled myself hand over hand, thankful for the frenzied burst of energy that gave me the strength. There were footholds, but the angle of the cliff was not yet fully vertical, so my fingers were the only thing keeping my body against the stone. One slip and I would fall backward into the bottomless chasm.

I forced myself to climb higher, higher, till I could see most of the way up, see a rope dangling above and hear frantic shouting from the boys. Inch by inch, breath by painful breath, until at last I clutched hold of the rope and hung on for dear life. I gave a hoarse call, and they began jerkily towing me up the side. I walked with the rope, finally catching my breath and giving my muscles a brief rest.

At long last, I took hold of the edge of the land and Kaen grabbed my good shoulder with his strong arms, Kymhar taking hold of my other shoulder, and they hauled me over the side. "Oh, Lyn!" Kaen gasped. "You're hurt . . . but alive! Ugh, lay off the meats!"

Kymhar pulled me to my feet. "You are lucky to be alive, lass."

"Where are the other two?" Oliver asked nervously, hands to his mouth. "I feel right terrible. . . ."

As we watched, Rhidea and Mydia's glider floated up above the island, having caught enough warm air to buoy their gravity-lightened load up to shore level. The two women awkwardly caught their footing and came to a stop. Mydia was practically clawing at her straps, shaking and pale.

"Lyn!" she shrieked, rushing over and tripping immediately.

"Mydia," I said raggedly but relieved, "Rhidea. You made it, too. Good." I allowed my head to sag, blurriness threatening to overtake my vision again. I had exerted a lot of myself, and my body was injured, but still the adrenaline pulsed frantically through my veins.

The men got Mydia and Rhidea out of their gear, and everyone rushed to me, helping me out of my broken glider and dragging me back toward the house. We had attracted a couple of frightened villagers, who sent for healers as soon as they saw me. Good neighbors to have, I thought numbly. Nice people.

Back at the house, Uncle Ben laid me down on a cot while we waited for the healers to arrive. I tried to protest that I would be fine, but my own mind and body betrayed me and I cut off into ragged coughing. I sure didn't feel fine. I had made it out of tougher scrapes before, but I had used up a large amount of my strength reserves and also beaten my body quite well.

On top of that, never before had I been faced with the utter terror of falling to my death in a bottomless abyss. (I know, I know, there was that time at the Hall of Eternity, but that doesn't count.) Who knew how far of a drop it was, if there even was a bottom? Would I have just fallen forever into an endless chasm? They didn't call it the Sea of Emptiness for nothing . . . but then again, no one knew that there was a continent on the far side of it, either. Ah . . . my brain was spinning in circles, and I really couldn't focus anymore. I simply squeezed my eyes shut and waited until new voices arrived.

A half hour later, they had me bandaged up in three different places. I'd been stripped nearly naked in front of, well . . . probably everyone except Oliver and Kaen, who had been shooed out by the healing woman. Kaen practically wouldn't leave my side, of course, the mother hen . . . but he was no match for the healer's forcefulness.

I believe her name was Lena? She checked me out and declared me to have no broken bones, bless my lucky stars. She then dressed me up in a simple gown, gave me lots of water and herbal tea, and laid me down to rest. Mydia insisted on paying her handsomely. Neither the queen nor Kaen would leave my side no matter how hard I protested.

Drowsiness overtook me, and the last thing I saw was a nervous Mydia clinging to Kaen.

- Chapter 33 -

The Orphan

The Sea of Emptiness, a boundary that encloses humanity, a border determined to keep us here. Be there more beyond the great expanse? Worlds unknown, or worlds past? Even Gaea, say the bards of old. Even Gaea, ancient home of the Legaleians. Even the Moon, a heavenly body lost in time. But who can brave that hollow chasm, perilous void that swallows man and beast?
— From *Legends of the Ancients*

(San'Hal 13, 997—Night Season)

I dreamed as I slept. In that bright, foggy dream world, White appeared, taking me to a memory of my mother.

In the memory, I was sitting on a tree stump across from my mother, who crouched in a field of tall, grey grass. She was talking to me. I kicked my chubby little legs idly as I tried to pay attention. Well, I didn't exactly try; I wanted to *move.* Every time I moved too much, she would steady me with her strong hands, a quiet reminder to settle down, and each time I grew distracted, she would gently prompt me to focus by turning my head with a finger.

"My little Lynchazel," she was saying, "you have to pay attention, please. I'm only telling you again so that you will remember. At least . . . well, someday. When you do, you'll be able to process what I'm saying more easily."

Actually, my sleeping brain was just barely understanding her words, mostly from the memories of my toddler self. The language was still foreign to me, but I could just make out her meaning.

"Gaea," she explained, "is not like this world. It's a scary world, full of volcanoes and earthquakes, magma fields and raging oceans. The thing you will have to get the most used to is the pull of the planet, which is far stronger than that of Mani. For a full-blooded Hellebes accustomed to it since childhood, it's not so bad, but . . . I worry for you." She stopped and coughed into her shoulder.

Some of the words that she spoke were hard for me to make sense of. Some, like earthquakes and oceans, I was able to grasp the meaning of from my child self, but . . . Hellebes? That one I certainly didn't recognize.

Mother sighed, brushing a stray lock of her silky white hair behind her ear. "I honestly don't know if you will ever make it back. I sense that it is your destiny, that you will one day return to Gaea, but . . . perhaps it's only my fears. Especially the fear of what will happen to you once you do reach Gaea. The people of my homeworld will try to use you, experiment on you as they did on me . . . but you must fight them, and you must win. You can win. I don't know what became of Zent, but some from his team are still out there, and I'm sure that all the time you are here, growing up on Mani, they will be planning for your return to Gaea."

Mother sighed and looked up past me, watching the grey grass sway in the breeze for a moment, and then she bent forward and kissed my forehead. "I wish I could live to see you grow up, my girl."

She smiled once more, and the moment was gone, my dream fading away.

❧⸲⸲❧

When I awoke later that evening, Kaen and Mydia were both still there. Kaen was up and pacing about, Mydia seated quietly on a stool by my cot. Oliver was poking his head around the doorway, probably wondering if he could come in now.

"Lyn!" Mydia whispered. "You're finally awake. How do you feel? Are you all right?"

"Unngh," I groaned. "I'm . . . I'll be . . . ugh, I feel horrible." I grimaced, reaching a hand to my bruised side. I sucked in a deep breath, wincing at the pain it induced in my ribs. "I'll be fine; don't worry." I managed a small smile.

I noted the tear stains on Mydia's soft cheeks, the haunted look in her eyes. She had been scared stiff over what happened to me, worrying the whole time about my recovery. But she seemed to brighten up now.

"Don't sit up yet, Lyn," Kaen protested, walking over just as I tried to sit up. "Careful."

I glared at him as hard as I could manage. "I'm fine. Really. I just—ouch!—need to stretch." I sat up and reached back tentatively to push my hair back behind my ears. "Whew. That was a thrill, huh?"

Mydia put on a pouty face. "That's not funny. I was scared half to death, Lyn! You almost *died*. I almost died! I mean, Rhidea probably had it all under control, but it was really scary. . . ." Her nervous smile died as she caught Kaen's disapproving stare from beside her, and she said, "Sorry. Rambling again. I'm just glad you're all right, mm'kay, Lyn?" She ruffled my hair and smiled, wiping at the tears on her cheeks.

Crybaby. I threw back the sheets to reveal my bare legs covered only by the short, simply-stitched healer's gown I wore. I was about to reach down and roll it up when I realized Kaen was still there, looking around uncomfortably. "Go on, get out," I muttered, and he did so. Then I rolled up the left side of the skirt enough to see the bandages that Lena had wrapped my upper-thigh in.

"Lena did a good job patching you up," Mydia said. "She's a very sweet woman, too."

Satisfied, I nodded and rolled my skirt back down to knee-length, swinging my hips painfully to rest my feet on the floor of the spare room. And then I rose to my feet shakily. Mydia steadied me with a hand on my good shoulder, a worried look on her face. I shook my legs slowly and proceeded to hobble around the room—equally slowly. The more I moved, the better I felt. The achy pain was still there, but I was able to function and my head, throbbing though it still was, was clearer than before.

"I'll be fine," I repeated to Mydia—and Kaen, who'd just reentered the room.

He nodded almost grudgingly. "You will. You're made of tough stuff. Lights and glory, but I don't think we know how tough of stuff . . . I'm just glad you didn't, you know, I'm glad you made it to the rope. That you didn't fall."

"Me too, Kaen." I approached my friend and embraced him tiredly, heedless of my attire. Then I backed away, feeling a touch of heat rising to my cheeks. "You know what, I should . . . find something to put on. Mydia, where are my clothes?"

Kaen glanced down at my gown and backed away. "I'll . . . leave you girls to that. I'll go tell the others you're up."

"Thanks," I said tiredly.

"Rhidea, Kaen, everyone . . . I want to go back out there. I want to fix whatever went wrong so that it doesn't happen again—and then I want to go back out there." I said the words with a fiery resolve that hadn't shown up in a long time, despite how tired I felt.

"Whoa, whoa, calm down, Lyn," Mydia said. "I know we need to get across, but . . ."

"Child, you just came close to dying because of a weak point in the design."

"Then let's find it," I urged them. "We'll go over the whole thing and see what we can improve. We can't just stop here when we're so close."

"There are other options to explore, Lyn," Rhidea said calmly.

I shook my head. "I think we're on to something here. You went out in a team of two and the glider performed fine. In fact, I'd say you were taking riskier moves than I was."

Mydia muttered something in agreement.

Rhidea rested her arm against the door post. "I was also the one with the better chance at recovering from a disaster with my abilities."

"Wait . . . abilities." My eyes widened. "The fire! I used fire magic to boost my height with hot air."

"Oh, that's right!" Oliver chirped in. "I know you said you wanted to try that and all, and it was impressive *looking*, but I never thought that was a very good idea. Fire used wrong can weaken the design. Not good for the glues."

"Let's examine the broken glider for scorch marks and weakness," Rhidea said. "As for design improvements . . . any ideas?"

Mydia's eyes roved back and forth over the floor. "Well . . . actually, I may be able to use my water magic to strengthen the wood of the fliers."

"Really?" I asked skeptically. "You can do that on dead wood? Your Authority is that strong already?"

"I'm not sure. But I can certainly try. I've done it to flowers. I think I can imbue it with a spell that will help it to . . . let's say remember the life it used to have. This would make it more supple and strong, a bit more flexible."

Rhidea pursed her lips. "Hmm . . . but it would be more resistant to heat and fire, if nothing else."

"Yes!" I exclaimed. "Mydia, that's brilliant!"

Kaen and the others immediately began checking the old glider diligently for any type of damage. They insisted that I go to bed early, however, even though my injuries were already healing. So I went back to the inn, ordered a giant meal, and went to bed.

I woke up the next day and sought out my companions. I took all my bandages off and threw them away, because my wounds were nearly completely healed. Only small aches were left.

I found the others at Uncle Ben's house. Oliver was still there, though I wondered when his parents would return and take him away from our project completely.

"Kaen! Mydia!" I called, coming up to the open workshop. "How's the progress?"

"So you're finally awake, huh?" Kaen said with a grin. "You look better."

"Yes, I feel better."

"You look like a new person!" Oliver said. "You don't look hurt or nothin'!"

"Well, let's just say Miss Lena did her magic well, hmm?" I gave him an innocent smile.

"Say, miss, I meant to ask you how in the great islands you managed to climb all the way up the cliff from where you were . . ." Oliver scratched his head.

Mydia gave him a flick in the head, prompting an angry yelp of pain. "Knock it off, kid. She's magic, okay? You saw her create flames."

The boy looked at me as though considering this for the first time—though I was reasonably certain his mind skipped right past the matter of my unnatural healing. "That means you're a fire mage?"

I studied the half-built craft on which they currently worked. "Yes. I have other abilities, too. You just don't know about them."

"Like . . . really fast healing?"

"Mm-hmm. Maybe."

Kaen interrupted to explain that they were modifying one of Oliver's old projects to be a bit stronger against gusts of wind and hard banking. Mydia was going to try her idea of imbuing the finished wood with water magic.

Old Ben, Rhidea and Kymhar worked on another one behind them. I wandered over to them and asked Uncle Ben, "When are, uh, Oliver's parents getting back?"

He froze and stopped his work, not looking up. "His parents?" He sighed. "So he told you that one. They're not . . . getting back. They died. I am his sole guardian."

I gasped. Rhidea nodded grimly, as though she'd already figured it out.

"What happened to them?" I asked in a shocked voice. I saw Oliver look up sharply from beside me, ducking it back down again just as quickly.

"It was two years ago. The boy doesn't like to talk about it, and neither do I. Let's just say they're the reason I don't like him going out flying. We'll leave it at that."

(San'Hal 14, 997—Night Season)

That afternoon, we stood once more on the cliff at the edge of Scathii, overlooking the majesty of the infinite starscape that faded into the dark fog of the Sea of Emptiness. The auroras' ribbonlike lights danced off the ashen particles that floated over the void. "It's so beautiful," I breathed.

"Uncle, please," Oliver was begging. "Let me go out just this once to flight test it. I'm familiar with these things like no one else is."

His uncle pursed his lips. "I know that, son, but . . . no, I can't have you going off alone like this."

"Then with someone else!"

"Someone like who?"

"I'll go with him," Kaen said. "He's talented, but impetuous. That's what you're concerned about, right? I'll keep him in check."

Yeah, sure, I thought wryly, *and you aren't.*

Uncle Ben grimaced. "Very well. But just this once."

Kaen and Oliver got suited up in the glider harness. Kaen was on top, just because it made sense, although Oliver would be controlling it for the most part with the steering ropes.

And then they were off, jumping from the edge into the misty horizon. They fell for a short distance until their glider's form became blurry to my eyes, and then they came up out of the dive, soaring away from the island and to the left.

Glancing up, I saw Rhidea put a hand on Uncle Ben's shoulder. "The boy is a natural," she said calmly. "He will be fine. A remarkable boy, really. Very intelligent and skilled for his age. I think he gets a lot from you."

Ben nodded solemnly. "He is a good boy. Willful and impetuous, but a good lad. He's all I have left. His mother and my brother, they . . . they fell on a skyship accident. It shouldn't have happened, as those boats are usually quite safe, but . . . well, there's no way to know how it happened. His father, their wind mage, must have fallen suddenly sick, or the mechanics failed. Who can say? The merchant guild tries to cover it up along with every other accident. I saw it fall with my own eyes, just as they were approaching port."

He said the words with such bitterness that I felt my heart wrench for him.

"I'm sorry," Mydia whispered from beside me, head bowed. "That must have been horrible, both for you and for him."

He looked away, then back down at the pair of fliers out on the horizon. "I loved them very much. And my fierce love for my nephew makes me protective of him. I'm sure you can understand. But . . . my, I don't often see him fly on these. He's . . . amazing."

Oliver was taking their glider in circles and swoops, probably using his Wind Authority to boost their speed, catching updrafts and soaring upward through the misty skies.

"Like a bird," Mydia said. "So graceful."

"He really is gifted," I observed.

As we watched, the boy righted the thin vessel and began to take them back to the island. They came in fast and pulled up at the last moment, slowing to land in an awkward run on the grassy soil of Scathii.

"Whew! We're back, Uncle!" cried the blond boy excitedly. "Wasn't that fun, Mr. Kaen?"

"That was . . . very exhilarating," Kaen said breathlessly as he worked to extricate himself from the gear. He straightened his wobbly legs and shot me a grin. "But really fun. The kid knows what he's doing."

"Oliver," his uncle beckoned him, arms open. The blond-haired boy ran to him and embraced him. "I want to apologize."

"For what, Uncle?"

"For never watching you fly. I might have changed my mind had I seen you do it before now. And . . . I think I've also decided to let you fly whenever you want now."

"Really?"

"You're almost a man by our standards, my boy. And I can see what a passion you have for it. You will become a great skyship designer in the future."

"So . . . what if I wanted to go on a proper trip?" Oliver glanced up at us. "With some strangers."

Uncle Ben squeezed his eyes shut, pinching the bridge of his nose, and then let out a breath. "That would be your decision, then."

- Chapter 34 -

Goodbye to the Last World

True Authority can trigger these ill effects, but is more an exercise of the mind than of physical stamina. Willpower, focus. Commanding the elements takes a mental toll, and enough of it will cause the mage to simply pass out or, with too regular of practice, begin to lose his own sanity. This is why a mage must always, always know his limits.
— From *Secrets of Mani,* by Sor the Lark

(San'Hal 15, 997—Night Season)

Oliver came with us in the end. It made the most sense. None of us wanted to put the life of a twelve-year-old boy on the line, but without a wind mage . . . it just wasn't going to work. Oliver was the missing key to our puzzle. Even Rhidea agreed.

So we welcomed on our sixth party member.

We left the very next day. We prepared special packs to put our luggage in, which would be strapped onto the gliders themselves next to the passengers. We took three gliders, distributing the weight as evenly as possible: Oliver and me, Kaen and Mydia, Kymhar and Rhidea. We wouldn't have divided it up quite that way, because of the discomfort of a female companion riding so close to a male companion, but it made the most sense since our gliders were of one common size. Plus, we would have a mage on board every glider in this case.

We waved goodbye to Uncle Ben, helpful soul that he was, promising to send Oliver back safely. Rhidea had already explained to him that, while we would do everything in our power to keep him safe, we couldn't guarantee that he would come back immediately.

We leapt off the edge of the last world of the horizon and sailed toward the unknown. Oliver twisted in his harness underneath, taking one last look at the island that had been his home for his whole life. "Goodbye . . . Scathii," he whispered. Then he looked forward, toward the somber sky that greeted us from the east. With a whoop, he said, "Yeah! I'm so excited!"

I sighed. "It's going to be a long ride, Oliver. Hang in there, okay?"

I could tell he was grinning, even though I couldn't see his mischievous face. "Oh, I'll be fine. This is going to be so much fun."

As we coasted toward the first air disturbance of a heat tunnel, Oliver worked his wind magic and I got to see it close up for the first time. He caused the wind to swirl around us, sending us high into the sky along with the other two gliders behind us. The updraft kept us aloft for a while as we soared toward the next one.

It was my turn to grin. "Yeah, you're right, kid. This will be fun. Come on!"

Rhidea's glider followed us behind and to the right, while Kaen's glider followed them, far enough below that I could see them by looking down. "Have you ever been flying in the dark?" I asked my companion.

"Nope! I've been out in the Night Season a couple times, but not after dark. The auroras ought to give us enough light till we get there, if there really is a far shore. What if I can't hold it, though?"

"What if . . . ? You'd *better* be able to." I was starting to think twice about how long this trip may take. "Well, kid, it all depends on how fast you can make us go. You said something about speed, right?"

"Heheh! I sure did. Here, watch." He wove the air around us so that it created a bolstering current that carried us along, faster and faster. Rhidea and the others got caught up in it as well.

"Now that's more like it. How far out have you been from the islands?"

"This is probably about as far as I've ever been," he replied. "I never wanted to scare my uncle too badly. Well . . . no, I just didn't want to get lost."

I smiled at that. "Well, for now we've still got the stars to point our way. Let's hurry. You keep an eye on the others to make sure they're getting the tailwinds and updrafts and staying with us, okay?"

"Roger that!"

An hour passed by, and then another, and we were still flying away from the continent of Argent. "They're still behind us, right?" I asked after a while, unable to see and unwilling to crane my head to look.

"Yep! And we're still making good speed. Wow, how far does this Sea go? Maybe it *is* endless, like they say."

"Don't say that," I grumbled. "Here, slow us down so we can talk to Rhidea and the others."

Oliver activated his Wind Authority, slowing our reckless speed and lining our glider up closer with Rhidea and Kymhar's.

"You two all right?" I shouted over the wind rushing past.

Rhidea nodded, and Kymhar gave us a thumbs-up signal. "My Earth Authority stopped long ago, and I've felt nothing since!" Rhidea shouted back. "So we're still a ways off!"

Behind us, Kaen and Mydia caught up, hovering below us and to the left. "Lyn!" cried Mydia in a shrill voice. "How much longer!?"

"We don't really know!" Oliver yelled back in a comically squeaky voice. "Do you guys want to go even faster? I can do that!"

"No thanks!" Kaen returned hurriedly. "Just keep the tailwinds steady, kid!"

"I estimate that we've traveled nearly a hundred and fifty miles," Rhidea shouted.

We broke up as Oliver summoned another tailwind to propel us forward. I couldn't believe it—one hundred and fifty miles . . . in two hours? Such speed. . . . I wasn't about to doubt the mage's calculations, approximate though they may be.

It was perhaps another two hours before we saw it. Oliver spied it first and alerted me: a faint, hazy wall creeping up over the horizon. Even as we drew nearer, it was hard to make out in the fading aurora light, but whatever it was covered the skyline in an unmistakable way, separating sky from ashen sea.

"Land," I said in disbelief. "We've found it!"

Oliver could hardly contain his excitement. To our right, I saw Kaen zipping up close, dragging a tired Mydia whose head hung on his shoulder. Kaen gave a nod. I could hardly make out his face in the dimness of the lighting.

We glided closer to the new land as the details became clearer and clearer. My heart pounded inside my chest at the excitement. Stronger still was the feeling of relief at the knowledge that the whole trip was not a fool's errand. Well, too early to speak yet . . .

Oliver sped us up, using a large updraft to boost our height, and then dove at a long angle toward the coast. It was a large, rocky cliff that trailed all the way down to blend into the mists below, with some few hundred feet visible, just like on the other side. A silvery-white stone seemed to be its makeup, though it blended into silver near the lower portions. Something poked up all around the top edge, and as we came closer, I could make out large trees, their leaves glittering in the last light of the auroras. Massive trees, unlike any others I'd seen.

"Uh, Oliver . . ."

"I see them," he said. "You'll have to help me with the landing, Miss Lyn."

He leveled us out and guided the winds to bring us over the edge at a safe speed and altitude, in between two of the larger, more territorial trees. We were enough ahead of the others to catch our footing and turn to watch their approach. I took most of our initial weight upon landing. Oliver scrambled to unhook himself from the harness, stumbling over shaky feet, and got ready to help the others land in much the same way. Kaen and Mydia were next in line, three hundred yards off, two hundred . . . one hundred . . .

They swooped in, a frightened Mydia staring wide-eyed at the precipice with a mix of fear and longing, hair streaming everywhere. They came up fast, but Oliver used his Wind Authority to slow their speed to a manageable one. They alighted on the ground and then their footing faltered. I caught them both, holding them upright and helping them out of their connected harnesses. Lastly, Kymhar and Rhidea sailed in, coming in low to swoop upwards and land almost gracefully. I had never seen the assassin do anything *un*gracefully, and Rhidea's gravity Authority was of the utmost help in such situations.

Once everyone was safely ashore on the new land, we took stock of our surroundings. Unfortunately, it was almost completely dark here in the cover of the mighty trees. Their trunks were as thick as three or four large men, towering upwards and spreading a dense canopy of leaves that completely blocked the sky and barred the light of the auroras from piercing its depths.

Rhidea sighed. "It's going to be a long, strange night, my friends. We've left the sunset far behind, and there's no way around this forest."

Only the fading glow of the auroras and the starry hosts remained to shine over the chasm, shimmering blue and green on the mists. I turned back to peer into the dark forest. The trees were giant but spread far apart, so that one could walk easily in the midst of them. "Well," I said tiredly, "time for a light, then." I summoned a small, careful flame in my hand and walked a short distance in, watching the flickering red light play off the craggy, silver-specked bark of the massive trees. "It feels . . . ancient here."

"Lyn . . . ?" Mydia's voice had an edge of worry in it. "Please don't go too far in yet. We don't know what might be lurking in this terrible forest."

"We will have to scout it out and explore its secrets," said Rhidea, "if we want to get through. I don't think there's going to be any getting around it. I had no idea that a giant, overgrown forest would block our way, but then of course . . . we had no idea *what* to expect, did we?"

Kymhar was glancing furtively around the place, inspecting every little detail. He said nothing.

Kaen came up and put a hand on my shoulder. "We did it." He turned to look at the others. "We made it! We found the new land. Rhidea . . . I have to say I'm impressed. You were right. And Oliver, we couldn't possibly have made it if not for your help."

"Mm-hmm!" The boy hopped around uncomfortably and then pointed into the woods parallel to the cliff. "I'll, uh, be right back." He disappeared, causing a smile to spring to my lips. A couple of the others disappeared for similar reasons, hopefully heeding Kaen's warning to be careful and not wander too far.

In a minute or two, everyone was back. I was still holding my flame for light, careful to not let it catch any of the surrounding forest on fire. Didn't want to accidentally burn down this whole side of the world. . . .

"So," said Rhidea. "Should we proceed into the woods tonight or make camp and set out tomorrow?"

I looked at Kaen and Kymhar, who shrugged. "Might as well make camp," said the assassin. "But we should head out at cloud-break. I will scout out the forest. I should be back in a half hour." With that, he vanished into the forest.

"Um . . ." Mydia pointed at where he'd disappeared. "Isn't that a little . . . dangerous? Going off alone in the dark . . . ?"

"Sure," I said, "unless you're Kymhar. He'll be all right. That's his specialty."

"But . . . how does he *see* in this?"

"Someone with his amount of training has learned to use every sense of the body to gather data about his surroundings," Kaen explained. "He's been teaching me things here and there, but I'm not nearly as good as he is."

I helped Kaen to make camp, starting a fire with the same flame that I kept going. By this point I'd trained myself to be able to hold a flame all day without tiring myself out. Coaction was all about practice. We laid out our bedrolls while Mydia set about finding sticks to hang our cook pot. Soon, we had a stew going, made from dried vegetables, fruits and meats. The smell was sweet and enticing. Kymhar arrived just in time to eat, bringing a report of the surrounding forest.

"The forest stretches on for miles and miles to either side as far as I can see," he said, "like a barrier to the cliff from the rest of this continent. But it appears to stop a few miles in, from what I could see from the highest vantage around. The vegetation appears consistent in the woods that I explored, with unknown berries and nuts that may be edible. There's a somewhat strong animal presence here, mostly herbivorous by the looks of the tracks I could find. Nothing too dangerous. And of course, no sign of human life."

Rhidea nodded. Mydia looked thoroughly impressed, and Oliver, incredulous, said, "You climbed a tree the whole way up?"

Kymhar shot him one of his classic impassive stares. "Yes."

"And you could actually see through the dark?"

"It's not as completely dark once you break through the cover of the trees, boy. The auroras helped a bit. Besides, there's . . . another source of light here. Another heavenly body lies in the east, like a dimmer, larger Sol. Blue. I . . . must confess, I don't know what it is."

I felt a chill run down my spine. *Another heavenly body . . .*

"Why didn't we see this anomaly on our way here as we got closer?" Rhidea asked, ever the practical thinker.

"It is in the far eastern sky right now, and may move with Sol or at a greater speed. I cannot say. But I theorize that it was hidden behind the cliff as we approached."

"And before that . . ." mused the mage. "It could have something to do with the angle, if indeed our world is round and not flat, as we suspect. On the other side of a sphere, one would see different sights, but only if those different sights never actually move much."

"Do you think . . . ?" I began. "Could—could that be the world we've been searching for?"

Everyone grew silent at the prospect.

Rhidea broke the silence. "We shall see tomorrow if and when we break free from this forest. This heavenly light will be more easily visible then."

We ate the stew—tasty stuff, I had to admit—and made our beds for the night. I fell asleep shortly after my head hit the ground. It didn't matter that this terrain was uncomfortable, or that I was excited about our arrival here on the newly-discovered continent; my body was so exhausted that it just wanted to recharge.

I awoke to sounds of movement. I opened my eyes to see Kymhar and Kaen up and about. Groaning, I arose from my bedroll and began to shake out my stiff limbs. Definitely not the most comfortable bed, but I'd slept on worse. But it was *cold*, just like most Sunless days. "Good morning, Kaen, Kymhar," I mumbled. "Ugh, I hate the Night Season."

"I like the night," Kymhar said in a quiet voice. He probably wasn't *trying* to sound creepy as he said it. "More cover, less noisy humans running around."

I shook my head and chuckled to myself.

Soon the others were up, and we ate some leftovers for breakfast while Kymhar and Kaen tore down the camp. Now for the big decision . . .

"Oliver," Rhidea asked. "Do you wish to continue on with us or depart to your homeland? You should understand that we seek another world. There is no telling what the dangers may be. We promised to protect you no matter what."

Oliver looked back at the faintly glittering mists of the Sea of Emptiness. "I . . . I want to go with you. I want to come."

"Are you sure?"

"Yes." He nodded with emphasis. "I wanted to see a new world. Why turn back just when I've gotten my first glimpse, ma'am?"

She smiled faintly. "Then welcome aboard our merry band of lunatic travelers."

"Let's stow the gliders here, then," Kaen suggested. "Put them safely in a recognizable location, hopefully one we can remember and find once more if we need them."

Rhidea nodded. "Good plan. Let's do it."

We stowed them right at the edge of the forest near an outcropping of the cliff that was fairly distinctive. Then Kaen and I took the lead through the forest, with me holding aloft my familiar flame while Kaen carried a burning torch. Together we lit up plenty of the forest to see by. The ground was littered with dead leaves, small sticks, nutshells and moss, old tree roots, and animal tracks. Birdcalls and sounds of wildlife mixed with the lonely moaning of the foreign wind that accompanied us. Unless that was just Oliver playing with us.

We saw small animals darting here and there, up and down the trees. One larger beast, hopefully not carnivorous, crunched a stick as it disappeared before we could get a good glimpse of it. I really wanted to see what some of the animals here looked like, but in this darkness, there was never a good enough close-up view.

We finally made our way out of the oversized forest and into a meadow dotted with smaller trees and thick brush and brambles. Some faint light shone just enough to see by, though it took some adjustment of the eyes to make out anything distant after all the darkness. And there, in the far sky on the eastern horizon, past the trees . . .

It was like a giant version of Sol, as Kymhar had described. It was the size of both my hands held out at arms' length. Glowing blue but dim enough to look at, it was most likely the source of the faint, blue light scattered about. It was . . . oddly shaped? Or lit as though from the bottom, with a small chunk having been eaten out of the top side by a celestial titan . . . I thought of where Sol was at the moment and realized that it could be an effect of the sun's current angle.

"I think . . ." Mydia spoke up, "I think Sol is . . . shining on it, just like on our world. See the really faint part at the top?"

"Marvelous," Rhidea whispered. "What a splendid sight. My friends, that is the world we seek, the one the writings call Gaea.

That . . . is our goal."

Oliver's jaw hung open. Kaen nodded dumbly.

I just swallowed and said in a small voice, "Okay."

\- Chapter 35 -

A New World

In the year 782, a mage by the name of Adullus Ta created the modern classifications of magic that we have today, dividing the seven branches—as well as the one we have lost, Silver— into sub-classes and compiling a list of the most common specialties among magi. Of course, there are the occasional oddities. Even today, new magi are born who exhibit different qualities or possess an entirely new specialty. Nothing is more exciting to a true scholar of magic.
— From *Secrets of Mani*, by Sor the Lark

(San'Hal 17, 997—Night Season)

Rhidea called it a prairie, the thick grassland through which we walked the next day—our second morning on the new continent, although it had been hard to judge time in the forest, as the thick canopy hid the auroras from view. We had left the thick forest behind by now, and were trudging through tall, papery grey grass that waved at hip height. We still hadn't found any water yet, and this worried me. Surely there was plenty of water in the soil here, but . . . none that we could drink.

Just as we were running out of our supply, however, we found the first small pond. Reeds paved the way down into it except for a few places where one could go right up to the water's edge. It was murky and strange looking. Kymhar had us all run it through charcoal first to purify it.

Mydia wiped her mouth after downing the last of her leftover warm water, making a face. "Ick. One of my favorite parts about

\- 350 -

traveling. Great water."

"We would've brought packhorses, your royal highness," Kaen said, "but we couldn't find a way to *ship* those packhorses across the sky, you see."

She turned a glare on him and crossed her arms. "I could've gotten us water anywhere," she grumbled. "You're the one who said we couldn't trust it."

I crouched down beside where she sat, crumpling all of the weeds around. "Mydia, I'm glad you're with us."

She smiled dully. "Thanks. I'm used to all this by now, of course. I don't mean to always sound like the whiney one."

I ruffled her black bob like a little girl. "It's all right." She had lost some weight over the course of our multiple journeys, still bearing the same rounded, delicate face but less padding. Traveling light would do that to anyone.

Rhidea was surveying the horizon, shading her eyes with a hand despite Sol being far behind us. Kymhar had told us that there should be water near here, but was not sure if the plentitude of it would increase or not.

Kaen took a small sip of the water. "I think it's probably fine to drink," he declared, taking another big gulp a moment later. "Just as it is."

One way or another, we all refilled our supply of water for the next couple of days. Surely, we would find a town before long. This was rich land, rich enough anyway, and yet so far, we had seen no people settling it.

"Rhidea," I asked. "Do you think it's really true that no humans live on this continent? That they've just . . . never even come here?"

"Well, child . . . that depends when and how they came to our side. It could be populated, or it could be unpopulated. If the tales of the Gate are true, humans originally came from Gaea to this side of our world, and only then found a way to cross to Argent."

I pondered this as we set off once more through the prairie. However, it wasn't much more than another mile before Kymhar said, "I'm seeing signs of people." As we went on, he pointed out tracks here and there. "Unmistakably human."

We continued to trample through the tall grass. It still stretched for miles in most directions. There was a little more forest toward the southern horizon. The only light came from the auroras, who twinkled helpfully as they did every day in the Night Season. And the stars, thanks to the clear sky overhead.

Eventually, we saw the smoke. Then the first house from which the smoke rose. Farms. And past the farms . . . a village. There was some discussion amidst our group over whether we should just approach them and claim we got lost, or circle around and approach from the north or south and say we journeyed far—or just tell the truth and say that we came over the Sea of Emptiness from the other side of the world.

We ended up just going with the first explanation, which was the simplest: we lost our way. The first farm we walked right past, as the farmers didn't seem particularly friendly when they saw us. More like . . . frightened? I suppose I would be, too, if I saw someone walk out of the forest at the edge of the world in the middle of the Sunless Cycle.

We made our way toward the village, arriving at the end of a rough half-circle of houses built from the nearby trees. The chimneys were of clay and stone, probably harvested from the tilled farmland nearby. There was an almost-road leading into the half-circle, which we followed into town. Children played with ropes and people walked to and fro in the starlight. Torch poles spaced throughout the village gave extra light. I supposed that would be their only light on a cloudy, pitch-dark Sunless night.

That is . . . depending on how well this Gaea's light pierces the clouds.

We asked some of the locals about the whereabouts of this place, saying that we were lost and got turned around in the forest.

One woman, bearing dark tan skin and dark hair like most of the locals, gave us a strange stare when we asked. "The forest? That is not a place many wander. Everyone knows that it is dangerous to go so close to the edge of the world." She spoke in a strange dialect, and it was difficult to make out what she said, but it was the same language.

"Why, because of the cliffs?" asked Rhidea.

"Yes," she whispered with a shiver. "Evil lurks in the depths, seeking to swallow any who come near. Everyone knows this."

I felt my skin prickling.

"What do you call this place?" asked Rhidea.

"Lor'Hav," she replied. She spoke the name in a sharp accent that I found fascinating. "We don't get many visitors, so my apologies are yours if we seem inhospitable."

Rhidea didn't ask what she'd meant about evil lurking in the chasm. I assumed it must be a sort of local superstition. However, once we were out of earshot of the townsfolk, she said to us, "I have heard tales of a 'Silver Beast' that dwells beneath Mani. Recalling those stories makes that woman's words a bit more chilling. But I doubt it will have any bearing on our journey."

I shared a glance with Mydia. A shrug from the young woman confirmed my recollection that her book hadn't said anything about this so-called Silver Beast.

We attempted conversation with a few more locals, and one of the more friendly men of the village gave us some directions for the journey inland, saying that we must cross the River Soul to reach the inner Duchy. (Whatever that was—apparently, we were on the far fringes?) He said that the river circled the world, which seemed a far-fetched claim. A few miles inland, according to him, was where we would encounter the first of the tributaries that ran into the Soul.

We purchased some interesting local crops for food and filled our skins with water at the village well, and then we departed shortly after, following the kind man's directions. Rhidea did not want to make the villagers any more uneasy than they already were at our sudden appearance.

The next day, after hours of climbing soft hills, we saw the first tributary. It was a shallow creek, only twenty feet across at its widest. It flowed eastward toward the center of the continent, terminating at a larger river called the Athalar, of which the village residents had spoken. On either bank grew short shrubs and trees of pale golden leaf. Animals poked their heads up here and there, mostly rabbits. There was a low valley sheltering the creek, fertile with all types of vegetation, and we chose to stay just on the inside of it, so as to follow it but not be seen too easily.

(San'Hal 20, 997—Dawn)

Nearly a week of travel on foot had brought us to our first river town. We didn't enter immediately, as it was already nighttime, clouds obscuring both the stars and the first light of dawn, so we decided to camp nearby. After we'd gone what Kymhar deemed a safe distance from the town, we crossed over the grassy ridge— tinged subtly green here—to find a place to camp. No fire, just our bedrolls, tucked in behind a copse of trees and thick brush. This could be hostile territory, after all. Mydia thought it was silly, and I certainly wasn't afraid, but Kaen and Kymhar didn't want bandits or hostile natives to have anything to find us by in the night.

Dawn had broken, and the first orange light reached up over the horizon, like Sol reaching to embrace her counterpart. Or perhaps attempting to swat down an imposter. Would Sol overtake Gaea soon? The Night Season was so much brighter here on the other side of Mani—whatever this new continent was called—due to Gaea's light. And it had only climbed higher in the sky since we'd come, by perhaps one outstretched handspan. I still wasn't used to the light from this "moon" (the locals' name for it) after our few days here.

In the morning, we entered the town to see about buying mounts for our journey. Wherever our destination turned out to be, we would not get there quickly on foot. The locals, who lived in crude wooden houses, did indeed have horses for sale, though not of any breeding that impressed Rhidea and Mydia. But, as our friend the queen eventually conceded, "A horse is a horse."

The villagers were kind enough to give us some more accurate directions to point us on our way. Rhidea had an uncanny knack for wheedling information out of anyone, as she had demonstrated on me back in the Nytaean Palace. And to think where we'd be if she hadn't . . .

Our destination, we learned via her carefully-worded questions, was a place called the Land of Storms, which lay at the center of the continent. It was like the Wellspring to the people of Darsor (their name for this continent), in that it was a forbidden place of history and mystery. It was also very close to the center of the Duchy of Halstar. Following this river, the Athalar, would take us eastward to the Soul, after which we would cross into the inner duchy. For some reason, they referred to this route as the 'Eclipse Path.'

Atop our new steeds, we set off for the day, same as we had been. Mydia hadn't complained in quite a while now. She was getting used to the traveling life, and had not only lost weight but had grown more fit as her body acclimated. Still those chubby princess cheeks, though.

Kaen said almost nothing until midday, when we stopped for a rest break to relieve ourselves. He was just coming back from the stream with fresh water in the waterskins. "How are you holding up, Lyn?"

I lay on my back on the grassy grey slopes of the river valley, dress crumpled over my bent knees as I watched the stars twinkle faintly in the dawn sky, running my hands over the cool, faintly moist grass—silvery mixed with green. With all the new sights, it was a relief to see at least something familiar. I supposed if both continents were composed of silver underneath, as the texts said, then that silver would bleed through into the plant life here just the same as on Argent.

I looked up, realizing Kaen had said my name. "Oh. I'm doing fine. A little . . . eh. Nothing. I'm fine." I gave him a decidedly fake smile, not on purpose.

He dropped the waterskins and flopped down beside me. "You always say that when you're all uptight."

I growled softly and glared at him. "Kaen, it's—"

He grinned, and I cut off. He probably knew. He was either playing with me or just trying to lighten up my day. Whichever it was, it was working in a strange way.

We stared at the sky together for a minute. The clouds earlier had contained an unfamiliar constellation, and I wondered if we would see a new one soon. I didn't understand how the constellations could be tied to specific positions of the sun, yet none of the ones we knew from Argent had appeared yet over Darsor. Given that it was a reaction in the magical Energy Field . . . who could put logic to it?

"It's gorgeous here, isn't it?" he said at length.

I nodded, hair rustling the grass as I did so. Then I said, "I miss Phoebe. And Mandrie. After our whole childhood together, we've gotten separated by circumstances."

"Yeah. I miss them, too. I even miss my squad, truth be told. Back when I was with the Nytaean guards."

"I miss Lentha."

Kaen grew quiet.

Then I snorted. "I even miss that stupid oaf, Cort Flanning."

Kaen echoed my snort. "Not that stick in the mud."

I groaned, rising to my feet and brushing off my skirts. They were utilitarian by design, comprised of eight overlapping quarter-sheets of linen sewn together over thin trousers. This made it a tad difficult to brush leaves or grass out. Of course, it was all sorts of dirty and stained from travel anyway. I helped Kaen to his feet and then took one of the water bags to carry back to the others.

"All right," Rhidea said briskly as we reassembled. "Let's go find that river. It can't be far off now, right, Kaen?"

He shrugged. "A couple more miles, if that soldier was right."

I wondered just how far inland we were at this point, and how much farther we had to go. The Soul River was supposed to run around the center of Darsor (I didn't have a clue how that worked), but I didn't know the circumference of the Soul. If Rhidea and the Archlord were right, then there were only these two continents, one on either side of Mani—but how big was each? We were supposing that this continent was the same size as Argent.

That night, I singled out Rhidea and asked to speak with her.

"What is it, child?"

"I . . ." I swallowed. My conversation with Kaen had brought something to mind that had been bugging me. "You remember the dreams I told you about?"

"Once, yes," she said. "Do you still feel they may be visions?"

"Well . . . actually, I think they're memories. I really don't know what they are, or why I have them, but I haven't had any since reaching Darsor."

Rhidea frowned, as though expecting to hear that they had increased dramatically. It surprised me as well, after all. "When was your last vision?"

"Back on Scathii. After I almost died."

The sorceress nodded thoughtfully. "So at a time when you would have been expending your otherworldly powers. Perhaps the visions come based on how much you utilize your powers?"

"That is . . . what I'm thinking," I admitted. It was the only explanation that fit. "I just wish I knew more about my mother, and who she was."

Rhidea gave me that look that said she was hiding something but didn't want to let on. I didn't care enough to press her. If I did . . . I might get some answers, but they would probably not be the ones I wanted. Eventually, she simply nodded. "I suspect it will all come clear when we reach Gaea."

We kept to our route, following the creek until we reached a larger one, a real river called the Athalar, which we traced for another week.

A few days in, we witnessed the most spectacular thing we'd seen since crossing the Sea of Emptiness. The sun chased Gaea, Darsor's "moon" up the horizon until they finally met. Sol slowly blurred out of sight behind the larger heavenly body, and we watched with unsettled fascination as the light dimmed until nearly complete darkness reigned.

"This must be the 'eclipse' the locals mentioned," Rhidea said quietly. "The Eclipse Path . . . proceed with care."

We guided our horses cautiously using magical torchlight to see by. The temperature dropped just enough to be noticeable, not as much as during the Night Season. It lasted for around an hour before Sol crept up and over the blue planet.

"Well, that was creepy," said Kaen, encapsulating the majority of our reactions.

(San'Hal 27, 997—Zenith)
Finally, we came upon the Soul River, breaking through thick golden trees at the top of a low rise in the land. The day's sunlight reflected off the river's rippling surface as it came into sight, stretching from the far horizon on the left to the near right and splitting off. Despite the glare of sunlight, the water was extremely dark. The Athalar, just as we'd been told, was only a small offshoot of the much-larger river—The Soul River—which was at least a half-mile wide here.

"Auroras above!" exclaimed Mydia upon seeing the large body of water. "I haven't seen so much water since Ti'Vaeth. This makes the Ardencaul look like a little stream!"

"The what?" Oliver asked distractedly, staring at the glittering stygian water.

"A river back home in Kystrea," I said. "It divides our home city of Nytaea."

"Now for the real challenge," Rhidea said, clutching one arm with the other. "Swimming . . . across."

Oh, no. I've heard she doesn't like water. . . . The mage had avoided swimming with a passion ever since I'd known her, and had since explained that she had harbored a fear of water ever since childhood.

Kaen shrugged. "Let's just swim across. How hard can it be? Well, Oliver probably can't swim, and . . . Rhidea, are you all right?"

"I'm fine," she muttered. "I don't like water. I don't like to swim." She lowered her head and squeezed her eyes shut in shame as she said it. I knew she didn't like to admit her fear.

"Um . . . I definitely cannot swim across that far of a gap," Mydia said uncertainly. "I'm no athlete, you know . . . I think we should see how deep and wide it is in certain spots. Perhaps we could just wade right across?"

"Oh, come on," Kaen protested, "You're supposed to be the royal water mage. You can't just part the waters and let us walk through?"

Mydia fixed him with an offended glare that said, *What do you take me for, divinity?*

Rhidea shook herself. "No, no, we may be able to do this an easier way. I apologize—I let my fear get the better of me for a moment. If we could only . . ." She took out her teleportation artifact and sighed. "It's much too far."

We gave up on fording the river and searched for the nearest bridge, which ended up being less than a mile to the north. Feeling a bit foolish, we camped on the far shore amidst a pine forest. We made no fire once again. No sense inviting all of our currently unsuspecting neighbors to come and investigate our presence.

As I did every night now, I looked up at the sky from my bedroll and gazed at the distant world suspended in the sky. My homeworld. Could it be? Gaea—or the Moon as the locals called it—had moved to a slightly higher point above us as we traveled inland. It was beautiful . . .

What kind of place was it? A land of scenery even more beautiful than Mani, full of strange people? A sea of colors and strange sights? Or a deceptively hostile world? Was it actually as blue as it looked on the surface? Who could say?

Gaea is not like this world. It's a scary world, with volcanoes and earthquakes, magma fields and raging oceans.

My mother's voice, from my most recent dream, rang in my head unbidden, causing a shiver to run down my spine. I'd been getting better at recalling my dreams lately. There was only one way to find out for sure what Gaea was like, however. And first we had to get there.

- Chapter 36 -

Beyond the Soul

Over the centuries, many different Mage Councils have come and gone. Each seeks a certain goal, held together by a common bond among the brotherhood, until such time as their goal has been met, enough of them have passed away, or no more young magi are brought in to take up the mantle, at which point a Council is disbanded. Most leave a legacy behind, recounted by historians and scribes. But there has been no Council in the city of Nytaea, where the first Council is said to have arisen, ever since the Archlord of Kystrea assumed control of it in 890.

— From *Secrets of Mani,* by Sor the Lark

(Quoi 3, 997—Waning Day)

"Behold, the city of Mogdael," Rhidea said as we came upon the first sizable city on the inside of the Soul River. We had decided to stop to resupply and learn what we could from the locals.

"Well, well," said Mydia, stopping to put one hand on her hip and stare up at the large, plank-walled city.

I say plank-walled, but the wall was over twenty feet in height and imposing, built strong and sturdy with cross-hatched planks. Two banners bearing a three-winged falcon symbol flapped above the gate, whose portcullis was wide open despite the supposed unease within the country. Two guardsmen outfitted in studded leather saluted us by tapping the butt-ends of their long pikes on the wooden bridge.

"Hail, good travelers," said the one on the right. "Welcome to Mogdael. What business have you?"

"We are passing through and seek to rest and resupply," said Rhidea, smoothly as ever. It was the truth.

The guardsman bowed his head respectfully and dipped his weapon toward the inner city. "Then pass on, and may you fare well."

We entered through the gate into a city unlike any I'd seen on our home continent. The architecture was nearly all of wooden design, sturdy but functional. I supposed they did have a lot more trees to work with around these parts . . . I wouldn't have called it crude, but certainly not as eye-catching as the stately stone buildings back in Nytaea. Flagpoles dotted the city, showing off an identical three-winged falcon emblem, probably the crest of the local city lord (whom we had no intention of meeting).

The city did not have the air of coldness to it that we were expecting, probably because it was inside the Soul and thus in an area deemed to be more well-protected. We made our way to the nearest small-time inn and booked a room for the night, and then set about exploring. I took Oliver and went to fetch food supplies, hoping that the locals accepted gold. Rhidea and Mydia went to find good prices on other supplies, while Kaen and Kymhar were searching for rumors and information.

Oliver took eagerly to the streets with me, taking in the foreign sights with his characteristic enthusiasm. "What a city!" he said in awe as we walked past fountains, hawkers and some very . . . let's say interestingly-dressed, if captivating, dancers. Oliver's head followed them for far too long, and I gave him a small flick on the shoulder.

He yelped and walked more quickly, turning his eyes back ahead just in time to dodge a man hurrying by with a push-cart. "Sorry. But did you see those—"

"Oliver, focus! And don't stare, especially not at women."

"But . . . why? You're a woman, too! I mean, not that I stare at you."

"I'm not dressed like a whore on holiday, though."

"What?" He sounded confused and almost innocent.

I picked my way through an especially tight throng of people, tugging Oliver by the hand to make sure he didn't get separated from me. Gotta watch the kid. "Never mind. Stick close, boy. Up ahead there. I think that's the market district."

"What kind of food do you think they're selling?" he asked excitedly.

I sighed, rolling my eyes toward Gaea. The expression was hidden from my young companion by my back. "We are about to find out."

We ended up roving from stand to stand, cart to cart, searching for dried goods and spices. I bought a pound of some local grain called rice, which was supposed to be very hearty but only grew in the wettest regions of the eastern Duchy. Oliver talked me into buying him some exotic sweets as well.

I was rather proud of myself upon returning to the square to wait for the others, proud that I hadn't lost Oliver in the crowds yet. We waited on a bench beside a large statue of an owl. Here in the south square, there weren't as many people, but I still kept a hawk's eye on the blond boy. He still seemed a bit intimidated by me, so that probably helped.

Mydia entered the courtyard from the north after a few minutes, and I waved to get her attention. She perked up and made her way across to us, taking a seat beside the same owl statue. "Where's the Wandering Mage now?" I asked. "Did you lose her already?"

She reddened slightly, murmuring a short protest to the contrary. "She's up near the city lord's palace. That tall building at the center of the city." She pointed toward it, and I followed her gaze. "She sent me to tell you that she'll be a little while. She said to see what we can find out about the city and the country of Halstar."

I nodded tiredly. "Sounds typical of her. All right, but let's rest here a while first. I'm sure she won't mind."

Mydia nodded back and reached out to pinch Oliver's cheek as he looked away. His head jerked toward her, and she giggled. "Oliver, you're so cute."

He blushed, turning away again and kicking his feet awkwardly.

"What do you think of Mogdael?" she asked brightly. "Bigger than you expected from a city?"

He perked up again. "Oh, yes! It's amazing! Lynx here has been holding onto me like a mother cat, of course."

Mydia laughed, and I asked, "Lynx? When did you pick up that nickname?"

He stuck out his tongue and grinned.

I snorted. "Fine. I don't care. But do you even know what a Lynx is?"

He hesitated briefly and then shook his head. "Some kind o' ugly bear?"

Mydia doubled over laughing.

I sighed, smoothing my hair back and adjusting my ponytail. "No, you dimwit. It's a kind of cat. A large, silver cat with tufted ears. A fearsome predator found in the southern forests of Argent. Somewhere in Torlega, I think. I . . . really don't know where I got the nickname. Mandrie used to call me that."

Oliver cocked his head. "Mandrie? Who's she?"

"She's about your age," I said. "An old friend of mine. Kaen's little sister."

"Oh. Is she as sour-faced as he is?" Oliver gasped as soon as he said it and clasped a hand over his mouth. "Oops. Sorry . . . that's a rude thing to say about a girl, isn't it?"

I smiled, ruffling his shaggy mop of hair as we'd all taken to doing. "A bit. But not as rude as 'ugly bear.'"

One hour later, we were all back in the *Falconer's Inn*, drawing up our attack plan. (So to speak; anything can be an attack plan if you just switch out a few words.)

We were in the room where the men would stay for the night, a sparsely furnished, plank-floored room with a small stove on one end next to a rough glass window. The floor, on which most of us sat cross-legged, creaked every time Oliver shifted. He had almost no attention span for boring things like discussions. I lay on my stomach with arms propping up my chin, wiggling my stockinged feet back and forth idly.

"Basically, nobody's heard about our entering the country," Kaen explained. "No one hears much from the outer side of the Soul."

"One kingdom, different regions," said Kymhar, examining a knife blade with dull interest.

Mydia glanced sidelong at the assassin. "Right. We pretty much knew that already, of course. I'd still like to know how we speak the same language. I mean, it's obviously a different dialect, but, well . . . how long ago do you think we came from this side of Mani? Or . . . the other way around? I don't really—"

"We came from this continent," Rhidea said matter-of-factly. "We've been over this—it's the only possibility that makes sense. If we, and all the people of Mani, came from Gaea originally, then we must have come to this side first, where the Gate is—and where Gaea is. It never leaves the sky directly over the center of Darsor. That's why it moves with us. Whether the chasm between continents formed from a great disaster or there was a land bridge originally . . . maybe our ancestors even possessed a teleportation magic like the Reality Authority known today, a more powerful form that was lost long ago? Who is to say?"

I rubbed my chin with one hand thoughtfully. "A land bridge, huh? But where would it have gone?" Then I cleared my throat. "Well, what is the plan for tomorrow? Where are we headed?"

In answer to my question, Rhidea took out a parchment map and rolled it out on the wood planks of the floor. "This map should help us out greatly. Here at the center, you can see the Land of Storms. That's where the Gate supposedly sits atop a high tower, though of course it's 'dangerous' to venture anywhere near it. So here should be our next goal." She pointed at a city labeled Redufiel. "The capital of Halstar, Redufiel, is said to be one of the largest cities in the Duchy, and pretty much the equivalent of Nytaea as far as holding a large amount of knowledge in its libraries. I'm expecting it to be pretty different from Mogdael, and we don't have much time, but . . . I think it will be worth the detour."

Kymhar nodded slowly. "If you say so, my lady. However, I suggest that we keep pace for the Land of Storms. The sooner we arrive, the better. If we do go to the Capital, we should be quick and careful. We should keep on our toes. If they make a big deal about all the magi in our party, or the wrong person decides they don't like foreigners prowling in their city, there could be further complications."

"But . . . no one has actually shown us any aggressive form of unwelcome," Mydia said hesitantly. "So why . . . ?"

"So we think," Kaen corrected her. "I don't know, I think he's right, Rhidea."

Kymhar folded his arms, posture straight, eyes on the floor, and nodded once. When he spoke, it tended to be in long bursts, and then nothing at all. Ever the mysterious figure.

Rhidea sighed. "I was afraid you would all say that. In which case our best option is to go here—" she pointed out a small town near the outskirts of Redufiel called Mannet "—and resupply, then make a direct route for the Land of Storms."

We ended up deciding on this second idea. I personally didn't care. The continent of Darsor made me uneasy, and I wanted to be through this odd duchy as soon as possible. Of course . . . I also grew more nervous the closer we got to Gaea.

"What word from the Archlord?" I asked, looking from Rhidea to Kymhar. "Anything?"

The Dalim raised his head but didn't say anything at first. When he did, he seemed to choose his words carefully. "My liege the Archlord was pleased to hear that we made it to Darsor, and warned us to watch out for dangerous species of monsters that may prowl these lands, and also hostile peoples. That was two days hence, his last communication to me. As you requested, I did not tell him anything of Oliver. I sent the last transmission yesterday, informing him of our encounters with the local people of Halstar."

I still felt uneasy about giving the Archlord so much direct information, but it had been one of his stipulations when we agreed to the bargain: he would be informed regularly, and sooner than Nytaea. Domon had not tried to backstab us yet—as far as we knew—but I still didn't trust the man, and probably wouldn't ever be able to.

Eventually, we adjourned the meeting to get some sleep, and we left the men alone with Oliver, heading to our room. I would be sharing one of the two beds with Mydia. Rhidea was too much of a lone wolf type, plus she snored too much for either of us. I was so tired that I zonked out in the middle of Mydia's intermittent chatter-ing.

(Quoi 4, 997—Sunset)
We left at cloudbreak the next day, the first day of sunset. We exchanged our horses for fresh ones, and then set our course for Mannet. We needed to ride as hard and fast as possible.

The trip took a week. Shortly after leaving Mannet, we left the sunset far behind, traveling in the aurora light of the Night Season as the land became flatter than the hills we'd traversed in the river lands. It was disconcerting how the Sol Cycle I knew back on Argent only got further and further ahead as we traveled around the world—it was now nearly two weeks off—but it certainly confirmed Rhidea's hypothesis about the size and shape of Mani. Of course, I had been persuaded already.

The outskirt town of Mannet was little more than a hamlet, but from its humble view, we could see the reaching walls of Redufiel in the auroras' light, a true city at last. A city we would not see, and my heart was all the more relieved at the fact. The lore and information we could find therein would surely help us, but we had decided it was not worth the time or risk to go to the capital.

There was only one final leg of the journey to go. We set out eastward for the last time without looking back.

On the fourteenth day of Quoi—nearing the dawn of the next Cycle in this zone of the world—we came to the dreaded Land of Storms. We could see the dark clouds looming ahead for miles in advance. As we approached, our horses grew even more skittish and Mydia and Oliver began to whine and shift in their saddle.

"Now that," Kaen said, "is a storm."

"Unlike any we've ever seen, if the stories are true," Rhidea said. "In we go."

Chapter 37

The Land of Storms

The weather of Mani can be unpredictable at times, but never harsh enough to create an emergency, save for the tampering of wind and lightning magi. This is why scholars are puzzled at the mention of great and terrible storms that have destroyed cities in centuries past, for no records of such events exist. Of course, if the theory is true that there are other landmasses out there besides the continent of Argent and the Sky Islands, then who could say what type of weather may exist there?
— From *Secrets of Mani*, by Sor the Lark

(Quoi 14, 997—Night Season)

The land of Storms was a wide, flat expanse, rocky and devoid of life as far as I could see. According to the map, it was approximately twelve miles across and roughly circular, barring entry to the very center of the continent, which none were said to have seen. We passed into thick cloud cover before reaching the actual storms. They were supposed to be patchy at first and then increase in intensity the farther in one went. No one was foolhardy enough to brave the storm all the way to the center.

Rhidea activated one of the Archlord's crystal spheres once we reached the first storm: the sphere that was supposed to suck in energy, magical or otherwise. We had been saving it for just such an occasion as this. She held the sphere aloft as she rode with one hand, and the rest of us followed behind. The hooves of the horses made a clattering on the rocks that would have been loud had it not been for the violent wind that whipped at us, blowing our hair around, and the crackling thunder—both near and distant. I had my hair tied back in my usual ponytail, of course. It wouldn't do to have it whipping all over my face. Mydia and Rhidea wore matching buns pinned up to keep their hair stable.

Lightning flared across the sky, branching and crisscrossing and then disappearing just in time for two more to sprout from other spots. The stars and even Gaea were completely obscured by this point, and so the lightning was all we had to see by. Unreliable and transient though it was, the lightning lit up the sky like daylight. Our horses neighed and whinnied, tossing their heads this way and that and testing our control. Mydia in particular had trouble with hers, since Oliver was clutching onto her for dear life most of the time.

"Hang in there, Mydia," I called to her from her left. "Just till Rhidea says that we can let them go, then we're walking, remember?"

She nodded, teeth gritted. Oliver's eyes were shut tight in a comical display of fear, his arms clinging around the queen's midsection. It was pretty terrifying, so I didn't blame him.

I spurred on my mount, coming up closer to Rhidea's black gelding.

"We're just over two miles in!" Kaen called from on my right.

"We've got to get farther before we release the horses!" Rhidea shouted back. "Keep riding!" The end of her words was drowned out by the biggest thunderclap yet, which came from a hundred yards to our right. And then came a lightning bolt, sparking from the *ground*, which arced through the air toward Rhidea's orb. Mydia gasped from behind me, ducking her head. *The crystal must be sucking in the energy like it's supposed to,* I thought with relief.

The storm around us grew more intense, the lightning flashes growing nearly constant all throughout the sky. Rain began to fall, slickening the stone underfoot and dampening our cloaks. I shivered. Great. Just what we needed, although in a storm it was to be expected. That was why we'd donned our overcloaks. I pulled up the hood on mine before my whole head got soaked.

Watching the lightning on the black horizon, riding against the rain over uneven, desolate terrain, I realized I'd never been so terrified since the day I'd crashed into the cliffs of Argent. We all depended upon one little trinket right now, bestowed upon us by the person I trusted least in the whole world. My stomach felt like it would cramp up from anxiety, abdominal muscles twitching rapidly.

We urged our horses faster. Rhidea, our lighthouse and beacon of hope, sat high in her saddle, crouched over against the rain, holding the orb high. I had never known her to back down, and certainly not now when the time was at hand to finally learn what we came all this way for.

"How much farther!?" Mydia shrieked from behind us.

"A couple more miles!" Kaen yelled back. "We've got to keep going a little longer!"

"The horses can't take much more—" I began. I cut off as a blinding flash lit up the ground around us for hundreds of feet and then vanished just as quickly, leaving behind afterimages. My poor horse bucked and snorted frantically. The following thunderclap was deafening. Immediately after, another bright bolt flashed in the sky a mile in front of us, and I saw it as a faint silhouette through the rain—our goal, rising high in the sky: A great tower. It was no longer directly ahead, as we seemed to have gotten a bit off-course.

"There it is!" Rhidea shouted. "The tower!" She corrected our course toward the distant landmark, now obscured once more. We slowed the horses a bit, giving them the chance to breathe. I could smell the sweat of my mount mixing with the rain.

As we approached, it became easier to see. In fact . . . was it just me or . . .

"The rain!" Kaen called. "It's letting up. I think the storm is growing less fierce."

Sure enough, the wind was beginning to die down around us and the rain was relenting. The clouds remained as thick and black, however, and the lightning only more frenzied than ever. "The rain is, anyway," I said.

Finally, we drew near to the great monstrosity of the tower, and I got my first clear look at it in the persistent lightning. Stone jutted from the earth for hundreds of feet around it in jagged spires, as though something had broken through the layers of rock long ago, tearing up layer after layer like a ridged hand. But there was a beauty to it, a wild and untamed majesty.

A winding path led through the ripped-up strata of dark-grey rock to the base of the tower. The structure rose hundreds of feet into the air, made of a reflective silvery rock with strange patterns like crisscrossing webs running up and down the sides.

We slowed our tired horses to a trot as we approached, and then Rhidea called the halt.

"This is close enough," she said in a clear voice. "We will unburden our steeds here and send them on their way. May they stay safe through the storm and find green pastures outside."

We removed the tack and saddles from the horses and sent them back on their way. Hopefully they would make it through the lightning without being burnt to cinders by a random bolt. We would have been struck on multiple occasions if not for Archlord Domon's crystal of Dark Magic, so I had my doubts.

I gazed up at the Tower of Mani. "And we're going to climb this

. . ." I whispered. I glanced at Mydia to see an expression of wonder and horror clear on her wide-eyed face. She mouthed the word, *scary*.

"Yes," said Kaen, putting a hand on my shoulder. I gave him a tight smile.

Oliver took my hand, squinting up at my face in the flashing light. It lit his frightened features from a thousand angles. "Lyn," he asked, unable to keep a tremble from his lower lip, "do you think we're gonna die?"

I shook my head, giving him a forced smile. "We'll be all right. Rhidea hasn't let us down yet." I pulled him into a hug, looking up at Rhidea. She stood facing us, giving us a moment to catch our breath and gather our courage. Then she motioned us onward, through the path of rock and spikes that led to the tower. We followed, boots clopping on the black stone and kicking up mud. The smell of ozone was thick in the air.

We wound past crags and spires of rock, looking down into holes that appeared to lead deep into the earth. "Ouch, better stay away from those," Mydia murmured fearfully, clinging to my arm.

I craned my neck to look into one of the holes. There was some kind of greenish light emanating from some of them, and I was trying to see what it was. As we got closer to the tower, the rocky landscape grew more dramatic, reaching higher with the spires and opening up off the side of the paths to reveal . . . nothing.

"Oh, that . . . that is *truly* unsettling," Mydia whispered.

"There's—it's open space underneath," I said. "What is this place?"

The craggy earth opened up in pockets of increasing size, revealing a glowing interior under the surface. The light was blue-green of the faintest color, both eerie and mesmerizing. The ubiquitous lightning flaring every which way did not help with the uneasiness in my stomach.

We tread upon what were essentially bridges of rock, misshapen and twisting, hanging down into the chasm like stalactites and stabbing upward from the surface like craggy spires. But the tower was unlike the rock, clearly built by hands . . . or by magic, at least.

Rhidea walked with the orb still raised in her hand, keeping the lightning from striking us. The sky seemed almost angry at our defiance. "Prepare yourselves for the climb ahead," she called over the storm. "We're almost there. The Gate will be at the top of this tower."

I gazed up at the looming spire, lit ever-so-dimly by the giant moon above it. *So tall . . .* and we were going to climb it?

We rounded the last jutting spike of earth, some thirty feet tall, and found ourselves at the base of the Tower of Mani. A stairway opened in front of us, circling up to the right around the wall of the tower. As I looked up, I could see that the spiral pattern continued up the wall, ever reaching toward the top. The stairs here were a good eight feet wide, and a three-foot railing of sorts ran up the side, so my worries of Oliver—or all of us—tumbling to his doom abated a bit.

Rhidea sighed, lowering her hand slightly as she tilted backward, looking up at the heights of the tower hidden in the clouds, and the frightening stairway winding up to the heavens. "Oh, this is going to be a long trek up." Breathing in deeply, she said, "Up we go."

"Up we go," Kaen agreed.

- Chapter 38 -

The Gate of the Moon

Scholars who hold that theory generally suppose that we, the Legaleians, came from that land. This could, perhaps, solve one issue, that is to say that if humankind came from this other continent, perhaps it would have been possible for life to exist before the Wellspring of Life at the center of Argent came to be. But then there is the same question—where did we come from before that? Scholars have a tendency to try and explain human origins with, "We came from somewhere else," but it's a rather circular argument. . . .

— From *Secrets of Mani*, by Sor the Lark

(Quoi 14, 997—Night Season)

The trek up the tower proved to be as long and grueling as we'd anticipated. The stone stairs seemed to never end, one after the other. The tower was perhaps a hundred feet wide at the base and tapered slightly with each row of stairs, but it was *tall*. So tall.

"So . . . tired," grunted Mydia. "I just want to—" She cut off with a yelp, clutching to my shoulder for probably the sixth time as a loud roll of thunder sounded, shaking the stone beneath our feet. We kept as close to the inside as possible, but every crash of thunder still sent a jolt of fear down my spine. Nerve-racking didn't begin to describe it. I wasn't really getting fatigued like the others—except perhaps mentally—but I wanted to be over with the perilous climb as soon as possible.

The lightning flared in the sky constantly, some thundering and others silent, lighting our way but in treacherous, shifting angles. I had tried my flame for light, but as much as it actually gave us light to see by, it also distracted our vision just the same. Kymhar and Rhidea led the way. We followed close behind over the slowly tightening curve of the stairway.

And . . . we tried our best not to look down.

Finally, Rhidea stopped and looked back. "Here it is: the top of the tower." She waved us up as Kymhar climbed the last steps to the top.

I wanted to hurry there myself, but instead I took Oliver's hand in my right and Mydia's in my left and helped them up the last bit. They both collapsed to the ground immediately upon reaching the top. I felt like doing the same, and looking at Kaen and Rhidea, I saw that they felt likewise.

"We made it," I said, looking around at the roof of the tower for the first time. It was roughly fifty feet across and circular, with a floor of the same cross-hatched silver stone that made up the walls. There was a low step up toward the middle in two spots, like raised tiers, and in the center stood an arched, empty doorway of stone. Eight feet tall, four feet wide. To look at it, one could not tell that there was anything special or magical about it.

I approached it hesitantly. "Is that . . . ?"

"The gateway to Gaea?" Rhidea asked in a tired voice. "We can only assume so."

Mydia picked herself up beside me with a grunt, and I helped her to her feet. "The Gate," she murmured upon seeing it. "But . . . how is it supposed to work?"

I shrugged. "One way to find out."

We approached the Gate and inspected it closely. Oliver caught up to us in time for his curiosity to get the best of him.

"Don't touch it," Rhidea muttered, swiping aside his reaching hand. She proceeded to run her own, more scholarly hand carefully down the side of the stone, and I gave Oliver a quick grin. He responded with a pouty face.

The sides of the Gate were curved all around except for the flat inner arch, and engraved with foreign letters on the side that Rhidea was looking at.

"Isn't that the same Gaean script that was on the mural in the Well?" I asked.

She nodded in response, brow furrowed in thought. "It must be of Gaea." Her tone seemed to imply that we would know more had we been able to browse the libraries at Redufiel.

A shiver ran down my spine. On a hunch, I went around to the other side of the Gate and looked at the opposite end of the arch. Sure enough, there were letters here that I could identify, although the writing was a bit old-fashioned and the engraving hard to make out, so I had some trouble trying to read it. "Rhidea, Mydia . . ." I waved them over.

"Oh, look!" cried the queen. "It's in our tongue! Well, it's High Legaleian."

"'The Gate of Mani,'" Rhidea read. She traced her finger farther down and began to read: "'Upon this ancient tor, this monument of trust stands. Between two peoples distant, formed by no mortal hands. Hold to these pillars and speak the name of the world you wish to enter' . . . there's more, but I can't make it out."

"So, the portal is activated by voice," I said slowly. "Do you think it still works?"

"One way to find out," Kaen said. He approached the arch and placed one hand on the left side, one on the right. "Gaea," he said in a commanding voice. "Take me to Gaea." He looked up at the great blue moon hovering in the sky among the stars, then back down at the arch. "Blasted door. Take us to Gaea! It's no use. It's broken."

I brushed him aside gently. "It might not be that simple, Kaen," I said. "Remember, there were more words. One must probably possess the gift of magic to open it, and . . ." I looked up into my teacher's eyes and saw the same thought there.

"It may take one from both worlds to open the Gate," she said. "You give it a try, Lyn. You've got the best shot at it. We can—" She cut off, looking around. "Kymhar? What are you . . . ?"

I glanced behind me and saw the assassin standing near the steps, the only exit from this high tower perch. He held the remaining orb that we had never used, whose use we never knew. He spoke now, so quietly that I could barely hear him over the storm. "Stay where you are. You have all done well to come this far. I couldn't have done it without you. On behalf of my master, I thank you." He gave a small bow and then raised the hand that held the orb.

"What are you playing at?" Kaen hissed, hand on his sword. "Your master sent you to help us because he believed in us. What purpose would he have to try and sabotage the mission now?"

"Ask him yourself."

"Wait!" shouted Rhidea. "Stop this at once, Kymhar. We trusted you. Was this trust misplaced? Should we kill you now?"

The Dalim smiled faintly and brought his hand up as though to smash the orb against the ground. Rhidea immediately cast her gravity Authority on him, freezing him in place. She approached him, Kaen at her side with sword pointed toward the assassin. "Give me the orb," she commanded.

Kymhar looked at her from his frozen position. "Too bad," he hissed. "It's too late."

The orb began to pulse just as Kaen reached for it, sending out a black shockwave that swept over the surface of the tower, causing each of us to stumble. It pulsed every second with the same effect, and then it shattered, falling apart in Kymhar's hand. A piercing whine sounded, and then a beam of light erupted from the sky right beside Kaen. He and Rhidea stepped back in time to see a figure emerge from the light in a crouch. He stood up as the light faded, revealing himself to be Kymhar's master, the Archlord.

"Domon," I whispered, still crouched in front of the arched Gate, where I had been trying to figure out the activation method before Kymhar's distraction.

"Well, well," he said, waving a hand dramatically in front of him. "What do we have here? Oh—the Gate of Mani!" He smiled in a pleased way. "I really must thank you all. I couldn't have done it without you." He touched Kymhar briefly and unfroze him.

"Domon, you *snake*," Rhidea hissed.

"Why, you can call me whatever you like, my dear," he said pleasantly. "But I'm afraid we can't let you through that Gate. After all, I've come to destroy it. And look, there's the hybrid freak. Kym, stop her."

"Understood." Kymhar zipped away toward me.

I stood up from my crouch to face him, but Kaen leapt in the way of the assassin, swinging with his sword. "Not so fast!" he shouted as bronze rang on bronze. "You'll have to get through me, traitor! Lyn, get that Gate open! We have to get through!"

"Traitor," Kymhar spat, trading blows with his protégé. "To my own master? You really think you can take me, boy?"

"Lyn!" Rhidea shouted from the far side of the tower. "He's right! Don't fight, just get that—just activate that portal!" She struggled with the Archlord, Authority against Authority, just like she had against Lord Kalceron. "I've always wanted this duel," she said with a smile. "For far longer than you know. To think I made a deal with the murderer of my family."

Mydia held Oliver behind me. "Don't worry, Oliver," she said in a shaky voice. "You don't know how strong my companions are. We'll make it through this."

"Mydia," I said, looking back at her, "protect Oliver. I'll handle the Gate."

She nodded firmly, and I turned my attention to the Gate. It was hard to ignore my friends who fought for me, but I couldn't fail them now. I racked my brains for something to do in order to get the Gate of Mani to activate. I spoke the name of Gaea, infused the arch with magic, heated it up, pushed on it, all to no avail.

Lightning flashed all around us, and whatever was going on between the Archlord and Rhidea was sending tremors down the tower and rippling the air. Sparks flew and explosions sounded, but I kept my attention fixed on the Gate. *How do I make it open?* I thought frantically.

Out of the corner of my eye, I saw Kymhar and Kaen leap into my field of vision for a moment, blades flashing in the light as they whipped them back and forth in a dangerous dance. I knew that Kaen was good, but could he really hold back Kymhar? Certainly not for long.

Focus. "Come on, come on, think!" I muttered to myself. Then it clicked. I was trying to use Coaction, but if I could somehow use my Gaean powers . . . but what even were those? I still didn't understand how they worked, aside from that I could metabolize food into energy far quicker than a normal human and could make my body perform at unnatural levels when needed . . .

But there was something else. I had felt it before, like a distant connection with something. The world itself . . . but no, not this world. Another. I looked up, gazing at Gaea. There was a connection between me and my homeworld that had always pulled me unconsciously, I'd just never recognized it as such. I searched within myself, looking for that connection, and finally saw something. I lowered my hands to the stone of the tower, feeling the cold dampness of it. Mani and Gaea . . . was there a link between them, too? Could I restore it somehow?

I closed my eyes and concentrated. Dimly, I began to feel it. Not because of my focus or the positioning of my hands or something silly like that, it just . . . clicked. I felt that same power within me that I had on only a couple occasions in my life, drawing from the power of Mani itself. It was weak, and not capable of much. In fact, it had never really helped me at all.

So I pulled on the power of Gaea as well. It came from the Gate itself, creeping into my hands like dew condensing on grass. As the two powers met, I felt the stone coming to life.

The connection was restored.

"Rhidea, I think I've restarted—"

I looked back to see the Archlord pinning her to the ground, a hand raised with black electricity crackling from his palm. But he stopped and looked at me and the Gate. His eyes widened. "Kymhar, I told you to—"

I watched as Rhidea shoved a hand into his side, blasting him up and off of her. She rose shakily to her feet. "Lyn, is it ready?"

"It's activating!" shouted Mydia from behind me.

I turned and saw Kymhar kick Kaen to skid across the slick surface of the tower, right up to the edge. Then the assassin turned on me.

I stood up, back against the portal, unsure of what to do. Mydia, holding Oliver, backed up toward the tower's rim, eyeing the

Archlord as he approached me. He held the orb that had been in Rhidea's hand—the same one that had absorbed the energy from the lightning around us—a wicked grin on his face.

"No!" shouted Rhidea, rushing toward him. Everyone seemed to converge upon me and Domon as he held up the crackling orb.

"Goodbye," he said, and vanished. The orb exploded a split-second later, hitting us with a shockwave tenfold that of the other orb. All of the pent-up energy it had absorbed from the lightning thus far condensed into a ball of shadowy essence that detonated in a blinding flash of light. I was knocked straight backward through the glowing Gate of Mani, feeling the stone of the archway breaking as I was pushed through.

The last thing I saw was a blazing white flash before I lost consciousness.

The last thing I heard was the sound of panicked screaming and pure destruction. And then nothing.

There she was, the girl I called White. She stood on a pale hilltop. The foggy land beneath, whatever it was, sloped gently up to the peak, where she stood an indeterminant distance from me.

But I could see her smile from here. "Come on," she said, so faintly that it wasn't audible, yet I knew what she was saying.

All I could do was wonder with a muddy mind, *What I am doing here? Where was I?* I was . . . reforging something. Had it worked? Or had it broken?

I shook my head. Slowly, a trickle of memory, memories of memories, came back to me, of these places with White, and why I was here. This time, I hadn't simply used my Gaean powers, but had drawn on the dormant energy inside Mani and Gaea and . . . fused them. It had triggered something in my mind.

A sense of purpose slowly built within me, and I knew what I had to do. And so I climbed. The hill was not steep, yet my ascent felt slow and tiring. But I didn't stop, and I didn't take my eyes off of White. I wouldn't give up now that I had a goal. I was here, and my mind was conscious—ironically, more conscious than I'd ever been in a dream. I would not give it up until I had the answers I wanted from White.

As I climbed, an image flashed across my vision of a foreign world, a desert place with windswept dunes. Roaring waves of a dark sea—an endless sea filled with water. A cave. A man and a woman. My . . . father and mother?

The images were gone almost as soon as they came, and my gaze was still fixed on the smiling girl ahead of me. She was closer now, still beckoning with hopeful eyes.

A new image, that of a troop of warriors in dull-colored, armored uniforms, bearing complex metal weapons I didn't recognize. They were marching toward me. The vision swept from my sight and was gone just as quickly as it had come.

I struggled on. So close—I could see the top of the hill now, and White's little hand reaching out. So close . . .

Fire and smoke. The stench of everything around me burning. I heard my mother screaming. And then that, too, was gone.

At last, I reached White. I grasped her little hand, and she pulled me up to the crest of the hill. I grinned and took a deep breath.

"You finally made it, Lyn," she said cheerfully, yet with a touch of sadness. "I can tell you've discovered something. You came of your own free will this time?"

I hesitated. "I'm . . . not sure. I think my plans were just ruined.

Either that or I succeeded. But I did discover something."

"Okay. And what have you come to see?" she asked.

"My memories," I said firmly.

"Which ones?"

"All of them. I want control again."

"Are you sure you want this burden?" she asked. "You've hidden me away all these years. It will be painful. It will be overwhelming at first."

"I need them. I can't hide from them anymore," I said. "I want them all back."

The little girl nodded. "All right." And she stepped aside, waving down toward the other side of the hill. I looked and saw a multitude of places and times and people, near and far, yesterday and distant past, of both Mani and Gaea.

It was disorienting, fatiguing, almost painful just to maintain my own consciousness, but I managed.

"Lyn? Are you all right?" White asked. I nodded, and she said, "You're not going to stuff me away again?"

I shook my head through the pain and blurriness. "No, not again. Although . . ."

"I know, Lyn. You can only see me in your dreams. It's the only place where you can handle your own Vault. Your mother's mind was stronger, but yours is only half Hellebes. But at least now you can see that you never forgot a single one. The Vault does not lose memories."

"I just stuffed them in here with you," I said, "a figment of my own imagination that I nicknamed White. You sit here in the darkness of my dreams—my Vault—and wait for me to come back. But now I have the key."

"So, what do you wish to see in this dream?" she asked.

I took a breath. "I want to see the day I came to this world."

"Very well." The little girl disappeared, and my dream changed.

(Mani'Tor 20, 984—Waning Day)

I was behind the eyes of a small girl, very small. Around me was the constantly jostling sight of a familiar city: Nytaea. Mother was carrying me, so I couldn't see anything too clearly, just over her shoulder and off to the sides.

I saw it all in a strange, detached way. The little me was staring around, as I had on that day, and focusing where she wanted to focus. I caught the details mostly as she did, except that I was able to process them with information I had now. So I didn't quite know how to feel when I saw my mother's face again.

She was gorgeous, as always. Features strong but refined, smooth-cheeked and point-nosed. Her eyes sparkled blue, like my own, and her hair, tossed to and fro by the wind behind her . . . it was like mine, but long and *vibrant*. Not just white. Not just white-like-the-sun as everyone described mine, but I could swear it actually shone, giving off a faintly . . . green? Yes, a green glow.

Mother's head was tucked against the wind, which blew cross-angled against us. She glanced side to side frequently. I realized that she was running fast, inhumanly fast. I heard shouts from bystanders around us, such as:

"Whoa, make way!"

"Why, look at that hair! How is she . . . wh-where's she going?"

Mother ignored them all, of course. In fact, my toddler mind in the memory couldn't quite grasp why, but I could tell that the shouts worried her. Somehow, I knew she was used to being hunted as a freak, a novelty, a monster.

But what a beautiful monster she was.

Mother stopped suddenly and ducked down a side alley. I experienced it oddly, looking from a child's eyes at an upward angle, but I could tell what was going on. She hesitated at the next inter-section, and then headed left. Was she . . . following directions? Yes, my child's mind thought just then. The kind man she had spoken with, he told mother where to go to find the orphanage.

And then we were there. Even from my poor vantage, I could tell where we were. As the child-me squirmed, I got an even better look. Unmistakably, it was Lentha's orphanage. Mother glanced down at me, stroking my head with hands that felt comforting, strong. "Darling, we're here: your new home." She didn't actually speak those words—it was in another language—but I realized with some surprise that I could understand it as a toddler. Better than a child twice my age would have.

Mother put me down gently, giving me a quiet order to stay put and not be afraid. And then she approached the door, hesitating be-fore knocking twice.

A moment passed, and then I saw her face. Lentha, the one who would raise me from this day forward. Her face, only slightly wrin-kled then, was as kindly as ever. She glanced up at my mother, down at me, and then doubled back to my mother's face. "Stars above," she breathed. "It's—it's an angel. Or a demon. Who . . . who are you?"

My mother shook her head, hunching her shoulders up slightly. I could tell that she didn't understand the woman's words.

Lentha opened the door and stepped out slowly, bending down to look me in the eye. One-year-old me looked aside bashfully, but I caught my mother's hesitant step backward. She must have been so frightened.

Lentha smiled warmly at me and reached down to pinch my cheek. "Hello, little one. What's your name?"

I looked up at my mother. She seemed as skittish as a kitten. Or . . . more like a mother cat with a human touching her kitten. Nervous about what would happen to her child, because . . . because she was planning to leave me here and never return. I could tell, somehow, even if my child self did not understand.

Lentha stood back up and looked at Mother. "No . . ." she whispered. "You're not a demon. I don't know who you are or where you come from, but . . . here. Here, you need a hug." She motioned with her hands, and when Mother did not oblige, she stepped forward and took hold of my mother in a tight embrace. I realized how much taller Mother was than she, so tall that she dwarfed the kindly woman. Strong though she was, she seemed to melt in that motherly embrace, and I watched as she carefully put her arms around Lentha and began to cry.

"It's all right," Lentha said as she pulled away. She smiled at my mother, and then at me. "You look like you've been through a lot."

Mother bent down and scooped me up in her arms. She smiled down at me through her tears and hugged me to her face. And then she held me out to Lentha. My child self was confused and a bit panicked, but I understood. Lentha took me gently, grunting at the weight.

I looked up from Lentha to Mother and back as Lentha asked, "Are you sure?"

My mother nodded as though she understood. "Take her," she said, tears staining her cheeks. "I cannot. Soon, my sickness will take me. Her name is Lynchazel." She repeated the name, and Lentha repeated it back. Mother reached out a pale hand and patted my head one last time. "I'll always love you, my dear, sweet Lynchazel," she croaked.

And then she turned and fled, gleaming hair trailing faint, green light behind her.

I looked up at my new mother, Lentha, and began to cry.

- Chapter 39 -

Gaea

Dear Mother,

There is something I must tell you, and I am too afraid to say it, not to mention I know that you would stop me. So . . . I am leaving you one final letter instead. I have decided to go. I cannot say if I will be back, so I will make no promises. Know that I love you more than all of Mani. But you know that this is more important than you or I or even this silver shell we call home. And so, I must go. I must. I will see you again, whether in this world, in the other, or in the afterlife.

Goodbye — Kallyn

Post Script: Please take care of Mydia. Perhaps someday when she is older, you can explain to her why I had to leave Mani.

(Planet Gaea—Gatewatch Isle
Koii 14, 2336)

I awoke in a strange world with a blazing headache.

"Mother," I murmured, unsure of why I said it. The word came out as little more than a moan. My vision swam as I tried to sit up, but a strong hand held me back. The effort of sitting up was so much greater than I expected. Was I really that weak? Well, I had just survived an . . . explosion? A flash of light and an explosion . . .

The Archlord. He had ruined everything and destroyed the Gate of Mani—probably killed my friends, too. Somehow, I must have made it through the Gate. Dimly, I wondered if it was even still there.

A voice spoke to me, a deep male voice in an unrecognizable tongue. No . . . I recognized it, I just didn't understand it. I shook myself and looked up to see the man who held my shoulder. He wasn't holding me down, I realized, but just steadying me. It seemed to be dawn here, and the only light I had to see by came from some lights shining from somewhere overhead. I couldn't see his face clearly, because he wore some sort of helmet with a dark glass shield over his eyes. It enveloped the sides of his head, crafted from a glistening metal of the strangest design . . . in fact, he wore a whole suit that was strange. White and dull, with plates almost like armor over his chest and shoulder. Instruments that I did not recognize were placed at his belt and on his chest.

The man spoke again, and I just shook my head, shrugging. Again, the effort it took was surprising. I wasn't so weak, I thought, it just . . . took more effort. The man, seeing that I could not understand him, raised his head and spoke something in the same foreign language to another man.

Looking around for the first time from my crablike position, I realized that there were three of them standing over me, all tall men of large build wearing identical suits and helmets. Overhead loomed an arch just like the one that the orb's explosion had destroyed, which could only be the Gate of Gaea, and far overhead in the sky loomed a distant planet, much like how we had viewed Gaea from the face of Mani. But it was . . . much smaller, and silvery-white, not blue. Gaea must be far larger than the other world. The stars twinkled faintly beyond it. Neither cast much light, but on one horizon, buried beneath long clouds, the sun was beginning to rise.

I was on some kind of island. The air was damp, as though next to a large body of water—in fact, I could hear it—and moss grew on stones around me. Moss and vines ran up the side of the arch.

"Is this . . . Gaea?" I asked. I groaned and rose to my feet with effort, shaking off the hand of the suited man. From my standing position, I could see over the rocks around me to discover that we stood on a small island. An ocean of water reached as far as the eye could see. An ocean. Not a river, not a lake . . . this was a true ocean.

Some hundred feet away, down a small incline, sat a large metal vehicle. I assumed that was what it was, though its design was completely foreign to me, and very . . . advanced. It had wings, and looked to be a flying machine. Between the flying vehicle and the devices on the men's suits, I could tell that these people's society was far more advanced in technology than any on Mani. *What kind of world is this . . . ?* I wondered with a rising sense of panic.

The man who had previously held me was eyeing me up with a wary posture. He spoke again, and somehow I could grasp the meaning without recognizing the words: *Who are you?*

I could tell by the way that they regarded both me and the archway, which must have just opened, that they were nervous but had an inkling of what was going on. Why were they here on this small, deserted island? Were they . . . guarding the Gate?

I drew in a deep, steadying breath, putting out my hands in a gesture that I hoped would look friendly. Or at least not menacing. Great auroras, it was a struggle even to stand. I was right—Gaea's gravity was much stronger than Mani's. It would take some getting used to. "I am Lynchazel. I mean you no harm." I pointed upward at the moon hanging in the sky, and then at the Gate. "I come from Mani. I came through the doorway."

The man, obviously the leader, spoke again in a harsher tone, pointing. I could tell what he was getting at: *Are more people coming through? Are we under attack?*

"No, no. It has been destroyed," I said, making as clear of gestures as I could. "No one can come through. The Gate, it's destroyed. No one will ever be coming again." Hopefully they understood at least somewhat.

The leader looked at his companions and spoke a couple of quiet words. Then he reached up and pressed a switch that caused his helmet to disassemble and retract almost like a hood, revealing his face. His features were strong, his neck thick. He was bald, with hard eyes and a large nose. His expression softened as he looked at me, uttering what was probably a welcome. Pointing at himself, he spoke one word, a name: "Zent." His next words and gestures gave the clear indication that they were going to take me into custody.

I sighed. I didn't care at this point. These men didn't seem overly hostile, and I certainly wasn't going to fight them. I let them lead me down a rocky path to the flat point where their flying metal ship stood. I looked down to see that the hill steepened and dropped off into a cliff. We were actually high above the water. I squinted, gazing over the breathtaking sea that stretched endlessly below us. More water than I could ever have dreamed of—water enough to fill even the Sea of Emptiness. What other kinds of wonders did this world hold? What kind of terrors?

Deep inside, between the dizziness and bewilderment evoked by even standing up on this heavy world, my heart ached for my lost friends. Perhaps they had made it out alive somehow . . . I could only hope.

But I would never see them again.

And that's . . . that's it. That's how I got here. There's more to tell, of course. If you were paying attention, there's a missing chunk at the end there, where I got imprisoned by the Senate for the crime of being born, but I think I'm just going to wait for now and tell it in my next record—that of my journey here on Gaea. We'll see how, um . . . how it all plays out. Hopefully, Zent will be back soon. I'm trying not to even think about what happened to my friends.

But I'm pretty sure I'm here for the long haul. Without the Gate, there is no escape from Gaea.

- Epilogue -

A Small World

Dear Mother,

This will be my final letter. I have so many things I want to tell you about, but unfortunately, I will not be able to tell you them in person. So I'd like you to meet your new daughter-in-law and grandchild, with whom I've sent this message: Lynchazel and . . . Lynchazel. I pray that their return to you is safe and swift. My wife does not yet know much of the Legaleian tongue, but I'm sure you will be a good teacher. I think that together you, she and Rhidea can come up with a plan to save two worlds. As for me . . . soon, I will sleep the sleep of death, here on Gaea. I love you.

— Your son, Kallyn

(Planet Mani—Nytaea
Quoi 14, 997—Night Season)

Archlord Domon strode along the wall of Nytaea, black cape cinched at his collar bone, displaying the blue flame of the Kystrean empire. His golden hair streamed freely in the wind; no crown. He was in the wall sector directly west of the Palace, right where he told Kymhar to lay the transport orb. Of course, he could have just come straight here at any point, but he had needed the group to make it all the way to the Tower of Mani in order to find it for him.

Now the Gate was destroyed entirely. No more doorway to Gaea. A successful endeavor. Now to begin the next phase.

Domon surveyed the city to his right. Light glowed in the darkness from a multitude of torches and lanterns, illuminating the alabaster buildings in all their glory. The starlight streaming down from the heavens blended with the torchlight, artificial mixing with the natural.

He looked directly in front of him at the tall, white Nytaean Palace, lit even more brightly, flags streaming in the steady breeze atop lofty towers. Despite tighter-than-usual guard patrols and the remnants of the recent unrest here in Nytaea, the city looked almost peaceful. The Archlord sighed. Such a pity, but someone had to break that peace. Someone had to let them know that his little parley had reached its term . . . prematurely.

Domon turned and leapt from the wall, landing on the Palace grounds directly outside the main gate. He glided to the ground softly right before his feet hit, creating a whoosh of wind. A couple of guards shouted, a torch waved upon the wall, and the two gate guards looked around frantically.

The two men clapped the butt of their spears on the stones as he strode up briskly. "Halt there! Name yourself, stranger!"

"I am the Archlord. I used to own this place."

The guards looked at him suspiciously, weapons held at the ready. Domon could see the fear in their eyes. In the background, horns were blowing. "The Palace is closed for the night, sir," said the guard on the left.

Domon shook his head as though in disappointment. "And I only wanted to pay a visit. Very well." He put out his hands to either side and then thrust them forward. A wave of darkness, visible only as a shadow that blocked all light in its area, rose from the ground and took hold of the guards, squeezing them and slamming them into the pillars of the gate. They barely had a chance to cry out before their armor crumpled in from the impact, cracking the stone with the force.

He let the men go, their corpses sliding down the pillars and leaving bloody smears. Domon pulled his shadowy hands from the ground once more and threw a fist. His corresponding shadow hand mimicked the motion, smashing the silver gate right in.

Cries began to rise from all around:

"Dark Magic!"

"Monster!"

"We're under attack!"

Domon simply dusted off his hands, shook his head as though in disappointment, and proceeded through the broken gateway. Bolts shot down at him, but they glanced off before they got within two feet of him, repelled by a shield of water and wind that he kept up at all times.

Soldiers were beginning to surround him by the time he reached the Palace, both spearmen and silver-armored mage soldiers. He blasted a few more who blocked his way and entered into the Palace foyer. "Now, which way . . . ?" he muttered to himself. He didn't have to wait long before Lanthar, Marshal of Nytaea, rushed in through the western doorway, bearing a ripple-bladed greatsword. He took in the scene in a second and then shouted, "Archlord Domon! What is going on here? What is the meaning of this?" Anger played on his hard face, accentuated by the torchlight.

Domon stopped. "Ah, finally someone in charge. I suppose some of your important leaders are out, hmm . . . on a little journey about now? You see, we had a deal . . ."

Marshal Lanthar stalked down the stairway into the room with his massive sword. Soldiers poured out behind him, taking up guarding stances. "Yes, I believe we did."

Domon smiled. "Well, you see, it's off."

❧ ❧

(Planet Mani—The Down Under
Quoi 14, 997—???)

Kaen awoke, dizzily shaking his head.

"Where . . . am I?" he mumbled, then gasped, glancing around him. Lyn, Rhidea, where were they all? How had he survived? He vaguely remembered the giant explosion from the orb just after the Archlord vanished, and being blown right off the top of the tower along with everyone else. They must have all fallen in different directions, down and down through the storm clouds and then . . .

He took in the strange scene about him. Sand. He lay in soft sand of the purest white color. The air itself glowed with a blue-green hue, which seemed to come from sparkling particles that drifted on the faint breeze. The light played on the sand in a surreal way. Had he seen it before?

Am I dreaming?

And then his eyes fell on the figure beside him. Kymhar, the assassin who had tried to kill him. Anger began to build within Kaen's chest. If the fool was dead, then he had only gotten what he deserved. If not . . . ugh, he had to find out, didn't he?

Groaning, Kaen lifted his arms from the sand and crawled to where his mentor lay, facedown. He was breathing. He rolled the man over, brushing sand off his face, and slapped his cheeks. It took a second, but then Kymhar's eyes snapped open and he reached up quickly to catch Kaen's arm. For a moment, Kaen felt a spike of panic, but he realized that it was just a reflex born of years of training. Kymhar was in no shape to fight.

Kaen brushed off the man's arm. "Enough of that. We came close enough to dying as it is." He resented the words even as he said them, but they were true.

Kymhar gave a groggy grunt. "Where are we, boy?" He sat up, spitting out sand and holding a hand to his side.

"I have no idea. But I think we somehow fell through one of those big holes in the earth around the tower."

Kymhar nodded. "That would make sense. This light around us, I recognize it. But how did we not die from the fall . . . ?" After a pause, he asked, "What of the others? Have you checked for them, or was your first instinct to help the traitor who tried to kill you?"

"I—well, you were the closest person I could see," Kaen stammered. "I figured I should make sure you were alive. I don't know about the others yet."

"Then . . . Lyn was blown through the Gate as it crumbled? So she's gone. My master, too, is gone. The others were all knocked off the tower just as we were—it is possible they have fallen down here somewhere."

Kaen grunted assent. He didn't understand why he was helping the assassin, but the situation compelled him to leave his anger in the back of his mind. He stood shakily and helped Kymhar to do the same. The odd-colored sand was awkward to get around in, yet he felt oddly light in this place deep beneath the world. The two of them, after stretching briefly, set about searching around for the others. They found Mydia and Oliver, hands still clasped together, splayed out in the sand. They looked a little beat-up from the explosion, but were otherwise all right. Kaen and Kymhar woke them up and then began to explain what little they knew about their situation.

Once Mydia and the boy were up to speed, they all set about looking for the last remaining member of their team. She had better be all right. Whatever fluke of nature had landed them safely to the ground may not have been enough to keep Rhidea safe. She had looked pretty worse-for-wear from her frantic battle of Authority with the Archlord. Kaen had never seen such a display of Authority in his life. . . .

"I found her!" Mydia shouted frantically from somewhere on Kaen's left, voice even higher-pitched than usual. "And she's hurt! Rhidea, Rhidea, can you hear me?"

Kaen's heart rate quickened. He rushed over to find Mydia kneeling over her teacher, tears streaming down her dimpled cheeks. "Oh, Rhidea . . ." Kaen took in the scene with horror. Their fearless leader lay sprawled in the white sand with one leg skewed outward at a horrible angle. Blood spattered the sand around her, staining it an unholy color.

Kymhar approached from the right, crouching by Rhidea's mangled body and taking in the scene. Mydia screamed at him hysterically, but Kaen pulled her back from the body and let Kymhar check her out.

"She must have struck either the side of the tower or a stone spike on her way down," the Dalim said. He inspected her body more closely, carefully feeling at her neck and putting an ear to her chest. "She is barely breathing, but she is alive. I'm shocked that this only happened to one of us, with all the stone bridges we could have hit."

"Oh, thank the heavens," Mydia whispered, clinging to Kaen's chest. He patted her on the back reassuringly, and Oliver took her hand.

"Of all the ones to get injured . . ." Kaen muttered.

"Is she gonna make it?" asked Oliver in a trembling voice.

Kymhar carefully rolled Rhidea over, trying to move her fractured leg as little as possible. "Perhaps. She bled a lot. We will have to cut her leg and realign the bones, and then . . ." He looked up at Mydia. "It will depend on the queen's healing magic. How good are you?"

Kaen could not look away from the bone that jutted from Rhidea's leg, now visible since Kymhar had rolled the woman over. Not because of how grisly it was, but because . . . "Bones aren't supposed to look like that," he murmured quietly.

"I . . . I have not used my healing often, so I really don't know . . ." Mydia said nervously in response to Kymhar. "But I don't think I can handle helping with the . . . the . . ."

Kaen shook himself, pushing Mydia gently aside. "I'll help. Let's be quick, before she wakes up. But . . . that bone."

Kymhar shook his head. "Doesn't matter—just focus, boy. Bones are bones, we just need to set it."

A half hour later, Kaen and Kymhar had the mage's leg back together and had persuaded the hemophobic princess to work her water magic on the wound, causing the bones and skin to stitch back together. Kaen held one hand over her eyes and guided her healing hand with his other.

"There," she said, rocking back on her rump and wiping her brow with the back of one hand. "That's all I can do for now. What about her other injuries?"

Silver bones . . .

Kaen shook himself. "They'll be fine as we've bound them," he said. "They're much more minor. What we need to do now is get her someplace to heal." He looked around, peering into the distance. It was hard to see much more than a few hundred feet ahead due to the glimmery effect from the particles in the air. "Come on. Kymhar and I will carry her. And Kymhar . . . thank you."

The assassin grunted. They carried the woman carefully between them as the party of four set out to find a different location. The sands had been shifted from here to there, forming small hills and dunes where the wind swept it. There was a refreshing, near-constant breeze down here in the belly of the earth, like the breath of the planet itself.

"So," Mydia said with a cough at one point, voice still shaking. "It might sound stupid to ask this right now, but . . . where exactly *are* we?"

Oliver perked up at the question, seeming as eager as the queen to get his mind off the situation with Rhidea. "Actually, I've been thinking 'bout that for a while now. There's no way to tell how far we fell, but I'd guess it was quite a ways since ya can't see anything in the sky, or air . . . whatever it is . . . above. Everything's so different down here. It's like another world within the world. The heart of Mani."

"The heart of Mani," Mydia mused.

Oliver nodded excitedly. "And I was thinking . . . well, back on the Sky Islands, we always assumed that a fall into the chasm was a death sentence."

Kaen gasped. "You might be right. The chasm—it probably just leads down here, to this place."

"Right! So, so . . . all the folks I knew, the folks my uncle knew . . . maybe even my parents! They might be alive down here!"

Kaen frowned as he carried half of Rhidea's surprising weight. "Wow. What a thought. Don't get your hopes up, kid, but . . . you might just be right. But how would anyone stay alive down here? How are *we* going to stay alive down here? I mean, there's nothing here but sand."

"You never know," Mydia pointed out. "We don't know how big

this underworld is, or if there are different regions—no, look, there's grass up ahead!"

Kaen looked up and saw that she was indeed right. They came into a region of water, with bright silver grass waving in the breeze and dotted with strange, twisted trees, their very bark streaked with silver. The land opened up into a valley of sorts that twisted down toward a foggy land lit by the same blue-green light—but brighter here.

"Life," breathed Mydia. "I *told* you. This is where all the water runs."

It wasn't ten minutes before they ran across another person, a man bent over and harvesting some kind of fruit from one of the plants. He wore a wide-brimmed hat that revealed his face only as he looked up. The man appeared to be in his middle years, with bushy eyebrows and a scraggly, grey beard. "Look, more visitors," he said brightly. "From the Sandlands! Now, that's new. Nobody ever . . ." he squinted, seeing that we had a wounded companion. "Blimey!" He put down his basket and rushed over to us.

"She'll be all right for a while," said Kaen. "She hit her leg on some rocks on the way down from the Tower."

"Tower? Youngster, where exactly were y'all up on the surface? You must be from that far continent, what's it called again?"

Mydia shook her head. "No, we traveled there from the Sky Islands on the east coast of Argent."

The man's interest was piqued even more. "Say that again, young miss? You traveled there? That is most impressive." He looked like he was going to say something else, but he stopped as he looked down at Oliver. "Now, ya look familiar, lad. Why is that . . . ?" He scratched his head, screwing up his face as though searching his memory. "Oh, I know! You remind me of those folks that crash-landed back in the woodlands two years ago. Heheh, that was a right mess, but they made it!"

Oliver's lip trembled as he asked, "What were their names?"

"Um, let's see . . . Lester and Marnie. Kinda young, kinda middle-aged fellas. A man and a lady. Why, ring a bell?"

Oliver gasped. "T-that's my mum and dad!"

"Nah, for real? Heh, to think . . . well, that must be a shocker," the man said. "Everyone always seems to think we just die when we fall. I mean, I suppose if you haven't been here before, you'd think that because, you know . . . the big fall and the giant Sea of Emptiness. All that. I'm Barry, by the way!" Barry held out his hand to no one in particular, looking between the members of the group, who mostly stood awkwardly by.

"Well, Barry," Kaen said with a small grunt, taking his hand. "Where do you live down here? We need a place for our friend to heal up. It sounds like you've banded together with others who fell, is that right?"

"Right, right. Just so. Everyone makes their way down to the Vale eventually after they fall. Not many do, mind you. A few every year. No one ever makes it back up because, well, there is no way up. Unless you can somehow climb the biggest waterfall in the world. We just make a new life down here amongst the other exiles."

"A giant waterfall?" Mydia asked curiously, but Kymhar cut her off.

"Barry, we are in a hurry. Can you take us there? To your home?"

"Oh, right! The wounded lady. Here, I'll show ya. It's just a mile away. Come with me." He retrieved his fruit basket and led the travelers down a path through the valley, muttering to himself all the way. Kaen thought with some amusement that it would make sense for such a place as this to make a fellow a bit . . . strange in the head. But a village down here in the center of the world? At the heart of Mani?

"Barry," Mydia asked as they all followed. "What's this subterranean world called? And how large is it?"

"Oh, this place?" Barry said cheerfully. "We call it the Down Under. Creative, I know. Folks have spent their whole lives down here. Heh, I've been down here for almost twenty years, I think. Kind of hard to tell after a while. Not so bad, really. It's a rich, fruitful land that no one knows about. Water comes down here and kind of . . . magically goes back up. Mist and cloudy . . . cloud things, that's our best guess?" He said that last part almost as a question, making hand gestures as he talked.

"We have the whole Down Under all mapped out by now," he continued, leading them toward the village. "It's only a few miles around. You can hike all the way around it in a day and arrive right where ya left! Heh, to think that some people up top think the world is flat . . . I mean, I guess since the two main continents up above are sort of . . . floating bread crusts, it's almost true."

"Bread crusts?" Mydia said with a laugh.

Kaen smiled despite himself as he listened to the banter. Barry was a little crazy, but at least he was entertaining. "How much farther to the village?" he asked.

"The village? Why, that's it just up ahead there." The eccentric man stopped and pointed down the hill, past some trees.

Through the mist, Kaen could make out light and chimney smoke. So it was a real village after all. He shook his head with amazement, still holding Rhidea's limp form over his shoulder.

Silver bones . . . could it really mean what he thought? His best friend was stranded on another planet, and he carried a woman with silver bones down to a hamlet beneath the earth.

Beneath the *entire* earth. The center of Mani, an unseen world.

"And here I thought our journey was almost at its end," Kaen whispered. "But it's only just beginning."

The End of Book One
(To be continued)

Whew, it's all done. Book 1 is out the door. I really can't thank you enough for reading, and I hope you enjoyed the ride! If you did, then I humbly ask that you consider leaving an Amazon or Goodreads review so that readers can know whether my obscure indie book is for them.

The good news is that Book Two, *Gaea*, is already well into the editing phase and nearing post-production. You can check out the excerpt at the back of the book if you're curious. It's been a long road, but *Gaea* and . . . Book Three . . . should be coming out this year. (Book Three may be pushed back to 2025, however.)

For those who haven't finished this book and don't want the whole story spoiled, please take this opportunity to stop reading, because I'm going to get into some details here that will ruin much of the experience. For those of you who like to skip to the back of the book and spoil everything, you just . . . keep doing your thing.

Background

When I first sat down in 2016 and wrote the prototype novel that became this trilogy, I had a few working ideas already. The oldest involved a young man on our world (it may have been a fictional one; I forget) who encountered some aliens from another, very close, planet. Aliens with the ability to "world hop." It was a pretty literal thing. This other world was called Luun, and was essentially the moon, but highly technologically advanced and populated by people with strange powers.

Then that became two other worlds, Ccalcitek and Legalei. Legalei was a world of magic, the other a sci-fi world of advanced technology. Ccalcitek was still the moon in that iteration. I thought I was a genius, because surely no one had thought to blend fantasy with science fiction before (yes, you can laugh).

2016 Camp NaNoWriMo rolled around and I decided, "All right, I'm going to finally give this a shot." I'd written one and a half novels at that point (throw in a couple dozen extra fractions for all the stories I had great ideas for but only ever started), but I wanted to write something new, and in one go.

Mani was a 41,000-word barely-novel, fast-paced at the start and totally rushed near the end. It followed a girl with super strength called Lynchazel—she went by Lynx, though—who lived in the city of Nytaea . . . all that stuff. Her powers were far more deadly, to a horrifying degree, and things went quite differently (e.g. Phoebe died on page seven). Around the two-thirds mark, it went off the rails and suddenly they were all off-world. Bing batta boom and the book was done.

Glad I rewrote it.

After splitting the story up into three parts and doing some actual outlining and a . . . little bit . . . of worldbuilding, years of working on that same project and answering the same questions with "Still working on it," *Mani* was done. A few trips through the transmogrifier and it was a workable story that made sense. I decided to go ahead and write *Gaea* before doing the final edits, just to make sure my continuity was right.

Inspiration

Anyway, now for the fun part: What went into it? Believe it or not, my first inspiration for this story was the 2013 film *Man of Steel*. Superman's backstory on Krypton captured my attention in a way few prologues ever have. *Final Fantasy VI* and *FFVII's* storylines also contributed, as well as my reading *The Wheel of Time* and some of Brandon Sanderson's works. I wanted to tell the story of two worlds linked by a strange history, one that wasn't tied down by genre conventions and traditional storytelling methods. I experimented with this along the way and eventually ended up with the final product of *Mani,* whose tone and viewpoint usage I think fit the book as well as it could.

Research

Yes, I had to do a lot of research for this project (even though it's very soft sci-fi). I combed through to try to make it as accurate as possible to the concepts I was drawing from. For instance . . .

Mani is Gaea's moon (in fact, named after the Norse god of the moon, Mani), as revealed partway through the story. There are hints throughout for the observant reader. Mani is just a hair larger than our own moon in circumference, about 8,000 miles, but of course there are . . . distinct differences. The reason day cycles are a month long on Mani is that, just like our moon, it orbits Gaea once per day, facing the exact same direction relative to its big sis, and takes a whole month (28 days on Mani, for author convenience) to make its own revolutions relative to the sun, Sol. According to my astronomy professor Wikipedia, this is known as tidal locking, which gives a moon such as ours or Mani a 1:1 orbital resonance—that is, it spins no more or less than the degrees of its orbit.

Therefore, the surface of the Moon that we view is always the same side. This inspired me to make a world whose people are trapped on the "Dark Side" of their own world, meaning they never see the planet they actually orbit. If someone lived on the Dark Side of the Moon, and you told him his world orbited a planet called Earth, he would think you crazy, unless he had been to the Light Side and seen it. Thus, on the continent of Darsor—the Light Side of Mani—Gaea dominates the sky and cannot be ignored, but I wanted that to be a surprise for the characters from Argent.

(Side note: a viewer from Gaea would be seeing the entire continent of Darsor—technically not a full face of a planet, but it would give the same effect. The gibbous and crescent shapes, etc., of Mani's phases would simply look slightly different from our own moon's.)

The aurora cycle, then, was invented to give the impression of days passing on Mani. (It's total magic, so there's no scientific basis for it, of course.) During the sunlit phase, clouds come in and cover the sky to make for artificial night, and in the sunless phase, bright auroras ripple in the sky to light their days. The Wellspring came about later, when I realized I wanted there to be a reason why a rocky, barren planet would be capable of supporting life after . . . well, no spoilers. But, as mentioned in the book, the Wellspring is the only way there can possibly be life on Mani. Just like the Energy Field in the atmosphere that controls the artificial day cycles, the magic of the Wellspring causes water to flow out over the face of Argent and then cycle back up from the depths of the Down Under.

What about the continent of Darsor? How does it receive water? We'll save that for the next book, among other things.

For the record, Lyn is stronger and has a different body composition than a full-blooded Legaleian because her mother was from Gaea—a world with a far larger mass and thus, heavier gravity. On Mani, actual planetary mass is tricky to calculate due to its unique shape, but a little fantasy helps one to pretend gravity works similarly to on our world. It's just a bit lighter. Technically, it is the silver in both continents' makeup that gives the land its power of gravitational stability (floating), same as the Sky Islands. The core of the planet is what regulates actual gravity experienced by humans, etc. Silver is the power that defies it. In the Down Under, gravity is lighter yet, and a strange force of magic protects people from impact when they fall.

One large challenge came when I went back and cross-referenced dates and times to see where I was describing the sun rising or setting and in between. Ugh, what a nightmare. Only then did I realize how far off it was. So . . . I tried my best, adding in dates and sun positioning for scenes and chapters. Any slight miscalculations can hopefully be forgiven. For those wondering, this was difficult because, as one travels a globe, one's position relative to the sun's angle changes, and on Mani, much more steeply because the circumference of the world is about one-third the size of Earth's while the day cycles pass 28 times more slowly. Therefore, one can nearly chase the sun around the planet. From Ti'Vaeth, the center of Argent, to the middle of the Sea of Emptiness in the east or west, there is a time difference of seven days (think of it like time zones).

I think I'll stop there, as I don't want to bore anybody to sleep. Hopefully this was a little interesting and/or explained some questions. See you on Gaea!

- Appendix A -

Characters

(And how on Mani you're supposed to pronounce them)

Adullus Ta (uh-DOOL-us TAH)—A famous High Mage credited with creating the modern classifications of magic in the year 782.

Aldyr Tolruin (ALL-deer TOLL-roo-in)—Syneria's elder sister, engaged to Ethas of House Gandel.

Alfred—A mage dwelling in the town of Snowbell in Fircas, whose talents are employed to facilitate a certain stunt.

Andra—Mydia's former handmaiden.

Bart, Big—His real name is Bartimaeus. One of the leaders of the Underground in Nytaea.

Bddo (b-DOE)—???

Ben—Called Uncle Ben by most, he is Oliver's uncle and a member of the Scathii Council.

Berta—A hearty young woman who eventually, with a certain young woman's help, fulfilled her dream of starting an orphanage.

Betty—The maid who shows Lyn the ways of the Palace maid.

Carth—A veteran sky sailor who doesn't take quickly to mainlanders.

Ccal (KAL)—???

Chara (CARE-uh)—Mydia's middle-aged handmaiden. She has watched over the princess for many years now. Squat and stuffy, always busy with something. Disliked by Mydia.

Charta (CHAR-tuh)—A bear-like, good-natured sky sailor.

Christoff—A lieutenant in the Nemental military.

Cort Flanning—A senior student at the Nytaean Mage Academy who is chosen by Rhidea to study at Randhorn. Thin and blond, he wears stylish attire typical of his noble family.

Domon, Archlord (ARK-lord DOME-uhn)—Archlord (emperor) of Kystrea, long feared for his magical strength and his ruthlessness, despite being a fair ruler overall.

Dudley—Duke of Halstar, popular and just.

Eivael Badon-Kalceron (AY-ih-vale BAY-duhn)—Mydia's late mother, and previous wife of Lord Kalceron. After her death eight years ago, he remarried to a sorceress named Lieda. [See **Kalceron**]

Ethas Gandel (EETH-us GAN-del)—Heir of his house, Ethas is 20 years old, tall and blond. He can't help being a bit better than most people, much like his fiancée, Aldyr Tolruin.

Feln—A sky sailor.

Fenwel—King of Nemental. He is aged and wise, possessing a keen wit and a good sense of humor. His hair and beard are white but not thin, his frame still strong, and he has some innate magic, though only a bit. Possesses the Perception-based gift of Truthseeing.

Fraid—A deranged fire mage and murderer, leader of a thieving band in Nytaea—the same who burned down Lentha's orphanage.

Gaela (GAY-luh)—A noblewoman who leads the Underground along with Mydia and a few others. She is tall, her blonde hair streaked with white, and her mild temperament conceals dark anger underneath. Very skilled at keeping a straight face.

Gendric—Master of the Nytaean Mage Academy. Old and wise, respected by Rhidea and feared by Lord Kalceron. Gendric despises the way Lord Kalceron rules Nytaea but tries to stay out of it. He once led a band of mage mercenaries who worked for whichever Kystrean State would hire them for the most money, then the Archlord offered to build him his own school in Nytaea if he would teach aspiring magicians the art of war magic so that Kystrea could build an army of mage soldiers. Gendric slowly came to detest the idea of using something as wondrous as magic for killing men. He made the school into a great academy where one could study all manner of magical arts, and only pursue a soldier's career if one so chose.

Glenidar—King of Ti'Vaeth until Lord Domon rose up and killed him in a duel, naming himself Archlord of Ti'Vaeth and setting out to conquer the other Kystrean city-states.

Gorman Sedler—A servant in the employ of Lord Kalceron who secures Kaen and Lyn a position among the staff at the Palace.

Hamia (HAY-mee-uh)—A maid in the employ of the Palace who shared a bunk with Lyn for a while. Both stocky and chubby, she has large hands, coming from a line of rural farmers.

Harcost—A carpenter working in the city of Nytaea, for whom Lyn and Kaen often do manual labor.

Harold—A corporal in Archlord Domon's palace guard.

Hespian—Captain of the Nytaean Mage Guard, answering to Lord Kalceron himself. Despite his air of joviality, he can be quite cunning.

Humphret—A nobleman of some standing in Ti'Vaeth. His main hobbies include pestering the Archlord and eating.

Inno—A soldier who joined the Queensguard in order to protect Nytaea's new ruler.

Jinna—A scholar friend of Eivael Kalceron. She died tragically in a magical experiment, prompting the queen to abandon her alchemical experiments.

Julia—A handmaiden to Princess Mydia, about the same age as Lyn, though she's been in her position for years now. She came from a poor home to the Palace to pay off her father's debts, but Lord Kalceron had them killed off a year ago, stranding her in service to

House Kalceron.

Kaen (KANE)—Lyn's longtime friend from Lentha's orphanage. Mandrie is his little sister. When Kaen infiltrates the Palace with Lyn to try to free Mandrie and Phoebe from the inside, he assumes the name of Roger. He has curly dark hair and intense expressions, and, despite his 17 years, carries himself like someone who has been through rough times and learned to harden himself against the world around him.

Kalceron, Edrius (EE-dree-us KAL-sir-on)—Governor of Nytaea, known for being crueler than the Archlord of Kystrea himself. His daughter is Princess Mydia. She and his firstborn son, Kallyn, were born to him of Lady Eivael Kalceron, his late wife. He remarried eight years back to a sorceress called Lieda. It is said that his first wife, Eivael, kept the worst of him in check, while his second, Lieda, only fostered that dark side.

Kallyn Kalceron—Son of Lord Kalceron and heir to the throne of Nytaea, Mydia's brother Kallyn disappeared fifteen years back and was presumed dead.

Keuda (KYU-duh)—Royal secretary of Nytaea.

Kyal (KYAHL)—Lord of the province of Imdek.

Kymhar (kih-MAHR)—An enigmatic member of the Dalim, the lethal servants of the Archlord. Dresses in dark leathers with many layers and keeps knives and kunai everywhere on his person. Trained in stealth, assassination and martial arts.

Kath—A fire mage soldier who joined the Queensguard in order to protect Nytaea's new ruler.

Lentha—The kind woman who raised Lyn from a small child, along with many other orphans.

Lester, Little—One of the leaders of the Nytaean Underground. His real name is Tomas.

Lhiard (lee-ARD)—Lord of the city-state of Uphel.

Lieda (LEE-duh)—The magician noblewoman to whom Lord Kalceron remarried eight years back, following the mysterious and sudden death of his former wife, Eivael. . . . Lieda is not well liked by Mydia, nor by the people of Nytaea. She is as much a thorn in the city's side as her husband. Hates Mydia and the sight of blood.

Lina—One of the senior Palace maids.

Lorta—A caustic, vulpine mage lieutenant who works closely with Captain Hespian in Lord Kalceron's Mage Guard.

Lyn (Lynchazel II)—A young woman with white hair and inexplicable strength. Said to have been brought by her destitute mother to Lentha's orphanage, where she was raised. Lyn barely remembers her real name, Lynchazel, for Lentha stopped using it early on when the other children at the orphanage picked on her for its 'noble' sound.

Lynchazel I (LINK-uh-zel)—???

Mandrie—Kaen's younger sister, who gets abducted by Captain Hespian of the Mage Guard.

Mydia Kalceron (MID-ee-uh)—Sole daughter of Lord Kalceron, heir of Nytaea ever since her brother Kallyn died fifteen years back (or . . . went missing). Her mother, Lady Eivael, died eight years ago of a disease. Mydia's hair is jet black, her form a bit padded from her pampered life, her skin a pasty white. She is shy but very talkative when encouraged, and has a mischievous side. Mydia possesses illusionary magic as well as green magic. Inherited from her mother, the latter is a type of water magic which includes accelerated growth and renewal of plants/trees/flowers, as well as healing.

Oliver—A twelve-year-old boy, sandy haired and freckled, who lives in the village on the eastern Isle of Scathii. He is an orphan and a rebel who loves to fly, characterized by his daring and cleverness.

Phoebe—a friend of Kaen and Lyn from back at the orphanage. She is sixteen years old and has brown hair that hangs down just past her shoulders, expressionless eyes and a beaklike, hooked nose. Phoebe dreams of having a family someday in a better Nytaea, but is also an incurable pessimist. No one knows the exact details of how she came to the orphanage, but she holds bitterness against someone close to her in her past.

Podda—A common girl's name that Lyn uses as an alias in the Palace.

Rhidea, Cae (KYE rye-DAY-uh)—A traveling magician, tall with deep red hair, once High Magister to King Fenwel of Randhorn. Now, she wanders about from place to place, seeking a solution to the dwindling magic of the world. She carries herself with confidence and addresses everyone equally, often as 'child.' Her features are beautiful but hard, her hazel eyes focused. Rhidea is also the most powerful mage to be seen in many decades. As a High Mage, she is versed in many branches of magic, but one of her specialties is gravitational control.

Rodessa—A young woman working at the Imperial Archives in the Ti'Vaeth citadel. She is a contact of Rhidea's.

Roger—Kaen's alias in the Palace.

Ruel (ROOL)—A soldier who joined the Queensguard in order to protect Nytaea's new ruler.

Sam, Skinny—One of the leaders of the Underground in Nytaea.

Shanagel (shuh-NAY-guhl)—A very strange sky sailor.

Sor the Lark—A scholar of an unknown era, author of the book *Secrets of Mani.*

Syneria Tolruin (sih-NEER-ee-uh TOLL-roo-in)—A talented student at the Mage Academy, best friends with Cort Flanning. Syneria is sixteen years of age, with shoulder-length golden locks and blazing blue eyes. She comes from the wealthy House Tolruin, and thus carries a heavy chip on her shoulder.

Teli (TEL-ee)—A young girl among the Palace maids who was sentenced to a harsh whipping by Lord Kalceron for dropping a plate while serving. Beaten by her mother as a girl, she learned to be timid and cringe frequently. Lyn later helps secure a better position for her.

Thames—A scholar friend of Eivael Kalceron.

Tom, Tall—One of the leaders of the Underground in Nytaea. His real name is Dossam.

Tommy—A young boy from Lentha's orphanage whom Lyn and her friends remember fondly . . . and with deep sorrow.

Trevias Lhordes (TREV-ee-us LORE-deez)—A famed general of Ti'Vaeth who fought for High King Glenidar along with a coalition of city-states to repel the invading Torlegans. Credited with bringing an end to the war and driving them over the Styrite Mountains for good in 794.

Tyiv (TEEV)—Lord of the southern Nytaean city-state of Dotham, and a member of the Umbra Council.

White—A small, pale-skinned girl whom Lyn sees in her visions. Lyn gave her the nickname after encountering her multiple times, having no other name by which to call her.

Zent—???

- Appendix B -

Glossary of Terms and Locations

(And how on Mani you're supposed to pronounce them)

Andeir (AN-dare)—A town in the province of Fircas.

Anteleth—A noble beast like a far larger gazelle, whose branching horns are breakable at every joint and could once be found scattered about the rocky outcroppings of the Plains of Nandaer where the Anteleth roamed. Now, they are thought to have been exterminated by monsters, and more recently humans, who hunted them to extinction, and their horns are prized items that serve to remember them by.

Aptitude—Magical talent.

Ardencaul River—One of the Four Rivers, fed by the Wellspring's water and flowing eastward from Ti'Vaeth. It passes through Fircas, Nytaea, Storklance, and finally the country of Nemental, before rushing over the eastern coast of Argent.

Argent (AHR-jent)—The major continent of Mani where the Legaleians dwell.

Auroras—A phenomenon that lights up the sky beneath the clouds during the nights of the Sunlit Cycle (very dimly and not consistently) and during the daytime of the Sunless Cycle usually without cloud coverage—thus creating light for the people of Mani to see by.

Authority—One of two schools of magic present on Mani, alongside Coaction. The two appear similar, except that Authority is far more powerful, but are quite different in practice. [See **Coaction,**

also see Appendix B]

Balrun—Situated along the banks of the Ardencaul in Nytaea, the Balrun sector is home to most of the Nytaean shipping industry, docks, warehouses, etc.

Branch—Magical term for one of the eight major classifications of magic present on Mani: Water, Fire, Lightning, Wind, Earth, Perception, Reality and Silver. Both Authority and the less powerful Coaction are categorized under these eight branches, though there are many subclasses, such as green magic (plant magic) and healing, Mydia's specialties born of her Water Aptitude. [See Appendix B]

City-State—One of thirteen small regions of Kystrea, each ruled by a king and dominated by one large, usually central, city. In the center of the empire is Ti'Vaeth, Archlord Domon's own city-state and the first of the thirteen to come under his control one hundred years ago. Before the Archlord took over, they were independent city-states ruled by a king, but now he likes to use the terms "governor" and "province."

Coaction—The lesser school of magic present on Mani, with Authority being its greater cousin. The two appear similar, except that Authority is far more potent, but are quite different in practice. [See **Authority**]

Constellation—A phenomenon of the Sunlit night skies, created by the Energy Field as Sol reaches certain angles, creating a shimmering image upon the thick cloud coverage not altogether unlike the auroras. They also appear in the Night Season, coming in different times of the day than in the Sunlit Cycle. [See **Auroras**]

Cryvad (crih-VAHD)—Westernmost city-state of the Kystrean Empire and birthplace of Mydia's mother, Eivael Badon. It is a land of plenty, as the Rudaens River forms a wide delta that spreads throughout it before spilling into the Sea of Emptiness.

Cydenges (sigh-DEN-jeez)—**???**

Dark Magic—A theoretical transversion of the power that flows from the Wellspring of Magic. Anti-life, anti-magic. It is extremely potent and destructive, but don't worry—Archlord Domon must have a good reason for creating it.

Darsor (dar-SORE)—The native name for a certain continent on Mani.

Dalim (duh-LEEM)—An elite order of assassins who work for Archlord Domon, trained in many ancient martial arts. Can refer to singular or plural assassins of the order, or to the order at large— though they are not many, and hold tightly to their bloodline.

Day Season—See **Sunlit Cycle**.

Dotham (DOE-thum)—A southern province of Kystrea, border- ing the Styrite Mountains on the south.

Energy Field—The outer portion of Mani's sky (atmosphere) that pulses with energy and is believed to contain much of the elemental power born of the Wellspring that is tapped by magi. The Energy Field is responsible for the auroras—the shifting heavenly lights that come and go along with thick cloud coverage, keeping the regular days distinguished throughout each Sol Cycle—as well as constella- tions and other such phenomena. [See **Sol Cycle**, **Auroras**]

Element—One of the five Elemental Branches of magic: Water, Fire, Lightning, Wind and Earth. Can also refer to any one of eight major forces at work in the world of Mani, though the magical term is 'branch.' [See **Branch**]

Faliday (FAL-uh-day)—A Nementali town located just south of Randhorn.

Fircas—A Kystrean province bordering Nytaea on the east and Ti'Vaeth on the west.

Four Rivers—The great rivers of the world that spring from the

Wellspring of Life in Ti'Vaeth and flow in the four cardinal directions to the edges of Argent.

Gaea (GUY-uh, JEE-uh)—A world whispered of by scholars and historians of the ancient days. No one knows what Gaea is like—but there is one who may hold the key to unraveling the mysteries that surround it.

Gaean Senate—???

Gantz River—One of the Four Rivers, running southward out of Ti'Vaeth through Imdek, under the Styrite Mountains, and through the country of Torlega before spilling over the southern coast of Argent.

Gatewatch Isle—A forbidden island which lies in the southeastern hemisphere of Gaea.

Ghartu (GAR-too)—Northwesternmost of the Kystrean provinces, bordering Uphel on its eastern side. Home to one of the harshest climates of Argent, dry and arid.

Governor—Official title of the king of a city-state (province) of Kystrea. Sounds less nationalist.

Hall of Eternity—The imperial palace of the Archlord, nestled deep within the Ti'Vaeth citadel. Three walls enclose it, rising higher toward the very center, where the tall stack rises from the Wellspring into the sky, whence issues the Sky Funnel. [See **Wellspring of Magic**, **Sky Funnel**]

Halstar—A duchy in central Darsor.

Hellebes (HEL-uh-beez)—The Hellebes are a race of people indigenous to Gaea.

Hellebes Mother—???

High Legaleian—An old language spoken by the first people of Mani, largely similar to the currently-spoken dialect but different enough to baffle the uneducated.

High Mage—A title given only to magi who have proven themselves both academically and in the arts of Authority. A High Mage possesses strong talent, carefully honed over decades, and is required to have mastered Authority in at least three branches of magic.

High Magister—Entirely separate, this is a royal court position bestowed on Cae Rhidea by King Fenwel some forty years back.

Imdek (EEM-dek)—A province of southern Kystrea.

Imperial Highway—A long road spanning the continent of Argent from west to east and breaking only with each major city encountered along the way. Highly traveled because it is safe, and vice versa.

Koiberries—Cultivated by farmers in the mountain slopes of Dotham and Torlega, these juicy red fruits grow on spidery brambles. They are oblong, ribbed end to end, and bear thin stripes of white between each rib. Clever Kystreans know where to find them wild in almost every province.

Kysedon (kih-SEE-duhn)—An island in the middle of Lake Lucia upon which the city of Ti'Vaeth stands. [see **Lake Lucia**]

Kystrea (KISS-tree-uh)—An empire spanning most of the map of Legalei (Argent) and comprised of thirteen city-states, ruled over by twelve lords called governors and an Archlord.

Land of Storms—A circular, barren rockscape which lies at the heart of Darsor, concealing the Tower of Mani at its center. Overhead is a great conflagration of thunderstorms, ever roiling and spewing deadly lightning everywhere, and no one ventures near for fear of being struck dead.

Legalei (leh-GAHL-ay)—An old term for the world of Mani. [See **Mani**]

Legaleian (LEE-guh-LAY-un)—Of Manese descent. Also, the language spoken by people all across Argent.

Legaleians—The humans who inhabit the magical world of Legalei, which is also called Mani. [See **Mani**]

Loftus—A northern Kystrean province.

Lor'Hav (lore-HAWV)—The first village encountered in Darsor, just east of the ancient forest that borders Darsor's western cliffs.

Lucia Lake—The largest standing body of water on the continent of Argent, this lake—affectionately called the Sea of Ti'Vaeth by idiot outsiders—surrounds the isle of Kysedon, and thus the city of Ti'Vaeth. Tall cliffs form a wall around the lake, which is fed from underground by the Wellspring. The Four Rivers run in each cardinal direction from Lake Lucia.

Lygellis (lye-GELL-iss)—An outlier nation to the southwest of Kystrea, partially bordering Torlega on the southeast. Lygellis is the largest of the outlier lands but sparsely populated. There isn't much there apart from the northern delta shared with Cryvad.

Monsters—Naturally, this word can be used to mean many different things, but to most Legaleians it refers to a range of specific, actual monster species that once roamed the face of Mani: fire-breathing snakes, enormous lions and bull-bears, to name a few. Some say dragons.

Magic—A force that drives the world of Mani and gives it breath. All magic comes from the Wellspring of Magic in Ti'Vaeth, which lies at the very center of the continent of Argent.

Manese (maw-NEEZ)—Legaleian; of Mani. [See **Legaleian**]

Mani (MAW-nee)—A silver world pulsing with magic, with which the Legaleians (the inhabitants of Mani) were blessed—or some say cursed. Mani's white sun, Sol, makes her rounds only once per month, so one Sol Cycle is four weeks long (28 days exactly). There is a reactive, pulsing Energy Field that surrounds the planet, creating powerful displays called auroras to light the two-week nights and also strange constellations that recur periodically. [See **Auroras, Energy Field, Sol Cycle**]

Mannet—A large town immediately south and within sight of Redufiel, capital of Halstar.

Moon—???

Nandaer (NAHN-dare)—A large plain in southern Sorfaen, near the southern edge of Argent, where the proud Anteleth once roamed.

Nemental (NEM-en-tall)—The kingdom bordering Kystrea's eastern flank, sandwiched between Storklance and the eastern cliffs of Argent. Her king is Fenwel of Randhorn.

Night Season—See **Sunless Cycle**.

Noduin (NO-dwin)—The largest of the Sky Islands, not far off the shore of Argent.

Nomu—Another Sky Island, lying just farther out than Noduin and not quite as large.

Nytaea (nigh-TAY-uh)—A city-state in Kystrea ruled by Lord Kalceron, the governor. Lyn grew up in this city, where she was raised from a baby by the kind woman Lentha.

Perception—The branch of Coaction/Authority that governs manifest (perceived) reality.

Polestone—A reddish stone whose natural properties cause it to point toward the center of Argent—more accurately, toward the Wellspring of Life. Not always as useful as it sounds, but using one in conjunction with the current angle of the sun can make pinpointing directions easier.

Province—See **City-State.** These terms are interchangeable.

Randhorn—Capital of Nemental, where King Fenwel rules and Rhidea has a seat as High Magister.

Reality—The branch of Coaction/Authority that rules physical reality.

Rudaens River (roo-DENZ)—One of the Four Rivers of the world, running westward from Ti'Vaeth through Thyria and eventually ending in a wide delta in the province of Cryvad.

Redufiel (ruh-DOO-fee-el)—Capital city of the Duchy of Halstar.

Secrets of Mani—A book of magical history once possessed by Princess Mydia's mother, given to Mydia by Cae Rhidea upon her return to Nytaea.

Scathii (SKAH-thee, with a hard 'TH')—Well known but rarely seen, the Isle of Scathii is hidden at the farthest reaches of the Sky Islands. Scathii is home to the world's highest density of wind magi, a secret they like to keep to themselves, and is also one of the few providers of wool to the outside world.

Silver—The most common metal in Mani, said to comprise a large portion of the continent of Argent deep below its surface. In places such as Nytaea, the ancient order of Silversmiths used their Silver Authority to wrest the raw metal from Mani's belly and create wonders such as the Nytaean Palace. In addition to being both a metal and a magical element, the word Silver (always capitalized) is also used to refer to a living force that is believed to represent the breath, or the will, of Mani himself.

Sky Funnel—A twisting waterspout that pours upward from the Wellspring at the very center of Ti'Vaeth. It issues from a long stack, walled in by the Hall of Eternity, but no one seems to know the exact source of the Wellspring's water.

Snowbell—A town in which Lyn and company stop on their way through the province of Fircas, experimenting with a new money-making stunt.

Sol—The white sun of Mani, which makes her rotation once every twenty-eight days. She shines for around two weeks during what is called the Sunlit Cycle, before dipping over the horizon and bringing on the Sunless Cycle.

Sol Cycle—A pattern of 28 days during which Sol passes around the world of Mani, providing two weeks of day and two weeks of night. [See **Sunless Cycle, Sunlit Cycle**]

Sorfaen (SORE-fane)—Southeasternmost province of Kystrea, bordering Torlega on the west, Nemental on the east, and Fircas, Storklance and Nytaea on the north.

Soul River—A river said to run in a circle around the continent of Darsor. To an outsider, it would sound mythical.

Storklance—The easternmost province of Kystrea, which borders Nytaea on the west and Nemental on the east.

Styrite Wars—A long war waged from 778–794 between a coalition of three Kystrean city-states (Ti'Vaeth, Dotham and Fircas) and the ruthless warriors of Torlega, who were attempting to expand over the mountains by conquering Dotham and other regions.

Sun Dancer—A constellation of the Sunlit night sky. [See **Constellation**]

Sunless Cycle—A period of two weeks on Mani where the sun drops below the western horizon and vanishes, causing the auroras and clouds to change their patterns. At dawn, the Sunlit Cycle, or Day Season, begins.

Sunlit Cycle—A period of two weeks on Mani where the sun travels from the eastern horizon to the west. At dusk, the Sunless Cycle, or Night Season, begins.

Synergist—One who practices Coaction, which is also called synergy. [See **Coaction**]

Synergy—[See **Coaction**]

Ti'Vaeth (tih-VETH)—The Capital of Kystrea, wherein dwells Archlord Domon. Encompassing the lush, vibrant surrounding lands both inside and outside the shimmering water wall called the Veil, Ti'Vaeth is the largest city-state of Kystrea.

Torlega (tor-LEE-guh)—A land to the south of Kystrea, hemmed in against the southern coast of Argent but defended by the jagged Styrite mountains. The Torlegans are well known for their earth magi, who use stonesung armor to protect themselves, insulating from most kinds of magic.

Tower of Mani—The mythical tower that lies in the center of the Land of Storms.

Thyria (THEER-ee-uh)—A western city-state of Kystrea lying between Ti'Vaeth and Cryvad.

Umbra Council—The Archlord's trusted friends whom he allows in on his plans and with whom he discusses them.

Underground—The largest group of rebels in the city of Nytaea, led by Gaela, Big Bart, Tall Tom, Little Lester, Skinny Sam and Princess Mydia. They plot to overthrow Lord Kalceron and his rule over Nytaea and retake control of the city to give it to the people.

Uphel (OOH-fel)—A northern Kystrean province.

Veil—A wall of water that covers Ti'Vaeth in a sheet, spraying upwards from the Wellspring at the center of the city and streaming outward, making the sky like the roof of a greenhouse. The water flows outward from there, forming the Four Rivers, and also feeds the giant lake that surrounds the capital city of Ti'Vaeth.

Wellspring of Life—See **Wellspring of Magic**.

Wellspring of Magic—Also referred to as the Wellspring of Life. The source of all magic—and water, so therefore life itself—on Mani. The Well has begun to dry up lately, and thus the magic of Mani with it, in part due to the Archlord's meddling with it.

Yan'Vala (YAHN-vuh-LAH)—A nation lying to the northeast of Kystrea, hidden in a mountainous region of crags and gorges that reach down to infinity, as though the continent were tearing itself apart. The locals assure any travelers that the cracks have stayed exactly the same for at least two centuries, mind you.

Yartel River (yar-TEL)—One of the Four Rivers, running northward from Ti'Vaeth and ending at the continental coast of the Uphel province.

- Appendix C -

Notes on the World

Coaction and Authority

Magic has existed on Mani for many centuries. How long exactly is often debated, but presumably for at least the one thousand years that humans have dwelt on the silver world. Magic is the essence of life and nature and the bond that holds the planet together—literally and figuratively.

Manese magic is split into two main classifications: Coaction and Authority. Coaction is the lesser art, a means of prompting the magical nature of Mani to produce for the wielder some effect, while the greater art, Authority, allows one to forcibly bend nature to heel and command the elements. The process is only technically different; it is mostly a difference in the strength of the results—and a prerequisite thereof. Any Authority at all generally takes years of practice to achieve.

High Magi such as the famed Cae Rhidea or the deceased Prince Kallyn (and his father, Lord Edrius Kalceron, for that matter) are skilled in even the highest magic Arts of Authority, able to bend the elements to do their bidding. To be called a High Mage, one must demonstrate mastery in no less than three branches of Authority. Lesser magi like the average mage soldier can only perform relatively small feats of Coaction, prompting nature into responding to their own actions in order to produce a certain effect. This is far less potent than actual Authority, but easier for those with little potential or training.

Those born with the gift—or Aptitude—of magic are called Adepts. This Aptitude is not distributed to all, though some Adepts miss their talent by not realizing they ever had it (the ability will eventually disappear if never utilized by adulthood), but those who have it also experience a longer life. It is for them to decide whether that is a blessing or a curse. The stronger the Aptitude, the longer the lifespan. Some of the ancient High Magi lived for multiple centuries.

The Eight Branches of Magic

Elements of Mani:
- Water—The element of water and the essence of life.
- Fire—The element of heat, combustion and flames.
- Lightning (Thunder)—The element of electricity and lightning.
- Wind—The element of air pressure and wind control.
- Earth—Manipulation of stone/ground, earthquakes.

The Dimensional Branches:
- Perception—the force governing perceived reality.
- Reality—the force governing physical reality.

Ancient:
- Silver—Manipulation of silver and its associated properties.

Silver is its own special case, as it predates elemental magic (while dimensional magic appears to have followed the elements to Mani). Since silver is embedded deeply into the makeup of the very planet, Silver magic is the most powerful by far, allowing the wielder near-complete control of the metal. As for its various abilities and the extent thereof . . . they are unclear, as the Silversmiths—the ancient order of magi who exclusively had this gift—died off long ago.

Dates and Times:

On Mani, the Sol Cycle is twenty-eight "days" long. Since these days are divided by the great auroras and the clouds, they are separate from the Sol Cycle. Each day in the Cycle, Sol progresses farther in her rounds, creating two seasons: Sunlit and Sunless; Day Season and

Night Season.

The Sol Cycle:
- 1–2: Dawn (Full sunrise on 2nd day)
- 3–8: Waxing Day
- 9–10: Zenith (Full Day)
- 11–14: Waning Day
- 15–16: Sunset (Dusk on Day 16)
- 17–28: Night Season

Naturally, all these figures vary depending on where on Mani you live. The farther north or south of the equator one lives, the shorter each Sunlit Cycle will be. The farther east, one will experience each stage of the Sol Cycle before those in Ti'Vaeth, Kystrea; the farther west, later.

There are thirteen months in the year, each with their own two seasons—Day and Night—which are warmer and colder. There are no traditional seasons on Mani, so the cycling of constellations is what tells the passing of a full year.

Months of the Manese Year:
- Mani'Tor
- Ae'Tor (AY-tore)
- Fynle (FIN-lee)
- Dri'Shal (DREE-shahl)
- Firvaen (FIR-ven)
- Norvaen (NOR-ven)
- San'Hal (SAHN-hall)
- Quoi
- Ver'Ta

Appendix C

- Herch'Ta (HER-k-tah—K standing for a hissing stop)
- Vendale (VEN-duh-lee)
- Henavaen (HEN-uh-ven)
- Sol'Tor

Excerpt from the Sequel:

GAEA

- Prologue -

Ancestor

(Planet Gaea—Anier headquarters
Soldor 14, A.E. 1459, E120)
Mother Gaea felt a hand on her shoulder. She jerked, swiveling her head to see a familiar man stepping up beside her. He was tall with neatly combed black hair, dressed tidily in a business suit. Everything about him was businesslike. "It's time," he said quietly.

She nodded. She tried to form a response, but it got stuck in her throat, so she shut her mouth and quietly followed the man. She was in the main Anier headquarters in what used to be the capital of Starklett, a grand city and one of the few places in the world the Anier had not yet abased. Well, aside from constructing their own buildings such as this. It was framed in metal and absolutely hideous to look at, with flat glass windows and no decorative style. As she followed the tall man through the hall, the electric lighting cast eerie, fuzzy shadows on the floor that flickered ominously.

Mother Gaea, as they called her, was not in the condition she once was. When they'd found her, she'd been but a girl of thirteen years, and she couldn't be certain how many decades had passed. One could almost mistake her youthful face for that of a girl, but for the

- 441 -

wrinkles and the scars, and her dark hair was now streaked with grey. On one hand, she felt as though she hadn't aged a day, but on the other . . . she was beaten and worn, and she could tell. How much longer could she keep living like this? How long until her body just disintegrated into dust and blew away on the wind?

"The creature is being kept under the tightest security," the man said out of nowhere, turning to look at her as he walked. "You are in no danger."

"Thanks," she mumbled. They had told her many things about these incredible life-forms that could destroy or save humanity, but she didn't know what to believe anymore. Did her beliefs matter? Her feelings? No. She couldn't save a single soul. But . . . danger to her? That was the least she was concerned about.

The tall man took her down one last hallway with warning signs labeling the walls, and finally through a door marked: *Test Subjects—Do not enter without armed protection.* Inside, filtered electric lights cast an unsettling blue light around a long chamber with many large glass tanks lining one wall. At the end was a T, and as they approached it, they met up with two more of the Anier and a half-dozen armed guardsmen, who stood watching something in a cage. A big cage, some ten feet tall and spanning the width between one wall and the other.

Mother Gaea frowned, trying to get a view of the cage and the creature it contained. A rising lump in her throat and a feeling of dread told her she didn't want to see it, yet at the same time it triggered her scientist's fascination. She glanced back at the man who had led her there, and then moved forward, maneuvering around the stout guards to get a view of the cage.

When she did, she gasped.

The two other Anier turned to look at her, and one said, "This,

Mother Gaea, is a Cydenges. Look well."

She wanted to tear her eyes away from it, but she couldn't. It was terrible . . . but beautiful as well, like an artist had skillfully designed it. A predator of enormous size, capable of mass-destruction.

The well-dressed man who had led her to the containment room said, "The cage is heavily reinforced and lined with copper, which has proven to be the only insulant effective at inhibiting their energy manipulation abilities. That is their most feared trait, after all."

Mother Gaea nodded with a gulp. They had already attacked multiple times, and she had seen the destruction the Cydenges could wreak upon Gaea, but never had she laid eyes on one. *Look well.* She did just that. This was the future of Gaea, after all. One way or another.

- About the Author -

Jacob Gamber grew up in Araluen, Alagaësia and Fablehaven, and spent the remainder of his childhood in rural Pennsylvania, telling stories to sheep. When the time came to embark on his own journey to a fantasy world, he botched it thoroughly several times and eventually got a full-time factory job. Presently, he lives in eastern Ohio with his wife and child. He enjoys music, role-playing games and puzzles, and is reportedly allergic to bad love triangles.

Visit www.jacobgamber.com for more info on his works, progress, and upcoming stories. You can also check out his personal blog, www.ideaengine.blog, where he posts monthly newsletters, behind-the-scenes content, and a weekly fantasy web serial called *Tales from the Earthen Sky*. You can also find him on Royal Road, where he posts *Earthen Sky* and other original works.

Sign up for the Idea Engine newsletter using this QR code: